The Devil's DEN

CAVALERI BROTHERS #4

LILIAN HARRIS

Editor: Ms. K Edits

Interior Formatting: CPR Editing

Proofreader: Judy's Proofreading

Cover Design: Covers by Jules

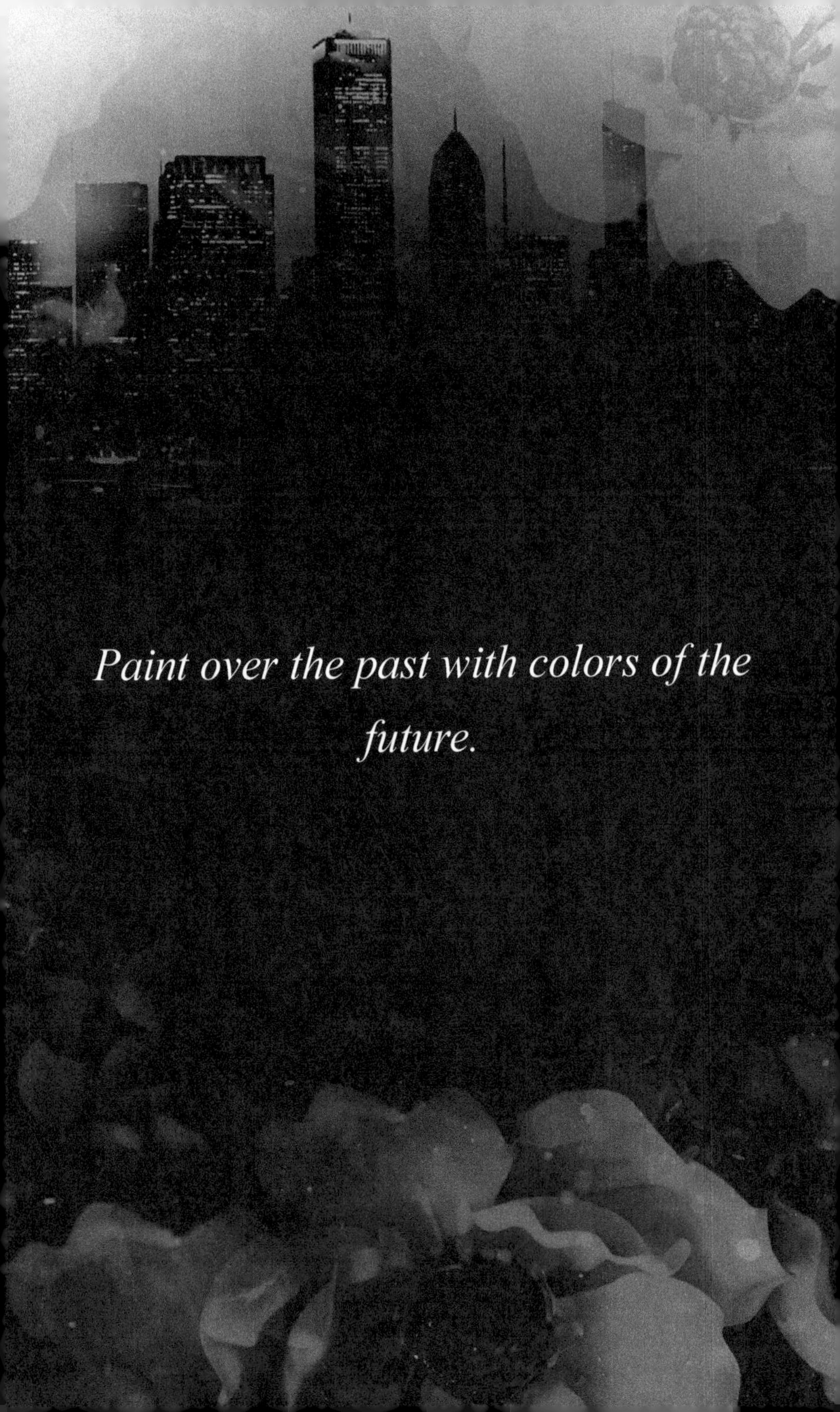
Paint over the past with colors of the future.

Everyone Dies

AIDA

"**T**ake the fucking gun!" he shouts.

Breathe.

In.

Out.

Just breathe.

Heartbeats echo in the chamber of my heart.

Quick.

Hurried.

Thump.

Thump.

I swear I'll drown in pain every single time I inhale.

His hand is on me now—that grip, it hurts.

"I can't do this." My body rolls with a shudder, every inch of me a cold, trembling mess.

"Take it!" The way he says it, it sends terror running down my spine.

"No!" My scream rips through the air, but it does nothing to stop him, to stop what's bound to happen.

"Take the fucking gun, I said!"

"Pl-please, d-d-don't do this!" My voice shatters with every dripping tear, the wave of emotion crashing over me. But he doesn't care. He likes it when I cry. When I'm hurting.

"If you don't shoot him…" The gun in his hand rises, level with the man I love sitting chained to the radiator. "Then I'll kill him and that other bastard. Choose."

I know he'll do it. His wrath knows no bounds. His hatred—that putrid rotting of his soul—it's been there since I've known him.

"Coward," Matteo taunts. "You were always such a damn coward. Kill me yourself." His upper lip curls. "I dare you."

But the man ignores him.

Is Matteo really not afraid to die?

I fear it often. Every time I go to bed and every moment I wake. How I've made it this far, I'll never know.

The man's thick laughter fills the space around us. "You think you're better than me, huh? You know, once upon a time, your dear old daddy thought he was too and look where it got him."

Matteo runs for him, yanking at the chain with a snarl, trying to get to him, but we're not close enough.

The man's attention is on me again. "You have to the count of three, then both of their deaths will be on your head."

My breathing is ragged, my fingers trembling as I stare at Matteo. Afraid for him. For me. I don't want to shoot anyone. Least of all him.

"One." His thumb lands on the trigger.

My body shivers with an ice-cold chill, my pulse hammering in my ears.

"Pl-please," I stammer, turning to his mud-filled eyes, hoping for some semblance of compassion, but there's nothing within them. They're empty, as hollow as his soul.

"Two." He holds my gaze, the gun still aimed at the only man who's ever cared for me.

"Leave her alone!" Matteo growls, his voice edged with force. I don't know where he finds the strength among the magnitude of his situation, but somehow, he does. He always does.

"I'd have killed you already," the man tells him. "But having her do it, knowing I can make her, well, that's a lot better." He pins me with a glare. "Your time is almost up."

"It's okay. I love you." Matteo's gaze lures me into the beauty of those large brown eyes, his lips slipping into a tender smile. "I'd never hold it against you. Do it. I'm ready."

"I'm so sorry." The never-ending tears spill down my cheeks. "This was never how it was supposed to be for you and me."

The man beside me laughs mockingly.

"Remember us and the life we swore we'd have," Matteo says, his raw emotions etched into and overflowing from his eyes. "Live it. For me."

"No! Please!" With tears leaking faster down my face, I beg for one more moment, another second, an hour, anything. "I can't say goodbye!"

"It's not goodbye. It's I'll see you later."

"Pinky swear?" I cry with gasp after gasp, unable to catch my breath.

"Always." He grins wide, his own eyes glistening.

"I'll never forget you. I couldn't even if I tried." My panting grows louder, my entire body shaking, my sobbing scraping up the walls.

I can't let him go. I don't know how. I just want to die.

With him, it was the only time I never felt alone. I reach my fingers for him. "You're the moon and the stars, the sun when it rises, the warmth when it sets," I say. My crying is heavy, sniffling, drowning in the pain, not caring that my tormentor will relish in my anguish.

"You were always so much better with words." His face turns with a mournful smile, stamped with the realization that he's going to die today, that we'll never have the days we once thought we would.

Freedom. There's none for us. There never was. Everything we imagined, everything we dreamed, was just that—a dream.

People like us, we don't survive.

Ticktock.

The clock on the wall, it bleeds seconds I wish I could undo.

Back.

I want to be taken back to a time I didn't exist, where nothing hurt. Where the world was numb. When you couldn't feel. Couldn't bleed. And this? It's an agony I can't describe—losing the only man I ever loved, the only one who loved me.

I'm losing him with every painful moment. Slowly, he's leaving, and I'll be the one to kill him. But there's no other way. That's what the man wanted. To make me a hostage to his will. To give me a choice without actually doing it. Who dies and who lives? I have the power to decide, but there's no power here at all. I'm always at his mercy.

"I—I'm sorry. I love you!" I weep, knowing it'll be the last time I get to tell him.

"Thr—"

In a flash, I tear the pistol away and without feeling, without thinking, I pull the trigger.

Pop.

He falls backward, his eyes rolling. "No! Matteo!" I scream his name, over and over, until my throat aches. I drop to the floor, reaching for him, tears trickling from the corners of my eyes, needing to hold him, to tell him I'm sorry. But I don't get far.

Hands tear me away until I can no longer see the death in his eyes.

Until he's gone. Until I am too.

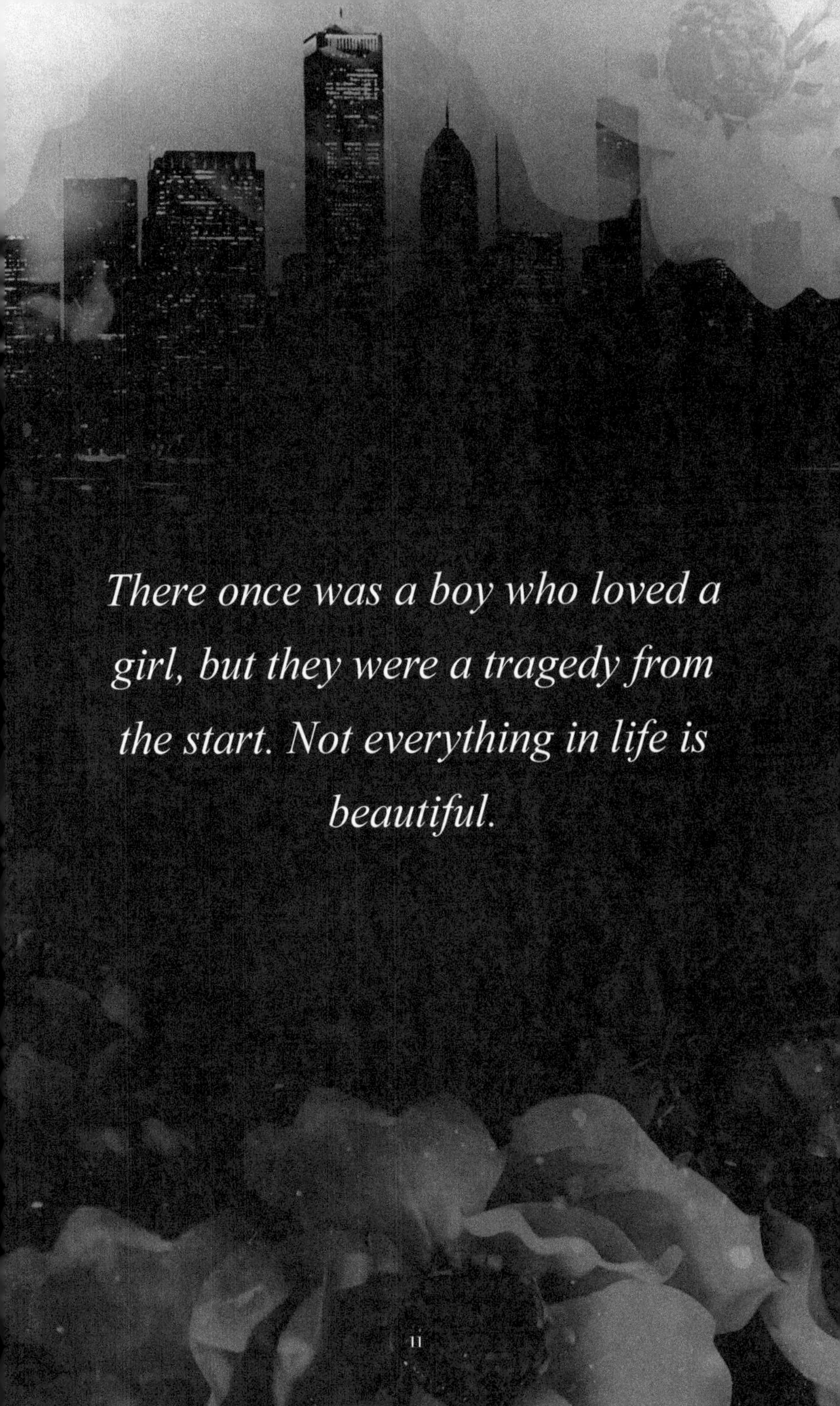
There once was a boy who loved a girl, but they were a tragedy from the start. Not everything in life is beautiful.

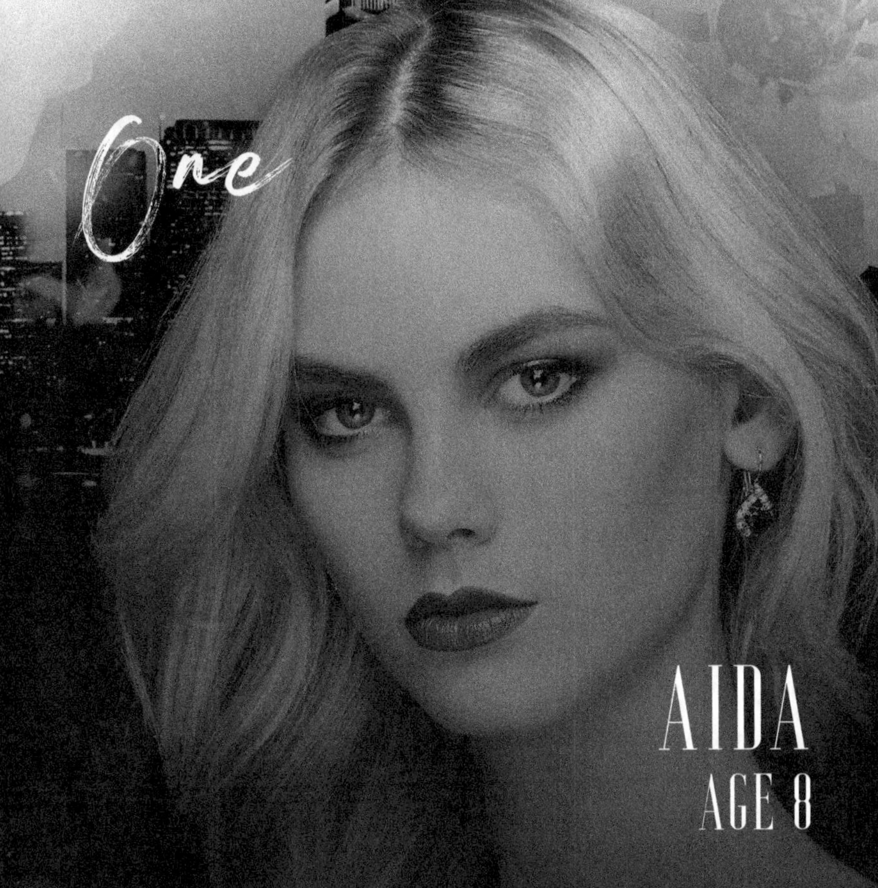

I never met my mom. I wonder if she's pretty. If I look like her. Daddy says she died a long time ago, right after I was born. He says it's my fault she died. That I did it to her when I came out of her.

I hate myself for killing Mommy. I wish I could see her, even a picture. But we don't have any. I want to have a mom like my cousins Chiara and Raquel do. They're so lucky.

I only have my dad. He isn't nice to me. I think he hates me for hurting Mommy. I don't blame him.

I play with the doll Uncle Sal got me for my birthday. There's no one here but me and Ms. Greco. She teaches me stuff because

Daddy won't let me go to a real school. He says it's better if I stay home. I don't know why. I just want to be like my cousins. They get to go to school.

I'm always here alone in our big house. He just goes and leaves me for most of the day. Ms. Greco sleeps over when he can't be home at night. She tucks me in. She's always nice to me.

She says I'm smart, that I read very well, but math is kinda hard. She buys me lots of books too. I like to read them when I'm not playing.

I want to see my cousins, have some friends, but Daddy won't let me. He gets mad when I ask too many questions. I only see Chiara and Raquel for holidays or birthdays. All the other times, I stay in our house. At least I have a backyard. I can go on the swing or play in my sandbox.

"Aida, honey," Ms. Greco calls from the kitchen. "I made some chocolate chip cookies. Would you like one?"

"Yummy!" I instantly jump to my feet, dropping the doll and running toward her. "Could I have two?" I rush into the kitchen, but she already has two on a plate, waiting for me.

I grin wide, grabbing one, and stuff it into my mouth. It's all warm and gooey. "Thank you," I mumble, crumbs falling out of my mouth.

"Welcome. You deserve it after all the hard work you did with your studies." She takes a cookie, placing it on her own plate, looking sweetly at me as she eats.

I wish she was my mom. Was my real mom as nice as her? Did she have blonde hair like me or black hair like Ms. Greco? I'll never know and it makes me so sad.

"What's wrong, honey?" Ms. Greco asks, and I look up at her, not sure what I should say. She works for my dad. What if she tells him? What if he gets mad at me for thinking about Mom, then yells or hits me?

"Nothing. I'm just tired." I start on the second cookie. "Will Daddy be mad that you made these?"

"No, don't worry." Her smile is pretty. It makes me happy. "He said it was fine when I asked yesterday."

"Good. I don't like it when he yells."

She sighs. "Me neither, honey."

"Will you stay tonight?"

She gets up, coming over to me, hugging around my shoulders from behind. "Not tonight."

"Oh." I can't look at her. I'll start crying. But she can tell I'm sad because she hugs me tighter.

"I'm sorry, Aida. I wish…" She takes a heavy breath.

I whirl my head up and it looks like she wants to cry. "You wish what?"

"I wish," she whispers, bending to my ear, "that I could take you away from here. You deserve more. I'm sorry I don't do enough."

"Don't cry." I quickly turn and put my arms around her stomach and hug her with all my might. "You do help me. You're nice to me. You teach me. You're my friend."

"Yeah, sweetheart, I am."

I hold on to her for a few moments longer until we have to get up and clean the kitchen together. If the house isn't spotless, my dad gets super mad at us.

"You can go play now, sweetie," she says once we're done. "Later, we can read some books together before watching a movie."

"That will be so fun! See, you do help me," I tell her with a big grin. But she still looks sad, even though she's kind of smiling.

We both walk back out into the living room. As soon as Ms. Greco sits and I plop on the floor to join my doll, the front door flies open, my dad, my uncles, and other men I've never seen before come rushing in, carrying someone.

Ms. Greco jumps to a stand. "What the…" Her eyes look like they're going to explode. "Who is that?"

"Shut up!" my father barks at her, and she instantly sits back down. A man with glasses walks in, carrying a long bed type thing. I don't know what it's called, but he puts it on the floor.

My uncle Sal is holding someone in his arms, but all I see are the person's feet from the floor.

Small feet. White sneakers.

I'm afraid to look, but I get up anyway. I want to see who it is.

Slowly, I tiptoe, scared my father will see me. Once my uncle drops the person on the bed, I gasp.

It's a boy. He's little like me. Why are his eyes closed?

I go to get a better look, hoping my footsteps don't make any noise. My heart is beating so fast, but I want to see what's wrong with him. I hope he isn't hurt or…dead.

I go even closer as the man with the glasses takes out a black bag with a bunch of doctor stuff, like a stethoscope, which he throws on the floor.

Is that who he is? A doctor? Oh, good. He's going to help the boy.

He puts his hand on the boy's neck. "He's still alive, but barely," the doctor man says, removing a blanket from on top of him.

"Oh no!" I yelp when I notice the blood on his shirt around his belly. I instantly cover my mouth because, in that instant, my dad's angry eyes are on me.

He caught me.

"Get the fuck out of here, Aida." He pushes my chest and I stumble, my eyes burning, my bottom lip trembling as I start to cry.

Why does he have to be so mean?

"Who is that, Daddy?" I whimper it so low, hoping he doesn't hurt me again. But I want to know. I want to help that boy. He shouldn't be here. Not in this evil house. Not with my dad.

"Are you deaf?" he yells. "Didn't I tell you to leave?"

"Come on, Aida," Ms. Greco faintly says, her hand reaching for me as she rises from the couch.

I glance at her once my dad stops focusing on me, shaking my head as I move back a step, huddling behind the sofa.

I can't leave the boy. He needs me. He needs someone who's worried about him to stay. I'm sure my daddy doesn't care. He doesn't like anyone.

"You better bring that kid back to life, doc," my uncle Faro warns, and the man looks terrified. He should be. Uncle Faro is mean like Daddy.

"I'm going to do what I can."

"No." He presses his teeth together and grabs a fistful of the man's shirt, pushing his face into him. "You'll do what I asked. If he dies, you die. And so will that pretty wife of yours, after I test drive her out for myself."

The man nods quickly, and it's like at any moment he'll burst into tears. "Whatever you say, Faro. Just don't hurt her."

"That'll be up to you. Now work." Uncle Faro drops his hand away. At least my uncle is trying to help this little boy, then maybe he can go home to his family.

The scared man fumbles with his stuff while he takes out some sharp metal things and something in a bottle. He pours the water out into a bowl. I think he's cleaning everything.

The doctor uses scissors to cut open the boy's shirt and throws it on the floor as he puts one of the pointy tools to the boy's stomach. I can't see what he's doing exactly, but he looks like he knows what to do, even with all the people around him.

I stop paying attention to them, staring at the boy's face. From here, I can see him clearly. He has such long eyelashes, even longer than mine, and his hair is brown.

Please be okay. I'm sure your mom and dad want you to be okay. Why aren't they with you?

"Aida," Ms. Greco whispers from her seat. "We should leave before your dad gets even madder."

"Shh! I can't leave until I know he's okay. He needs me. He has no one."

"Oh, sweet girl. We can only stay for a few more minutes, then we have to go."

"A few more minutes, yes." But I don't tell her I won't leave. Not until he's awake.

"We gonna use him for the club," Uncle Faro tells my father.

What club? Is it fun?

Daddy laughs. "Yeah, he'd be perfect, a cute kid like that. They'll eat him up."

"Why don't we use him for something else?" Uncle Sal asks this time. "We need men. Killers. We've never built one from the ground up. We can have the guys train him. Make him into whatever the hell we want."

What are they talking about?

"Hmm." Uncle Faro's mouth twists to the side as he slowly nods. "You have a good point. But we can't keep him with the rest in case the law comes snooping. I don't want that little shit to ever be found."

"I'll keep him here," Dad says with a tight smile. "The basement will be perfect. It hasn't disappointed me yet. And my kid goes nowhere, so she won't talk. Neither will that one." He tilts his head, staring in Ms. Greco's direction.

The boy will stay with us? For how long? Why? Where's his

family?

Maybe I can keep him company while he gets better. Will he want to be my friend? But I'm not even allowed in the basement. Daddy says that's his private place.

"It's done, then," Uncle Faro says. "Cavaleri is ours. Too bad we can't bring his daddy back and show him what will become of his youngest." He smiles meanly.

Even though I want this boy to be my friend, I don't want him to stay here. This isn't a nice place. He has to go home. He has to get better.

"Open your eyes," I whisper quietly, looking straight at him, his face tilted to the side. "Please. You have to get out of here."

Maybe he can hear me if I think it loud enough. But that's silly. People can't hear each other that way.

Can they?

"Shit," the doctor says.

Suddenly, I gasp.

The boy, his eyes fly open, and they're staring straight at me.

Two

AIDA
THREE WEEKS LATER

He hates me. The boy. Dad calls him Matteo. He's been locked in a bedroom we never use upstairs while he gets better. One of Daddy's men is always there with a gun, probably guarding him to make sure no one hurts him. But it's not like me or Ms. Greco would.

Whenever the doctor comes by to check on him or when Ms. Greco brings him food, I follow. I tried to talk to him, but he just glared at me like I'm the one who hurt him. I even brought him some books to read, and he threw them rather unkindly on the floor. He's probably just sad he can't be with his family.

"I want to go home!" Matteo shouts at my father as I quietly tiptoe up the stairs to listen better, crossing the hall and hiding around the corner of the bedroom. There's no one up here but my dad, which is a good thing, or one of his men would catch me and tell.

"That's not possible, I'm afraid, kid. There's no one there."

"Yes, there is! My dad, my brothers. They will be looking for me."

"Yeah, sorry to be the one to tell you this, but they won't be. See, your daddy is dead. I made sure of it when we shot him after shooting you."

My eyes bulge, and I quickly cover the gasp from my mouth. And there, in the silence, the boy cries so loud it breaks my heart.

My dad shot Matteo? Killed his daddy? Why? How could he shoot anyone, especially a kid like me? What's wrong with him?

"Di-did you kill my brothers too?" His voice sounds crushed, and I'm hurting right along with him.

"Oh no, they're very much alive, but they want nothing to do with you. I actually cut them a deal. They told me I can keep you in exchange for not hurting them. They're long gone by now, kid. Far away from here. You're on your own."

Matteo sniffles. "I don't believe you. My brothers love me."

"I guess they love themselves more."

"No! Let me go! I need to find them!" he cries on a shout.

"I'd calm down if I were you, kid, or I'll gag you."

But he only screams harder. "They want me back! You're a liar!"

"I don't give a fuck what some eight-year-old punk thinks. I'm your new family, so you better get used to it. You have no one else left."

My father's evil laughter does nothing to block the sound of the boy's sobs, loud enough to crack the walls between us.

MATTEO
AGE 8

The pillow is wet under my face as I remember what happened. My dad can't be dead.

No, Daddy. Please. You have to be alive. You can't leave me like Mommy did! You can't leave me here.

Inside, my chest hurts like I'm being punched. Why did these men hurt my dad? He never did anything to anyone. He was always nice to all the people who came to the store.

And what that man said about my brothers, it can't be true. They'll find me. They won't give up. Maybe I could send them a message somehow.

But I don't know where I am or who these people are. I just want to get out of here. But everywhere I look, there's someone watching me.

Agnelo, that bad man, left after he told me about Dad and my brothers. They would never just let these strangers have me. Maybe he hurt them like Daddy.

I remember the bad man. I remember the others too. There were four of them the morning they took us from the bakery. Dad and I were there very early. He was setting up everything before people started coming in.

He wasn't going to take me that day, but I begged to come. My brothers were always saying I was annoying, so I wanted to be with my dad instead of them.

But then those men knocked on the door and nothing was the same again.

"Matteo, could you hand me that box next to you?" Dad asks, putting out some cupcakes on a round plate

I hop off the stool, pick it up from the counter, and bring it to him. "That looks so yummy! Could I have one?" I look at the chocolate Oreo cupcakes and wish Dad would let me have one for breakfast.

"Maybe after lunch," he says, ruffling my hair as he takes the box from me.

"Fiiine!" I go back to the chair so I can look at my comic book. As I try to get back on the chair, I slip, the chair collapsing on top of me when I fall on my behind.

"Ow!"

"You okay?" Dad rushes over, lifting the chair off me and helping me up.

"I think so." I rub my cheek where I got hurt.

"Let's go sit on the couch instead." Dad places a hand on my shoulder, and we walk side by side.

"Hello, anyone home?" someone calls from outside, knocking really loud.

My dad stops moving, and when I look up at him, his eyes are round and huge.

"Who's that, Dad?"

"Shh!" he warns, his chest moving up and down real fast. And that's when I become super scared, too.

"Francesco, yoo-hoo!" There's another loud knock, but more like a bang this time. "I know you're in there. Open up before we break the door down and cause a scene you don't want."

My body jerks as I inhale, my heartbeats pounding hard. We can't see the men from here. The shutters are still closed since Dad used a key in the back door.

"Matteo." Dad kneels, gripping my shoulders. "I need you to

hide. Go in the back and hide in the closet until they leave. Do you hear me? Don't come out for anything. And I mean nothing."

"No. Daddy. Y-you can come with me. We can go together. P-please." I sniffle, panting while my heart squeezes.

He shakes his head, his eyes full of tears. "I can't, son. They'll come for me. But they don't know you're here and we're going to make sure of that. So go now, and remember"—he holds me tighter—"no matter what you hear, no matter what they do to me, you don't come out."

"No," I sob in a whisper, shaking my head, not wanting to go. He has to come with me.

"You have on the count of three before we start breaking things."

Oh no.

I tremble.

"I love you, son. Never forget that."

"Daddy?" The tears fall down my cheeks, and when he stands, they only come faster.

He smiles weakly. "You remind me of your mother. Every single day she's been gone." He's crying harder. His tears stay in his eyes, filling them, until there's nowhere else to go but down.

"I can't go," I wail, wrapping my arms around his belly, holding tight. "Please, don't make me."

"Hello!" I jerk as one of the men bangs hard on the shutters. "We're getting impatient."

Dad pushes me away by my arms, placing his palm over my cheek, staring down at me. "Matteo. Listen to me." His voice is urgent. Fast. "They're very bad men. They'll hurt you, and I'd die twice before I let that happen. Please, you have to go in that closet. Do it for me. Your brothers need you."

Boom.

"Oh God," Dad gasps. "They're breaking the back door. Go. Now!"

My hands shake as he lets me go. "I love you, Daddy." I snivel, my body shuddering.

"I love you, son. So much. Tell your brothers I love them too, okay?" He closes his eyes and I look at him once again. His tears come even faster.

Boom.

This time, I rush to the back, leaving my dad, running into the closet and shutting the door just as something hard bangs from the outside, then footsteps march in. So many of them.

"Ahh, there he is," a man says, and then my dad makes a noise like someone hurt him. They keep hitting him I think because he screams for them to stop, the men cursing at him as he grumbles.

He sounds so bad. I have to do something. Maybe if they see I'm here, they'll leave. But Dad said not to come out, no matter what.

Glass shatters with a heavy thud. "You thought you could fuck my wife and I wouldn't know? That you're gonna help her and my daughter run away from me and I'd let that stand? You never learn, do you? I took your wife from you, and now, I'm taking your whole family. You'll pay for this," the man says, and my dad screams like he's hurt.

Oh my God, what are they doing to him?

"You thought you could get away with it? From me!" He shouts so loud, I shiver, something warm dripping down the inside of my leg.

Things continue to break across the floor while my father begs them to stop. But they don't. They hit him harder as he groans in pain.

"Give me the bat," another voice says.

"No! Please!"

"You won't die. Not here."

My hands are moving before I could stop myself. Daddy will be mad, but I have to help him. I can't let these people keep hitting him.

Carefully, I push the door open, my teeth clattering, my fingers shaking as I walk out, step by step, scared more than I ever was. Not even when Benny from school said he'd punch me if I sat next to Laura.

"There's someone back there, Faro."

I pull in a breath, my eyes practically falling out. I stop, wanting to run back into the closet, but it's too late. My pulse hammers as footsteps thump in a hurry until a man with black hair stands in front of me, a nasty smile on his ugly face.

"Look who we've got back here."

"Get away from me!" He's on me in a second, grabbing my arm hard while I try to get it off me. But he's too strong.

"Please, Faro, let him go. He's just a child," my dad begs from the other side.

"Let me go, you animal." I punch him with my other hand, but he only laughs as he drags me out where my dad is on his knees, blood coming out from his eyebrow and bottom lip.

"Your son's got a mouth on him, Francesco." The man yanks harder as I come to stand in front of Dad. "You let him talk like that?"

"He's a good boy, Faro," Dad sobs. I've never seen him like this. "Let him go. He's done nothing."

"Maybe not." One of the men guarding the door gives Faro a bat. "But you have." Raising the bat, he smashes it into my dad's head until he falls.

"No!" I yell so loud, hoping someone hears me. "Daddy, wake

up!" But he doesn't, even as someone else throws him over his shoulder. "Where are you taking him? Put him down!"

"Shut the hell up." Faro closes my mouth with his palm while I kick his leg and bite his hand.

"You fucking little shit!" he shouts, slapping my cheek. I give him my meanest face. I won't cry.

He glances at another man to his right. "Give me the tape, Benvolio." When the other jerk tosses it to him, he cuts some off with his teeth.

"Get away from me." I back up a step.

"Where do you think you'll go?" They all circle me. "There's four of us and one of you." He chuckles.

Suddenly, someone grabs my shoulders from behind, keeping me in one place while Faro puts the tape on my mouth and lifts me in the air. He brings me out the back door while I scream through the tape, punching his back, doing what I can. But I'm not strong enough. They toss my dad inside an SUV and then I'm next, thrown in beside him.

One of the men sits behind us while another is next to me, staring like he's trying to scare me.

It's working.

"Wakey, wakey." Faro smacks Dad's face with a flashlight as he mumbles, both of us on our knees in a cold, dark place.

I sniffle, sobbing hard, unable to move my hands tied behind me. Dad's bound too.

I want to go home. I want my brothers. I want Daddy to be okay.

Please, Daddy, wake up. Get us out of here.

"Maybe I should kill your son now. I think that'll wake you up." Faro lifts his gun, pointing it at me. My whole body shakes as *the weapon nears my forehead.*

Daddy, you have to open your eyes! Please!

But with the tape around my mouth all he'd hear is mumbling.

I don't want to die. I try to scream. But it's no use. He can't hear me.

"Mmm," he suddenly groans, his eyelids fluttering, tape around his mouth too, then his eyes jump to me and to the men.

I scream, rocking on my knees, trying to get closer to him, but I can't. My legs hurt too much.

"Ahh, he's risen." Faro rips the tape off his mouth. "Finally, I'll get to hear you beg for your son's life before I kill you both." Abruptly, Faro whips his head in another direction. "You hear something?" he asks his friends.

"It's that damn pipe, I'm tellin' you," another guy says. "Fuckin' annoyin'."

The flashlight jumps back to our faces, and I close my eyes to stop it from hurting.

"It's okay, Matteo. Daddy's here." His voice trembles, and when I'm able to peer at him, his tears are falling fast.

"Daddy won't be able to do shit for you, kid," Faro says with a scary laugh.

I want to go home. Please.

I fall facedown on the floor, crying for someone to help us, but no one comes. No one even knows we're here.

"Please, Faro. Please don't hurt the boy. He did nothing wrong," my father wails. "You can do what you want to me but leave him out of it. He's innocent."

Faro chuckles like one of those villains in the comics I read. "The mistakes of the father always come back on the son, Francesco. You should know that. Say goodbye to your son before it's too late."

Goodbye? Where am I going? I breathe so hard, my chest hurts, my stomach queasy, prickles all over my arms.

"N-no. No. Please no," Dad screams, moving his legs to get close to me, leaning over my shoulder, both of us crying.

"It's okay, Matteo. It's okay. Shh." *But the more I look at Dad, the more I cry, the more I want to hug him. To let him kiss me on the forehead like he does.*

"Want me to do it?" another man asks.

But I ignore them as my dad whispers with a cry, "I love you for always." *He fights so hard to smile, to finish saying what he tells me and my brothers every night before we go to bed.*

And forever after that. *I say it for him, even though he can't hear it, even as the man raises a gun, pointing it at me.*

"Don't look, okay, son?" Dad tells me. "Ju-just look at me and close your eyes." *His voice breaks with a sob.*

"I love you, my boy. You hear me? Papa's sorry. I love—"

Pop.

Three

MATTEO
TWO WEEKS LATER

I hold on to the pillow, my fingers clutching tight, trying to close my eyes and hide away, but I can't. I'm stuck on this stupid mattress, on this stupid floor, in the basement. And it's not even comfortable.

After my stomach started to feel better a few days ago, Agnelo brought me to the basement. He said I wasn't allowed to sleep on a bed upstairs. The trash sleeps on the floor, he told me.

A guy with glasses has been checking on me. He told me he was a doctor and that I got very lucky. If this is what they call luck, then I don't want it.

There's also a lady named Ms. Greco who was making me take

medicine for a lot of days. I forgot what it's for, but she said I would feel better if I took it, so I did.

Moving around, I get up, and my stomach still hurts a little, but not like before. I yank my left hand too hard, the long silver chain pinching my wrist when I pick up the bucket I have to pee in. It's gross. This place is gross.

Every day I'm still here, I try not to cry, but I can't stop. I want my family. I want my brothers. Why haven't they come for me? Could they really have given me away?

When I finish using the bucket, the chain clanks as I pull my pants up and sit back down. A man comes to empty the bucket once a day, then he throws me in the shower. It's always cold. They don't let me use warm water. I shiver as I think about it, hating it every time. But I go really fast and try to think about sunshine. It doesn't help though.

I can't even run away. There's a key for the chain, a lock at my wrist, and the other end around the radiator. At least I get food. Ms. Greco brings me down stuff on a tray. She makes really yummy things, like Dad used to make. She even quietly asks me what I like to eat, and sometimes she gets it for me.

There's a girl who lives here too. I saw her once a few days ago, when they brought me down here from the bedroom upstairs. She was just staring as they dragged me to the first floor, like I was a monkey in a circus or something.

But I haven't seen her around since then. She's tiny with very light brown eyes and blonde hair. It's so yellow and shiny, it reminds me of the sun.

But if she lives here, she must be bad too. Even the lady who brings me food must be bad. If she was nice, she would let me out.

How long will they keep me here? Maybe if I act nice, Agnelo will let me leave. But each day I'm here, I don't think that's true.

I think he's going to keep me here.

Forever.

AIDA

Dad is home today. He's usually gone during the afternoons, out with my uncles or doing work stuff, whatever that is.

He hasn't let me see Matteo since they put him in the basement. I was hoping to say hi or something, maybe share some of my toys, if he likes dolls that is. I do have a police car that lights up. Maybe he'll like that.

I asked my father if I could go see him down there, but he shot me down. I'm too scared to sneak without his permission. I don't want to make him mad. He's already always so angry.

Ms. Greco just finished making spaghetti and meatballs for lunch, putting some into a small bowl for Matteo. She picks up a tray, walking it out to the living room, where Dad sits, scrolling through channels, and I follow her out.

"I—" she says to him, clearing her throat, stopping at the back of the couch. "I'm going to bring lunch down to him, Agnelo, if that's okay with you."

"Yeah, fine. Make sure you don't give that shit too much." He continues watching television.

"Daddy, may I please go with her?" I put on my sweetest puppy-dog face as I jog up to him, my hands in a praying position, my head slanted to the side. "Pretty please."

"Didn't I already tell you no when you asked yesterday?" His voice gets scary loud.

"Okay." I drop my chin and pout, looking up, hoping he'll feel bad and change his mind. "Sorry."

"Hmm." That one word has me lifting my head. His eyebrows do this thing, like he's thinking about something. "You know what?" He smiles, and I instantly get excited because he doesn't do that a lot. "I think you should go see him. He could use a friend."

"Really?" I grin excitedly, and for the first time in a long time, I'm happy.

"Oh, yeah. And you know what else?"

"What?" I clap, practically jumping.

"From now on, it'll be your job to bring him the food. You think you can do it all by yourself?"

"Of course, Daddy! Thank you! I'm not a baby!"

"You can start now." He turns to Ms. Greco. "Give her the tray."

"I—ahh." She peers at the food. "Maybe she can carry the bowl first, then come back for the water bottle?"

"She can han—" he starts to snap.

"Don't worry," I interrupt them. "I can hold the water under my armpit and the bowl in my hands. I got it!" I quickly grab the bottle off the tray, tucking it under my arm, then pick up the bowl. "See?" I glance at them both. "Easy-peasy."

Ms. Greco looks nervous, so I smile really big at her, with my teeth and all.

"Go, Aida," he says. "You gotta clean up the kitchen after, so don't waste time. In and out."

"Yes, Daddy!" I rush toward the basement, down the hallway, to the last door on the right.

Ms. Greco comes after me, opening the door. "Please, honey. Be careful."

"He's just a little boy." I roll my eyes. "I'm not scared of him."

She sighs. "I don't mean of Matteo." Her hand lands on the top of my head and she glides it down my long hair. "We'll clean after, then do some reading when you get back. Okay?"

"Sure, yeah. I gotta go. Bye!"

My feet land on the first step, and carefully, I go down each one, not wanting to drop the food, or Daddy will never let me do this again. I can't believe he changed his mind in the first place. He must be in a really good mood, which doesn't happen a lot. He even smiled at me. He never does that!

I don't see Matteo at first, but when I climb down the last step, I finally do. "Oh no," I gasp, the bowl rattling in my palms, the bottle almost slipping, but I tighten my arm around it, careful not to let anything dirty the floor. Inside, my heart, it beats like crazy.

He doesn't see me, not at first. But I see everything. The long, silver chain he's locked to. The dirty mattress with not even a sheet on it. A small, thin blanket bunched up at the end.

A black bucket is in the corner of the room, not too far from where he sleeps. What is that for? Why would my dad do this? My lower lip trembles. This is awful.

I have to help him. But how? What can *I* do?

His face snaps to mine. "Why are you down here?" Those big brown eyes appear angrier than the last time I saw him when they brought him kicking and screaming into the basement.

He saw me then, while I stood, scared, at the end of the stairs. I didn't understand why my dad and uncles were moving him, but Dad said it's safer for him there. I now see he lied. He always lies. I don't know why I still believe him at all.

I want to run back up and ask how he could do this, but Ms. Greco told me to never question him. *Don't involve yourself in grown-up stuff, Aida. It's not safe,* she'd say. Maybe she's right. Daddy would probably hurt me if I asked.

"I…" My feet tread closer. "I came to bring you food."

"I don't want your stupid food. I want to go home to my family." He kicks his foot out against the tiles, his eyes darting to the floor.

"I'm sorry." I near him some more, afraid to go any faster in case he gets mad.

"Who are you?" He looks back at me. "Why do you live here?"

Suddenly, I'm embarrassed to admit this is my home, that my father is the one doing this.

"Because… This is my house." My voice grows small and croaky.

"So that bad man who locked me here, is who? Your dad?"

I nod, biting inside my bottom lip, my brows pinching tight.

"Well, he's not a good person. And neither are you!"

"Hey!" I fight back. "I'm not like him."

"Then let me go." He rattles the chain on his left wrist.

"I can't," I whisper sadly. "I don't even have the key for the lock. And even if I did, how could I get you out of here? My dad has a man out by the front door when he isn't home."

"Fine. Whatever. Just leave me alone." He stops looking at me again, but I want him to. He has kind eyes. Other than Ms. Greco, I don't have anyone who's kind to me.

My throat aches as I edge a step backward. "I'm really sorry. I wish I could help you. I swear." Tears fill my eyes. "I don't know why my dad would do this to you. It's not nice."

"Okay. Okay. I believe you." He huffs. "Just don't cry."

I nod, unable to stop the tears from falling.

"Maybe you can ask him to let me go?" He looks so hopeful, like I could actually do something, but I'm nothing. Not to my dad. Not to anyone.

"My father doesn't like me very much."

His eyes widen. "But you're his daughter."

I shrug. "I killed my mom, so he hates me."

He frowns, but I continue anyway.

"When I was a baby, my mom died when she gave birth to me."

"That's not your fault." He glares.

I shrug again, not knowing what to say.

"Your dad's a real jerk. Whenever I get out of here, I'll take you with me."

"Really?" I breathe, afraid my dad is listening, the door still open.

"If you want to," he whispers.

"I want to." I let a tiny flicker of a smile line my lips and one makes it to his mouth too.

"Then it's a deal. When I find a way out, you'll come with me."

"I will."

AIDA
THREE DAYS LATER

In the past three days, whenever I bring him food, he talks to me. We don't spend too much time together in case my daddy catches me and gets mad that I stayed too long. But it's enough. I'd like to think we're friends now.

He told me about his parents, about how his mom died a few years ago, and about what happened to him the day one of my uncles killed his father.

I don't think I ever realized how bad my family was until I found him chained up like he's a dog. I've told him about my life too. How I wish I knew my mommy. How I wanted my daddy to love me. How I wanted to have friends and be normal.

I don't know how many days we have together, because knowing my dad, he could change his mind and stop letting me come down here. So today, I decide to sneak something to Matteo when I bring him lunch. With a pen and a small notepad in my pocket, I carry a bowl of rice and fried chicken down to him.

As soon as he sees me, he sits up straighter and smiles the brightest one I've ever seen. I can't help it, I smile right back.

"Hi," he says.

"Hey." I take a seat next to him, not understanding why I'm suddenly shy.

"Thanks, Aida." He takes the bowl from me, putting it in between his thighs so he can use the spoon.

Seeing him eat while locked up like this… I just wish I could do something. But there's nothing I can do.

"I never asked how old you are," he asks, his mouth full.

"I'm eight."

"Me too." His eyes light up.

"We're twinsies!" I giggle.

"Yeah." He laughs as he takes another spoonful.

"Oh, I brought you something," I say, reaching inside my cardigan and pulling out the stuff.

"What's that for?" He glimpses at my hand.

"It's a pad for you to write on. You know, in case you ever need to send me a message and I can't be here. Maybe you can give it to Ms. Greco or something and she'll give it to me. Like a secret."

He nods, wiping his mouth on his sleeve. "Good idea." He drops the spoon into the bowl. "I can hide it under my mattress."

"Make sure he never finds it," I whisper. "I don't want us to get into trouble."

"Don't worry." He grabs my hand and holds it, staring up at me, his long lashes flapping. "I'm sorry you're scared too. But one day, when I'm bigger, we'll run away together. I'll keep you safe."

"Pinky swear?" I hope he does. I'd do anything to go with him.

Looking straight at me, he holds out his finger and I hook my pinky through his. "Pinky swear," he tells me.

And I think, he means it.

MATTEO

They only let me have two shirts and two pairs of pants. That lady takes my dirty ones when I change after the shower and brings me the clean ones.

I once asked her to help me get out of here, but she told me she couldn't. Then she cried as she left. Why can't she do something, like call the police? She's a grown-up!

But no one wants to help me. No one cares. Except Aida. But she's too little to do anything. Plus, I don't want her dad to hurt her.

"Let's go!" the man who unlocked my chain yells as he bangs on the bathroom door. "What the hell is taking you so long?"

My teeth clatter while I quickly scrub the shampoo off my head with trembling fingers, the water freezing as I try to get it all off. My body swarms with goose bumps from the icicles forming on it.

"Seriously, if you're not done in the next minute, I'm dragging you out of there!"

Fear tumbles into my belly. I hate that man. He isn't as old as Aida's dad but he's just as mean. And he has a gun.

He told me he would kill me when I once screamed for help from the basement, so I never did it again.

But I won't be little forever. One day, I'll grow up and I will hurt them all. They'll see. They'll pay for it. For killing my dad.

For hurting me. For hurting Aida.

She's not like them. I was wrong when I told her she was. She's just a scared kid like me. It's not her fault.

No matter what, I'll protect her. She won't have to be sad anymore, not when we escape. Once we're big, we'll hurt them all, together, and they'll be the ones crying.

I shut the water off, shaking as I grab the towel from on top of the toilet bowl lid, and quickly dry before putting my clean clothes on.

The door flies open and that awful man with the brown mustache walks in, his upper lip curling like a monster. "Took your stupid ass long enough. What the fuck were you doing in there, huh?" He yanks my upper arm, dragging me back to the bed, throwing me harshly on top of it. "Not only do I have to clean your shit and piss, but I gotta babysit you while you fucking shower."

Don't cry. Don't cry.

But I can feel it coming. I bite down really hard as he picks up the chain and wraps it tight around my wrist, locking it up with a key he keeps in his pocket.

"What happened? You can't fucking talk now?" He smacks my chin with the back of his hand.

Don't cry. Think of Aida and those funny faces she makes when I tell her about the pranks my brothers would play on each other.

I start to smile. That helps. She helps me. She's my only friend now. The only person I have.

"You're dumb too, I guess." He laughs cruelly, moving away from me, but I just stare at him. "I should take the bucket away and make you piss your pants, but Agnelo doesn't want your stink dirtying up his house. Too bad we can't cage you like the rest of them."

My heart races. My breathing going faster and faster. "I'm

going to kill you." The words slip out of my mouth before I have a chance to stop them.

He laughs. "You? That's cute. Well"—he comes right up to me, his disgusting breath wafting over my mouth—"my name is Louis Esposito. You can try, kid." He shakes his head as he stands straighter. "Man, maybe Sal wasn't wrong about you. Maybe we can make you into one tough and crazy son of a bitch. You better hope so, or your life will get a lot worse."

I can't wait to hurt him. He'll be the first, right after I kill Agnelo.

He finally leaves me alone, going up the stairs, the door closing behind him. A little bit later, I stand, reaching under the mattress to get out the pad and pen Aida gave me.

But there's something else I've hidden there too—a photo. The only one I have of my family. The only sad thing about it is my mom isn't in it. It was taken after she died. Gerard, the man who works in the candy store next to Dad's bakery, took it of us while we were there. I'm sitting on Dom's lap, all of us smiling and happy.

I always keep it in my pocket wherever I go, and the day Agnelo and those others came, I still had it. If they had found it, I know they would've thrown it out. I'm lucky it didn't fall out of my pants pocket when they had me upstairs.

I stare at the picture another second, the back of my nose burning when I remember that my brothers left me. My chin quivers. How come they don't love me anymore? Wiping under my eyes, I quickly stuff the photo back under the mattress in case someone comes down.

Still holding on to the notepad, I plop back down, starting to draw, then scribble a message on the other side once I'm done. It's not perfect, but I think I spelled it right. And that's when I remember I may never go to school again, and I start crying quietly against the pillow. I miss my friends, my teachers.

"I want my family back," I weep with a pant, unable to catch my breath. "Please!" After a few minutes of feeling bad, I rip off the piece of paper with my picture on it and hide it under my pillow, before stuffing the pad and pen under the mattress.

When Aida comes down again, I'll give her the picture I made. I really hope she likes it.

Five

AIDA

"**H**as the boy said anything?" Dad asks as he slips into his black shoes, his back to me, getting ready to leave for the night.

"Not really." I twirl a strand of hair around my index finger.

"Nothing at all?"

"No."

He takes out a jacket and puts it on, facing me this time.

"You lyin' to me?" His thick, black eyebrow rises.

"No, Daddy. I would *never* do that."

"Mm-hmm. If he says anything that you think is important, you better tell me. You hear?"

"Of course, Daddy." I grin. Obviously I'd never tell him anything. Matteo's my friend, and whatever he tells me is our secret. "Why is—" But I immediately stop talking as soon as the question begins rolling out of my mouth.

He stares coldly, flipping a hand in a what-do-you-want motion. "Well, what were you gonna say?"

"Never mind." I puff out a breath.

"I don't have time for this shit. I have places to be. Goodnight." He sets for the door, his hand on the handle.

"Why are you keeping him locked up?"

"What did I tell you about minding your business?" He comes near me, his footsteps pounding across the floor, my pulse now popping in my throat as I swallow. His finger is on my chin, lifting my face up to his. "Don't question me ever again or else you'll never see him anymore."

I gasp, my eyes bulging.

He drops his hand. "Make sure you're in bed in an hour."

Then he's out the door, the lock clicking, the engine roaring a minute later as he speeds away. I knew he'd never tell me why Matteo is here. I'm an idiot.

While Ms. Greco is busy in the kitchen, prepping food for tomorrow, I decide to creep into the basement with a few books in hand—textbooks Ms. Greco teaches me from. I don't know what Matteo knows, but I figure maybe I could teach him what I'm learning. That way he isn't missing out on school.

With a math and grammar book in hand, I stomp down the stairs, making sure to close the door behind me in case Dad comes home and catches me here. Louis, the man who stays in the front during the day, goes home once it's bedtime.

"Aida?" he calls, the chains clacking as I take the last step.

"It's me," I whisper. "Miss me?"

"Kinda." He smiles. "What's that?" His attention jumps to the books in my hand.

"Since you can't go to school, I brought school to you."
Walking over, I sit down beside him, his knee touching mine. "Ms.
Greco is my teacher," I explain. "I don't go to a real school, and I
thought—"

"Why don't you go to school?" he interrupts.

I shrug. "My dad won't let me. I get homeschooled."

His expression turns serious. "Do you wanna go to school?"

"I think it'd be fun, but I try not to think about it much. There's
no point being sad about it. He won't ever change his mind." My
stomach gets all twisty from embarrassment the more he looks at
me. "Anyway, back to the books."

"Okay." His gaze lowers to the page as I open the math book.

"You're in third grade like me, right?" I ask, just to make sure.

"Yep."

"Good. What do you know about adding three numbers at a
time?"

"I'm guessing you'll show me?" He laughs.

"Sure will!"

"Are you any good?"

"Sometimes." I grin wide, getting one out of him too.

We go through a few pages together, laughing, as I show him
the method Ms. Greco taught me, jumping to pronouns for a little
bit before the door opens and Ms. Greco calls for me to get to bed
before I get into trouble. She leaves, giving me a moment to say
goodbye.

"Before you go, I wanted to give you a picture I made." He
reaches under his thigh and takes out a ripped paper from the pad
I gave him. On it is a photo of two kids who look exactly like us.

"Whoa," I whisper. "Did you draw that?"

"Yeah, do you like it?"

My eyes bug out as my gaze dashes from him and then back

to the picture. "Are you some kind of whiz kid or something?" I snatch the drawing. "This is really good. Like *really* good. Is that us next to a house?"

"Yep. When we're bigger, we'll have our own house, and no one will keep us from anything we want to do or boss us around."

"I like that." I giggle. "Can I keep it?"

"Yeah. I made it for you. Oh, and turn it around. I wrote something on the back."

Matteo and Aida. Friends Forever.

My heart bursts from how sweet he is. "I'm going to keep it safe. Somewhere no one knows about," I say with a quiet breath, placing the paper against my heart, my palm squeezing at my chest.

"Can you also take this?" He says it so low, I almost don't hear him as he removes something else from under his leg and hands it to me.

"Is that your family?" I ask, as I stare at three older boys with him, and a man who looks like he could be his dad.

He nods.

"I'll keep it safe. I promise. No one will find it."

"Thanks."

The next thing I know, my arms are around his neck, holding tight, and he hugs me back.

I kind of like it.

MATTEO
THREE DAYS LATER

When I used to sleep in my own house, I could tell when it was day or night, but in this basement, with no windows, I don't know. When Aida brings me breakfast every day, that's when I know it's morning.

It's nice to have a friend in this stupid place. The chain hurts my wrist. It leaves a red mark on my skin. Whenever I'm allowed to shower, it feels nice to have the cold water on it, even while I shiver.

The door squeaks as it opens, and though I can't see her from here, I know it's Aida bringing me breakfast like always. I hope it's pancakes again. They're not as good as Dad used to make, but they're pretty close. They even have chocolate chips in them like his did.

She comes in with a plate of pancakes. "Yes!" I whisper-shout. "I was hoping that's what she made again."

But instead of her usual smile, she frowns. Getting nearer, she hands me a plate, not even sitting down like she usually does.

"What's wrong, Aida?" I grab the food, taking a bite, my stomach growling.

"There are some men upstairs with my dad." She looks to the floor, biting into her bottom lip. "I think they're here for…"

"For what?" My heart beats fast.

"For you," she whispers, staring big-eyed at me, tears gathering inside. "I tried asking my dad what they're doing here, but he told me to get lost. I kept listening anyway and heard them say they'll take you out of here. You can't go!" she cries, kneeling on the floor, clasping her hand over my chained-up one. "I won't let them take you."

I place the plate down. "It's okay, Aida. No matter where I go, I'll always find you. Forever means always."

"Pinky swear?" Her eyes are full of tears as she holds hers out for mine.

"Pinky swear." I fasten our pinkies together.

The door booms open, like someone kicked it. Multiple footsteps traverse over the stairs, so I stuff a pancake into my mouth, eating quickly while Aida gets up, staring at the men now in front of us.

She blocks them from me, her arms out. "Stay away from him!" The men shove her away, and she falls hard onto the floor.

"Hey! Don't touch her!" I jump to my feet. "What's wrong with you?"

A man laughs, pulling up the sleeves of his black t-shirt. "Shut up, kid." The other jerk grabs my arm, and with a key in his hand, he unlocks the chain from my wrist and drops it on the floor with a heavy clank.

"Let me go!" I kick him, stomping on his foot.

"Fuck! You stupid brat!" He whacks me on the face with a palm and I fall back down on the bed, clasping a hand over the pain.

"Get your damn shoes on!" He picks them up from the opposite corner, throwing both at my face, causing me to hurt more.

"Get away from him!" Aida throws her fists onto his back, while the other man yanks her away.

"Agnelo!" he calls. "Get your damn kid out of here."

Another set of footsteps descends until we see him, the man who brought me here.

"Didn't I tell you to get the hell upstairs?" Agnelo yanks her by her hair, dragging her up the stairs.

"Matteo, no! Please, Daddy, don't hurt him!" she screams, her voice growing distant, but I can still hear her calling for me, even as the door bangs shut.

They put a blindfold and a bag over my head once they threw me inside a black car with four doors. I tried to remember everything I could about it right before they did, like the big scratch on the passenger side door.

Once the ride ended, someone grabbed me and brought me inside this building, where more men waited.

They all have guns—big ones, small ones. Some are even on the ground. Are they going to shoot me? I breathe out really hard and my arms go prickly, but I'm trying really hard to be brave.

My heart races as a man drags me to a chair, pushing me onto it, while another eats a sandwich while standing in front of me. The way he bites and chews, it's so gross. He eats like a gorilla. He wipes his mouth on his sleeve, throwing the wrapper on the floor before he pulls over a chair and places it backward in front of me.

"So, kid," he says, plopping down on it, scratching the side of his light brown hair. "You ready to become a man?"

"Wha—ahh, what do you mean?"

"You see this, right here?" He reaches for a gun beside his foot. "You ever shoot one of these?" The weapon flips in his hand and he almost drops it, causing me to jerk back with a pant. "Don't worry." He laughs, his body shaking. "I ain't gonna shoot you with it." Suddenly his face turns serious. "Not yet. Not unless you give me a reason. Do you wanna give me a reason?"

I shake my head very fast, my heartbeats hitting me from the inside, like I'm being punched over and over.

"Good boy."

"Will you let me go?" I whisper so low, but in this big place, it sounds louder.

He mocks with a snicker. "Let you go? Like out of here?"

I nod and he laughs some more. "No way, kid. You work for the boss now. That's why you're here." He glares. "To prove yourself."

"How do I do that?"

"I'm Stan, and I'm gonna teach you. When I'm through with you, you'll be able to fire one of these bad boys in your sleep."

"B-but I don't want to use a gun. They're dangerous. They can hurt people."

"Ain't he cute?" He looks over at the men behind me before firing a stare at me. "That's the point. To learn to hurt people. To become a weapon yourself. And with me as your teacher, you will be. When I'm done with you, your own mama won't recognize you."

"My mama is dead." I scowl.

"Well, if she came back to life." He chuckles, and I want to punch him in his eye.

"Stand up." He pushes the gun toward me, like he actually wants me to get it.

I jerk away, forcing myself into the back of the chair. "Please. I don't want to."

"Fine." He shrugs, and for a moment I think he really is fine with it. That is until he gets up, coming over to me, the gun digging in between my eyes as I gasp wide-eyed, holding my breath. "You ready to die, then? Because that's your only way out of this. Death. You can join your mommy and your daddy." His mouth lifts at the corner and my stomach stirs the more he pushes that thing into my head, my chest flying up and down with quick exhales.

"Three. Two. On—"

"Okay!" I jump. "I'll take it." My body trembles, tears burning my eyes, but I still get off the chair, my fingers on the gun before I hold it in both hands.

"What do I do now?" I frown, the thing feeling like it weighs a million pounds.

"Follow me."

And I do, not having a choice, following him all the way down until we stop in front of something which comes out of the ceiling, with circles on them.

"We're gonna shoot these targets together so you can see how it works." He comes up behind me, his hands wrapped around the weapon, putting mine on it the way he wants. Without warning, he pulls, and the sound of the gun, the vibration from the bullet causes my hands to jerk, my body to stumble backward, bumping right into Stan. I huff like I just ran.

"Whoa, kid. Relax. You'll get used to it." We go again and again, so many times, my hands get tired. But he doesn't stop. He keeps having me shoot more targets. Then a mannequin-looking thing is brought out.

"Shoot it anywhere."

"I—" It looks so much like a person. It even has eyes and a mouth. "Do I have to? I'm tired. Please," I breathe. "I want to take a break." I want to stop forever. I don't like guns. I don't like shooting them. My eyes quickly wander around, and I know I can't run. There are too many men here.

"Do it!" he yells, his face getting red, a gun pointed at my head. "I'll fucking kill you right this second if you don't do it, pussy."

Someone help me! Please! Please get me out of here!

"Kill him," another man shouts.

"Yeah, kill the kid." Someone else laughs, the voice further away.

I turn this way and that, my heart pounding, my breathing heaving out of me.

My hands shudder. But with tears slipping past my cheeks, I take the gun from him, lifting its weight with both hands. Slowly, I raise it, aiming it at the mannequin, closing my eyes, and I pull.

With a gasp, I stare out to where I shot, just as Stan gets up, marching all the way down to the mannequin. "Damn, kid." He examines the stomach area. "That was either a lucky shot or you're a natural."

I don't want to be a natural, whatever that means. I don't want him to be happy I shot good. I want to be bad at this, because maybe then, they'll tell Agnelo I suck, and I can go back to be with Aida.

"Can I leave now?" I ask with hope in my voice.

He makes it back to me. "As long as you can pass the last test of the day."

Another test? Ugh!

But whatever it is, I'll do it, as long as I can go after.

"Yo, Carlito," he tells someone. "Bring it out."

Footsteps pound behind me, my pulse slamming even louder. He gets closer now, coming over, holding a brown box.

"Remember how you shot that target?" Stan asks.

I nod.

"Well, you're going to do it again, but this time…" That's when this man, Carlito, faces me and takes out the cutest white bunny I've ever seen.

My mouth spreads into a giant grin. "Will you let me keep him if I do good? Please? I promise to take care of him!" But when I try to get near the bunny, someone else behind me holds me back around my chest.

"You think we're gonna let you keep a bunny?" Carlito snorts on a laugh. "Where? In Agnelo's basement while they got you chained up like a stray dog?"

"Why would you bring the bunny here if I can't keep him?"

Stan answers, "Because you're gonna kill it."

I stumble back with a whimpering cry. "No! No! No!" My entire body shakes. "I won't do it!" I scream, swallowing my tears with every breath I take. "You can kill me! I don't care! I won't hurt this poor animal!"

"Ahh, but see, I know for a fact that you will," someone else says—the man whose voice I hate, the one whose daughter hates him too. His feet shuffle to us, getting nearer as he comes to stand next to Stan. "He do good today?"

"Acceptable." Stan folds his arms over his chest, both of them staring at me with their monster eyes.

"Now, Matteo," Agnelo calmly says. "You're going to take that fucking gun and you're gonna put a cap in that bunny and you're gonna like it. Because if you don't…" He removes his cell phone from his pocket, and as he comes closer, he plays a video. In it is Aida, sitting on a chair in a kitchen, a man behind her. In his hand is a gun just like this one, but she has no idea it's pointing right at the back of her head.

"No! You can't hurt her!" I shout, huge tears blurring my vision. *How could her dad do this to her?*

My pulse hits me hard in my neck, like it's going to explode out of me, the room spinning.

"That's all up to you." He winks with a cruel sneer, making himself look even uglier than he is. "So, kid? What will it be?" Carlito drops the tall box in front of me. "The bunny or my daughter?"

I stand there, wide-eyed, panting loud as I look at the bunny, hopping around in there. "I can't hurt an animal. I just can't."

"Well," Agnelo says. "I guess you made your decision." He picks up the phone and starts to dial.

"No! I'll do it! Don't hurt her!" The words fly out. "J-just leave her alone."

He puts the phone away. "Do it, then." His gaze narrows. "Show me what you've got."

With the tears dripping out slowly, my feet weighing a million pounds, I take that fluffy bunny and place it against my chest. Those little ears wag, his eyes staring back at me. "I'm sorry," I tell him, petting his soft hair, before putting it back in the box.

With the gun in my hand, I point it to its head. "I'm so sorry." Then I close my eyes and pull the trigger, hoping I missed.

But when I look back at the bunny, I realize I hadn't. Something cold runs up my arms and my chest hurts because I can't seem to breathe while staring at the animal I killed.

Agnelo claps. "Not bad for your first day."

Blood. So much of it, I could barely see the white fur anymore. My stomach wobbles and I instantly throw up. But nothing seems to come out.

No… What did I do?

I killed something. I hurt someone.

Am I bad now too?

MATTEO
AGE 10

My breaths blow out in a rush while I'm running like crazy, looking over my shoulder as they chase me. *Faster. Go faster.*

They're coming closer.

"Better think of something quick," Stan mocks as I round the corner, running up the metal steps of the warehouse, not sure where I'm going since I've never been up here before. I enter a pitch-black area, their footsteps not far behind.

"How are you ever going to be tough when you're so scared?" the other man taunts. I have no idea what his name is. I've never met him before.

They want me to fight them both, as if I could. I'm short, small, and they're huge. They say I have to be tough if I want to work for them, but I don't want to work for anyone.

These last two years have been nothing but hell. I'm still in that shithole basement with no way out, because no one will help me.

They take me here every day, teaching me to fight. To shoot. To kill. I hate it all.

When they bring me back to the basement, all I do is silently cry, missing my family, the way things were, like my brothers picking on me for getting in their way. I miss that. I miss them. All of them.

I blink away the tears, knowing I'll never see them again. If in two years they haven't found me, it probably means they don't want to.

Aida's the only good person in my life. She's pretty and nice. We talk all the time. I love her more than anything.

Their hard footsteps crash up the stairs as I gasp, my panting loud.

Crap! Stop thinking about her before they kill you.

I widen my eyes, looking this way and that, but there's darkness everywhere. I run anyway. I can't wait around for them to catch me. I turn a corner and—

"Boo!" Stan jumps out, a flashlight under his chin, a frightening smile on his face. "Lookie who I got, Drew." He grabs my hoodie, yanking me back down the stairs, my feet practically tripping over each other while I try to keep up.

"Oh, it's our little friend." Drew pouts and his black mustache does too. He's scarier than Stan. "We missed you. Gotta say, you're some runner though. Now, we're gonna see how well you punch."

I shake my head as Stan throws me to the cold floor. "I don't want to fight."

"Too fucking bad." Stan kicks my back.

"Ow! Stop!" I cover my face with my palms.

"Owww! Stooop!" Drew mocks in a baby voice. "I'm a wittle pussy."

Stan kicks my back again, harder, right before Drew lifts me up, balling my hoodie in his fist. "Punch me! Show me what you got."

"No!"

"You have one more chance to do it before I hit you."

With my rough inhales, I form a fist at my side.

"Don't want to disappoint Agnelo, do you? If Daddy isn't happy, his princess is in lots of trouble." Stan chuckles.

At the mention of Aida, my fist lands without a thought right into Drew's cheek.

"Fuck!" He grits his teeth, and when he punches my chin, I crouch on the floor as he lets me fall onto it.

If protecting Aida wasn't the only thing I cared about, I would've killed them all by now, or at least tried to. But over the years, Agnelo has threatened to hurt her if I don't do what they want. So I have to. It's the only way to protect her.

"Stupid kid has a good right hook." Drew massages his cheek. "He's got potential," he tells Stan as though I'm not there.

"Agnelo wants you to start today."

"And I will, right after I give him a good ass beating."

Once his foot connects with my stomach, I don't remember much after that.

AIDA
AGE 10

I pick up my books after completing another reading lesson with Ms. Greco, needing to take them to my room before Dad gets home. Just as I'm about to climb the stairs, the front door opens and in comes Stan, a man who's been in the house a few times, carrying—

"Oh my God!" The books drop with a bang as I run. "What did you do to Matteo?" I shout as he brings him toward the basement.

"My goodness," Ms. Greco whispers in a trembling way. "Is he still alive?"

"He's fine." Stan rolls his eyes. "Drew got a little too happy with his fists. Kid's gotta toughen up."

"You assholes beat him up?" I grit as we reach the basement. I'm boiling with fury tangled with rage.

"You better watch your tone with me," he snaps. "Don't want your daddy finding out what a little bitch you are."

"Don't speak to her that way!" Ms. Greco opens the door, while he brings Matteo down.

"I'll speak to her however I want." His tone's ice cold as he throws Matteo onto the mattress, getting in her face. "What are you gonna do about it? Spread your legs?" He snickers.

I wander my gaze from him to her, and she's glaring just as hard at him.

"Yeah," he says on a laugh. "That's what I thought." He turns, locking Matteo up, the chain clinking as he takes out the key, then roughly brushes past her, going up the stairs.

"Are you okay?" I ask her once the door closes.

"Yeah." She forces a smile, but in her eyes, there are tears. "His poor face." She clears her throat, her attention on Matteo. "His cheeks are so raw. I have to clean him up."

When I finally look at Matteo… "Oh God." My chin quivers. "Do you think he'll be okay?"

"We're going to do everything we can to make sure he is." She tucks me to her side with a squeeze. "Now, run upstairs and get me two towels from the closet and a big bowl from the kitchen with some lukewarm water in it."

"Yeah, I'm on it." I nod, then I'm gone in a flash.

Together, we cleaned the cuts on his face. He finally woke up about an hour after we finished. He knew where he was and who we were, which was a good thing according to Ms. Greco. He even drank water but refused to eat anything.

I wouldn't be hungry either if someone just beat me up. If I could, I would hurt those men just as badly as they hurt him. How could they do that? What's wrong with these people? It's like my dad made them all crazy. Like him.

In the past two years, Matteo and I have gotten very close. We're literally inseparable, and it's not because he has nowhere else to go. We laugh. We read books to each other. We dream about the world outside of ours, wondering what it feels like to be in it, to be one of those people, the lucky ones. I'd do anything for him, and I know he'd do anything for me.

I lie beside him, refusing to leave him alone, in case he needs something. We hold hands as we face one another, one of his eyes swollen almost shut.

"I'm so sorry, Matteo." Tears bathe my lower lashes. When he doesn't say anything, I continue, "If I knew how to get you out of here, you know I would. I'm sorry my dad and my uncles are doing this to you." I lower my head, too ashamed to face him.

"It's not your fault," he finally whispers, squeezing my hand once. "None of it has ever been your fault."

"They're my family." I snivel with a gasping breath.

"But you're not them. You're you, and you've always been a good friend."

But I'm not, I want to argue. I haven't called the police for starters. Not that I could. We have no phones in the house, and Ms. Greco is too afraid of Dad to ever do it herself. What if calling the cops causes more awful things to happen to him? To Ms. Greco? I don't know what to do.

He inhales slowly. "Could you stay a little longer?" He closes his eyes. "It'll help me sleep."

"Anything you need."

I glide my hand up and down his arm, the way Ms. Greco does when I have a rough time going to bed. When his chest falls peacefully with his breathing, I stare at him one last time before I shut my eyes, and hope the nightmares stay far away—from the both of us.

That boy I met so long ago is gone. He's older than he seems. Colder. Harsher. It's as though my father sucked out all the joy he once possessed.

We're still close. And he's still here. In the basement. Chained. Locked away from the world.

We still spend every single day together. My father somehow lets me. I don't question it. I take it as a gift, one of the few he's given me. Except it's not really a gift, now, is it?

It's suffering and pain wrapped in a pretty bow. Because in my gaining a friend, he's suffered. Horribly.

They've beaten him countless times, so badly once, the doctor thought his ribs were broken. Those are the only times they've allowed him to rest.

The other days, they take him, and there's blood when he returns. On his face. His hands. Sometimes even his clothes. Sometimes there's a little, and other times there's so much. He won't talk about it, the stuff they make him do. But I don't have to hear it to know it's bad.

Yet, no matter what they do to him, I can still see shreds of that little boy I care so much about. They haven't managed to rip him away from me completely. I don't think they can, though they try with all their might.

My friend. That's what he is. The only one I have. I can't lose him. He can't die. But every single day they drag him away, I'm afraid that'll be the day he doesn't come back.

He hates for me to see him hurt. Whether it's his cut-up knuckles or the bruises on his face, he tries to hide it all. But that's not something a person can hide. He'll tell me to go, that he's tired, but I know what he's trying to do.

I wait for him to come out of the shower, sitting on the bed. Louis, the man who still watches the house during the day, stares at me, leaning against the wall, waiting to chain Matteo back up. Why can't my stupid father just lock the damn room and let him move around like a person? He can only walk right past the mattress and to the corner of the room.

The door clicks open, and Matteo comes out, his hair still damp. He's fully dressed.

"Finally." Louis huffs like he had to wait longer than the damn five minutes it took. "Let's go." He grabs Matteo, who shoves his hand away with a snarl. "You fucking do that again and I'll cut your arm off," Louis warns and Matteo grits his teeth in response, glaring hard as he's yanked to the bed, the chain enveloping his wrist.

"Your father said to come right up in five minutes. Don't piss him off."

"Mm-hmm." I roll my eyes in annoyance. "Bye, now." I shoo him away with a hand, popping my brows as I sit next to Matteo on the mattress.

He bites down while eyeing us cruelly, cursing as he heads for the stairs. Once the door shuts, I breathe a sigh of relief.

I hate these people—my father, my uncles, their men. Why can't something bad happen to all of them so Matteo and I could run away like we planned to when we first met.

"Why do you still want to be my friend?" Matteo asks, staring at his own hands while playing with his fingers.

I jerk back. "What kind of silly question is that?"

"A serious one." He drags in a long inhale, finally looking at me. "I'm not a good person, Aida."

"Bullshit. You may have forgotten, but we're friends forever. Remember? Friends don't give up on each other."

He peers down onto the floor.

"Why don't you talk to me?" I whisper right into his ear so no one hears. "Why can't you tell me what's been going on? Maybe I can help."

His head shakes sadly as he pitches back with a mournful stare. "You can't. If you wanna help, then run, Aida. Leave this place when no one's looking, or you'll never get out."

I scoff. "Even if I could, I'm not leaving you. Ever. You're stuck with me." I shrug. "We either go together or I don't go at all."

His hand lands over mine, holding on tight. "You have to think about yourself."

"I'm sorry." I look him hard in the eyes. "I can't do that."

"I'm sorry too." His face turns into a frown.

"Aida," Ms. Greco calls. "Come on up, we have homework."

"Ugh!" I groan.

"Go." He gazes onto his lap as I reluctantly get to my feet.

"I'll come back, okay?" I incline my head, angling it toward him, hoping to catch his eyes. He finally glances up. "We'll study together later, once my father leaves."

"Yeah, okay." He sighs. "I'm gonna sleep for a bit though." He begins to lower onto the bed, giving me his back like I'm disturbing him.

My heart clenches and my palms fall against my chest. My poor Matteo. Why did you ever have to end up here? I'd give it all away—knowing you, loving you—just so you never have to suffer.

I whirl toward the stairs, running up before I start to cry, making it to the kitchen just as the first quiet sob rips through me. Sliding down onto the floor against the kitchen island, my palms covering my face, my body trembles while I break with the force of my emotions.

Why am I such a loser? Why can't I help my friend? Why am I afraid of him—my horror of a father? I should kill him in his sleep. I want to. I could. Maybe. *Ugh!* No. No, I can't. I'm not a killer. But maybe I should be.

Footsteps creep closer, but I don't have the energy to discover who it is. "Aida?" Ms. Greco's concern spills from her voice. "Sweetheart, what's wrong?"

"Everything! I wish I was never born," I cry lowly, swiping my palms over my eyes as I peek up at her. "How could you not help Matteo? Why can't you do something? I'm just a kid, but you're an adult."

"Shh. Your father will hear you," she whispers, looking around before dropping beside me. "You think I don't want to? You think seeing that poor boy down there year after year doesn't kill me every time I walk into this house?"

"Then why?" I demand. "Why haven't you done something?"

"Because…" She shuts her eyes. "You're still a baby. I shouldn't even say a thing."

"I'm thirteen. I'm not a child. I know my father isn't good. But I want to know why you don't help. Because you, Ms. Greco, you're good." My brows dip as our gazes align.

She lets out a defeated breath, wandering straight ahead as she starts. "I have a sister. She's about ten years younger, and when she was really little, my parents borrowed a lot of money from your uncle Faro to get her a kidney. They couldn't pay him back. Not all of it. So Faro killed my father, and as a way to earn what we owe, he's enslaved me to work for his family in whatever way they need. Over the years, I have been through hell, living through the most horrific things." She tilts her head with a glance at me. "Being here with you is the best job they've given me so far. If I do anything, like report this, they'll kill my sister and my mom." She tugs my hand over her lap and squeezes, her brows tugging tightly. "I'm sorry, Aida. I'd help if it were just my life on the line, but—"

"I get it now." I nod, my voice hoarse. "I'm sorry I doubted you." The tears trace down my cheeks.

"You never have anything to be sorry about." She looks tenderly at me. "You're nothing like him and thank goodness for that."

MATTEO
AGE 13

"Again!" Stan shouts over my shoulder as I pummel fist after fist at the man lying under me, his nose cracked, his eye swollen, but I don't stop. I don't know how to. It's what I've done these past years. What they've wanted me to do.

"Harder! Show me what you're worth!"

I roar, as another punch lands over the man's cheek, picturing Aida being hurt, them doing stuff to her.

I'll never let them hurt you. Never, I growl to myself, as I almost kill the man who's no longer defending himself. Not that he had much left in him after they brought him here. I've never killed a person yet, but I've done other things.

Thanks to Stan and Drew, I've not only killed animals, but I learned how to fight. To hurt people well enough to make them cooperate, which means do whatever the Bianchi assholes want.

After the bunny they had me murder, they moved me to cats and dogs. Now, I hurt people. But I'd do anything for her. Anything at all. Even kill.

And they all know it.

"Whoa, kid." Stan wraps an arm around my chest from behind, pulling me back. "Didn't say to ax him yet. You can relax now."

"Is he dead?" I breathe heavy, my chest burning as I try to calm my inhales.

The man groans, as though answering my question. I didn't want to hurt him. I don't want to hurt anyone, but I don't have a choice.

Stan rises over the man. "You better have that money you owe us or else we're coming after your kid next. And my friend right here"—he pats my head even though I'm almost as tall as him—"will do far worse to your boy than he did to you."

The guy cries as two others drag him away.

"You ready for your next job?" Stan asks.

Sure, if that involves breaking your nose.

"Yeah." My reply is calm.

"Bring him out," he tells someone else. A man appears, yanked by his shirt. His sneakers drag across the floor as he mutters with a sob, his mouth covered with black tape, his hands tied up behind him. He fights the hand that holds him, his eyes bulging once he's next to us.

He's probably the same age as the other guy I just hurt. They're all usually older. My knuckles throb. I don't think I can handle giving another beating, but I'd never complain. Not if they'll hurt Aida as punishment.

"The big boss is here for this," Stan warns. "So you make us proud." That's when more footsteps pummel, until they get nearer, until their faces are clear as day. Faro and Agnelo stand beside each other, staring into me with an empty look in their eyes.

The man groans and fights as he's taken to a chair and pushed on top of it. But as I come at him, readying a fist, Agnelo laughs.

"No, kid. This time"—he reaches into his coat pocket and whips out a pistol—"you're going to blow his fucking brains out."

I jerk back, my lungs rattling with heavy breathing, my stomach winding with knots. "I can't do that." I keep retreating, step after step, until someone grabs me from the back and holds me down.

"What the fuck did I tell you?" Stan barks in my ear. "You fucking do this and do this well or you know what they'll do to your precious girlfriend."

"She's not my girlfriend." I glare back, grinding my teeth as I look straight at him.

These people, I want to kill them all instead. I want to take Aida and run away with her. But I can't, and she'll never go anywhere without me. She's made that clear. So we're stuck here, in this world where I'm forced to do the most awful things, not for me, but for her, the one person I have left in this world to protect.

That girl is the only one who still makes my heart feel happiness. I don't know how not to be when she's around. Even when I push her away, even when I want to hide the evidence of what her family makes me do, still, I want her around. She's a part of me I can't let go of, and I'll protect her always. Because no one else does.

"Take the fucking gun," Agnelo shouts as he walks up to me, pressing the barrel of the weapon into my throat while Faro watches from behind him. "You'll do what we fucking tell you. It's the only damn reason you're not working the club. You remember it, right?" His upper lip curls. "The place I showed you?"

I refuse to answer. Just thinking about that disgusting place makes my heart race. The sick things those people were doing with each other, to the kids.

"Answer me, boy!" He slaps me hard, my head whipping to the side. "Not only will I send you there for being a shit…" His hand curls around my jaw, the gun digging into my neck. "But I'm going to send Aida there too."

"No!" I pant, shaking my head over and over until my neck hurts. "Don't do that to her."

"Then you pick up this gun"—he pulls it away and stretches it out for me—"and kill that scumbag."

"Wha—what did he do?" Maybe if he's bad like them, I can do this.

Faro chuckles. "You work for us. You don't fucking ask questions." He steps up to me, grabbing a fistful of my hair and yanking hard. "It doesn't matter what he did. Hell, we could've picked him up off the street and you'll still have to kill him. You have no alternative. You either kill for us or we send you and Aida to work the club. It's your choice." He drops his hand away, returning to where he first stood.

My shoulders tremble with loud exhales as I take a peek at the man I have to kill. He stares at me, his eyes pleading, his head jerking, the chair rattling as he tries to run, his muttering getting louder.

My mind instantly goes to Aida—that long golden hair, that smile, which always lights up the room, erasing every awful thing I've done and will have to do. For her. And without another single thought, I take the pistol from Agnelo, line it to the man's forehead, and…

"I'm sorry," I whisper as I pull the trigger, the rip of the bullet piercing the air.

Instantly, his face falls forward.

He's dead. I did that. I killed a person.

An arm drapes around my back, a hand falling over my shoulder, but my eyes are glued to the dead guy.

"You never apologize," Agnelo says. "You kill without hesitation. Without an ounce of regret."

I glance over to find him glowering at me, the fury in his eyes forcing me to swallow down my fear.

"If you ever apologize again, I'll fucking kill her. Then, I'll kill you."

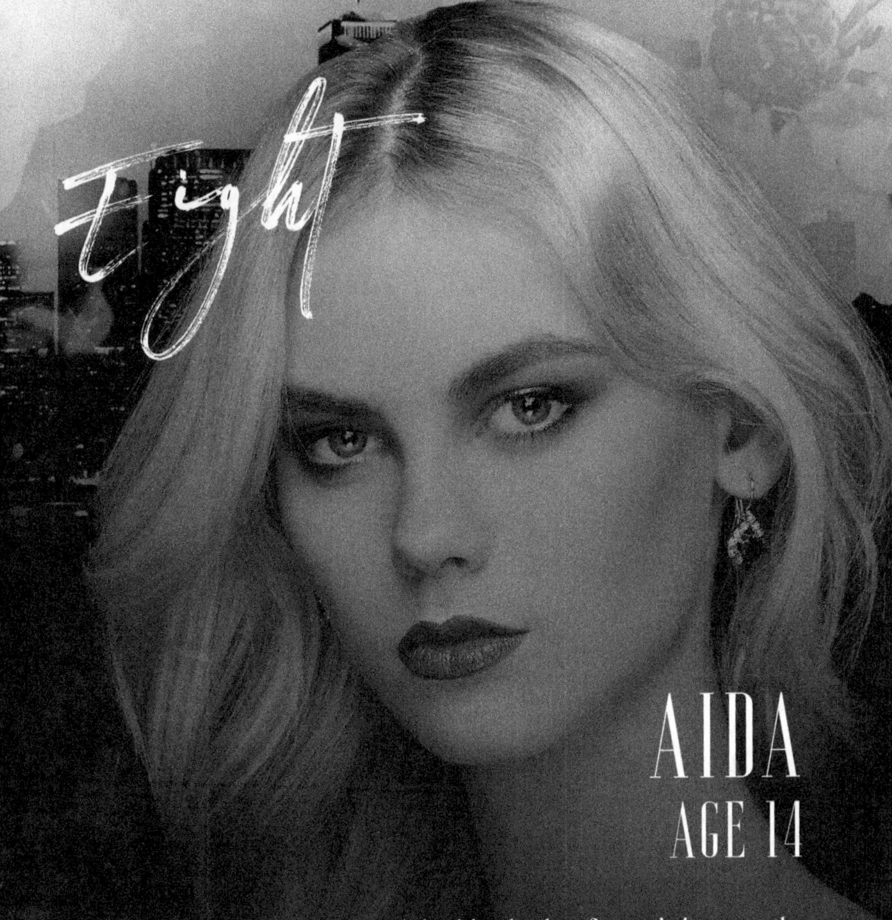

He holds my hand in his, both of us sitting on the mattress still on the floor like it's always been, the same one we both know quite well.

Every year that passes, I think this will be the year my father changes his mind and lets him go. But I'm foolish, aren't I? Evil has no bounds. No restraints. It'll eat away until there's nothing left. And from Matteo, they've managed to take everything.

He's only fourteen, but his eyes, those kind brown eyes, they lack the sweet touch of the little boy I once met, and every year, I find less of him.

But no matter how much he may change, our friendship never

does. He's still my Matteo. And lately, I think… I think I'm starting to like him, like more than just a friend, which is weird because I never even liked a boy before. Not that I'm around any or anything, but still.

I could never tell him though. I could never say that when I'm near him, my stomach does this flip thing, like a swarm of butterflies have somehow made it there. Nor could I tell him that whenever his lips roll up in the tiniest of smiles made just for me, it makes my entire heart burst. I'm even grinning as I think about him. I can't tell him any of this because I'm sure he doesn't like me that way. Why would he? He's cute, and me—not so much. My hair is too thin and pale for starters. What boy would like that?

"What are you thinking about?" he asks, rubbing his thumb over the top of my hand, my head lying over his shoulder.

"That I have ugly hair."

"What?" He jerks his head back in an instant. "Who gave you that idea?" The way he stares, it's not with anger at me, but for what I just said.

I shrug, avoiding his gaze by staring at my bare feet. After a few seconds, he snakes a hand under his pillow and retrieves something. In his palm is the notepad I once gave him.

But as I look at it, as he turns to open a page, I let out a small gasp, my stomach flipping all over again.

I can't stop staring.

My breathing goes ragged.

I'm there on the page, in a long wispy dress, my hair caught in the wind, skipping among flowers, butterflies floating around me, like he knew that's how he makes me feel. But that's silly, of course, there'd be butterflies in a meadow. That's what this is. He continues to turn, page after page, and I find more of me on every single one.

He's been drawing me this whole time? Why?

He gazes straight at me, the crooked smile reaching the far corner of his mouth. "Your hair reminds me of the sun, and the sun is beautiful."

My heart flutters in my chest, tears growing within my eyes. And his face, the one that barely ever smiles anymore, grins so wide for me now. "Did you just call me beautiful?" I whisper with a thread of shock, because there's no way he said that.

He raises a shoulder with a smirk. "I may have."

My mouth spreads into a smile of my own, those butterflies in my stomach flying higher. And my head, it falls right over his shoulder, his arm draping around my back. "I think you're kinda beautiful too."

With a deep sigh, his head slants over mine and we stay that way until it's time for me to go, wishing I didn't have to.

MATTEO
AGE 14

Is this how it feels to like a girl? To want to see her every waking moment, not being able to wait until she's here? Because that's how I constantly feel. Every single second.

She's so perfect. So pretty. Why would she ever say she has ugly hair when I think she's the most beautiful girl in the world? And sure, I haven't been around any, but I don't need to see them to know they don't compare to her.

I've been drawing Aida for a while now. It's how I've been coping with all this shit they put me through. It's the only time I can get out of my head whenever she's not around, to help me through the mess inside it. And she does help, more than she realizes.

If she weren't here in this house, I'd want to die. It'd probably be easier, for it all to end. No more pain. No more killing. I've killed too many. I don't want to do it anymore. But they continue to threaten her if I don't, and so I do it. Over and over.

"Wake up." Stan smacks the back of my head, the van jerking to a stop. "Time for daydreaming is over. You've got work to do."

"Yes, sir." I strain the words out, hating them as soon as they come out. But I do it all for her, no matter how sick it makes me. She's still the most important person in my life. None of them matter. No one but her.

Two men hop out, Stan following them, grabbing my arm and tugging me out too. We're back in the warehouse, the same one we're always in when they make me kill people. They don't take me anywhere else.

But during these drives, it's the only time I can see the sun shining brightly through the passenger side window. It's the only time I get to see the world, even though it's only through a lens of their making.

We head inside, reaching two men on chairs, zip ties around their wrists over their thighs. Their faces are barely recognizable from the beating they obviously got before we came.

Stan takes out his gun, handing it to me as he faces one man while I face another. "They're all yours, kid."

The cool metal clings to my palm as I lift it up in the air, aiming it level to the chest of one man.

Pop.

Done.

That's all it takes to kill someone. Just a flick of a finger. And this time when I kill, I feel nothing at all.

Blood spills from the hole in his chest, and when I move to the next guy, he kicks out with his feet, dragging himself back in the chair.

But he can't escape me. No one can. My footsteps are almost silent as I move on him. The further he goes, the more I do too. When he falls backward, looking up at me, he starts to cry, knowing that this is it, that as I lift the gun this time, it'll be over.

Pop.

No more screams. He's quiet now. Those empty eyes, they stare at me, and I wonder if they see the monster I've become.

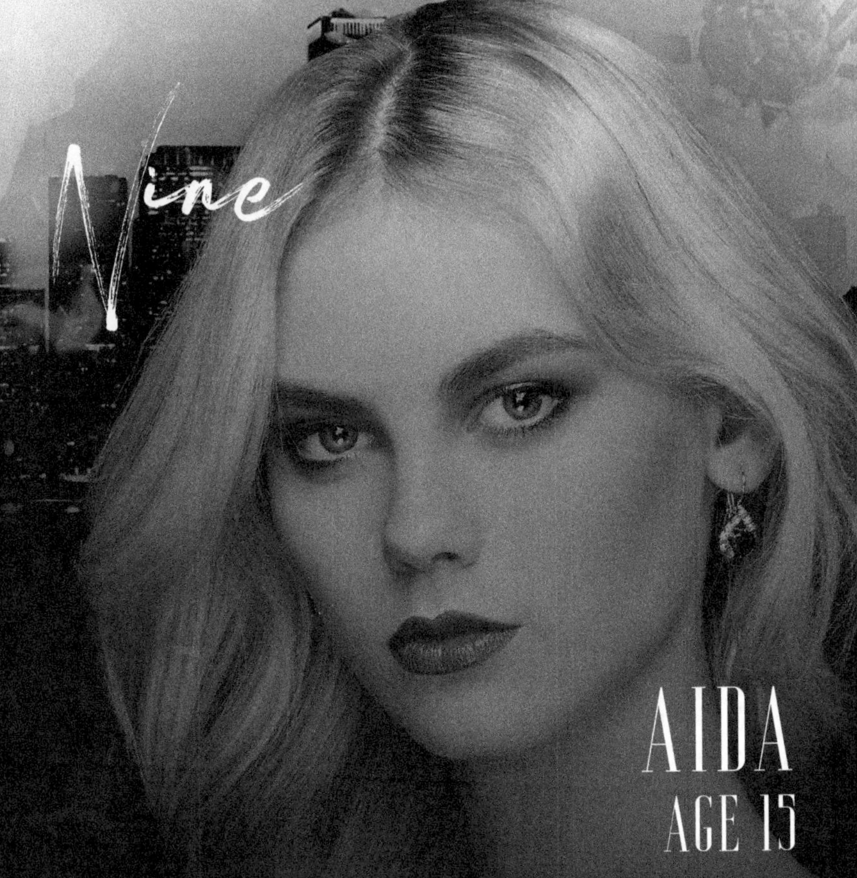

AIDA
AGE 15

A heavy clattering wakes me from my sleep, my eyelids heavy as I rub at them, groaning, and stuffing my face into the pillow. From the corner of my eyes, I find darkness out the window, wondering why my father would be up this late. Unless he left after I went to bed and is coming home now.

I ignore the stomping of his feet as they get near, yawning, attempting to fall back asleep. He bumps into something else with a groan, and that's when the sound of a baby's cry erupts.

I instantly sit up, turning on my bedside lamp, my heart racing. "What the…?"

Did I imagine it? I must've. Why would he have a baby? I shake my head. But just as I'm about to plop down onto the bed, my door swings open, and there he is, a soft bassinet in one hand, the kind for the floor, and a real-life baby in his other.

"Dad?" I yawn again as the baby wails. "What's going on? Whose baby is that? Why do you have it?"

"Shut the fuck up, you little bastard!" He throws the bassinet on the floor beside my bed, placing the baby into it, a blue blanket wrapped haphazardly around his body.

The little one continues to cry, his little pink mouth curling pitifully. I swing my feet onto the floor, staring at him, not sure what to do. I've never held a baby before. What if I break him? Drop him?

"Why is he here?" I glance at my father. "Where are his parents?"

My dad crosses his arms and glares. "He's mine."

I freeze. "I'm sorry, what?" I'm sure I misunderstood.

"He's my kid. He's going to be living with us."

No! No! No! He can't live here.

"What?"

"You heard me," he barks. "You know how much I hate it when you question me."

"I don't understand," I continue. "Where's his mom?"

"She's in prison."

"Prison?" This has got to be some kind of joke.

"Are you gonna repeat everything I say? Are you stupid or something?"

"Who will take care of him?" My father sure won't. He doesn't have a caring bone in his mean body.

"He's your brother. *You're* gonna take care of him."

My brother? Oh my God. He's my brother…assuming my father

isn't lying that this boy is actually his.

"Dad…" I grimace as the baby screams with all his might. "I'm only fifteen. I know nothing about babies. I can't do this."

"What the fuck is so hard? You feed it, change it, and put it to sleep. Stop acting like it's damn complicated. Your great-grandma was fifteen when she had her first baby. You could learn a damn thing or two."

"I don't even know how to hold one," I whisper, not sure if my father could hear me over the loud sobs of the little boy.

"Alison will help you," he says of Ms. Greco. "I texted her already. She'll see it in the morning before she comes over tomorrow."

"What about food? Diapers?"

"I got that shit. It's in the kitchen. One of my guys got everything his wife told him to get. Got some bottles and pacifiers to shut that kid up too." He lifts a fist in the air. "You make sure he's damn quiet when I'm home, you hear?"

And what if I can't? I want to ask. *Will you hurt him?* My brows bow as I get off the bed, kneeling beside the baby, stroking his soft cheeks, and suddenly he stops crying. Just like that. This poor thing just wants someone's touch. My heart, it aches.

You shouldn't be here.

I reach for him, both arms cradling him as I tuck one beneath his tiny head, the other one around his butt, like in one of the books I've read, hoping I'm doing it right even as I try not to tremble.

I'll take care of you, I promise.

"What's his name?" I ask, unable to rip my gaze from this beautiful boy.

"Robby."

"Nice to meet you, Robby." I grin. "I'm your sister, Aida. And I'm gonna love you."

"My guy is gonna give me his baby's old crib and some other shit, so I'll put it in here tomorrow." I stop listening to him, focused on the new life in my arms.

He turns for the door.

"What if I need something?" I quickly ask. "What if I need help with him?"

"I don't fucking know," he spits out, his face twisting with a snarl. "Figure it out with Alison."

He stalks out, slamming the door behind him, but Robby doesn't pay him no mind. He falls asleep against my chest like nothing else matters.

"So you want to use the sponge gently on his head," Ms. Greco explains the following day, both of us on the floor in the bathroom as she shows me how to give him a bath. Once my father brought the things for the baby, Ms. Greco and I organized it around the house.

"And you never ever touch the baby's soft spot." She gently runs a fingertip around it. "Right here."

"Okay. Could I try washing him now?" I pivot to get more comfortable around the infant tub.

She hands me the sponge, and I go to work, squeezing some bodywash into it before rubbing it on Robby's hair as he coos, his hands moving robotically.

"That's great. That's exactly how you do it. You're a natural." She smiles like she's proud of me, like I'd imagine my mom would look at me if she were alive. Is it bad I wish Ms. Greco was actually my mother? I love her more than my own father.

"Thanks. I can't even believe this. I have a brother."

"I can't believe it either," she says quietly, sitting up on her knees as she watches me with him. "He seems to really like you."

"He's just so adorable. And he has the most beautiful blue eyes I've ever seen."

"They're pretty special." She sighs as I drop the sponge at the corner of the tub.

"I'll be there to help you in every way I can. You're not alone in this." She places a palm over my shoulder. "I'll sleep over as much as I can when I'm not helping my mom."

I nod, looking up at her, feeling the relief wash over me. Her mother isn't well. She has diabetes. "Thanks. I can't do this alone," I breathe.

"No one can, especially a child. What he's doing is wrong," she whispers. "And I don't believe for a moment this baby's mother is in jail."

My eyes widen. "You think he stole the baby?"

"It's your father after all."

My pulse pounds. "Oh my God. That's awful if it's true."

"I know. But knowing him, I don't expect any different."

Once we're done washing Robby, she carefully scoops him up while I grab the towel from the counter.

"You ready?" she asks, moving him toward me, my heart hammering as I get ready to hold him against me, nervous I may drop him in this position.

But as soon as he's in my arms, I wrap the towel around him, and place him gently over my chest.

"You're doing great," Ms. Greco reassures as I caress his back, his little head against my shoulder, making my heart explode. He doesn't make a sound, just lies there, like he's content to be with *me*. Like I'm somehow special, which I'm not. Maybe he just doesn't realize it yet.

We head for my bedroom, placing him on my bed as Ms. Greco

grabs one of his one-piece pajamas from the closet.

She helps me dress him, lifting his head when I'm too afraid to do it myself. But I'll have to get used to it. She won't always be here. With the bottle already made and sitting on my nightstand, I pick him up, cradling him like the first time.

He sucks on the bottle, looking up at me, staring sweetly the entire time, his body small and fragile. This perfect baby has got to be one of the unluckiest. Because to end up here, you have to be.

MATTEO
AGE 15

When she visits me today, she isn't alone. In her arms is a baby named Robby and all I do is stare. Compared to us, he's so small. Too small for a place like this.

"I don't get it. How the hell did he get the baby?" My eyes are unable to look anywhere but at him, curled in her arms with a dinosaur shirt which snaps around his diaper.

"His mom is supposedly in prison and my dad's the father."

I shake my head, huffing out a breath. "You can't keep him here, Aida. They'll hurt him. You know that. He's too damn small to defend himself."

She tilts up her chin. "I'll defend him."

"Aida…" What do I say that she doesn't already know? That she's just a kid herself? That if her father wanted to kill them both, he could in a second?

"He's my brother, Matteo. What else can I do? It's not like I can pawn him off to someone safer. He's stuck with us, as bad as that is."

I release a long sigh. "You're right. I'm sorry."

"Don't be sorry." Her brows knit as she takes a step closer, standing over me.

"You're sure your dad didn't steal him or something?" It wouldn't shock me if he killed some family and stole the kid.

"I hope not, but that's what Ms. Greco thinks." She rocks Robby in her arms, her golden hair swaying as she hums "Twinkle, Twinkle Little Star," those hazel eyes glimmering in the sparkle of the light above.

"Can I hold him?" I ask, which is probably stupid. Why would I want to hold a baby? But he's just so damn cute.

"Umm…" Her gaze widens.

"I promise, I won't break him." I chuckle. It's adorable how protective she is of him already, even while only having him a day.

"Okay." She clears her throat, biting into the inside of her lower lip. "Make sure you secure his head, just like I am." She kneels so I can see better. "And also, hold him under his legs."

"I think I got it." I smile, loving how cute she is when she's serious.

"Okay." But she still doesn't hand me the baby, her gaze darting between us, like at any second, she's gonna bolt.

"Aida, I don't have to hold him if you don't want me to."

"No, no, it's fine." She giggles nervously. "I'm being too much of an annoying big sis, isn't that right, Robby?" She lowers him into my arms. "I think we'll be okay if Matteo holds you for a minute."

"Maybe two minutes?" I tease.

"Ha, ha." She rolls her eyes mockingly.

"Hey there, buddy," I say, my eyes now wandering over this small thing in my arms. "How you doing in this crazy world?"

He yawns in response, his little fingers spreading out before forming a fist. He's going to need that fist to survive here.

"I'll protect him too, Aida." I look to her with all the promise in my eyes. "I swear."

"Pinky swe—"

"Pinky swear." I grin as I curl our fingers together in a vow that I have every intention of keeping.

"**D**o you have a boyfriend?" my cousin Raquel asks me a few days later as we sit in her parents' kitchen for her mom's birthday. The grown-ups are all talking loudly in the den, while Chiara and I join her here where it's quiet.

"Umm…" I play with the bowl of potato chips, avoiding both of their hard stares. What do I say? That I'm crazy for a boy I've known since I was eight? That he's a prisoner in our basement? Oh, and I also have a baby. Well, he isn't mine. My dad just brought him home one day. Oh, here, Aida, you should know what to do. Bye. "No, I don't have one."

"That sucks," she says, her mouth twisting in pity. "I mean, I don't either because of my stupid parents." She rolls her eyes. "But at least I could go to school."

Ouch. I know she didn't mean it that way, but ouch.

"Your dad is such a douche," Chiara adds. "I'm sorry. I mean my dad is Satan, so I sympathize, but at least I can escape mine in school. You can't even do that."

Okay, guys, just keep piling it up.

I simply nod, tightening my lips.

"You could talk to us, you know?" Raquel adds, placing her palm over the top of my hand.

No, I can't. If I tell you the truth, my father will hurt Matteo or maybe even Robby. He told me as much many times throughout the years. Threatening to kill Matteo and me both if I ever opened my mouth to anyone about anything. I believe him.

"I know I can." The words are a whispered lie. "Do you have anyone special?" I ask Chiara, hoping to change the focus away from me.

She shakes her head, her features growing depressed. "I have no one. No one but myself."

"You have me." Raquel bumps her shoulder.

It suddenly makes me sad we aren't close, but we couldn't be. I'm just as much my father's prisoner as Matteo is. He's never let me have a friendship with them, no matter how much I've begged. I think it's because he's afraid I'll spill his secrets. But I'd never do that, not when Matteo's safety is at stake, and Robby's too.

I wish they got to know Matteo like I have. I bet they'd love him just as much as I do. He's got the kindest eyes when he looks at me. It's like the ice in them thaws away, leaving the boy he once was behind. But it doesn't last. Whenever he goes with my father's men, he comes back different.

But I'll love him anyway. Like I once told him when we were younger, friends don't give up on each other. No matter what.

"Whatcha girls doing in here?" My father suddenly appears, like a ghost haunting me, no matter where I try to hide.

"Nothing much, Uncle Agnelo," Chiara throws in. "Just eating chips and discussing school stuff. Math sucks." She laughs as her eyes land to me, hiding the truth of our conversation.

He chuckles dryly. "Yeah. Never cared for it either." His attention zips between us, a suspicious glint in his eyes. "We're leaving in ten," he tells me. "Make sure you're ready."

"Yes, Dad." But he's already marching out of sight.

"You think he believed you?" Raquel whispers to Chiara, flitting a peek to where he just came from as though afraid he'll return.

"I hope so," Chiara says. "I don't know who's scarier, Aida, your dad or mine."

With a deep sigh, I say, "It's a tie."

"You're not kidding." She snickers.

We remain hushed for a moment until Chiara speaks again. "I miss my mom." Raquel grips her hand, pinching her lips tight. It's been two years since Chiara's mom disappeared. No one knows what happened.

"I'm sorry," I say and meaning it. "I don't know how it feels to have a mom, but I bet it was nice."

"She was pretty great." She smiles big, looking distantly, wiping quickly under her eye. "Anyway, you got ice cream in this place or what?" she asks Raquel, blinking rapidly. "I want a bowl full of chocolate."

"I think so." Raquel giggles, standing up to check the fridge. "You're in luck, cuz," she calls, pulling out a carton, lifting it in the air. "Let me grab some bowls."

"You know what," Chiara retorts. "Just get some spoons. We'll eat right out of it. I think we've earned it."

"I think you're right," I say, meeting her gaze, a threaded smile between us, like she sees me, the silent hurt I carry in my heart.

Raquel brings over the spoons and we dig in, laughing together, having the best time as though our life is normal like all the other kids our age. But there's nothing normal about us, especially me.

MATTEO

"Did you get to eat?" she asks as soon as she's down here. A pretty flowy blue dress hits her knees, the straps thin at her shoulders. I shouldn't look at her the way I am right now, but I can't help how beautiful she is.

Her blonde hair falls over both shoulders, pinned back at the center, away from her face, which is a good thing, because her face is too breathtaking to hide.

I clear my throat, gesturing with my head at the empty bowl on the other side of me.

"Oh good." She moves forward, playing with her hands, clasping them tightly in front of her. "Sorry I wasn't here to bring it to you. I was out with—"

"A date?" I cut her off, gritting my teeth so damn hard, it fucking hurts. I don't want her out with anyone but me. But she has to live her life.

The chain cuts into my skin as I pull, reminding me that I'll never be with her. I'm the secret she keeps, not the boy she falls for. I run a hand down my face, avoiding her gaze.

Everything I know about the world, I learned from her, and she's one good teacher. Being secluded here, I would've wasted away, been a moron who knew nothing, but she taught me all of it. So yeah, I know about dating, and sex, and all that shit. When she pulled out a health-ed book last year, or whatever it was called, and explained that whole business… Yeah, it was damn awkward.

I don't want her doing any of that with someone else. I want that with her. Someday. When it can be the first time for both of us. Together.

Nice to dream, except it won't ever happen. She's free in more ways than I am. That's the way it should be. I'd never wish my life on Aida.

She doesn't know I like her. I never admitted my feelings. Because what's the point? What could we do about it? Not like I could take her on a date or buy her flowers.

I want to take her on a picnic, hold her hand, our faces to the sun. The warmth… I could feel it. My eyes fall to a close. Deep breaths. We're there now.

Her soft footfalls approach, yanking me from the fantasy, and I manage a glimpse at her.

"Me? A date?" she finally answers. "Please, who would want me anyway?"

My pulse races as I give her a long stare. And once I find that doubt in her eyes, I can no longer hold it in, and it comes spilling out.

"Me!" I slap a palm against my chest. "I'd want you. That's who."

"Wha-what?" she stammers, her brows tightening, mouth trembling. "Do you—do you really mean that?" Her steps draw closer.

"Of course, I mean that, Aida," I whisper. "How could you not see it?" My heart tilts with emotion, gripping me with more than I've ever felt before, especially when I look into her unsure eyes.

"I just…" Her lashes go downcast.

There's that doubt again.

"Sit with me." I pat the empty space, needing her close. And when she does, when she lowers right beside me, clasping her hands on her knees, I slip mine between them, threading my fingers through hers. "I like you, Aida, even when I shouldn't. I've liked you for a while now. I just haven't had the guts to admit it." She finally looks at me, her expression stunned, those long lashes fluttering.

"I—I like you too," she confesses with a hushed breath, like she's afraid someone will hear it. "There's no one I like more."

My mouth quirks up at the corner, my stomach dropping in that nervous way I only get with her.

She likes me. It's a relief to hear her say that. For so long, I thought she'd never see me that way. Sure, we're friends, but I'm the boy locked away in her basement, and she's the daughter of the man holding the key.

We're complete opposites in that way, but we're also the same in the ways that count. We like the same jokes, have the same wishes for what our life will look like when we're out of here, and most importantly, we like spending time together.

I often wonder if we'd be friends had we attended the same school. Would she give a boy like me a chance? Would she be shy the way she is now? I bet all the guys would follow her around, desperate for even a bit of her attention.

I can't believe her asshole of a father won't let her go to school. That's got to be against some kind of law.

"What do we do now?" she asks, her gaze dancing between the floor and me.

"Get married?" I tease with a smirk.

"I'm serious." She giggles, swatting me lightly on the chest.

"I don't know, Aida. We just exist. Here. In this basement. Dreaming of another life."

Her eyes bore into mine, glistening with tears as she forces a smile. "I'd never want to exist with anyone but you."

"I wish I could give you more." My voice is steady, yet there's a tiny crack in it.

She gives my hand a squeeze. "You've given me enough."

"Somehow I don't think that's true."

Her eyes dance between me and her fingers playing on her lap. "You…um…you can give me something else."

"What's that?" I sit up straighter, wanting to give her everything.

"I've never…" Her voice is a barely there whisper.

"Never what?"

"Never kissed anyone."

My pulse quickens. "Do you want to kiss me, Aida?" I breathe.

"Yes." She nods, her gaze tucked into mine.

Slowly, with a soft exhale, I lean into her, and I do.

I kiss her.

Eleven

AIDA

I replay our first kiss time and time again, even though we've had many in the months since then, shared whenever we're together. And sometimes, in those brief moments, it feels as though we're normal. Like I'm a girl who met a boy she's crazy about. But then I remember where we are, like the storm chasing away the sun, and it hurts so bad.

And sure, I wish Matteo didn't have to be here at all, but if he had to be anywhere else of my dad's choosing, I'm glad it's with me. At least he has Ms. Greco and me looking out for him. And today, I plan to make it special for him, because it's not any ordinary day.

My father has never celebrated my birthday. He doesn't even acknowledge it. If it weren't for Ms. Greco, it'd be just like any other day.

When I was little, maybe seven or eight, before Matteo, I had asked him if I had a birthday. Everyone in my family was celebrating them, and it made me wonder why I wasn't.

He told me I was born on March third and that was the end of the conversation. I always just assumed he didn't want it celebrated because that's the day Mom died. I get it. I accepted it.

But Ms. Greco hasn't. Every year, she'd get me a cupcake and we'd sing happy birthday when Dad wasn't home. It was nice to have at least one person care. She'd also sneak me a gift.

This year, she got me winter boots and a bunch of books. Last year for my fourteenth birthday, she got me a diary. I never had one before, but it's been fun to keep my thoughts in one place, locked with a key so that no one can read what's inside.

I never asked Matteo for his birth date. What a friend I am. I guess because it's been so insignificant in my life, I forget it may matter to others. But when I had finally asked yesterday and realized his was like two weeks before mine and I missed it... God, that look on his face. It broke my heart.

I promised myself that every year he's here, we'd celebrate it, and though he may have turned fifteen already, it doesn't mean we can't celebrate it late.

So, I asked Ms. Greco to make him a cupcake of his own today, and I also asked her if she'd buy him a notebook and some colored pencils. My dad will probably kill us both if he ever found them, but I've kept them hidden under my mattress. A lesson I picked up from Matteo.

"They're done," she says, as the timer on the oven beeps, and I instantly hop off the stool as she retrieves a tray full of chocolate cupcakes. He once told me how his father owned a bakery and how he'd made the best Oreo cupcakes, which were his favorite.

Ms. Greco and I were so excited to make them for him. I just hope they're close to what he remembers.

Robby giggles on the high chair, throwing pasta on the floor, his face covered in tomato sauce, a toothy grin you can't help but love.

"Robby!" Ms. Greco tsks playfully, cleaning up his mess while the cupcakes cool. Once he's happily playing with his teether, we start on the frosting. "Do you think he'll like them?" I ask as I mash up a bunch of Oreos.

"You know what I think?" Her smile drapes her entire face with warmth, as she cuts up some butter before tossing it into the bowl.

"What?"

"I think that boy is going to love anything you make him."

"You think?" My cheeks heat up as I try to hide them by peering into the bowl, not wanting her to know Matteo and I like each other, that we've kissed. A lot.

She laughs, shaking her head. "Oh, Aida. You have to see the way he looks at you when we're down there together. It's like he can't stop staring, even when you're not staring back."

I instantly look up, wide-eyed. "Don't tell Dad, okay?"

"Of course not. I'd never say a word." Her focus returns to baking, using the mixer, her voice growing low. "You're allowed to like people, Aida. No matter what your father says or does."

"That's kind of hard to do." I bring over the Oreos and pour them in with the butter mixture. "He doesn't let me have a life. Matteo's the only kid my age I can hang out with and that's not even hanging out."

Turning off the mixer, she places a tender palm over my cheek. "I know, sweetheart. Your life is cruel, and still, you make the best of it. You both do. I'm really proud of you for that. Not everyone would be this strong. I know I wouldn't."

"You're strong too," I say, instantly swinging my arms around her middle in a tight hug, loving her so much. I don't know what I'd do without her.

We get to frosting all the cupcakes. She only made four, not wanting my dad to flip out when he didn't okay this. Ms. Greco has to inform him of what she plans to cook and bake each day. If he doesn't give his approval, she can't make it. He's insane.

She took a big risk for me and I adore her for it. We're lucky my father's man, Louis, doesn't guard the house anymore like he used to. Maybe my father realized we're too scared to run, and he wouldn't be wrong. Louis still comes once each morning to empty Matteo's bucket and let him have a shower before storming back out.

I finish up the last cupcake, placing two in a bowl for Matteo, both with a candle in it, but neither is lit. We can pretend though. And I'll sing him the best happy birthday song anyone has ever sung.

"Alright," Ms. Greco nervously says. "Hurry, before your father surprises us and comes home."

"Yeah, okay." I scoop up the bowl, carrying it out of the kitchen, starting for the hallway. But before I could make it down into the basement, the front door swings open.

Oh no!

I suck in a breath, my body creeping with a shudder as I try to hurry out of sight, the bowl rattling in my palms, almost slipping.

"Where you rushing to?" My father's fiery tone skitters up my spine. A tight knot forms in my throat and my knees buckle. "Hello!" he shouts. "What the fuck are you doing? Turn around and show me what you got."

"Nothing, Dad." I discreetly start removing the candles while numbed in place. One quietly hits the bowl but as I slip off the other, it falls out of my jittery hand and lands on the floor beside my feet.

His footfalls are rough as they approach me from behind, my breathing going ragged. I will the fear away, swallowing it down where he can't see it, where I don't feel it, but it doesn't work. Because fear is all I've ever known. His hand hits my shoulder as he tightens it until it hurts.

"Did you really think you were going to get away with this shit?" He drops the hand away, crouching to retrieve the candle. Once he rights himself, he violently turns me around. I hold on to that bowl for dear life, my lungs heaving with short breaths.

He levels me with a glowering look. "Where the fuck were you going with that?"

I instantly shrivel up, my arms slithering with goose bumps. "I was just going to bring one to Matteo." I sweeten up my voice, hoping to pierce that rock of a heart he has, but it's no use. Nothing could make him love me. Nothing will make him human.

"Who the fuck told you he's allowed dessert in my fucking house? Does this look like a damn restaurant to you?" His face nears mine and nerves roll in my stomach, heavy, thick dread crawling up my throat. "He's not our fucking guest. He's our prisoner. I allow him to eat my goddamn food and that's all he's gonna get!"

"But, Dad!" I plead. "It's his birthday. Can you please do this for me?" Tears sting the backs of my eyes.

"Put those cupcakes in the trash." He backs away, straightening his blazer. "I won't repeat myself."

"Why do you have to be so awful!" As soon as those words fall, my eyes bug out. His hand is quick as he slaps me hard across my cheek.

My teeth clench as I fight the onslaught of tears already

swarming in my eyes. Panic sucks me in, my pulse throbbing heavy in my neck.

Don't cry.

"You talk to me like that?" He grabs the bowl away with a rough tug, smashing it onto the floor as I whimper, his foot pounding over the cupcakes, again and again, the frosting running up his shoe.

"You stupid, little ungrateful bitch!" His hand finds the back of my head, snatching my hair as he yanks. "You want a damn cupcake? Go fucking eat it!"

I let out a snivel.

"Agnelo!" Ms. Greco screams. "Stop!"

He ignores her as he throws me on the floor, his shoe landing on the back of my neck as he pushes my face into the cream, bits of cake making it into my mouth.

"Eat it." He stomps harder, my nose and my mouth covered with what I thought would be something Matteo and I would share. Instead, I suffocate on the flavor, the taste now corrupted by the man who's supposed to protect me. But he's always been a monster disguised as a man.

A bout of a sob falls from me, and in the background, Ms. Greco cries too, begging him to stop, to have pity on me, blaming herself.

"Hurt me, Agnelo!" she pleads. "I did this. Not her."

He pushes me in deeper instead, a shard of the porcelain puncturing my cheek. I can feel the ache, the burn as it enters. The tears come heavier now, like the pounding of hail on the ceiling.

"I'm gonna deal with you later." My skin comes alive with a tremor, afraid for the both of us. "You little cunts think you can do whatever the hell you want when I'm not here, huh?"

"I'm sorry," she weeps. "I'll never disrespect you again. It was wrong. P-please let her go. She can't breathe."

"Go get some rags," he barks to her. "And both of you better make sure this mess is cleaned by the time I finish with my shower."

He finally removes his foot from my nape and takes off both shoes, throwing them at my head. I sob as he stalks away, leaving me there like I don't matter at all. But I never did, did I?

In his bedroom, she screams. He has her there, and I can't do a thing about it. I wish I could stuff my ears and stop hearing it, but I can't. I refuse to. I should listen. I should hear her suffering. It's all my fault. Wanting to do something nice for Matteo has caused her pain—the only other person who's ever given a damn about me.

My father's room is right next to mine. I can hear every grunt, every cry. My insides curl and I'm ready to vomit, snatching the small garbage pail from the corner of my room and hurling into it.

Grabbing a pillow, I lower it over my face, wailing into it, my entire body shaking as I do. The small cut on my cheek throbs, but I ignore it, unable to stop from shattering.

If there was a gun in my room right now, I'd rush right into my father's bedroom and shoot him dead. I continue to sob as she does too.

The door next to mine creaks open, then slams shut. Heavy footsteps crash across the floor, the stairs squeaking as someone goes down them. When the front door bangs shut, I know he's finally gone.

I sit up, wanting to run in to see Ms. Greco, to make sure she's okay, but I'm afraid. What if he comes back? What if she doesn't want to see me after what he did to her?

A wave of nausea impales me again, but I manage to keep it down this time. How could he do that to her? To anyone? Why do I still wonder? How could my mom ever love him? Why would she have a baby with someone so awful? I don't doubt he treated her badly too.

Maybe she got the easier end of the deal. She's gone, not having to deal with his cruelty, while I'm here, endlessly tormented, wondering when it'll all stop.

Minutes trickle by, until a whole thirty minutes have passed. I've been tracking it on the clock on my wall. There's a soft knock on my door and I instantly jump off my bed, knowing it's her.

My hand on the doorknob, I pull it open. When I see her, my bottom lip trembles, and hers does too. Mascara runs down from her lower lashes, past her cheeks, her eyes glossy, her hair matted. Instantly, my arms come around her, and I hug her tightly to me as she cries.

MATTEO

"Aida!" I shout, pulling at my chain, trying to get it off the radiator as it cuts into my skin, wanting to run to her. To save her. He's hurting her, while I'm here, unable to do a damn thing about it. Her desperate cries penetrate through the ceiling as something heavy shatters on the ground…and the way Ms. Greco screams for him to stop… My hands ball into tight fists, my lungs heaving, begging for air.

"Aida! I'm here!" I growl in frustration, knowing if the chain was off, he'd be dead. I'd kill him and not even blink. It's who they taught me to be. End lives without feeling. Without thinking. And he'd be my easiest kill. I just need thirty seconds. Then it'd be over.

He tells them to clean the mess, then it's silent. But the quiet doesn't last long. When he returns, so does his yelling.

"You missed a fucking spot!" His voice is like a hammer built for destruction. Ms. Greco screams as Aida begs him to let the woman go. I yank at the chain with a roar, my skin ripping, drops of blood slipping down to my feet.

"No!" Aida shouts with a deafening cry and my heart slices in two. She sobs as footsteps stomp further away until they're distant. Until she's alone. Until all I hear is her pain until she's gone too.

I don't know how long I remain down here, anger swirling inside me, pacing back and forth in front of the mattress because that's as far as I can go.

After some time, my door opens. At first, I think it's him, coming to give me a piece of what he gave them. I dare him. I'd rip his goddamn throat out with my teeth.

"Aida?" I ask, as someone gently climbs down the stairs.

"It's me." She sounds so small. Like a bird with her wings clipped, like the sun darkened by the rainy sky.

Her face lowers once she's before me, and when she looks up, my eyes zap to the cut on her cheek.

"He did that?" My exhale howls out of me. "He hurt you?"

"Don't," she cries, those warm, golden eyes that radiate with the glow of the stars, now clouded with darkness. "I can't stay long, but I couldn't not come and wish you a belated happy birthday. Again." She sniffles, avoiding my gaze. "I really tried to make it special. I'm sorry."

"Hey, come here." I reach a hand for her, my brows tightening with my own bout of sadness. "What happened?"

"I had Ms. Greco make you a cupcake. But he found out and…" Her chin trembles. "I'm sorry I ruined your birthday." Large tears slip past her eyes, sloping down her cheeks as she lets out a single sob, punching me in the chest.

"No, Aida, don't cry." My arms are around her, holding her close, knowing I can't keep him away. The only thing I can do is do whatever he says so that he doesn't send her to the club or kill her.

"I don't care about my birthday." I pitch my face back to look at her. "I only care about you, okay? Don't do anything else to piss him off."

"So I guess I shouldn't have brought down your birthday present?" She swipes across her lashes as a tiny, pained smile curls over the corner of her mouth.

"Aida…" I slant my face. "You shouldn't have gotten me anything. I just like spending time with you. That's all."

"I know, but I wanted you to have this. He can hurt me all he wants for this. I don't care."

"But I do." I grasp her shoulder, locking her in a stare. "I will *die* before I let that happen."

"Well, if you die…" Her voice goes faint, fresh tears pooling in her gaze. "I'd really have no one at all."

I pull in a long breath, rage filling me. Every time she cries, I get the urge to murder her father.

She reaches under her shirt, confusing me, until she removes a notebook and a box of pencils.

"Whoa. This is great," I say as soon as I see them.

"Yeah?" Even through the hurt, she still manages to smile, to make me do it too.

"You kidding?" I take it from her. "You know drawing is my thing. Now, I've got a lot more to draw you on." The corner of my mouth tilts up.

She sighs brokenly. "Make sure you hide them well."

I grab hold of her hand just as she gets set to go. "I will. Promise." Her eyes fall to mine and that familiar flip in my stomach hits me hard.

"Could I kiss you?" I ask in a breathy tone, afraid the world will somehow slip beneath our feet and I'll never get another chance.

She holds my cheek in the softness of her palm. "You can always do that, Matteo."

So I do.

For as long as she lets me.

Twelve

AIDA
AGE 16

Watching Robby grow into the funny, sweet, and beautiful one-year-old he is today has been more than I could've asked for. And with him, I grew up too. I had to. I had a child to take care of.

Having him and Matteo here with me has kept me sane. My father has only gotten crueler in the past years, and he's not softened to Robby either. How could anyone not burst with love when that boy giggles?

I feel sorry his mother is in prison, missing him grow up. Sure, she gets her monthly visit, and I hate that Robby has to go to a place like that, but that's her baby. I'm glad he knows her. I know

I had my doubts about his mom being alive, but where else would my father's men take him every month?

"Where are you, stinky butt?" I call, tiptoeing around as though I can't hear his laughter under the table. "Oh, boy, when I find you, you're going to get so many tickles." That gets him rolling. "Oh, man, what is that noise, I wonder?" I creep around the table, pretending I can't see his little legs right next to me. "Could it be…" I pop my head down. "There you are!" He giggles. "I got you!" I tug him out by his feet and he instantly jumps into my arms.

"Yav you."

Yep, my heart just turned to mush. No one has ever loved me, except Ms. Greco. But this is different in a way. He's actually my brother. My flesh and blood.

"I love you too, baby bro." I hug him tighter. "We gotta get changed so you can see your mommy, okay?"

"No!" He giggles, running away from me as soon as I drop him down. "Oh, you can run but I'm gonna find you." Then I'm laughing too, chasing him around, finally snatching him up, taking him to our room so I can change him.

It's nice when my dad isn't home. Robby and I can play without him screaming for us to shut up. He hates hearing that boy's laughter. It's like he's allergic to joy. I'd be too if I was a sadistic piece of shit.

Over the past year, Ms. Greco has been my saving grace. She's helped me with Robby more than anyone in her position would. And it wasn't because she feared my father. It was because she wanted to. She adores Robby, genuinely. I'm glad he has us, especially while being exposed to my father's temper.

A month ago, when Robby was coloring on the floor, he yelled so loudly and knocked over the crayons, telling that poor child he'd kill him if he did it again.

Robby didn't understand the words, but he knew rage. He had to living here. His face broke with the saddest eyes, before he began to cry. It shattered me. I lost it. It was the first time I really stood up to my father.

"Look, Robby, this is a turtle." I point. He just started saying words, and it's stinking cute.

"Tootle."

"Sure, let's go with that." I laugh, gliding a hand through his blond hair. Ms. Greco just gave him a little trim, but it's still so full and beautiful. "How about we color it? What color should we use?" I ask, as I spill the box of crayons into a paper bowl. "What about red?" I wag my brows playfully.

"Wed!" His eyes glisten with innocent joy and I want that. To feel this much for something as simple as coloring with someone I love.

"Do you mean red, silly?"

He giggles, his dimples popping out on both sides. "Wed!"

"Okay, wed turtle it is."

"Tootle." He looks all serious as he corrects me.

"Tootle. All right. Let's color that tootle wed."

"Yay!" He picks out the red crayon, sticking it into his mouth, sitting there on the floor, while I color the sun purple.

"Don't eat it, silly!" I tickle his belly and the crayon rolls away. He wobbles to retrieve it.

The main door opens and my father struts in, my uncle Sal with him as I turn. "Hey, Aida," my uncle greets.

"Hey, Uncle Sal. How are you?"

"I'm good, kiddo. Raquel says hi."

"Tell her I said hi too. How is sh—"

"What the hell are you two doing on the damn floor?" My

father's voice booms like a crack of lightning pouring from the sky. Robby drops the crayon from the shock of it, his eyes frozen with a frightened stare at him.

"It's okay," I breathe. "Come here."

He runs into my lap as my father rushes to us. Kicking the bowl, all the crayons rapidly scatter across the floor.

"Are you trying to get this damn floor dirty, you stupid bitch?!"

He grits his teeth, his nostrils flaring as he bends his face close to mine.

"We were just drawing," I say in a calm whisper, holding on to a trembling Robby. I wish I could take him out of this place, but how could I run away without Matteo? I can't leave him behind. My father will definitely kill him if I do.

"Pick up that fucking shit and throw it out. There will be no more drawing. And if you"—he points a finger at Robby, who dares a look at him—"ever draw on my floor again, I'll kill you!"

Robby bursts into tears and runs off under the table in the next room. That's his favorite hiding spot.

My heart pounds, my entire body breaking with seething rage, the kind that makes you dizzy, blood boiling, skin tingling.

I stand up, my jaw pulsating. "You sick, pathetic excuse of a man! How dare you tell a little child that you'll kill him? What the fuck is—"

I don't get to finish because the next thing I know, his hand is around my throat, squeezing hard.

"You're done. I'll fucking ruin you." His fingers tighten and I claw. I fight. But he's strong. Too damn strong. My lungs burn, my throat bursting with agonizing pain. I can't catch a breath, my eyes rolling.

"Agnelo, let her go," Uncle Sal says. "You're killing her."

"Shut the fuck up, Sal!" he yells. "Do I tell you what the hell to

do with your own kid?"

My uncle backs away. Asshole. That's what they all are. Every single one of my uncles is a monster. They have to be for killing Matteo's father, for allowing him to be imprisoned.

If Ms. Greco was here today, she'd try to stop him, not that it'd do any good. My father would only hurt her. I'm glad she's with her family right now.

I don't know how long he keeps me hostage to his torment, but he finally drops me to the floor like a rag doll, spitting at me before he paces back out the door.

"Robby?" I call, my chest heaving as I cough. "Come here. It's okay." My hand falls to my neck as I fight the ache there. "He's gone now."

But he doesn't come, and that only makes me want to die.

MATTEO
AGE 16

"Again!" Stan shouts as I kick the man on the ground, his face swollen so badly, you wouldn't be able to tell if he has his eyeballs in there or not. His lip is busted up to the point that blood gushes out like a fountain.

The only good thing about being taken to the warehouse is that it gives me some time away from the chain, which is a relief, even while knowing the dirty things I'll have to do when I'm out of it.

There's nothing left of the man I'll have to kill. My only purpose is to hurt the people they bring me. No questions asked. And I never have any. Not anymore.

I kick the man again and he doesn't make a sound. "Check his pulse," Stan tells me, and I do, leaning over, two fingers on his neck.

"It's still there."

"Good." He kicks the man himself, just once. Then he removes a small flip knife from his pocket.

"Cut his fucking throat."

I grab the blade from him. They've never had me use a knife before. Bullets are easier. Shoot and you're done. This is more personal.

"Let's go. Hurry up. I have places to be," he snaps.

I kneel, opening the weapon, lowering it to the man's neck. My hand's steady. They don't like weakness. They'll punish her for my mistakes.

With a quick breath, I let the knife slice from one side of the man's throat to the other. Blood oozes with thick drops, seeping steadily.

"You're gonna fucking bleed out like a pig," Stan tells the man, slamming his foot into his nose.

I drop the knife beside the body, hoping he's dead already. This is more suffering than anyone should take. And knowing these people, I doubt he did anything at all.

"Take him back to the house," Stan tells another, who's already yanking me away.

Every time I hurt a man, I can't wait to leave, needing to be with Aida. She's the only one who makes the world seem right even as it crumbles.

Thirteen

AIDA
AGE 18

From the moment he entered my life, Robby has been my world. I often wonder about his mother and whether she knows who her son is with. I've come close to writing her a letter that I know my father would never give her, but I wish for her to know her boy is loved. That he has people who fiercely protect him.

I've done my best to care for him, with Ms. Greco's help. And when she isn't staying over, I'm all alone with him. The first year was the hardest. I barely slept. He was an awful sleeper. On those days, Ms. Greco was here, taking over night feedings. Thanks to her, I was able to actually catch up on sleep, which is a weird term, because you can't catch something that's forever lost.

My father never bothered with him and still doesn't. I don't think he's held him once. Not even as he played on the floor, smiling at him, reaching his little hands for a man who despised him. But Robby didn't need my father, he had me, Ms. Greco, and Matteo. We gave that baby all the love he ever needed.

"Come on, poop head," I tell Robby, holding his hand, heading down to see Matteo. "Let's show him what you made him. He's going to love it so much."

Robby's skills may not be that of Matteo's, but the kid makes the cutest scribbles I personally have ever seen.

Since I gave Matteo those colored pencils, he's made picture after picture of us. Pages filled with how he sees me, and in those pages, I'm actually beautiful. I don't see it, but Matteo says he sees it for the both of us, and it makes me love him even more.

And I do love him. I kind of always did, in one way or another. I don't know how not to. But every time I try to say those words, they get trapped in my throat. I'm scared. What if my father hears us and stops me from seeing him after that? What if he sends Matteo away or, worse, kills him for it?

Another part of me fears Matteo wouldn't see me that way, that our kisses have been nothing more than two people who've known each other for most of their lives, trapped together.

He's the only boy I've ever been around, felt this much for. He makes me feel like I'm floating. Like the world is something it isn't. That monsters don't lurk in the open. I forget it all in his arms.

We make it down to him, and as soon as he sees us, his face instantly brightens.

"Hey there, buddy." Matteo opens his arms and Robby runs into them, that paper gripped in his fingers. I don't know which one of them loves the other more, but Matteo is crazy about him.

"Is that for me?" Robby nods with a grin. "Whoa, let me see that," he says, placing Robby on his lap and taking the drawing from him. He examines the rainbow of colors, no space on the paper left untouched.

"Is that the sun?" Matteo points to the scribble of yellow in the middle.

"Yeah!" Robby flaps his feet excitedly against Matteo's calf. "This a car." He points to something I can no longer see.

"A brown car. I like it. Hey, soon you're going to be drawing better than me."

Robby giggles, bowing his head into Matteo's chest.

"I told you he'd like it," I interrupt, moving closer.

"I totally love it, buddy. May I keep it?"

"Yeah!" He bursts with excitement.

"All right. You can't take it back now," Matteo teases.

"'Kay." He continues to swing his feet, yawning.

"I think it's someone's nap time." A lazy smile falls over my mouth.

"Oh man, I could use a nap too." Matteo throws his head on the pillow and pretends to snore.

A fit of laughter erupts from Robby.

I let them fool around for a bit more before Robby rubs his eyes, and Matteo lifts him up with a kiss to the top of his head, handing him to me.

He looks deep into my eyes, a thumb stroking down my cheek. "Come back?" My heartbeats still or surge to life, I can't quite figure out which one.

"I'll always come back to you." With Robby lying over my shoulder, I slice a hand through Matteo's and I kiss him.

Slowly.

Tenderly.

And I don't have to wonder what love is because he's love. He always has been.

MATTEO
AGE 18

She's right. She always comes back, and I love it and hate it all at the same time. A girl like her should see the world, experience everything on that globe she's been teaching me from. All those countries she could visit, even move to, away from here. From me. From all this awful shit. But fuck if it doesn't hurt just thinking about not seeing her ever again.

She lies beside me, her head resting on my bicep as she looks up at the ceiling. "You ever wonder what other people are doing in this exact moment?" she asks. "Not just here. I mean, like everywhere, in all parts of the world."

"Not really." I stare down at her, my face settled in my palm. That sparkle in her eyes has me wanting her to keep talking. I once told her that her hair reminded me of the sun, well, that wasn't entirely true. She is the sun. My sun. The bright ball of light in my messed-up life.

"Well, I think about it all the time." She smiles, lost in her own thoughts.

"What else do you think about?" I brush a thumb down the side of her face. Touching her sends a jolt across my body, right to my dick, and instantly, I feel damn dirty for even getting hard, especially here in this basement. The thought of doing anything like that with her down here makes my dick shrivel back up. If

I ever get the chance to show her how much I love her, it won't be on this mattress. It'll be somewhere beautiful, somewhere she deserves.

"Well…" She pivots to me. "I think about us. Like how much fun it'd be to stroll the beach together, somewhere warm and beautiful."

Like you.

"And where do we live?"

"Oh, that's a great question!" Her bottom lip gets caught between her teeth as she contemplates an answer. "I never actually thought about a specific place, but if I had to, we'd live on Corvo Island."

"Where's that?" I gaze intently into her eyes. "I don't think you taught me about it."

"No, I don't think I have." Her expression goes all dreamy, and I promise myself that when we're free, that's the first place I'll take her. "It's one of the smallest islands, west of Portugal. We could watch the volcano, go hiking after our stroll on the beach. We could even go fishing."

"We fish now?" I chuckle.

"Duh, it's our fantasy." She rolls her eyes with a small grin. "We can do anything there."

"I like this fantasy." A smile casts over the shadows of my face, igniting my heart with something it desperately begs for—a life with her. "What else do we do in this fantasy?"

Her lips part, her cheeks catching sight of a hint of pink. My thumb brushes over it, and in her eyes, I find something she's afraid to say. "Tell me, Aida. What else do we do there?"

"Maybe—" Her breath catches as she swallows harshly, glancing away.

"You never have to be afraid to tell me what you're thinking, no matter how big or small. 'Cause I bet you anything," I whisper, my lips landing on the tip of her nose as I draw back, "I've thought of it already."

"I don't think you've thought of *that*." Her voice becomes soft and breathy.

"Try me."

With another tug of an inhale, her eyes align with mine, and the emotions within them cause me to still. "I've thought of marrying you one day," she finally admits, and my heart swells because I want that too. "Living in a house big enough for us and Robby, maybe a few kids of our own. We're hugging on the sofa while they play, making too much noise, but we don't care, because we're happy. Together. Finally, the way it should be."

"Do we kiss a lot? Because I plan to kiss you *all* the time."

"We kiss like mad," she breathes, rubbing her nose with mine.

I groan, my palm landing on the back of her head, tugging her closer. "Yeah, I like this fantasy. A lot. And marrying you…" I brush my nose down her neck. "…is on the top of my list."

She sighs, her hands tangled in my hair, pulling me up, her lips capturing mine in a greedy kiss, her tongue sweeping into my mouth.

I pitch back, both of us breathless.

"One day, we'll have it all." But even as I say those words, I don't know if I believe them. It's a damn dream. But sometimes, dreams are all we have in the nightmares of our reality.

Fourteen

AIDA

AGE 19

I promised Robby we'd attempt to make the highest tower we can from the big blocks Ms. Greco got him. We decided to build it in the spacious hallway upstairs. That way there isn't a mess if my father comes home early.

These days, he likes to surprise me. I think he does it on purpose, wanting to catch me doing something I'm not supposed to.

Ms. Greco's downstairs making chicken parmesan for dinner before the almighty lord arrives and demands his plate.

"It's as big as me now!" Robby shouts excitedly.

My eyes widen and I grin. "We should make it even bigger!"

"Yay!" He claps, skipping toward the bag full of blocks, and bringing them over, placing one on top of the others.

We continue building for a few minutes longer when the front door opens with a creak before slamming shut. I gasp, any breathable air evaporating from my lungs.

"I'm sorry, Robby," I whisper. "We have to clean up quickly."

"But I wanna play," he whines, while my quivering hands start taking off the blocks as fast as possible, throwing them into the bag. If my father sees this, he'll be furious.

"I know you do," I say quietly. "But we can play later, okay?"

"No!" he cries with a scream, stomping both feet so hard, the floor shakes. "I want to play!"

"What the hell is that noise?" My father storms up, and my pulse races, blocks slipping from my fingers as my entire body rattles.

"Are you fucking kidding me?" he shouts as he reaches the top step. "What the hell did I tell you about making a fucking mess of this house?"

Robby's eyes pop wide and he runs into our room and shuts the door. Thank goodness.

"I was cleaning it," I tell him, trying to remove every damn block, timidly glancing up, my heart ripping out of my chest and riding up my throat.

"This is what you call clean?" He stomps closer, kicking the rest of the tower, blocks scattering everywhere.

"I'm so fucking sick of you and your disrespect," he grits, crouching down until we're face-to-face, his hand reaching for my neck, tightening his fingers until my skin burns with a violent ache. "You're more trouble than you've ever been worth."

My breaths heave, my throat in agonizing pain, but he only clutches tighter.

"I should've gotten rid of you when I had the chance." And

still, after all these years, his rejection of me hurts. To know I never meant a thing to him.

I blink back tears that swim deep in my eyes, staring at him, wondering what I ever did to make him hate me this much.

"I'm your daughter," I barely manage to breathe out.

"Daughter." He snickers, finally releasing me, standing straighter, while I pant.

"Clean this mess up and go serve me my food when you're done," he throws out calmly before walking away from me like he's done my whole life.

MATTEO
AGE 19

I was about to fall asleep when the door creaks. Those bastards had me training late, then killing two others. I often wonder how good it'd feel to use those weapons on myself instead, but then she stops me.

Aida.

When those thoughts hit me, it's like she knows, jumping into my mind as though she's there, begging me to stay, to love her even when it's hard.

And I do. I love her so goddamn much, I'd raze the world to see her smile. But lately, she's been drowning with the weight of her father's cruelty. And fuck, I want to murder him for the way he treats her. He deserves to die painfully. Slowly. And he will. We will rise.

But with every damn year, I fail to convince myself that I'll ever kill him. But I can't give up either. I gotta believe it'll happen.

One day.

"Aida? Is that you?"

She doesn't answer, but I can tell it's her from the way she moves over the stairs, so elegantly. She lets out a sniffle and the muscles in my entire body instantly harden as I rise to my feet.

"What happened?"

She appears, tears streaking down her cheeks, her neck an angry red.

I inhale a fiery breath. "Did he do that?" I snap, my tone razor sharp. "Did he fucking hurt you?"

She nods slowly, her chest rising and falling with gasping exhales.

Fuuuck!

"Come here. Let me hold you." Because that's all I can do. She rushes into my arms, her fingers clasping the back of my neck as she cries.

Even with the amount of rage that's in me right now, for her, I soften. Because she needs me that way. I lower us onto the mattress, and instead of sitting beside me, she straddles my thighs, crying into the crook of my neck.

My hand brushes up her back, my fingers threading into the long, waves of her silky hair. "I've got you. I'm right here. I'll never leave you, not if I can help it."

She draws back, a palm curling over my cheek. The way her tear-filled gaze delves into mine, I can't help the intense feelings surging through me. There are so many of them and they hit me all at once.

I love her.

My breaths labor out of me, each one more difficult than the last.

My cock stiffens, even while I don't want it to. She's upset.

How could I get hard now? I try to maneuver her, so she doesn't feel it, but when I attempt to, she pushes her hips deeper into it.

"Fuck, Aida…please don't," I plead, my voice hoarse, desperate. For her. We've never done that. Damn, if I didn't think about it constantly, but the way our life is, it's not possible. "We can't do this here."

"Why not?" she whispers, her brows bowing. "I want my first time to be with you."

And that confession, that no one has been with her, it wrecks me. Because I want that too, for her to be my first. Yet I know it'll probably never happen, that her first time will be with someone else.

It has to be.

Damn, does that realization hurt like hell.

"Because you deserve more than this mattress. You deserve someone who can give you more than I can." I swallow against the lump buried in my throat.

"I don't want more. I want you." Her palm clasps tighter over my cheek, her eyes glistening. "It's always been you, Matteo. That'll never stop."

My heart shatters because it can't be me.

In our years together, we've never discussed her dating or getting married to someone else. She's never brought it up, and I was too afraid to. But soon enough, even with her being locked up here, in this prison, her father will eventually want her to marry some asshole, right? And I'll probably still be here. Or dead.

I curl my fist at my side.

I can't think about not being around and leaving her alone in this world where nothing good happens.

But she and I, we aren't destined for each other. It's the truth I'll carry with me because I can't break her heart and say those words out loud.

Nothing about us is normal. Stolen kisses every day, hand holding and tender touches, that's what we've been.

But now as we've gotten older, things have changed. Our bodies have too. And goddamn, I may not know what the hell to do, but as she rocks her hips against my cock, I have the urge to rip off her clothes and pretend I do.

"Matteo," she whispers, her arms draped around my neck. Her lips tentatively reach for the corner of my mouth, kissing softly as I groan, both of my hands spilling in her hair, my fingers tightening around the weight of it, pushing her further into my straining hard-on.

In all this time, neither of us has told the other that we love them. I don't know if she feels it like I do, like she's embedded in the marrow of my soul, but I feel it. Every damn day. Like she was born to be mine.

I've been afraid to tell her. Not because she'd reject me, but because I never saw the point in confessing it when there's nothing we can do about it. That's always been my fear. Feeling the weight of our love and not living it.

But now, with the way she looks at me, I realize I had it all wrong. We may not be able to love each other the way others do, out in the world, but we can love each other here. Our way. However long we have. I'll love her always. Until I can't. Until my heart stops beating.

It's then I realize, maybe we can find these small moments of love in between fragments of tragedy, like they're actually there, reminding us they still exist.

"Aida," I growl, fisting her hair as I find her mouth, kissing her desperately, my lips moving in sync with hers as she grinds over me, my cock throbbing, wanting to know what it feels like to be that connected with her body and her heart.

My tongue sinks into her mouth, teasing the tip of hers. Damn, this feels so good. Like it's right. The way it's supposed to be.

Her moans only give me more courage, and I suck on her lower lip while her hips ride circles over me. I'm aching to be inside her, wanting to show her just how much she means to me.

I move a fraction, cupping her cheek in the palm of my hand, finding those heavy-lidded eyes. "I love you, Aida. So damn much." She gasps, her brows snapping. "I'm sorry I never told you sooner, because I've wanted to. So badly." I push her forehead against mine, her hot breaths rushing past my lips. "I've loved you before I even knew what that word meant." I pull away, needing to look at her. "And if it weren't for you, I'd have died a thousand times over." Her eyes gleam with a fresh coat of tears, her hand resting against my neck, my pulse speeding even more. "You're the only one keeping me here, and I'm not sorry about it. Because for you, I'd endure all the torture in the world. Because you're worth it."

Her chest rattles as her arms jump around my neck, her face burrowing in my shoulder as she cries, her body swaying with emotion.

"I love you too, Matteo," she pants, looking back at me. "I'm sorry I didn't say it either. I think I was afraid you didn't feel the same, that you didn't think of me that way. That I wasn't..."

"Wasn't what?" My eyes widen.

"Wasn't pretty enough." She lowers her gaze, those auburn lashes fluttering.

"Aida..." I give her a tiny smirk, lifting her chin up with my index finger. "How many times do I have to prove to you that I think you're the most beautiful girl in the world? Why the hell would I kiss you the way I do if I didn't think you were pretty?"

She shrugs with a small smile. "Because you're bored?"

"I'm not *that* bored." I chuckle, leaning my lips forward, kissing her forehead. "But you couldn't be more wrong. I'm very much into you." My voice lowers. "Or I wouldn't be hard right now."

She bites into her bottom lip with a gasp, palms against my chest, her breathing growing tattered.

"You're perfect. Not just for me. For anyone. And I'll always love you, even when I'm not here to do it."

"Don't say that," she cries, laying her lips to mine, peppering my mouth, my face, with more kisses than I can count. I smile, the warmth filling my veins like only she can provide. "I don't ever want to think about you being gone. Okay?" She gazes back at me. "I want to think about us old and wrinkly together."

I chuckle. "Am I still cute when I'm old?"

She scrunches her face. "Who said you were cute?"

"Wow." My body rouses with deep laughter as hers does too. I flip her over, pinning her underneath me, and I kiss her some more.

Fifteen

MATTEO
AGE 20

Every time I leave this house lately, I don't want to go. I used to like the car rides to that warehouse, the sun, the world almost at my fingertips, but I no longer look forward to them.

I'd rather stay back home with Aida and Robby. It's like having a family again, as fucked up as that family is.

I know she hates when I go. The worry stitches up her face like it's visible, for everyone to see. She asks about my bloodied knuckles when I return, and I don't tell her how I got them. I can't. What will she think of me when she finds out I not only hurt people, but I kill them too?

I've killed more in my young life than grown men have killed in a lifetime. I don't dwell on it anymore. If I did, it'd haunt me. I have to bottle it up. Keep it contained. Or it'll explode and send me straight to hell.

I shut my eyes as the SUV rolls over the bend in the road, remembering her lips, that smile of hers lighting up my world like it could burn every awful thing to the ground.

She keeps wanting us to sleep together, but how could we? Even if there was a chance we wouldn't get caught, I won't touch her chained up against the radiator, on the ratty mattress they call a bed, with my piss bucket right there.

She deserves more. I've told her that countless times and she tells me she's right where she's supposed to be. But that's a lie. She deserves a guy who could take her out, give her flowers, go to a restaurant. I distantly remember those places exist, and she's told me about the world. Every part of it. I want her to experience it all one day, with or without me.

No matter how badly I wish she'd forget me, I hate the thought of her with someone else, making a future that doesn't include me.

I've begged her to run away with Robby countless times, to find someone to protect her in the ways I can't. But she continues to reject the thought, saying if the tables were turned, I'd never abandon her. And sure, she's right, but this isn't about me. I don't care what happens to me.

The vehicle comes to a stop and the driver I don't know gets out, Stan in the passenger side. Drew, who's been seated beside me, pulls me out by my arm. They don't bother tying me up. They know I'd never run, not when it puts Aida in danger.

We march inside, me next to Stan, Drew and the driver behind us. The warehouse is dark until Stan pulls on the overhead string, illuminating the space that may as well be my second home.

Someone drags multiple chairs in, the whimpers coming from them heavy as though they've realized their time on this planet is about to come to an end. By me. I'm always the one doing the killing, while the others stand around and watch.

My heart is no longer my own. It's been corrupted by the chains that have been branded on my soul. I can't erase what's been done. I can't hide from it. I am what I am now. A killer. A man with no future. A boy with no past.

I walk up as the chairs are finally before me. At first, I don't understand… Why is there a kid in one of them?

I glance back at Stan, who nods, stretching out his hand with a blade in it. Not a gun, a fucking knife. He wants me to gut a little kid, who's probably no more than twelve.

I eye the boy, seconds drifting by, his brows huddled tight, his snivels louder, those eyes green like Dom and Enzo's. I run a hand down my face.

I can't do it.

I'm not that far gone. Not animal enough to end a kid.

The man beside him screams through the gag in his mouth, shaking his head, the chair clattering. I can only assume it's his father.

"Take the *fucking* knife!" Stan hollers.

But I could barely move, legs buried in concrete while I continue looking at the boy, not sure how I could get him out of this.

His small chest jumps every time I move, and he stares right at me. I think of Robby in that moment. Is that what his life will be like? Either becoming a murderer or being murdered?

My stomach stirs.

"You have one more chance to do this," Stan grits, slithering closer, a hand clasping my shoulder so roughly, I want to rip his entire arm off.

Every second that passes is as heavy as eternity.

"It's okay, Stan." A voice I hate with every fiber spills throughout the room. "I know what'll motivate our boy." Agnelo arrives from the shadows like a demon you don't see until it's too late.

He drags his phone out of his pocket. "I can call one of my men right now and have him throw Aida in the car and let her get ripped apart at the club. Is that what you want?"

"Fuck you!" I roar, coming at him, face-to-face. "Fuck you to hell! She'd never want a kid to die just to save herself! That's one thing you'll never have in common with your daughter. A conscience."

But I don't know how I could refuse when there's a chance he means what he says. How could I let that happen?

His punch to my jaw comes quick, and my fist lands square into his eye before the men have a chance to hold me back.

Damn, that felt good.

"Fucking motherfucker!" he bellows, rubbing where I hit. Stan and another grip my arms behind my back as I fight their clutches, snarling at Agnelo like a beast.

"You're gonna regret this, you ungrateful little shit. Your whole fucking family is a bunch of ungrateful bastards, starting with that father of yours." He removes his blazer, throwing it to another guy, rolling up his sleeves. "I should've sent you to the club from the beginning. I'd never have to look"—he slams his fist to my cheek—"into"—he lands another hard hit to my nose as it starts to bleed—"your damn face again." He punches me in the jaw this time. "But I let you live in my fucking house while you ate my food!"

I don't react, my eyes on his as he hits me, again, then again, until the raw pain blends with the roaring of my skin. I can still see, but it's blurred, my cheeks swelling right under my eyes.

The boy looks at me, gaping, his body trembling as another hit comes to my stomach. He cries heavy now, and his father does too.

"String him up," Agnelo demands, his voice even. I'm being dragged by my shirt, my sneakers squeaking against the floor.

At first, I have no idea what he's talking about, not until seconds later when Stan and Drew remove my shirt and lift me up in the air, tying my wrists together.

Then I'm raised in the air, feet dangling. The pain to my wrists comes rough, and I groan, peering up, seeing the metal beam where the rope is attached.

Will it hold me? Could I escape?

"You think you have choices here?" Agnelo asks, standing a couple feet from me as I zap my eyes to him. "You're nothing. I'm gonna show you what you're worth."

His belt comes off, clinking in the silence, the quiet heavy, and I know what's coming, I know what he'll do before the first whip hits my back. But I'll take it. All day. As long as he leaves her alone. As long as he doesn't send her to that horrible place.

Blow after blow, my flesh tears as he slashes it with the heavy whip of his belt. But I don't make a sound. I won't give him the satisfaction.

She appears before my eyes, her face, her smile, the feel of her lips on mine, her hands in my hair. I hold on to her—our love, her beauty. I don't stop thinking about her even as he removes the pistol from his waistband, aiming it at the boy in the chair. Not even when he shoots him in the head, his father's muffled screams reminding me of my dad's the day they killed him.

Once the father goes too, they all walk out, and I'm bathed in true silence. I'm alone now, drops of crimson leaking onto the floor, tormenting pain on every inch of my body, not knowing if I'll survive it.

I'm sorry, Aida. I love you. It wasn't supposed to be this way.

AIDA
AGE 20

I haven't told a soul, but I've been having nightmares. A lot of them. I can't explain them all. Sometimes I'm alone in a dark, empty place with no end. I just keep running, screaming for help, trying to find a way out. But it never comes.

Other times, there's a woman, her hair long and blonde, her features not so clear, like she's been blurred. But her hand reaches for mine, and she asks me to come with her. But fear envelops me and I don't go. She pleads with me, saying my name. When I ask her who she is, she just disappears. Then I wake up, sweat drenching my forehead and my back, breathing heavy, trying to remember every detail of that woman. But it never comes until I see her again the next night.

"Are you okay?" Robby asks, patting my knee as we sit beside one another, me with a book in hand. I realized I had stopped reading, consumed by thoughts of my nightmares.

Clearing my throat, I try to push them away. "I'm fi—"

The door flies open as we startle, my father's heavy stomping coming toward me. "Get dressed." He throws a bag on the floor, looking irate, his forehead wrinkled with rage-filled lines.

"What?" I sit up straighter. "I am dressed."

"Put the dress on," he grits. "The one in the bag."

Ms. Greco walks in, wiping her hands on the apron as she looks questioningly at him.

"What's going on?" I ask. "Where's Matteo?" An eerie feeling in my gut tells me something is wrong. It's been hours. He should've been back already. But I was so distracted with Robby, I hadn't looked up at the clock until now.

"Put the fucking dress on!" he screams so loud, Robby runs under the table, like he does every time my father loses his temper.

"What's happening?" Ms. Greco's voice shivers. She's afraid of him just as much as I am, but her worry for me shrouds the need for her own safety.

"Are you questioning me?" He rushes up to her in an instant, roughly yanking her hair with a snarl. "You're gonna shut the fuck up and stay here to watch Robby. Don't piss me off."

He drops the hand away as I glance at her, my brows furrowing, fear settling like a plague in my stomach, curling with a rotting taste of my demise.

"Pick the bag up and go change," he snarls. "We're leaving."

"Leaving where?"

"Go. Or your boyfriend dies."

I gasp, quickly standing up, grabbing the bag. "What have you done to him?"

"Nothing he didn't deserve. Now, if you want him to stay alive, I suggest you hurry."

Oh my God, what has he done to Matteo!

Before going upstairs to change, I rush over to Robby, kneeling as he trembles, his arms tucked around his knees. "Hey, buddy. I gotta go for a little bit, but Ms. Greco will be here with you, okay?"

His body only shakes, his lips quivering.

"I love you," I muster with a smile.

"I love you too." Tears gather in the powder blues of his eyes.

I quickly stand, my throat aching from the onslaught of my own emotions, not wanting Robby to see it. My heart tightens, not knowing if I'll see him again.

Who knows what my father has planned for me? With him, it's impossible to say. But if Matteo needs me, then I'll do anything I can to save him.

Rushing upstairs, I quickly remove my clothes, taking out the dress from the bag, but when I see it, my eyes expand. It's black and short, shorter than I'd ever wear. There's another box inside and I open it, finding black strappy heels. Not too high, but enough for me to fall in. I have never worn heels. Where could I be going?

I slip on the dress, pulling it as far down as it'll go, making sure it covers me, my face burning crimson from the discomfort of being in something this revealing.

Lowering onto the bed, I fumble as I try to get the shoes on, unable to strap them on right away. Once I do, I attempt to stand normally, feeling as though I'll tumble if I take a step.

But I try, prodding around the room, practicing for a bit. I'm not that tall, but these make me feel like I'm on top of the world. Is that why Ms. Greco likes heels so much?

"Let's go!" My father's bellowing comes loud and clear. With a long breath, I come out and close the door behind me.

Carefully, I hold on to the banister for dear life and clack my way downstairs.

My father is there waiting with a cruel smile. "You could've brushed your hair, but it'll do." His gaze assesses me from top to bottom, and I suddenly have the urge to hide. That's not how a father should look at his own daughter. My stomach flips, taking my heart with it.

Ms. Greco gasps as she makes it to us, Robby slinked over her shoulder. The sudden panic on her face sends a shiver down my spine. "Agnelo, no. You can't do this to her." She gapes, begging him for something I don't understand.

But his eyes, the devil in them, they don't leave me. I feel naked all over, like I'm wearing nothing at all.

"I can do anything I want." His gaze finally narrows to her. "I'm damn sick of you telling me what the hell to do. I should kill you and that kid, right here right now."

"No!" A gasping inhale flies out of me. "Let's just go." I don't care what he does to me as long as they're all safe.

He snickers before giving her his back. With one final look at her, her face drowning in sorrow, she mouths *I'm sorry*, before I'm out the door.

I know, wherever I'm going, it won't be good.

At all.

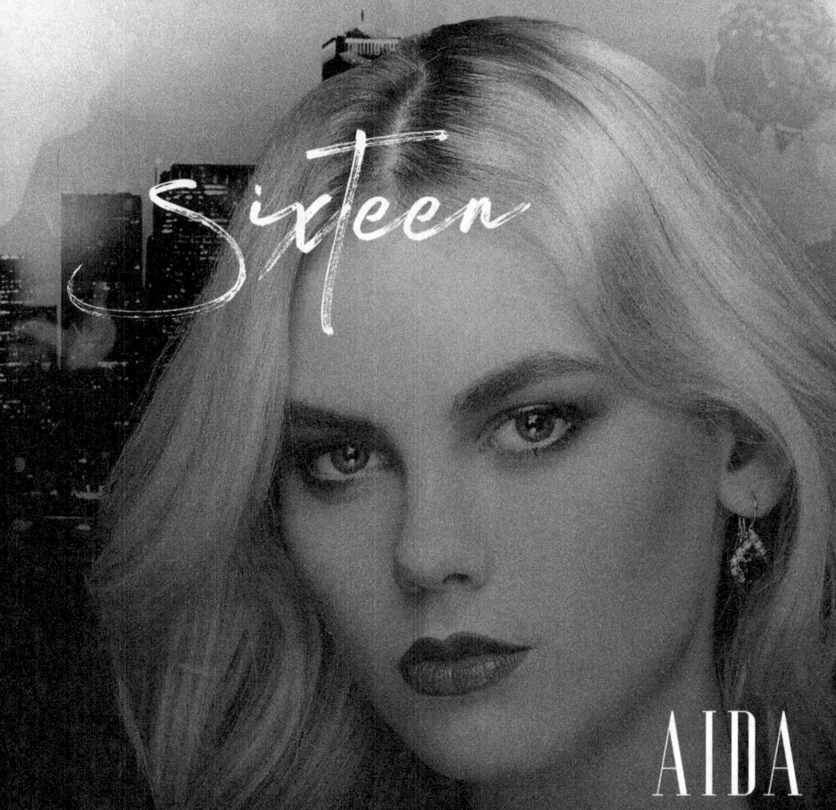

Sixteen

AIDA

I'm shrouded in darkness. It's all around me. Like in my nightmares, the black dread skitters up my body. The pounding of my heart warns me of what's to come. It hammers loudly, goose bumps zipping up my spine.

My legs race with a chill, and it's not from the air conditioner inside my father's SUV. It's the fearful anticipation. The unknown. What am I stepping into and why do I need a blindfold to get there?

The car finally halts, his feet crunching until my door opens.

"Let's go," he snaps, grabbing me by the arm and pulling me out. As soon as he does, I stumble, my knees hitting the ground, tiny pebbles digging into my palms. "Are you fucking kidding me?" His anger sways the incoming hurricane brewing in my heart, the roll of the tide before I drown in it. I'm pulled to a stand, my knees burning with a raw ache.

"I—I've never worn heels before, Dad." *Especially on rocks. Asshole.* "Where are you taking me?"

"Somewhere I should've sent you a long time ago, instead of—" But he cuts himself off.

"Instead of what?" My body tingles with nervous energy.

"Nothing. The point is, you'll be working here when I need you to. It's time you earn this family some money."

"What are you talking about?" My stomach dips as he opens a door and we step inside, the air current changing into something warmer, draping me in false safety. Fear like I've never known slams into me full force instead, as though it's right there, taunting me, knowing I can't see it at all.

"We'll be hitting some steps. Try not to fall this time." He scoffs as I carefully maneuver myself around his hold on me, feeling for every slope downward until he tells me they have stopped.

Music drifts from everywhere, the simmered conversations bathing the room.

"Agnelo!" someone calls with laughter in his tone. "What have you got there? A new one?" His hand runs down the side of my body and I flinch with a gasp. "Been holding out on us, huh?"

"Yeah." He chuckles. "Something like that. Is Faro here?"

"What is this place?" I ask, but I may have whispered it. Did he even hear me?

"Yeah, he's in with two in a room. Doesn't want to be disturbed."

"All right. I'll see you."

"You coming to the show?"

"Wouldn't miss it."

A sudden coldness hits me at the core. *What show?*

"Cool. See ya, man."

"Where the hell are we?" I shout at him. "Where have you

taken me?" I yank the blindfold off, not caring that he warned me to keep it on.

But as soon as I do, I wish I hadn't. Because this place, it's ugly.

Cruel.

"Oh my God…" I plant a palm over my mouth, disgust riding up my throat as I take it all in. My father doesn't say a word, his mouth rolling with a vile grin as I continue staring wide-eyed around the vast space.

Sofas line one side while rooms draped open, some closed, are on the other. Men, so many of them, but they're not alone. Young children are beside them, on their laps. Naked. Scared. Women too. Looking just as frightened.

"What have you done?" The question hurls out of me with venom.

He comes at me, his clenched teeth nearing my face. "Whatever the hell we want. Your uncles and me, we own this place. We've owned it for years."

A heavy feeling sinks into me. "You're sick! I knew it all along, but now, I know for certain. You're all monsters."

"Call us what the hell you want, but you'll be getting to know this club pretty well."

"Screw you!" My palm reaches his face, my fingers clawing into his cheek to shove him away, to hurt him. "I wish I had the guts to end your pathetic life."

He catches my hand, bending my fingers until I scream. "By tonight, you'll wish I had ended yours. Now let's go. You have people to entertain."

Terror settles thickly over me, my body breaking into a full tremor as he drives a palm into my back, pushing me all the way down to the end of the room, until we reach a black, unassuming door. With two knocks, it parts slowly, a masked man behind it, only the bottom half of his face uncovered. My throat closes as my father shoves me inside.

"She's new. Completely fresh. Never been touched before."

I gasp, my eyes widening, tears welling as I back away, but my father holds me down with an arm enclosed around my throat. A horrid smile slinks over the man's face, his knuckles running down in between my breasts, and nausea churns in the pit of my stomach. "We'll take care of her, don't you worry."

"I'll be back to get her in an hour," my father tells them. "Make sure you're dressed by then," he says to me, his voice swarming up my neck, causing me to wince, my fingers trembling.

Once he drops his hand away, he's out the door, leaving me among the ruins, as though I don't matter at all. But that's because I don't.

I stand there, shivering, my arms rounding the front of my body. Hiding. Wanting to disappear. I almost miss the other man in the same gold mask, sitting down on the chair, a leg raised over his other, a glass of something in his hand as he watches us.

"You're a pretty little thing, aren't you?" The hand of the man before me lands on my ass, squeezing my body to him, another reaching under my dress, a finger sliding where I've never been touched before.

No, no, no! I scream in silence.

Heart stabbing. Skin prickling. My father can't be this vicious. He can't do this to me! "Please! Let me go!" I fight his hand away, trying to run, to escape, but with a sinister chuckle, his fingers bite into my flesh until it hurts.

"Why would I ever do that?" He squeezes harder. "I paid good money for this and we're going to enjoy every last dime."

The tears…they're falling now, trickling out of me, while his hands split apart the dress. What will I wear home now? That's the first thought which hits me when he grabs my arm.

My bare skin is on full display as he yanks me toward his friend who places his drink down on the table beside him, patting his lap.

I don't have to guess what they'll do. I'm not naïve. These men, they're going to tear away the one thing I promised to save for Matteo, the one thing we promised to save for each other, and my father, he managed to take that away too.

I'm thrown on top of his lap, and a hand slithers from the back of my head, down my spine and to the very depths of me.

When they touch me, when their bodies invade me, I close my eyes. I dream of better things, a better life, filled with Matteo, with Robby.

And I go there, and I don't let go.

Not until it's over.

MATTEO

I groan, my wrists throbbing like hell while I hang there, unsure what time it is or even what day. I'm thirsty, my mouth dry. My face and my back still fucking throb, but none of that matters. I have to get to Aida. I have to make sure she's okay.

"Aida," I call to her, but I could barely hear it. "Let me down," I say, louder, but I don't think anyone is even here. Minutes blend into one another, hours probably trickling away. And I think I'll die here. That this is it—until footsteps draw near.

"Hello?" I can hardly lift my head. It wobbles as I do, but through one eye, I see a man.

"Damn," Stan's voice mocks with a laugh. "You look like shit." He drags a chair toward me and stands on it, cutting the rope from my hands. "I guess you would be, considering you were here for nearly twenty-four hours."

I fall to the ground with a heavy thud. "Fuck," I mutter. Everything hurts.

He laughs as I stumble.

"W-w-where's A-Aida?" I slur.

A smile slides to his face and I want to carve it out. He doesn't say anything for a minute, but when he does, it's as though he's shot a bullet straight to my heart. "Her dad sent her to the club yesterday."

Something inside me shifts, it's sudden, like a flip of a switch. "What did you say?" The adrenaline courses through me, giving me the strength I've lacked.

I rise to my feet, lifting my head in slow motion, a fist curling at my side, my chest widening with pummeling breaths.

He snickers. "Kid, you heard me. Your girlfriend was sucking cock yesterday, definitely getting some too."

With a roar, I'm on him at lightning speed, like my body has been reborn, forgetting the scars of the day before, forgetting everything it endured. And before I know it, he's underneath me at my mercy.

I pound his face, over and over until his screams for help and his features are distorted. But I don't end it there.

He attempts to get his gun out of his pocket, but I snap his hand back, bones cracking as an animalistic growl rips out of me.

If he's telling the truth, if Aida had been sent there to be.... *Fuck! No!*

My hand clutches his throat, his eyes filling with terror, my teeth baring.

"You're gonna die," I tell him. "I've wanted to kill you for so long. I'll enjoy this." When I notice a knife only inches away, I stretch out my fingers to retrieve it, my palm tightening around his neck.

"Hey!" someone shouts, running up to me, his weapon cocked. In that instant, I reach for Stan's gun and shoot the asshole before he even has a chance to pull the trigger. He dies on impact, the bullet entering his chest cleanly as he falls backward. It was stupid of the Bianchis to underestimate me. I'm stronger than they think. They made me that way.

I pick up the knife, aiming it at Stan's eye, and slowly, I puncture it as he tries to scream but his voice is no longer there. This time, I'm the one who's smiling.

It goes deeper, the blade sinking through his flesh until only the handle shows, until he's dead.

"Fuck you!" I spit into his face, then grab his car keys from his pocket as I dash out of there. But I'm not running, I'm coming back to the den. For her. It's always her.

Aida's my lifeline, an extension of me. Without her, there's no boat. There's only fire. And I'm sick of being burned.

They thought I'd never get the chance to escape, so they'd let things like Agnelo's address slip, not thinking I'd ever need it.

It's thanks to their stupidity I'm able to drive back to the house. At first, I had no idea what the fuck I was doing at the wheel, but I watched them every time they drove me to this shithole. Saw how they started it, what they did to drive it. I memorized everything. Every damn detail of the outside. I ate it up. Spit it out. Then chewed it up again. Until I could taste it.

Sure, I'm nowhere near good enough to drive, and I'm definitely afraid of going fast in case a police officer stops me, but it's good enough.

They've got one of those GPS things too. After taking five

minutes to figure it out, I realized they had Agnelo's address programed in here, even had his name.

Finally pulling up to the house, I run to the door, banging on it so hard, I almost break the glass.

Ms. Greco opens it, Robby huddled to her side, but when she sees me, her eyes bug out. "Robby, sweetie, why don't you go and finished building our tower?"

"Okay." He frowns at me, darting off.

"Where is she?" I push past her, running into the house. "We all gotta go. Now! Aida! Where are you?"

"Matteo, you're bleeding," she whispers. "Your back. Your face. Oh my God." She clasps a hand around her mouth.

"Is she upstairs? Why isn't she down here with Robby?"

"Matteo…" She shakes her head with sorrow permeating her eyes.

"Tell me." I walk up to her, gently clasping her shoulder, bending my head to meet her gaze as she lowers her face to the floor.

"She's upstairs. Hasn't come out since…" She pulls in a trembling breath, tears trapped in her lower lashes.

"Since when?"

"Since Agnelo brought her home yesterday…from that vile place."

"Fuck!" I shout, stepping back, pulling at my hair. I don't want to think of what they did to her there. The fury, it fills me to capacity, my chest expanding with every ravaging breath.

"I'm worried about her." She wipes some tears away. "She told me to leave her alone, so I did. Every time I bring food and leave it outside her door, letting her know it's there, she never touches it. I've heard her crying in there. That place…" She swallows, shutting her eyes. "It still gives me nightmares."

I clench my teeth. Hard. "We all have to leave now before they figure out I got out." I start for the stairs, needing to see Aida, to hold her, to make sure she's… She's what? Okay? How the fuck could she be okay?

"I can't go." She shakes her head. "I can't leave my family. But you take her and Robby and you go, as far as you're able. You hear? This is your only chance."

I nod, running up the stairs in a flash, banging on her door. "Aida! We gotta go now! Open up."

But there's not a sound coming from inside, even as I place my ear against the door. The ugly thought hits me fast.

What if she…

She wouldn't. She told me she'd never leave me.

My muscles go rigid, my heart crashing in my ribs as I run at the door. Once…twice…slamming my shoulder into it with a gut-wrenching roar. I keep smashing the door, ignoring the pain running up my arm, until the wood cracks at the center, giving way as the latch breaks.

And when I'm inside… "No! Aida! No!" My heads spins as I rush to her unconscious body on the floor, a bottle of pills scattered beside her outstretched hand. "This is all my fault," I howl, feeling for a pulse, my own filling my ears.

She whimpers. It's low, but enough to know she's still alive. "I'm so sorry!" Emotion clings to my throat as I scoop her small body up into my arms. "I'd take it all back if I could."

I should've killed them, the boy and his father. They ended up dead anyway. If I did it myself, I would've prevented all of this.

"Oh my God!" Ms. Greco gasps. "I have to call 9-1-1!"

"We'll take her now! I'm not waiting. She has a pulse, but it's weak." There's panic-filled pain at my chest, my lungs, my throat. I can barely breathe. I can't lose her. "It'd be faster if you drive," I tell her. "I could barely do it earlier. I won't be able to at all now."

"O-okay." I hand her the keys as we rush down the stairs. She grabs Robby from the kitchen, slips into her shoes and snatches her bag from the closet as we open the front door.

But in that moment, we're no longer alone.

"Where do you all think you're going?" Agnelo looks smug, a snarl planted over his mouth, six of his men beside him, their weapons drawn at us. "You thought you could get away?" He takes a menacing step toward us. "From *me*?" His eyes narrow.

I come at him closer. "I'm not afraid of you, cocksucker."

"You should be." He lets out one small chuckle. "I'm not nearly done with either of you."

"Your daughter needs a damn hospital," I tell him. "She tried to kill herself because of what you did!"

"That's too bad." He pops a brow. "Always knew she was weak. Nothing like me."

"There's nothing strong about you. You prey on those who can't defend themselves." If she weren't here, if I were alone with him, I'd take them all. Every one of them would die. But I can't. I have to sit on my revenge for when the day of reckoning comes.

"Really brave opening your mouth when I could shoot you all dead right now."

"I don't have time for your games." My tone is sharp. "I'm taking her to the hospital. I won't let her die."

"Like hell you are." His men move in on us, and Robby starts to cry. "She made her damn bed."

"Shh." Ms. Greco rubs Robby's back as he hides in her thigh.

Every second we're still here, she's fucking dying! What the hell do I do? The vein at my neck pounds.

Aida jolts in my arms, eyes closed, gasping until she lurches forward and hurls. Relief washes over me, hoping she gets out everything she swallowed.

The men jump back, afraid of some fucking vomit.

Gently, I let her down so she can throw up the rest on the ground outside instead of the house. "I've got you, Aida. It's okay." I hold her hair in my fist and use my other hand to keep her upright.

She groans once she's done, crying while slowly turning to me, and I lift her back up into my arms. "I'm putting her to bed."

"Well, let's hope she makes it through the night." He pushes past me, strolling inside. "She doesn't look too good."

My nostrils flare, my jaw pulsing from the clenching of my teeth. There's something wrong with him, to treat his own daughter this way. It's fucking sick. But what's the damn point of telling him that? He'd probably take it as a compliment.

His men stay outside, while he shuts the door, whistling a tune, like nothing happened. Before I head for the stairs, he calls to me.

I turn reluctantly, Aida's chest falling slowly. Too slow. But at least I know she's breathing. That she'll be okay. I hope.

"I should take her from you for taking two of my best men, but I'll do far worse." He marches up to me, so damn close I smell the stench of his foul breath. "I'll make you both suffer worse than you've ever suffered before. You thought your first time fucking would be with each other?" He barks out a chuckle. "It's cute."

"How the fuck did you…?" But I already know.

His laughter bursts through the room. "You think I was stupid enough to let her see you for years without recording it?"

Aida whimpers, trying to lift her head, but she's too weak. I know in that moment, she heard what her father said.

"I listened to everything. That was my plan all along. When she begged to see you when you first got here, I had a brilliant fucking idea. Why not let you two get close? So when I take her from you, you'll crack like a weak, pathetic Cavaleri that you are. And I *will* take her from you, my boy." His palm lightly pats my cheek, his mouth twisting in a vicious grin. "And it will hurt." Then he strolls away. It takes everything in me not to place Aida on the sofa and go after him.

Ms. Greco stares wordlessly at his back until he disappears out of sight, then we climb up the stairs, and I bring Aida to her bed, tucking her in, kissing her forehead.

I check for her pulse and it seems strong. "I love you, Aida. I love you so damn much, it hurts not to." I swipe a thick piece of her hair away from her mouth. The back of my eyes sting. "Don't do this to me again. I can't lose you."

"Mat-t—" She sighs, but she can't finish it, her eyelids fluttering.

My knuckles brush down her cheek. "I'm here, beautiful. Don't talk. Just rest. I'll be right here. I'll never leave you. Not if I can help it." It's the only real promise I can make her, time after time.

I climb into the bed beside her, and as soon as I'm skin to skin, her head falling to my chest, I drown in the most intense kind of love.

I keep my emotions at bay, not understanding how a boy like me ever deserved a girl like her. But she's mine and I've always been hers, from the moment I saw her when they dragged me down to the basement. I remember her, staring at me with those tawny eyes, worry filling them. She was the first person I wasn't afraid of at the house. I never imagined she'd be the one to steal every piece of my heart away.

I hold her, a hand curled around her as she sways with every peaceful breath. I realize she'll never meet my father, nor my brothers. I'll never have that with her. I wonder if my brothers still think of me.

I try not to dwell on it. If I do, it'll carve a hole bigger than I can handle. I don't want to think of my brothers as abandoning me, but fuck, knowing what I know now, could I even blame them? One life versus three. What would I have done, especially being a kid?

The photo of my family I gave Aida is still there under her mattress. It's the only piece of my family I have to cling to. Agnelo would've burned it all if he knew where it was. Lucky for us, he must not have heard it on the recordings.

The door barges open, and in walks one of Agnelo's men, a pistol in his grip. "Get up," he demands. "Vacation's over. You're going back to the basement."

I pitch him a glare, kissing the top of her head.

"Boss said I can shoot you both if you don't act right." He lifts the weapon at me, his mouth set with a snarl. "And believe me, I want to for what you did to Stan. I should fucking kill you anyway."

"I love you, Aida. You come see me when you're better."

I rise, gently sliding my hand from under her, lifting the blanket higher around her shoulders. At least she'll have Ms. Greco watching out for her.

Strolling up to this asshole, I near him, his weapon hitting me in the center of my stomach. He's short, where I'm tall as fuck. "Do it, cocksucker. Whatcha scared of? Daddy?" A mocking laugh rips out of me.

"I should," he grits. "If I didn't have kids. I would."

"I bet I'd kill you before that bullet ever made it inside me." I back off, striding for the door. "Come on, you can tell Daddy what a good little boy you were, chaining me up." I wink with a chuckle, enjoying the enraged look on his face.

Seventeen

MATTEO
ONE WEEK LATER

I haven't seen her since I left her in her room. Alone. Scared. It's like I abandoned her, but I know she doesn't think that way. At least I hope not.

Ms. Greco has told me she's eating now, even though she still won't leave her room. But that's a start. I've asked her to send notes up to Aida, but she's said Aida won't read them. It breaks me that she's hurting without me there to help her through it. I can only imagine what they did to her at the club.

I remember the place, seeing that shit when I was a kid. It was a scare tactic the Bianchis used to keep me in line. And at that age, it worked. Though Aida's safety alone would drive me to do just about anything for those bastards.

Will she ever forgive me when she finds out what happened to her was my damn fault? Maybe her fucked-up father told her already and that's why she won't read my notes.

From now on, I'll do whatever the hell I have to, just to keep her from getting hurt again, no matter who has to die for me to do it.

Ms. Greco managed to clean and wrap the wounds on my back. It fucking burned like acid, all six lashes. The scars won't be pretty. But the ones inside me, those are far scarier to look at.

I have been stuck here in the basement for the last week. Other than Louis coming to let me have a shower, no one has taken me to the warehouse. I haven't killed a soul.

For most people, that'd be a good thing, but in my world, it isn't. A break in routine isn't good. Agnelo must be planning something.

I have to be ready for whatever that is.

AIDA

His notes lie scattered on my bed. Unopened. I'm too nervous to read them. To feel them. Because I know he'll make me feel, and I don't want to feel anything. It's easier that way.

I smell their breaths. Taste their salty skin upon my tongue. I force myself to forget. To close my eyes and pretend nothing happened. That the burn between my legs was nothing but a nightmare. It didn't happen. No, it couldn't have. I made it up. But when I wake up, they're still there. Their hands. Their taunting. There's no pretending anymore. I can't hide.

After those men raped me repeatedly, they left me on the cold floor. Naked. Crying. My father walked in, yelling at me for not being dressed, ignoring what he had allowed to happen to his own child. I'm nothing after all. Small. A shell that barely holds a life. He didn't care. He never does.

I had no clothes. I'm sure he saw what was left of them on the floor. He grabbed a robe from a closet, threw it over my face, and ordered me to put it on as he watched. I shook all over as I did, but I managed to get my hands to work. Somehow.

Those men, they found ways to torture me. To make me want to die. Not only did they use their bodies, but they used objects too. I screamed, but it drowned out with the music.

I was alone. Dying. My soul shriveling. And I knew, right then and there, I was gone. A piece of me unrecovered on that very floor.

My father took me home, threw me on the bed, and left me there. When Ms. Greco found me, she wanted to help me bathe, but I refused. I shouted for her to go. To leave me alone. I'd never yelled at her before.

She cried as she strode away, and I quickly locked the door behind her. When I went to the bathroom the next day, when I saw those pills in the medicine cabinet, I knew then I had to die. Not because of what happened but because it'd keep happening. I knew my father wouldn't stop. He'd send me back. He told me in so many words when we first arrived there.

You'll be working here when I need you to. It's time you earn this family some money.

I'll never forget those words. They'll haunt me, just as much as what those men did. That's another reason I can't bear to read Matteo's notes or to face him. I'm sure he knows where I went. He must know what was done to me. My first time, it was with someone else and in the vilest way. I can't bear to look at him after that.

How could he want me, knowing what was done to me? He'll feel obligated to still be with me. I know he will, and I don't want that.

My door opens, now left unlocked at my father's command, and Ms. Greco walks in, a tray in hand. "I've brought you some food." She gently places it on my nightstand, tiptoeing away, like she's afraid to say the wrong thing. It wrecks me to see her this way because of me.

"Wait," I whisper. "I'm sorry."

She turns sharply, walking up to me. "What? No!" Her head shakes, her eyes glistening with tears she won't shed, adorned with tenderness. "There's nothing to forgive. Ever."

"But the way I spoke to you, it was—"

"Normal." She clasps her lips tightly. "If you ever want to talk, I'm here to listen. I know of that place and what happens there."

"He sent you there?" My tone drops low with a tightening in my chest.

"Yes." She forces out a sigh. To know she went through what I did, it nearly kills me, because no one should have to. "It was the first place he sent me when my family had no money to give him." Her brows lower. "I'm sorry, Aida. I'm here for you." She strides to the end of the bed, lowering to the edge as I sit up. "I'll always be here for you. I love you like you're my own daughter." Her eyes shut and she pulls in a long inhale, tears slipping past her cheeks. "If there was a way I could've taken your place, I would've. I'd give my life for yours and not think twice."

It's my turn to cry, the tears falling faster as I jump off the bed and into her arms. She holds me tightly as we both shed layers of our pain.

All those days, I've wanted a mother, I didn't realize I had one all along.

I inch back so I can peer at her. "I love you like you're my mom." I sniffle with a sob. "You've always been there for me. Without you, I would've died a long time ago."

"If anything…" She places a palm against my cheek. "You're the one who saved *me*."

"Then I guess we saved each other." A crestfallen smile glides up my mouth.

"That we did." She nods, tightening her arms around me. "That we did."

Minutes trickle by, or maybe seconds, all I know is I'm content, knowing the warmth of a mother I never had. "How did you live through what happened to you…there?" I stare up. "Will I ever be okay?"

"You take it a day at a time. You tell yourself they don't define you. They're nothing. You hear me?"

"Yeah." A heavy sigh causes my shoulders to slump.

"Robby misses you," she goes on. "He keeps asking about you every second. I guess I'm not good enough." She rolls her eyes with tearful laughter, and a flicker of one falls out of me too.

"He loves you, you know. Matteo? He's crazy worried about you." Her attention scatters to the notes left behind. "You should read them, then you should go see him while you still can."

My heart leaps. "What do you mean?"

"I just… With your father, time is precious. He may change his mind and send Matteo away or—"

"Or kill him."

"I don't even want to think about it because I love that boy too. He'll always be a little boy to me." A fond smile grips the edge of her lips. "Go see him. He needs you just as much as you need him."

"I can't." I bite the inside of my cheek. "He's going to want to know what happened and I don't have the heart to tell him."

"I have a feeling he'd be patient and understanding. If you explain that you don't want to talk, he won't pressure you. I think he just wants to see you walking and talking for himself."

My gaze goes downcast, riddled with shame I know I shouldn't feel, yet I do. The weight of it is heavy. I don't know how to get rid of it.

"You have us, Aida. You're not alone in this. Your father doesn't get to own us." She raises her chin. "He may think he does, but one day, he'll realize how wrong he actually was. Every tyrant eventually falls on his own sword."

"I wish I believed that."

"You have to believe it. Don't give up. That's what he wants."

I suck in a sharp inhale, wanting to trust that he'll find damnation one day. But how long can I be patient?

"Hey, look at me." And I do. "You *will* be okay. You *will* survive. Your battle scars may be deep and they still bleed, but you're a warrior. And warriors don't give up, no matter how many battles they have to face."

I let out a quiet sob, closing my eyes, letting the agony envelop me so completely, I can't see beyond it. My body trembling, I cry with a heavy ache encroached upon my soul.

And she's there, holding me, like she's been holding me since I've been a little girl, because someone had to. And she doesn't stop until my tears do too.

I pick up the first folded-up note, written from the same paper I gave him for his drawings. He tore them into squares, folding them up so they're easily transported to me without my father seeing.

My fingertips tingle as I open his message.

I love you.

With a whimper, I read the next one.

I miss you like crazy. If you can't see me, I understand. But I needed you to know I won't stop loving you, no matter what.

Tears slip down onto the paper, pooling at the center. Could he really love me after what they did to me? I pick up the other note.

It's my fault what happened to you. I'm so damn sorry. I was supposed to kill this young kid and his dad. If I did, they wouldn't have hurt you, but I couldn't do it, Aida. Those kid's eyes, they fucking haunt me.

I still, my hand falling over my mouth as I try to comprehend what he wrote. My family had wanted him to murder a child? Of course he couldn't! I continue reading the same note.

He was maybe twelve. But they shot them anyway. If I did it, you would've never been sent there. I hate myself. I won't blame you for hating me too.

My chest tightens. *It's not his fault. How could he think that?* Quickly gathering up all three notes, I fold them over one another before getting up to lift the mattress. I hide them among the growing collection of Matteo's drawings and the single photo of his family. Once the notes are tucked away safely, I slip out of my room.

Anxiety swirls in my stomach, my heartbeats ramming within me, hoping I don't see my father as I climb down the stairs. I take my time with every step, glancing in every direction. When I'm down there, I don't find him in the den. He must be out. I breathe the biggest sigh of relief.

The sounds of Robby's giggles coming from the kitchen fill me with blissfulness. I go there, needing to hug that boy with all my might.

"Aida!" he yelps, running to me as I crouch down, my arms outstretched for him, my heart so full it might explode. If I could adopt him and run away with Matteo and take Ms. Greco with us, I would. But that's not possible. We're stuck in a never-ending loop of horror.

With my arms around him, I raise him up, hugging him tightly as I spin us around. "I'm sorry I was gone for a bit. But I'm back now," I say, but my eyes, they're on Ms. Greco as she grins from ear to ear. She looks so proud. Of me.

"What are you guys doing in here?" I kiss his little nose.

"Baking cookies!" he tells me excitedly.

"Of course. Why didn't I suspect that already with this yummy smell?"

"We saved some just for you." Ms. Greco hands me a warm one. The taste of chocolate chips is like heaven.

"Maybe Matteo would like some," I tell her.

"I suspect he does." A knowing smile dances across her mouth as she places a few cookies into a bowl.

"All right, buddy," I say to Robby. "I'll be back in a bit. Don't eat all the cookies." I narrow a playful gaze as he giggles.

I retrieve the bowl and shuffle toward the stairs. Suddenly, those nerves in my stomach are back, forcing me into the ground like pounds of brick. But with a long, tattered breath, I gather the courage to make it to the door. To open it. To climb down the first step, even as my throat dries, my arms breaking out with a shudder.

"Aida? Please tell me it's you." His voice stitches up with an ache as raw as mine. Our torment bound, one and the same.

I continue downward, each step its own journey.

"Come here. Let me see you." His words are soft, like he always is with me, no matter how hard of a man he's become. Underneath his broken body is a beautiful soul meant just for me. And like everything else he's given me, I promise to keep that safe too.

I climb down the rest of the way, faster now, needing him more than he knows. When I see him, I gasp. "Your face…" It's covered in black and blues, the top of one of his eyelids swollen.

"I'm fine. It's okay. Just come here." Those eyes glisten as his hand reaches for me. "I fucking need you." I ignore everything else—the fear of rejection, the trauma—and I run, right into the safety of his arms, needing them still. Needing them always.

"God, I've missed you so damn much." He palms the back of my head, his exhales rough and deep against the curve of my ear.

"Matteo…" I breathe, clinging to his back, and he winces. "Are you okay?" I pull my head back.

"I'm just fine." He smiles and brings me back against him. My body roils with silent tears that I can't quite get rid of, but there's no shame in them, not with him.

He moves us to the mattress, holding me over his lap, letting me cry as long as I need to. And I do for a while, and in a way it's cathartic.

I draw back, kissing his forehead. "I missed you too."

A smile wraps around his mouth, and it's a Matteo smile. Big. Beautiful. So full of life. His mouth moves to my ear. "Before you say anything else, you have to know he's been recording us this whole time. He told me."

I sharply jerk back. "Bastard!"

"We'll be careful," he whispers, his gaze fastened to mine. He tugs my hand into his, his thumb rubbing circles over my skin. "I'm so happy you're here."

"Do you mean that? Because if this is too weird for you now, to be with me after what they—" I gulp down the lump in my throat. "After what they did. You can tell me, Matteo. I won't be mad."

"What?" His face twists with confusion. "No. Never." He tucks his knuckles under my jaw, his eyes filled with the truth seeping into me, giving me the courage to believe him. "You're mine. I'm not going anywhere because I don't want to. I'll *always* love you, Aida. Every single time and in every single lifetime."

My body rattles with another bout of tears. Because this kind of love, this acceptance, devotion—I've never had it.

"I—I wanted my first time to—" But I can't finish that sentence. A sudden aching hits the center of my chest and I look down to avoid him.

"Hey." He tips up my face. "Don't do that. That doesn't count. Our first time will still be together. The other stuff doesn't change how I feel about you. I love you." His lips move toward me tentatively, like he's worried they'll scare me.

When I don't back away, he kisses me with a tenderness I've come to enjoy, tasting my lips like it's the very first time he has. But in a way it is. It's the first time since everything changed.

Once his hand spills into my hair, his fingers pulling me deeper, I groan, not caring if my father hears it. Let him know he hasn't taken Matteo from me.

And he never will.

Eighteen

MATTEO
AGE 21 - THREE MONTHS LATER

"**M**y money's on the kid," a man whose name I don't know says, chewing on tobacco.

"I have a feeling they'll take him." Drew snickers as three guys surround me. The fear is there in their eyes, evident as I glare at each of them.

They know to survive, they'll have to kill me, and that's never been easy to do. I have no weapons. My fists, my body, are all I have. They have none either. My victims used to arrive tied to chairs, but now, they throw them on the floor and make me kill them with my bare hands. It's my punishment for killing Stan and the other man. But I haven't failed once in the last few months, and I don't plan to start now. It didn't take Agnelo long to have me back in the warehouse after that first week, and I was right to assume he had something up his sleeve. But at least she's been safe. That's all that matters.

I gesture for them to come at me, and stupidly one does. When he gets near enough, I run at him, kicking him in the face, and he goes down with a groan. The other two decide to attack me at once, each from the side, and while swiping the legs of one, I punch the other square in the jaw.

"Oh, damn! Looks like I'll be winning that money," Drew's friend mocks on a laugh, and from the corner of my eye, I find Drew glaring, drilling a hole in my head.

"Fuck!" he barks. "I hope they kill him. If Agnelo would let me, I'd end the bastard myself."

I ignore them, coming at the one I just punched, jumping over him, landing hit after hit to his face until he grunts.

Another man jumps on my back, his arm circling my neck, trying to get me in a choke hold, but he fails when I twist his hand backward and crack it.

"Ahhh!" he screams, while I deal with the other one, now backing away.

But he can't get far, not here, not when the people who want him dead will stop at nothing to see that happen.

With a hard kick to his stomach, he goes down, and I take the time to destroy him. My fists fly unrestrained as I growl like an animal, hitting him until he's unrecognizable, his nose shifting as it breaks, my knuckles bloody and raw. I don't realize he's dead, not until I ease off him, finding no pulse.

With a heavy rise of my chest, my attention is on the guy holding on to his damaged hand, still there on the floor, the fight in him gone.

He covers his face with his good arm, a serpent tattoo marking his skin there. "Please, do-don't!"

"I promise to make it quick," I tell him as I grab the collar of his shirt and raise him up in the air. My forearm rounds his neck, cutting off his breathing. His body fights, the oxygen slowly leaving him as he does, and gradually the movements diminish, until they still. I drop him to the floor with a thud.

There's only one left. Then I'm done until the next day when they'll make me fight them or kill someone new. Every day is different. And every day fucking sucks.

The last man is huddled at the far end of the wall, his body shuddering with harsh exhales as I descend on him. He knows he won't win. He'll die. Here. And there's nothing I can do to help him. This is my hell as much as it is his. I can't refuse the Bianchis. I learned that the hard way. So I'll fight and I'll slaughter. I'll do it all to make her life that much less unbearable.

Every night I close my eyes, I wonder what I can do to give her a better life. If I get near enough to kill Agnelo, his people will kill me in an instant and his brothers will come after Aida.

There's literally not a goddamn thing I can do. We lost our one chance to escape, and there's no way we can do it now. That's probably another reason they no longer give me any weapons, too afraid I'll kill them and disappear with her. It's too risky. If I fail, she'll be sent back to that hellhole or be killed. My only option is to do whatever Agnelo wants, in the hopes that he spares her that agony again. I can't lose her.

"Hey, you!" Drew calls to the soon-to-be dead man. "Grow some balls and fight! What the fuck? You know how much money I'm losing?"

"Sorry." Drew's friend chuckles. "Told you. That kid could kill anyone."

"I taught that fuck everything he knows. I can take him." Drew folds his arms over his chest.

I advance on the man who shakes his head, pushing himself further into the wall.

"I don't want to hurt you more than I have to," I tell him. "So stand up. Let's end this because you're not getting out of here alive."

He weeps as he tries to climb up, falling to his knees instead.

"I'm sorry," I whisper as I lift him up, my arm suffocating him, his body growing limp. I let him fall to the floor. Walking up to Drew, looking straight into his eyes, I ask, "Anyone else you got for me, or can I go home now?"

AIDA
AGE 21

I've been waiting for him alone in the basement, hoping he comes back soon. Worry is my permanent state of being. In the last few months, I've pushed what happened to me somewhere so deep, it's like I blocked it out, like it never happened. But when my head hits the pillow, it all comes back with a vengeance.

I find myself awake, tears streaked down my face, realizing I wasn't crying solely in my nightmare but in my reality as well. Talking about it will only make it more real, so I don't.

Last night, I saw that blonde woman again, but this time her face was clear, like she had wanted me to see her. Those charcoal-brown eyes gazed at me, her long, shiny hair swaying over her shoulders. She was gorgeous, and when she smiled, her hand reaching for me, I took it. But then I suddenly woke up, wondering who she was and why I keep seeing her. Was my mind conjuring up what I think my mother looks like? That's probably it. But even still, knowing she isn't real, I want to see her again. She brought me a sense of comfort among the chaos, like a quiet wave of tranquility.

The basement door swings open, multiple footsteps climbing down, and Matteo comes to view, his white shirt streaked with red. I widen a stare at it, knowing it's blood. My pulse pounds at the sight as Drew pushes him toward the mattress.

"Your boyfriend lost me a lot of money today." He throws him on the bed, grabbing the thick silver chain and clasping it around his wrist.

"Poor you," I hiss, my face turning up with disgust.

"Bitch," he grits.

"Call her that again," Matteo growls, "and I'll have you on the ground with your throat slit open."

Drew breaks into laughter. "Funny kid." Then his face goes hard as he grabs Matteo by the neck, pinning him into the mattress. "You may have balls, but I'll break them. Try me, bastard. I fucking dare you."

I jump to my feet and smack Drew's back. "Let him go!" But they both ignore me.

Matteo's glare goes cold. He doesn't even flinch as Drew practically chokes him. Just when I think I'll have to find something hard to hit Drew with, Matteo kicks up his knee and lands it square into Drew's crotch, flipping him under and positioning himself on top. A grin grows as he wraps the long chain around Drew's throat and yanks hard.

Drew's hands claw into the air that won't quite enter his lungs. "I really want to fucking kill you," Matteo adds. "Aida's the only reason I won't. But the next time you call her a name, you'll die for it."

Matteo lets him go, sitting down as though nothing happened, while my heartbeats explode in my chest. Having never seen this side of him before, I should probably fear him, this boy who somehow became a terrifying man, but I'm not at all afraid. If anything, I feel just a little bit safer.

Drew tries to stand, but wobbles for a few seconds before finally managing to right himself.

"Agnelo…" He coughs, holding on to his neck as he chokes out the rest. "Agnelo will hear about this, you fucking little punk."

"He has this room bugged." Matteo winks. "So he probably already knows."

Drew huffs out a breath, his teeth gritted, then he rushes up the stairs, the door slamming behind him.

Once he's finally gone, I instantly run into Matteo's arms, straddling him chest to chest. My hands slink into his thick, chestnut-colored hair as I peer down at the chiseled face of the man I'm madly, insanely in love with. "Thank you," I whisper.

"For what?" He jerks his head, tucking my face into his palms.

"For standing up for me. No one has ever defended me that way."

The familiar throb behind my eyes is back from this immense sense of adoration for him, too great to even comprehend.

"I'll always defend you, Aida." His thumbs brush the tops of my cheeks. "My only regret is that I didn't do more. I let what happened to you go unpunished."

"It's not your fault." I place my hand over his.

"But it is." His expression turns into one of anguish, guilt, and self-hatred as though branded there. He grabs me to him, hugging me tight, inhaling sharply as though trying to steady his emotions.

I draw away a fragment, my eyes boring into his. The way he gazes at me, his eyes full of turmoil and tenderness, all I need in this very moment is to feel his lips, to capture them in mine. As I slowly lean into him, I do just that.

He cups my nape, his fingers sinking into my hair, tightening, grasping roughly, turning my face so the kisses are deeper. His tongue charges into my mouth, swirling, tasting. And all I want is more—of him, of this, of us.

His groans flirt with my own as the passion spills from the wounds ingrained upon our souls. I could kiss him until the sun no longer rises and the moon withers and dies.

But there's something else I desperately need. Something he's never given me, and I'm afraid to ask for it. But after what those men did at the club, I need him to be the one to give me something that they'll never give me.

With a palm against his chest, I push him onto the mattress, my body weaved around his, like a puzzle that fits just right.

"Aida," he grunts, his cock thick and heavy, straining against my core. "What are you doing?"

My lips are on his neck, dotting him with kisses, the bravery spilling like blood from my veins.

"Fuck," he hisses through clenched teeth, arching his hips, the pads of his fingers rubbing my scalp. "Your mouth feels damn good."

I peer up at him, loving him aroused, wanting him so badly. "Touch me?" I ask in a breathy sigh.

"What?" He immediately props himself on his elbows, his brows tugged.

"I want you to touch me," I say with a heavy pant.

When he looks confused, I grab his wrist and lead his hand between my thighs.

"Aida…" His eyes drift shut for a moment before he stares at me again, like he's not sure what to do. I know him well enough to see it. "I can't. I—I don't want to hurt you."

"You won't." I press his fingers into me, stroking them against the throbbing there. "Please, Matteo. I need this. I need you to give me that. With them, I never—you know…" My cheeks grow hot. "I want you to be the first to do it. I want that to be my first with you."

He nods like he understands. "If you're sure…" He grips the back of my neck, his full lips hovering over my mouth, his gaze fastened to mine.

"I don't care who knows or who hears. I want this," I tell him. "I've never been surer of anything more, except that I love you. Please, Matteo…" My teeth tug at my bottom lip, that pulsing in my core growing needier. "Make me feel good."

"Shit," he groans, his lips lining my jaw, nipping, before he kisses me again, rolling his cock around my achy center.

What I wouldn't do to feel him inside me. To know what it's supposed to be like. But that's been tainted by the men who ruined my life, by a father who never gave a damn.

But this, him giving me an orgasm that I never had before, not even with those men, it'll be something that's mine, something they can't take from me.

Every day I worry that I'll go back there, and they'll force it out of me. So I need Matteo to give me this. So I can hold on to it when things get bad, when the nightmares come.

With his hands falling to my hips, he flips me over until I'm underneath, all the muscles of his body pinning me to the bed. I grow deliciously aware of our proximity, the way his large frame overpowers my smaller one.

As he gazes, those heavenly eyes searching my face, it takes everything in me not to cry.

I'm safe. I'm wanted. I'm loved. No one can take that away

from me. No one can tear away our bond.

There's this weight in my heart, this mountainous level of devotion seeping into my soul and all I want is to get lost in it. Lost in him.

"You're the most beautiful girl I've ever seen," he promises as he looks at me with awe, his voice hoarse and full of aching emotion, like he could barely contain the way he feels.

My mouth parts in a pant as he braces himself on his elbow, his other hand sliding down my arm, my skin tingling from the wake of it. He cradles my knee, his fingers circling there until he nudges it outward, his hand continuing to journey higher, climbing into my inner thigh.

Our eyes can't seem to part, clinging to one another as his fingers meet my waistband, stilling there. "If something doesn't feel right, you tell me, okay?"

I nod, nervous butterflies springing to life, mingled with deep desire. His hand slips under my leggings, cupping me there, as a moan flies out of me, arching into him, my nipples suddenly hardening beneath my tank top.

With his index finger, he pulls my panties to the side, and I feel his touch.

Warm.

Masculine.

Like every inch of him is.

The muscles in his bicep ripples, the vein there straining as one finger sinks past my wet lips, running up and then all the way down, like he's discovering it, remembering.

"Yes…" I cry on a sigh as the pad of his finger meets my clit in a tantalizing touch.

"Is this what you like?" His growl is rough as his teeth rake my jaw, my eyes closing, my hips rocking to the beat of his touch.

"Yes, I—oh God, keep doing that." My hands bite into his back, gripping tighter, the more he works me. Another finger meets my pulsating flesh, running both of them around my clit, and I wither in sheer ecstasy as his tempo grows more confident.

I open my eyes, drowning in his heavy-lidded gaze.

"You feel damn good," he whispers. "So wet. You like this, don't you, my beautiful girl?"

"Yes… I've never felt this good." I groan on a gasp, my nails clawing his skin the faster he rubs me. My body grows hot, my toes curling. A finger enters me as I cry out in a hushed breath. "Kiss me, Matteo. Please."

"Never have to ask me that." His mouth crashes over my ravenous one, kissing me roughly, his teeth tugging on my lower lip like he's never done before, those fingers moving faster, two of them stretching me, filling, thrusting. And I don't think about those men, not once, even as they try to fight their way out, to remind me what they took from me. But I don't let them. I allow my body to feel the touch of a man who's been my everything, who'll always be.

The warmth within me grows until it's something I can't explain. It's too much, yet not enough.

His palm is on the top of my head now, his eyes sultry, starving, as he takes me so deeply, I know it won't be long. Spreading my thighs wider, I let him go even deeper.

"Matteo!" I cry, my body tingling, coming alive like it's never been before. As he pumps his fingers into me once more, I fall. It's foreign and beautiful, and I never want him to stop.

I try to quiet the sounds coming out of me, remembering who's listening, feeling depraved knowing that, but I don't seem to care right now.

He kisses me, swallowing up every single moan and gasp of

pleasure, his fingers slamming harder as he takes everything that I wanted him to take so long ago.

Slowly, once my tremors still, he slips his fingers out of me, kissing my forehead, his cock still hard. I want to touch him, to make him experience what he just gave me, but I'm too shy to ask.

A lazy smirk turns up as his knuckles stroke down my face. "Wow." His eyes spill with adulation.

"Yeah." My lips spread with a smile of my own. "That definitely was."

He sighs, dropping to his side, tucking me into him, his front to my back. After our breathing slows to a natural pace, we hold each other and talk about his life before, whatever he can remember, so that way he never forgets.

Over the years, I've asked him to talk about his family on purpose. It's the only part of himself he has left before my father and my uncles took it away.

"My brother Dante was always trying to copy Dom," he tells me with a chuckle. "They were one year apart and Dante hated it. I remember once they were competing over who could carry the most cupcakes and they both dropped them on the floor at the shop."

"What did your dad do?" I ask, knowing mine would lose it.

"He gave them each a towel and told them to start cleaning. And they did, muttering while Enzo and I ate some of the ones they managed not to ruin, high-fiving each other."

"Your family sounds amazing." Melancholy builds in my heart and I instantly hate myself for it. How dare I feel that way when his entire life was stolen.

"They were." His fingers glide up and down my arm, and a sense of calmness drapes me. I'd give the world to feel this every day. To feel his unending love.

"I wish I knew my mom, but there aren't even photos of her I can look at."

"I'm sorry," he murmurs.

I twist in his arms, facing him. "It's okay. It's just how it is." I release a rough exhale, taking a long pause, wanting to tell him about my dream of her. "I keep having a dream about a woman who looks so much like me." He eyes me with immense concentration, like he wants to know everything. "At first, I couldn't see her face clearly, but now I do. I'd like to believe that's her, my mother, that she's coming to me, knowing I need her. Do you believe that's possible?"

He ponders over my words. "I don't know, but I'd like to believe it is, because maybe then, there's a chance I can see my parents too. Just one more time."

AIDA

The warm air billows around me, and I look down at myself, barefoot, a long white dress fluttering at my ankles. The grass is cool, the dew has long set in. I move slow, not sure where I'm going, but it's as though my feet do.

She's there if I keep walking. I just know it.

Suddenly the clear blue sky is replaced by a storm rolling in. Darkness glides across, thunder booming from every side of me.

"Hello?" I shout. "Are you here?"

There's no answer except the heavy raindrops now falling to a chorus of its making. Running away from it, I try to seek shelter, but the trees are bare and listless.

"Is anyone here?" I call. "Please, I need help!"

The grass is muddy now. I keep running and stumble on a small *pebble, falling to my knees. Blood trickles out, washed away a second later by the rain dripping down my soppy body, trickling from the ends of my hair, the dress now sticking to my skin.*

Thunder strikes hard and I jump back, my heart racing. It's there in the clearing, a light from what looks like a cottage.

With renewed courage, I go faster, knowing that's my only safety in this cruel world. I'm alone. There's not a soul here, except in that house. If there's a light, there's life, and I have to find it. Almost there, the house grows larger in my view.

My lungs ache but I fight it. Thunder tumbles with laughter and I fear it with a tremor running down my spine.

The house is finally there and I don't knock as I push the door open. Whoever lives here must've known to leave it unlocked for me.

With my breathing labored, I step inside, shutting the door, my palms against it, trying to catch my breaths.

"I thought you'd never come," a woman says from behind me, and every hair on my arms stands up, my heartbeats roaring loud enough to outshine the rumbling of the storm.

Slowly, I turn, facing her—the blonde woman, the one from my dreams.

Am I dreaming now? Is that where I am?

"Who are you?" I tremble.

"You know who I am, Aida. You've always known." She takes a step toward me, her dress matching mine. No, not matching, it's exactly the same.

I swallow down the panic in my throat, my pulse thrumming in my neck.

"No, I've no idea who you are. Just tell me. Please."

"Remember." She's closer now, her hand reaching, and mine goes to her.

"Remember me." When she touches my fingertips, I jolt, my eyes rolling into the back of my head, my body trembling as I grow dizzy.

Falling.

Drifting.

I drop to the floor, and I find her there when I close my eyes, but she looks different this time. I can see her beside a child whose hair is blonde.

Like mine.

As I look around, I realize I'm somewhere else entirely, no longer in the cottage.

"Mommy? When can we go home?" the child asks, walking around. And the room...

"Oh God," I breathe, clasping a hand over my mouth when I realize where I am. The very basement that's been Matteo's home. The little girl wanders across the bare floor, nothing here at all, except a mattress. An eerie feeling creeps up my back.

"Hello?" I call. "Can you see me?"

But they ignore my voice as though I'm not there at all.

"Shhh!" the woman cries. "Please, baby. Stay next to me and be quiet." When she lifts up her arm, I hold my breath, because her wrist is chained up just like his.

"Will he come back?" the girl asks, wide-eyed.

"Yes, so you have to always stay with me. You hear? Never go with him, even when I'm not here."

"But what if he makes me, Mommy?"

The woman sobs. "Aida, listen to me, you..."

What did she...? No! *I break into a shiver, panting, not hearing the rest of what she said.* This is all wrong... N-no.

"Mommy!" The girl runs to her mother and falls into her lap, arms clasped around the woman, and on her small face there's

fear. Too much of it. "He's coming. The door—it's…it's opening."

Heavy footsteps crash down, and when he appears, I stumble backward, my eyes gaping, my chest clattering, inhales and exhales fighting within me.

Because the man is none other than my father.

Why would he do this to us?

"Please, don't hurt her," the woman chokes out. "I'll give you whatever you want."

"You don't make the rules no matter how good your pussy is." He chuckles. "Now get up. You gotta get some work done."

She stands up willingly, clutching the girl in her arms, kissing her hand before kneeling down.

"I love you so much, baby girl. You don't ever forget it, okay?"

"I love you, Mommy. Please come back. Pinky swear!" The girl sobs. "I don't like being alone down here."

"I know you don't. Pinky swear." The woman holds out her finger and the girl hooks hers through it. "I'll do all that I can to come back soon."

My father takes the chain off her wrist and drags her out, and my eyes can't stop staring, the tears I didn't know were there, drifting down my cheeks.

Once our mother is gone, the girl sits alone on the mattress, her knees tucked up to her chin, her arms around them. She rocks slowly as I trek toward her—toward me. That's when I fully realize…that's me. That—that was my mom.

My stomach whirls. Nothing makes sense.

So he lied. Mom never died in childbirth. So where is she? Why would my father keep us in the basement? Did he kill her? Where else would she be?

"Mommy," the little girl whimpers. "I need you. I'm scared."

"Hey," I call, my hands quaking, new tears beginning to fall

down my cheeks as I make it in front of her. "You'll be okay. I know you're scared. I am too. But you'll find people who love you. I promise."

Gradually, she lifts her head, swiping under both eyes and that's when she looks at me as though she sees me. Her brows scrunch as she fits me with a measured stare. "We'll never be okay."

I jump up to a seated position, my body rocking, sweat beading on my forehead, my breathing rough as I stare around the room. "What the…" With a palm against my chest, my heart pounds.

The basement. I was in it. With…with my mom? That pinky swear. "Oh God…" I whimper. Is that where I learned it? From her?

Nothing makes sense.

Why would we be there at all? Did he keep us locked away for shits and giggles, just because he could?

I looked maybe four? I have to find out what the hell is going on, if what I saw is even real. Maybe Ms. Greco knows.

I hurry off the bed, realizing my nap took longer than I wanted it to. I'm supposed to cook lunch for Matteo and me today, kind of like our own date. I even planned to bring down an old CD player I got for my birthday from Ms. Greco. Food and music, that's how people do dates in the real world, right? At least that's what my cousins have told me.

I don't care if my father finds out. He can fuck right off. Hopefully, he won't be here for that. He left about twenty minutes ago, not saying a word, not even looking at me.

I haven't been sent to the club since that day months ago, and a part of me hopes that maybe my father felt sorry for me. That somewhere in his withered heart is a place for a daughter, even if he kept her and her mother trapped in the basement.

I wonder if he ever thinks about what he did to me—having

men rape me so he could get paid for it. Does he feel any bit of remorse? I doubt it. He doesn't have an ounce of a soul and I don't know why I still think he's redeemable. I wonder where it went and when? I don't think I ever saw it.

Do my uncles know what happened to me? Do my cousins have to do this too? I hope not. I don't want that for them. For anyone.

I head down the stairs and right into the kitchen where Robby is busy eating meatballs while Ms. Greco cleans up.

"Aida? You okay?" She looks questioningly at me.

"No. I—" My eyes peek at Robby, but he's not paying attention to me. "I had a dream or a nightmare. I don't…" I run a hand down my face as I pace away. "Did you ever see me in the basement when I was little?"

"What do you mean?" She narrows a stare.

I let out a nervous laugh. "It's probably crazy, but ahh…" I pause in front of her. "I had a dream about a woman, a blonde woman who looked like me and she gave me this memory of when I was small, maybe Robby's age. I was locked in the basement here, with her. My father was there and he took her away. Then I woke up."

Her eyes widen.

"It's dumb, I know." My lips tremble with a reluctant smile.

"You poor thing." Her chin quivers. "That must've been awful. Let me um—let me get you a glass of water." She turns from me, her steps hesitant before she heads off to grab a cup from a cabinet, pouring some water into it from the fridge.

She takes her time getting back to me, completely avoiding my gaze until she returns.

I take the cup from her outstretched hand. "You didn't answer my question. Did you ever see me locked in the basement?"

"I don't—"

"More!" Robby yells over her. "Please, give me more."

"Sure, sweetie!" Ms. Greco rushes to the stove, grabbing the pot and bringing it over to the table, adding some more meatballs onto his plate.

"Are you going to start on that lasagna for Matteo and you?" she asks me.

"Yeah, I should." I shake my head, realizing how ridiculous I'm being. Of course I wasn't locked up in the basement with my mom. That would really be crazy. I'm sure I'm projecting with everything that Matteo and I have been through and how badly my dad has been to me. It's no wonder I'm having crazy dreams.

Rolling up my sleeves, I go to the cupboards, grabbing the pasta, then head for the fridge and snatch the rest of the ingredients.

"You need any help?" Ms. Greco appears beside me. "I can mix the sauce for you."

"No, that's okay. I want him to know I made it from scratch." I smile at her with a turn of my head. "I hope he likes it. He once said his mom would make the best lasagna."

"You're so kind, making him things that remind him of his family."

My shoulders sway with a heavy sigh. "It's the least I can do after what my father has done to him."

"Yeah," she ponders with a nod. "He's an awful man." Her voice lowers as though she's afraid he's listening. I wouldn't be surprised if he has the rest of the house bugged too.

In the next hour, I cook the best meal I've cooked anyone in my life. I've never cooked anything from scratch without Ms. Greco there to guide and assist. But I've made lasagna with her in the past, so I remember how to do it.

With a beep from the oven, I know the food is ready. I cut two generous pieces for us, placing them on a plate, another one stacked under it.

"Okay, here goes nothing." My stomach spins with nerves.

"It smells amazing. I'm sure it tastes just as good. I'll have a piece too."

"If not, I'm telling him you made it." I giggle.

She rolls with a warm laugh. "I'll gladly take the blame. Now go. Enjoy your date."

"Thanks." With the CD player in my pocket, I tread into the basement, carefully opening the door.

MATTEO

As soon as she climbs down, her hair high in a ponytail, the ends hitting past her shoulder, I get up, the biggest damn smile on my face.

"Is that lasagna?" I finally look at what she's holding, taking the plates from her outstretched hand.

"Yes." She grins, a hint of pink on her cheeks.

"You made that? For me?" Placing the plates on the mattress, I gather her in my arms, cupping her cheek as I kiss her, inhaling her clean scent.

"Mmm," she groans, her nails raking into my back as her lips slide over mine, her tongue slipping past my mouth.

I capture her hip, pulling my face back, while yanking her body closer, both of us tempted.

"You're gonna get us into trouble with the way you kiss me," I groan, my nose brushing over hers.

"I'd say I'm sorry, but I'm really not." Her lips meet my jaw, her mouth hungry as she peppers me with soft kisses. "Just so you know"—she peers up—"if the lasagna sucks, Ms. Greco made it."

I burst into a laugh. "You're amazing, you know that?" I hold her to me, my eyes drifting closed as I appreciate this moment, lost in it.

"I don't." She sighs. "But thanks for always making me feel like I am." I kiss the top of her head, imagining us together someday, really together.

"I brought us something," she whispers and that has me reluctantly drawing away just enough to see what she's got.

She slips a hand into her pocket and retrieves a CD player.

"I figured we could, you know have like a date or something…" She shrugs. "I don't know. Is that dumb?" Her nose scrunches.

"Dumb? You kidding?" I slant my forehead against hers. "Do you know how badly I want to take you on one? Fuck, Aida." My voice nearly shatters, emotions scratching up my throat. "I'm sorry that this is all I can give you."

"Hey…" Her brows tighten and both her palms slip over my face. "You're the most incredible man. You never have to apologize to me for anything. You will always be enough. And this, sharing a meal, music, it's just stuff. I can live without them. But you? I could never live without you."

Her eyes glisten with unshed tears, and I kiss her again. Deeply. With quiet passion. She moans in a hushed breath as I suck on her tongue, knowing all the ways she likes to be kissed, because in these past years, that's all we could do.

When I touched her yesterday, hell, I had no idea what I was doing. But I'm a quick learner. Her body told me what she liked, and I knew just how to listen.

She has taught me so much, but most of all, she taught me love, and for that, I don't think I could ever repay her. With another peck to her lips, I gaze into her eyes, the color of the golden sun as it gets ready to set, and I don't ever want to look away. Her stomach growls, and it zaps me out of my thoughts.

"Come on, let's eat," I say, tugging her hand as we finally sit beside each other, one leg on the mattress, the other on the floor so we can look at one another.

It's easy to forget the torture, the pain, when we're this way. My vision grows hazy, and even though I'm strong enough to kill a man, she makes me weak. It's drowning and saving me all at once.

There's fragility in love, I know that now. It'll make you sacrifice everything for her. But it also makes you strong—that fierce protection for the one you cherish, overcasting everything else.

She's the one I'd give up my life for and she'd never even have to ask.

Pain echoes in the chambers of my heart, wishing I could show her all the ways I could love her outside of this place, where we could be free to do anything. And if we ever get there, to freedom, I'm gonna marry her, and I know she'll say yes.

I hand her one of the plates, and place one of the pieces of lasagna onto it, taking the other. She waits for me to try it, staring hard as though holding her breath.

Cutting off a sliver, I place it into my mouth, chewing thoughtfully, pretending I'm still trying to figure out if it's any good. But this is the best thing I've tasted.

"So, how is it?" She tilts an eager brow. "I really tried, just so you know."

"It tastes like shit." I wink, popping another bite into my mouth, grinning wide as she feigns a gasp.

"Hey!" She giggles, dipping her fingers into the sauce on her plate, then smearing it down my nose.

"I hope you're gonna lick that off."

"Nope." She starts to eat, sucking on the fork as she stares at me in defiance.

"Okay." My lips slant up as I grab her plate and place it on the floor by my feet, moving in on her, my nose getting closer.

"What do you think you're doing, mister?" She laughs, backing away, but I gently grab her wrist and keep her just where she is.

"I'm getting you dirty." Before she can move, I rub my nose on hers.

"Hey!" she yelps, but she's not the least bit mad, her face shining brightly with her smile.

"Twinsies." I chuckle, remembering how she called us that when we were kids.

"You'll pay for that." She swipes a finger past the tip of her nose and sucks it into her mouth.

"I hope so," I whisper, watching her watching me, and when she slides her finger out, I take that very same hand and glide that very same finger down my nose. Her eyes pin mine as I guide her hand into my mouth, sucking the finger clean.

Her mouth parts as I do, her chest rising the more I suck. My cock grows stiff from her widened look.

I slip her finger out while she just stares. Now, I'm wondering if I did the right thing. What the hell do I know about girls?

"I'm sorry, Aida. I shouldn't have—"

"You can do that to me *anytime*," she breathes, her gaze still caught in a daze.

"Maybe I will." I crack a smirk, hit with relief.

We eventually finish our food. I get up before her, a palm outstretched for hers. "I think I'd like to ask you for a dance now, my lady."

"Yes, dear lover." She rises, giving me her hand with a bow. "I shall grant you this dance."

"It'll be my honor."

We both let out a laugh, and she removes the CD player, placing it on the mattress. With a press of a button, a soft melody drifts, washing over us.

My arms are around her waist, hers draped over my shoulders, and we sway together, our gazes aligned into one. This moment, the look of happiness on her face…it'll stay with me forever. Because every moment with her is even better than the last.

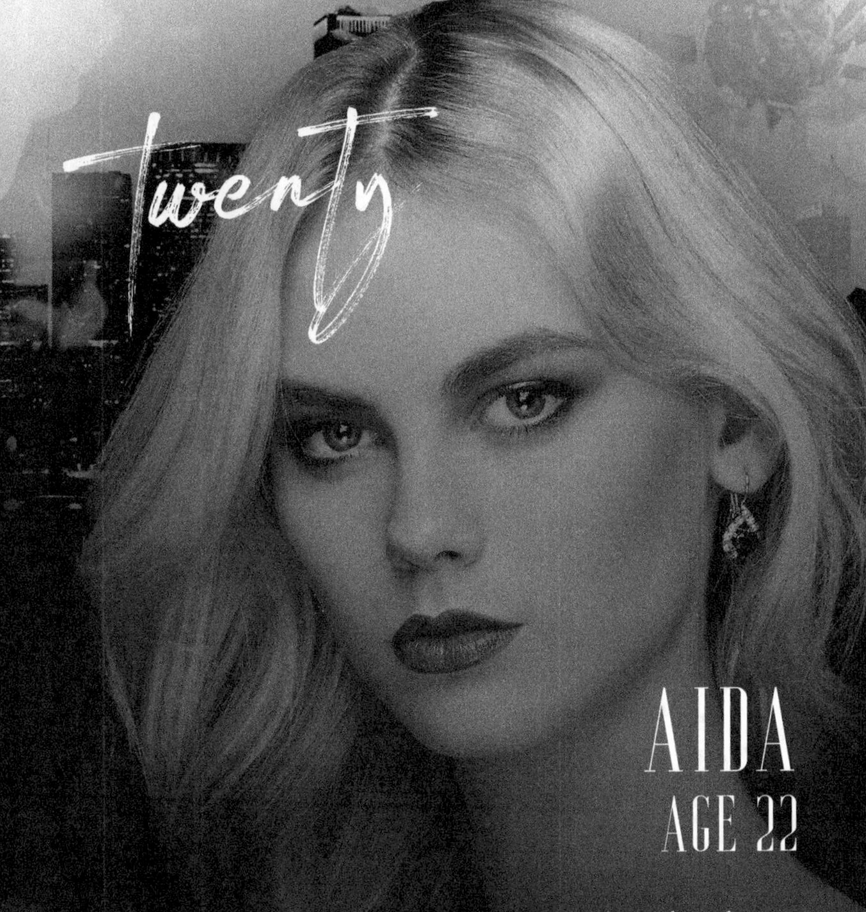

AIDA
AGE 22

I don't see that blonde woman anymore. It's as though once she was done with the message she had for me, she left. Every night I go to sleep, I hope I see her again, just once. I still have so many questions with no one to give me answers. If she's my mother, if that's who I saw, then I want to get another chance to speak to her, to let her know that though I may not know her, I love her anyway. But she never comes. The dreams have stopped claiming me, and I'm afraid it's over for good.

Hearing a bang in the hallway, I slip out of the warm bed, the clock reading midnight. I should've been asleep long ago but I couldn't get my mind to relax with all these riddling thoughts.

Robby breathes easily beside me, his little face peacefully asleep. I leave a small kiss over the hair on the top of his head, so as not to wake him. Then, I rise out of bed, my bare feet hitting the cold wooded floor.

The creaking outside is louder now, someone coming up the stairs. Before I can make it to the door, it barges open.

Drew appears, a hoodie on, black sweats, and in his waistband, there's a gun.

"What the hell are you doing?" I whisper-shout, darting a glance back at Robby who rustles before turning the other way.

"Your father needs you. We're going for a drive."

"What the hell are you talking about?" I start toward him, gesturing for him to leave the room, but he won't move.

"The car's waiting downstairs," he stresses, a flash of rage overshadowing his tone. "Hurry up."

My insides shift, curling from the danger lurking all around.

Where could I be going? The club? Again? No. I can't.

My breathing hastens, an ache lodging in my heart, moisture building in my eyes. "I'm not leaving Robby alone." I stifle the tears.

"Alison's downstairs. Let's go before I shoot the damn kid."

"Aida?" Robby whispers, rubbing his eyes and sitting up.

"It's okay, sweetheart." I rush over, tucking him back down. "Go back to sleep. I'll be back soon." I stroke his cheek and he smiles soundly.

"I'll go. Okay?" I tell Drew. "Give me a few minutes to get dressed."

"No. You won't need to do that." He comes forward just as Robby's eyes flash open from the harshness of those words.

Robby stares wildly at him. "Don't go, Aida," he begs, his hand clutched to my wrist. "I'm scared."

"Shut up, kid. We've got grown-up business to do. Go to sleep and dream about ponies or some shit."

"I love you, Robby. I'll have Ms. Greco come up to be here with you, okay?"

"Okay." Tears glisten in his eyes. "I love you so much," he cries, jumping into my lap, and I hold him as tight as my arms will let me, painful emotions running up my throat. I gulp them away. I don't want him to see my fear. His is enough. He shouldn't carry mine. He's been dealt with more than any child should and I don't want to add to that.

I lay him back down, tucking the blanket tight around his neck as his eyes stitch up with worry. "Everything's okay. I promise." But as I go to the closet, glancing over at him, I find I haven't alleviated his anxiety. It's still there, cast over his face.

Slipping into my sneakers, I hurry back to him, leaving a kiss on his cheek. "I love you." With a final look at him, my face forcing the hardest grin I've ever had to make, I walk out the door, hoping I haven't left him forever.

We make it down where a pacing Ms. Greco waits by the foot of the stairs. "What's going on? Where are you taking her?"

Matteo.

My tears fall and I can't make them stop anymore.

"Take care of Robby," I say to her. "He's scared."

"Let's go!" Drew shouts, grabbing my arm as I look back at her

Her tears slip down her cheeks, and in her eyes, I taste the fear like it's my own. She thinks I'm going back there and she's probably right. My hands tremble, my body breaking out in a shudder as I'm dragged out the door and into a black SUV. A driver I don't recognize is behind the wheel.

Drew puts on my blindfold and a bag over my head this time, then throws me into the cold seat. One of my worst fears is confirmed: I'm going back there.

My panting breaths tremble out, heavy as the thundering of my heartbeats. A door shuts and his voice drifts from the front. "Don't think of escaping. If you do, your father has instructed me to shoot her and the boy. Your boyfriend too."

"I wouldn't do that," I say with whispered words.

The car sets to a roll.

"How could you all do this and live with yourselves?" My question comes out before I fully thought about asking it.

"We do what we gotta do to survive."

"Is that what you tell yourselves?"

He doesn't say anything else as the drive continues, and all I can do is wait for the torment to begin once we arrive.

The car jolts before it turns right, and then it stops. Doors open, then mine does too as he clutches my forearm. "Come on. We're here."

I climb out, the same small pebbles at my feet, the ones I remember all too well. Drew pulls me inside, dragging me down the stairs before the music scratches up my skin. I don't remove my blindfold, not this time. But he yanks it off, stuffing the bag and blindfold into his pocket.

"My God…these kids. They're so young." I sniffle. "Monsters. All of you."

"I don't do that shit," he tells me, as though that absolves him in some way.

"You haven't stopped it either."

"Whatever, bitch. Watch your mouth. Your boyfriend isn't here to protect you this time."

A tremor rolls down my body as he leads me to a black door, a different one this time. When it opens, a tall, beautiful woman greets me.

"I've got this," she says to him. He lets me go and marches off.

"Come on, we don't have much time. Your clothes are in the bathroom. I'll do your hair and makeup after you're dressed."

I back up a step, my eyes scanning what looks like a dressing room. Two floor-to-ceiling mirrors line one side, a clothing rack in the corner, and a black leather sofa against the other wall. There's a vanity there too with all kinds of makeup on it.

"Who are you? Why am I here?" My stomach heaves and churns, my lungs growing tight.

"I'm Destiny. You're going to be in a show tonight, so hurry before boss man gets mad at you. Believe me, you don't want him mad." Her long, shiny black hair brushes down to the small of her back.

"A show? What kind of show?"

She laughs once. "You're new, huh? Well, one piece of advice…" She slaps her hand on my shoulder, her gray eyes lined with a thick row of black liner on the top lid. "Do whatever they say. You want to please the master." She rolls her eyes as she goes to the vanity, sharpening an eye pencil.

"Who's the master?"

I don't even have to ask. I already know.

"Agnelo of course. Faro is the boss, boss, but Agnelo is the one who runs everything and everyone here."

"And this show? I'll have to have se—sex with someone?"

"Mm-hmm. So come on, go get dressed before they come in here and flip out."

My head violently shakes, my skin growing clammy. I fight the feeling to run, to go anywhere but here, but I can't.

"I'm sorry, sweetie, but you don't really have a choice." She shrugs as I blink back tears, knowing she's right.

There's no one in this world who matters more than the three people in my life. So I slog into that bathroom and I put on a white mini dress and slip into another pair of strappy heels, gold this time. I come out, knowing when I do, I'll never be the same. That the nightmares I had after the first time will turn into something even worse.

"Wow!" Destiny's eyes skim my body. "You look good. Hiding a body behind those baggy clothes, huh?"

I swallow, trying to step over to her in these shoes, but it takes me a while.

She threads her hand through mine. "Come on, I'll help you." I take a seat before the vanity as she comes to stand behind me, gathering my hair in her palms as she assesses it, peering at me through the mirror.

"You look terrified."

"And I shouldn't be?"

"Well, no, I guess you should. I've been doing this for a very long time, so I'm immune now." She picks up a curling iron. "I have stuff you can take. You know, to make the experience duller? It helps."

"Drugs?"

She nods. "They give it to us if we want it. I have a lot for the new girls who come here."

Picking up the spray from in front of me, she adds some to my hair.

"No. I'm not interested. If my father wants me to be raped, I'm going to remember everything."

She stills, her movements paused. "Your father?"

"Your boss. Agnelo."

She gapes in shock, her full, bright red lips stunned like the rest of her. "My. God. I thought my life was bad. That's some sick shit."

"Tell me about it."

She curls the ends of my hair, then starts on my makeup. I don't even know what she's putting on, but it's a lot of stuff. From my eyes to my chin, she covers every part of my face. I've never worn makeup. I never wanted to.

"You ready to see yourself?" She grins like she just prettied me up for a school dance.

I nod, and she turns me toward the mirror.

"Holy crap," I whisper.

"Good, right?"

I can't stop staring. It doesn't even look like me. My brows are thicker looking, my lips a soft pink, while my cheeks a darker rosy hue, touched with a shimmer. There are also shades of brown on my lids.

"You're really good at this."

"I know." She stands taller. "I used to be a makeup artist before…"

Her eyes grow distant. Sad. But instantly she erases it, as though that mask has melted right back into her face, helping her to forget someone she once was. "Anyway. You're ready," she announces.

But that's the last thing I want to be. My pulse beats so loud, it pounds in my ears. "Do you know who I'll have to…"

"I don't know. They don't tell us. Just ignore the crowd."

"Crowd?" My eyes grow with a wild stare as I spin toward her, gut roiling.

"Shit. Sorry. I forgot to mention that. Yeah, there'll be a crowd. They'll have masks on though, which is the only good thing, because at least you can't see them." She kind of frowns. "I'm sorry. I really am. But you'll be okay."

But when the door opens and Drew shows his face, I know I won't be. My stomach falls, my body erupting into a burning chill.

I pull away as he advances. "Please, don't do this," I sob. But he grabs my arm. "No!" My fingertips reach for Destiny, my eyes glued to hers as I'm yanked out the door.

"Don't cry," she calls. "You'll ruin your makeup."

MATTEO
AGE 22

They woke me up in the middle of the night—two of Agnelo's men whom I've never seen before. They took off the chain and brought me into a van, telling me Agnelo had demanded my presence.

We finally reach wherever we're going, the blindfold on me with a bag over it. The only other time I ever wore it was when I was a kid, taken to that club they run. But why the hell would I be going there now? I've never had to do shit there, but what if that's what he wants? What if that's further punishment for offing his men? But better me than Aida.

Someone opens the door, and a hand pulls me out. "Move." The voice is gruff.

They push at my back and I keep up with them through the darkness surrounding me. We enter inside, the air changing, the door creaking shut.

"Watch the stairs," one says as though I can see them, but they haul me down and I try not to trip. My blindfold and bag are pulled off, my eyes blinking, adjusting to my surroundings.

The soft pounding of music blends with the moans, disgust piling in my stomach, seeing men abusing those they have no business touching.

A hand drives at my back and I keep walking until we reach another door they open. We enter a small room where Agnelo waits with a smile on his face, two others beside him.

"Sit," Agnelo demands harshly. "Get comfortable. You may be here a while." Mockery is in his tone, a vicious glare on his face.

"What the hell is this?" My attention wanders from the single row of six seats before me, to the partition reaching the ceiling, keeping us away from the round stage with lights pointed to it.

I take slow steps, catching sight of more men seated in this circular room, set up like it's a theater. I plant my palms on the plastic partition. The observers, they're all in suits and black and gold masks. The place is filled to capacity.

"What the fuck?" I snap, facing him. "Where am I?"

"It's a show." There's humor grating his voice. "You remember those from when you were a kid?"

He sets a hand over my shoulder and shoves me down onto one of the red velvet chairs, then takes a seat beside me.

My eyes jump from him and the stage, my head swimming with confusion. "Why the fuck am I here?"

"I just wanted to give you something you may have been missing." His mouth thins as he looks onto the stage just as a bell rings, like a call. In the silence, it sounds louder. Ominous.

My pulse races and my ears buzz. As the doors from within the stage open, loud with a bang, it kicks up even more.

Two men march up to the stage, the same masks on their faces, and music starts to drift. No words. Just the sound of it. On any other day I would've enjoyed it, but not today.

Turning, I speak low, my fury seething. "You want me to go and join them, is that it?"

He chuckles, patting my knee. "You really would do anything for her, wouldn't you?" His cold, brown eyes fill with disdain. "It's too bad you always fail. She'll never be yours, my boy, and I'll prove it to you."

"What the hell does that mean?" But before I could wonder, the crowd erupts in a hushed whisper, and that's when I see her.

"Aida!" I jump to my feet, banging on the partition. "I'll get you out."

"It's soundproof. She can't hear you." He pulls one leg over the other as I stare at him from over my shoulder. "But she sure as fuck will see you."

Yet she doesn't look at me, her eyes swiveling around the crowd. I could only see the left side of her face as she stares ahead at the two men. She backs away with trembled steps, hitting the door.

The men grin viciously, enjoying the fear riddled in her expression, and every single muscle in me fills with rage. My teeth gritting, fists clenching, I look at Agnelo.

"You can't fucking do this to her." I march to him, grabbing the collar of his shirt. "I'm begging, please don't do this. She's your *daughter*."

"Daughter?" He snickers. "She's not my fucking daughter. I have no daughter."

I jerk back, my hand falling away. "What?" I stare hard, not understanding, glancing at Aida at the same time the men advancing on her as her body jolts with a tremor.

"She's not my daughter. She never was. It was the biggest con I ever ran." He leans back, his arms crossed. "Her mother worked for me."

"You mean you…" I trip back a step.

"Kidnapped her?" He shrugs with a chuckle. "Yeah, I kinda did."

Oh fuck…this can't be happening. I jump back another step, my body growing ice cold.

"When we took her mother, she had a kid with her—cute little thing. My men had no idea what to do, so they brought them both to me. As soon as I tried out her mother…" He slumps forward. "I told myself she was gonna stay with me, where I could have her whenever I wanted." He inhales, his mouth lifting at the corner. "Mmm, mmm, still the best pussy I ever had. They lived in that basement. Her mother knew the chains like you do. And Aida, well, she hated me. Not much has changed, I guess. Even when she's forgotten about how she came to be with me." His laugh grates up my insides. "She was probably four… I don't fucking remember now. They were on the news for a while until the family gave up hope. I hid them well. No one could find a trace of them." He looks damn proud of that.

"Where's her mother?" I spit out, constantly glancing back at Aida, the men now slowly marching at her side by side.

"Dead. Of course. Bitch had a mouth on her."

"You fucking asshole," I roar on a harsh exhale, wanting to kill him right here. What else do I have to lose?

"If I was so bad, I would've sent her here when she was a kid, but I didn't. *I*"—he slaps a hand across his chest—"took care of that girl!"

"Yeah, some father you are."

"Never wanted a kid, but I kept her. Me! You should thank me, you ungrateful bastard." He pops up his chin with a snarl. "I don't even know why I pretended she was mine, but I'm tired of it. I should've told her and sent her away to be a whore like her mother was."

"I'm gonna ki—" I advance, but suddenly two men are at my side, clutching each one of my arms as I attempt to fight them off.

"Shh." He holds out a hand as the lights dim more. "Let's

not get your throat sliced open tonight. I want you to enjoy the performance. If she's anything like her mother, I'm sure she'll put on a good one."

My vein pulsing at my neck practically rips out of me, as the room fills with my animalistic growl.

The men try to push me back onto the chair, while I fight them like hell, punching one while another lands a hit to my chin. Something hard smacks the back of my head and that's all they need to shove me down onto the chair, holding me there while I stir.

Another rushes up to me, a corded rope in his hand, and I know exactly what they're going to do. I try to get out, but they overpower me, wrapping the rope around my body, binding me to where I sit.

"I knew we'd have to use this," Agnelo chides. "Your behavior has always been much to be desired."

"Let me out!" I shout, my fists balling, my eyes on the woman I love as the hands of other men are on her, gliding up and down her arms.

I'm restrained, yet fighting it anyway, shouting her name as one throws her onto the floor, another pulling down her dress, exposing her breasts as she sobs.

"Fuck! No!" I scream, my chest piercing with a deep, raw pain, stinging at my eyes. I want to burn this entire place, slice my knife across every person here, lining the walls with their blood.

"Please, don't do this," she begs, her voice small, shredded into pieces of her broken soul. But the crowd continues to watch, still, like statutes, nothing inside them but sin.

A man takes something out of his pants pocket and I realize it's zip ties before she does, and the tears behind my eyes swell.

"No, Aida!" I scream, breaking, the strength in me gone. "You can still stop this," I urge him, every word punctured with agony.

A man ties her wrists together in front, but she fights them. "No! Stop!" she screams, kicking at them while the other son of a bitch holds her legs with his knees, yanking her dress all the way off.

"Pretty thing," he groans, his knuckles running over one of her breasts. "Can't wait to have a taste."

"Let her go!" I rattle in the chair, pulling at my wrists, fastened to my sides.

Their clothes come off, and when they touch her, feel her, the vomit and shame, it slices up my throat. All I can do is stand by while they violate her. I deserve death for this.

Unable to stand another moment of it, I close my eyes. My fucking tears spill and flow.

Agnelo's hand is around my jaw, his fingers pushing into my flesh. "Open your fucking eyes, kid. Look at her!" But I don't. I can't. "Look at her with those men," he continues, his fingers clawing at my eyelids.

But I don't have to see what's happening to know. The grunts of the men... *Goddamn it!* My body heats up with pure rage, my throat closing in from the paralyzing pain as I catch the sight of one man moving on top of her.

Aida...I'm sorry

"This is what she likes." Agnelo chuckles. "She doesn't want some kid in her basement. She wants a real fucking man. She loves it. Look at how she spreads her legs for them."

"Fuck you! You're sick!" I choke on the words.

They flip her over, forcing her onto all fours, one man in front, his dick in her mouth, while the other is inside her.

"No!" I shatter. My eyes shut again, tears filling them, shaking as the back of my throat throbs, my body silently shriveling.

"You look at her, I said!" He pulls at my eyelids once more. "This is all you two will ever have."

I shake my head, my vision marred by the anguish drenching the very depth of me. "I'm sorry," I cry openly, and his laughter is one of victory. "I'm so sorry, Aida."

She screams. Their hands are everywhere. So many hands I can barely see her. After a while, she stops crying, stops screaming. She just lies there, letting them do whatever they want. And I get it. She's hiding behind the pain the way I do. But you can only hide for so long.

Twenty-One

AIDA

I've been in the shower for hours, the hot water sluicing down my body. I can still feel their hands. Everywhere. My insides ache, my skin burning from the mere thoughts. The tears have long been replaced by silence and I don't want them to get out again.

The bathroom is like a false safe haven, where no one can touch me. But my father, he can do anything. Anytime. He proved that today.

His wickedness knows no bounds. He tears me down every single time I think I've finally built myself back up. I'll never escape him. I'll never be free. Not unless I die.

After tonight, I wish I were. If only I had ended my life when I swallowed those pills. Why the hell didn't they work? Why did

Matteo have to save me? If he hadn't, maybe I'd have choked on my own vomit instead.

It's well past morning the following day. I only know because of when I arrived home. Destiny cleaned me up after they were through with me and helped me get dressed before one of my father's men drove me home.

I can't get all those people out my head. How could they just sit there and do nothing as though I was just an actress? It's sick. It's as though they've lost their minds to their depravity.

Those men, I can still feel their breaths on my neck, their groans in my ear. My stomach rolls and I dry heave in the shower, gasping for air, clawing at my chest.

My skin at my arms is a bright red from how hot the water is, but I barely feel a thing. I stay here as long as I can, then shut off the water and open the glass door, stepping out into the chill. My body shivers as I grab a towel, drying off with shaky hands, putting on an oversized hoodie and sweats.

When I exit to my room, Ms. Greco is there with a mug in hand. "Drink this. It's chamomile tea."

I take it and plod to my bed, sitting on one side while she sits on the other.

"A-Aida…" She trails off. "I'm sorry."

"Yeah, everyone is always sorry." I laugh bitterly.

"Your mother, she loved you so much," she whispers with a cry.

"What?" I jerk, drops of tea burning my thigh. "Wait a minute, are you saying…" I swallow, my mouth dry and sandy.

Thump. Thump. Thump.

My pulse beats in my ears for several seconds.

She stares down, avoiding me, and when she peers up, there's shame within her gaze. "I—I'm sorry for lying… I…" Her voice echoes with whispered cries.

I jerk back, a sudden eerie feeling creeping up my arms.

"When you asked me about that dream," she goes on, "I froze. I didn't think you'd ever remember, and I didn't want you to. And your mother, she wouldn't want it either. She had me swear if you ever asked, I'd lie."

"W-wha— Are you saying I saw…my memories?" I recoil. "No…" I breathe.

She nods solemnly. "You were almost five when I met you. Such a smart girl. Beautiful like your mother." She smiles sadly, her lips tight. "I just started working for him when I met you both. That's why he brought me here, to take care of you."

The cup trembles in my hands and I slowly lower it onto the nightstand. I didn't want my dreams to be real. I didn't want that for my mother. For me. It was better when I thought she died in childbirth…but now…

Oh God.

Tears slam past my defenses even when I swore I was done crying.

"Whenever I'd come down to bring you two food, your mom and I would talk. I'd like to think we became friends. She had me promise that if anything should happen to her, I'd look out for you. I hope I've done that. I hope…" She sniffles. "I hope I've been able to do that one thing for her."

"What happened to my mother?" I whisper, edging to the middle of the bed. "Where is she?"

"Oh, Aida…" Her brows pinch. "I don't think you want to hear this."

"Tell me." My words are fitted with agitation.

Her eyelids drift to a close. "One night after he…"

"Raped her?" I finish.

"Yeah." She pulls in a long, heavy breath, like reciting it is difficult, and I'm sure it is. "A few weeks after you two arrived, he was dragging her across the hall upstairs and she started yelling at him, calling him names, so he…" Her chin trembles as she shakes her head, a palm landing over her mouth as tears outline her cheeks. Mine roll down too. "He bashed her head into the wall, over and over until she stopped crying. Until she was no longer moving."

"Oh God." A snivel rolls out from me, drenched with her own. "Where's her body?"

"I don't know. I'm so sorry." Her hand lands on mine. "You're very much her daughter. Tough. Kind."

My fingers dig into my eyes as I quietly fall into despair. My mother, she was his victim too. And the only light in this tunnel is knowing I don't share his blood.

"Do you know who my father is?"

"No, I don't. Your mother never opened up about her life before. She was probably too scared to fully trust me and I don't blame her. There's no one you can trust in our world."

"How could you keep this from me for so long? Knowing how badly I wish I knew my mother!"

"Aida, I thought I was keeping you from more pain. I thought you thinking your mother died in childbirth, like he led you to believe, was far easier to swallow than the truth. But I was wrong." She cradles my hand in both of hers. "Your mother, she thought keeping the truth was the best for you too, so I honored her wishes. For that I'm truly sorry. I hope you can forgive me, because I'll never forgive myself."

A new throbbing builds behind my eyes. "Of—of course, I forgive you." My tear-filled sobbing slices the room, the pain coming in from all sides. I don't know how much I can handle as my torment permeates every living cell in my body, my palms drenched as I cry into them. Her arms hold me still as we huddle together in shared agony.

I often wonder, why evil rises when goodness falls?

MATTEO

I haven't slept a wink since they brought me back to the basement. I've paced for hours, cursing, screaming, swearing to kill them all. She hasn't been down here and neither has Ms. Greco.

I don't fucking know what time it is anymore. I'm on an endless loop of seeing her hurt by those animals. It's lucky they had masks on because I'd find and kill them all. My heart beats so loud, it practically jumps out of my throat. I don't know how to contain my rage. It grows with every second, every hour, until I bash my head against the wall.

Someone's at the door, and I freeze, my fists balled at my side. "Aida? Is that you?" I want it to be her so goddamn bad. I need to hold her, to keep her with me, away from the clutches of the sadistic man who she thought was her father, and in this basement is the only way I know how.

The stairs creek and she's finally at the end of them, a hoodie over her head, her eyes streaked red, her eyelids swollen.

"Hi, beautiful—" I break with a cry, and I run to her, reaching just beyond the mattress, just as she runs to me with a sob.

I hold her as we both shed layers of insurmountable agony. I need her to know I feel it too. Her pain. It's mine just as much as it is hers. Our love has tied our suffering into one loop, and when she bleeds, I do too.

"He brought me to the club a-and…" She wails on my shoulder, her breaths warm, her tears soaking up my shirt.

"It's okay. You don't have to tell me because I already know."

She pushes out of my grasp, her brows snapping. "How?"

"He…" I inhale slowly, shutting my eyes for a second to gather the damn courage to tell her. "He brought me there so I could watch… Fuck!" I explode, punching my forehead with my fist. "Fuck!"

Her hands still over my fist. "Stop. Don't do that," she cries.

"I'm sorry, Aida. I'm sick of fucking apologizing to you, but it's all I've got." My lips lower to her forehead, and I keep them there as seconds drift by, my heartbeats pummeling like crazy.

Once I move back, I stare deep into the brokenness of her gaze. "I swear, if I ever get the chance, I'll rip out your father's heart and give it to you while it's still beating."

"He's not my father," she says.

"Shit. That's right. He told me that last night. My mind, it's all…" I swipe a hand past my face.

"It's okay." She swats at the tears brimming in her eyes. "Ms. Greco told me after I got home today. She's known all along but didn't want to hurt me."

My palm slides to her cheek, my thumb wet as it rubs under her eye. "She loves you."

"Our life. It's—it's all wrong," she stammers, her lower lip trembling. "I want to die. I wish I did that day."

"No, don't say that." Tears blur my vision as I stare at her, the dull look of a woman who's no longer there. "I know what he's taken from you, but you can't let him win. We gotta keep on fighting. Corvo Island. It's waiting for us."

"Matteo." She laughs bitterly. "It's time we realize we'll die before that ever happens."

"I refuse to believe that." My other hand cups her cheek.

"Well…" She shrugs. "I guess that makes us different."

"Don't give up on us," I plead, refusing to let the woman I love go. She's still in there. I just have to give her time to see me again.

"The next time I'm close to death…" She throws me a hard, unblinking stare. "Don't save me."

"Aida…" My voice rolls with emotion. "Don't ask me that."

"Pinky swear," she demands, clenching her jaw, holding out her pinky for mine.

But I don't give it to her.

"Matteo! Please!" The desperation scrapes up her features.

I don't want to promise her something I can't do. I'll never be capable of letting her die. Yet, I can't refuse her in this moment either.

With regret piling onto me like heavy stones, my hand slowly crawls toward hers, and I hook her pinky through mine. "Pinky swear."

Twenty-Two

MATTEO
SIX MONTHS LATER

She's breathing against my chest, and I watch her sleeping for far longer than I should, but I can't seem to close my eyes whenever she does. It's like I'm afraid she'll try to hurt herself or something. In the past months, she's grown inward. The light in her eyes, slowly flickering until it'll blow out completely.

He hasn't sent her back there, but he likes to toy with us. He may do it again when we least expect it.

Later today, they'll come for me as always, with more training or more men to kill. My back aches from the workout they had me go through yesterday, Drew pushing me, wanting me stronger.

But that's not a bad thing. The stronger I am, the harder it'll be for them to destroy me.

She jolts, moaning as her body quivers, her head thrashing. "No," she whimpers. "Leave me alone."

"Aida," I whisper. "Wake up. You're having a nightmare."

Again. She has them all the time and it breaks my damn heart.

Her eyes flash open and she jolts to a sitting position. "Matteo?" She looks around the room.

"Hey." I swipe away the hair from the sweat settled on her forehead.

"I'm sorry I fell asleep." She sighs.

"No, don't be sorry."

"Sleeping is useless anyway." She shoves my hand away as she gets off the mattress. "I see them in my nightmares. I can't run from it, no matter how hard I try."

I rise to stand beside her, my fingers inching toward hers, but she pushes past me, leaving for the stairs.

Just as she's about to go, she pauses, her back to me. "Why do you even bother with me, Matteo? When are you going to learn I don't matter?"

She runs up the stairs as I scream her name. "Aida! Don't say that! Aida! Come back."

But the door shuts and I'm alone, wondering when I'll see a glimpse of the girl she once was. But with each passing day, I'm afraid she's gone.

For good.

The day after, she doesn't bring me breakfast, nor lunch. Instead, Ms. Greco comes down with a bowl of soup and a salad.

"Where is she?" I ask as she places the food on the floor beside me.

"She's not well, Matteo. I tried to talk to her, but she only looks past me, as though she's not even listening." She takes a deep sigh.

"We can't give up on her."

"I'm not giving up. I'm giving her room to breathe and so should you. She needs that right now."

"You have to watch her. She may try to—"

"Don't worry." She squeezes my hand. "I am. I promise. I'll do everything I can to keep her safe from herself."

She starts for the stairs. "I care about you too, Matteo." There's sorrow etched in her eyes, her smile the same. "I hope you know that by now."

"I do."

She thins her lips as she nods. "I wish I had known you both at a better time, when life wasn't so cruel. But we have to make the best of things."

"That's what we've been trying to do," I tell her. "And look where it got us."

The day has turned to night, and Ms. Greco returned hours ago to bring me dinner. Though I tried to sleep, it never came. I've been awake for longer than I should've and the house has gone quiet.

I think about what Ms. Greco said, giving Aida time. I know she's right but what if we don't have any time left? What if all we have are stolen seconds, dwindling away until they're gone? Every day, I wonder if today I'll die. They don't need me to kill for them. They do it to torture me. That's all I am, a toy. When they get tired or bored, I'll have no value left. Then what will become of Aida and Robby?

The door suddenly opens.

"Hello?" My body stills into ice.

Footfalls crash heavy.

"Who's there?"

Louder now.

It's not Aida or Ms. Greco. I know how they walk by now.

The person gets nearer until the last step brings me face-to-face with Agnelo.

"What the hell are you doing here?"

He never shows his face down here. "I wanted to retrieve you personally. Today is a very important day." He marches slowly, grabbing my wrist and undoing the chain with a key in his pocket. "Come on," he orders with a wicked grin. "We've got places to be and people to kill."

Fucking great. "What time is it?" I ask.

He doesn't answer, not even when we make it outside and into a white van.

"No blindfold today?" I try with another question.

But his mirthless chuckle is all he offers in return.

All the muscles in my body turn rigid on alert. Something bad is about to happen.

The cruelty of his stare only amplifies that knowledge.

He slides open the door and shoves me beside a man I met once. Carlito I think his name was. It's been so long since he brought out the bunny I was made to slaughter as a child.

"Nice to see you again, kid." Carlito's mouth curls in a vile way. Everything about him smells like shit. I really want to gut him.

Another man's behind the wheel, Agnelo in the passenger side, as we drive for a while until the warehouse comes into view. It's the perfect place for murder. Nothing around it but trees.

They all hop out first, then I'm ordered out, Carlito clutching my arm, yanking me out. We trudge inside, the place dark, muffled sounds falling closer from the distance. At first, I think it's a child, and shit, my body recoils. I can't go through that again. I can't murder kids. That's not right. But when someone turns on the light, the air from my lungs completely evaporates.

There are no kids here. Not at all. Instead, in front of me, I find Aida and Ms. Greco, each with a gun pointed to their temples, their mouths covered with black tape, tears caked down their cheeks.

"What the hell is this?" I roar, darting back at Agnelo, his arms crossed over his chest as he smugly stares me down.

He finally comes over, standing in front, obscuring my view of Aida sobbing. "I swore to you that I'd take everything from you until there's nothing left. Remember that?" He clasps both his palms over my shoulders as I widen a stare, my heart pounding, my teeth gritted and bared. "Well, that time has come." He roughly pats my cheek. "You have some big decisions to make."

My heart slams into my rib cage, my body cold inside, but my skin, it burns. "No." I rapidly shake my head. "I won't do it."

He jerks his head back with a snicker. "I haven't even told you what you have to do."

But I know. I knew the moment I saw them.

"You'll choose who lives and who dies. That will be on you." He turns to the two women he never gave a damn about, and with a slice of his hand through the air, as though presenting me with a gift, he says, "So who will it be? The girl you love or the woman she loves?"

"Fuck!" I roar, my hands balled into shuddering fists. "I can't! Goddamn you!"

"Sorry, but in this game, that's not an option." He tilts his chin to his men, who whack both women on the side of their heads with the pistols in their grips.

"You asshole!" I pounce as he jumps back like the coward he's always been. I don't even get a chance to hit him. Carlito and another guy hold me down even as I fight them.

"You're wasting time, kid. You have two minutes to decide or they both die. And if you try that shit again, it's game over for them both."

They finally release me, and this time, I don't move.

The men pull their gags down. "Matteo," Aida cries. "Please kill me. Not her. I beg you!"

"Aida, no!" Ms. Greco screams, turning to her. "Don't you dare! You can't give up! I won't let you." Her sobs grow heavy. "You have to live for your mother! You have to let me go!"

"Don't listen to her!" Aida retorts, not meeting her gaze. "You promised, Matteo. You pinky swore you wouldn't save me."

"Stop!" I shout, gripping my face in both hands. "Both of you just stop. I can't... Fuuuuuk!" My roar rips through like an echo, setting off avalanches I can't yet see.

"Time isn't your friend," Agnelo whispers near my ear.

I can't choose. Of course my gut says to save Aida, she's the damn love of my life, but hell, I can't kill Ms. Greco. She's been like family to me. And if I hurt her, there's no way Aida will ever forgive me. I know that to be true. How do I save her only to let her go?

"One minute." He removes the gun from the holster and holds it out for me. I take it because there's nothing else I can do. I could shoot him, then try to take out his men, but none of that will guarantee that either Aida or Ms. Greco will survive.

"Thirty seconds."

"Matteo," Ms. Greco calls, choking on her tears. "Listen to me. You two need each other. You have to kill me. It's the only way.

I'm ready to go. I swear, I won't hate you for it."

My breathing rolls out harshly as my attention darts from her to Aida, an ache battering behind my eyes…in the back of my throat.

My vision grows hazy by the second as I lift the gun in the air, and never has my hand shook this badly, not even when I first held a gun they gave me when I was a child. But right now, with the magnitude of who I have to kill, I can't make it stop.

"Matteo, please!" Aida wails. "You promised me. You swore. Y-you can't break that p-p-promise." Her chest climbs higher with every breath.

"Ten, nine…" Agnelo counts with excitement, the light dancing like a flame in his eyes as he stares at me, then at them.

"Do it!" Ms. Greco yells. "Kill me!"

"No!" Aida fights the man's grasp, her whole body shaking violently.

I level the gun, my pulse exploding in my neck.

"Three. Two."

Pop.

The bullet roars to life, like it's in slow motion, and once it hits her right in between the eyes, she falls on the ground with a heavy thud.

And Aida, her scream, that gasping cry—it's a sound I'll never forget.

Twenty-Three

AIDA

There was a time I thought I could trust him, that he'd never be the source of my pain, but how wrong I was. He swore I could always count on him, the one to protect me, but instead, he took the only mother I ever had, and murdered her before my very eyes.

My lashes flutter to a close, the tears staining my cheeks as I silently cry. Robby plays with some Legos on the floor, not realizing anything is wrong.

It's only been a day. Why would he think her not being here would be cause for alarm? But she's gone forever, and Matteo took her from us. My heart, it hurts so bad. It's like he reached inside and ripped it out, the emptiness gnawing at the wound in my soul.

How could he do this? How could he betray the promise he

made me? Instead, his deception was like a double-edged sword. He lied. He didn't give me the mercy of death. Instead, he brought more hell right to my feet by taking her away.

"Do you think Ms. Greco will make brownies today?"

I choke on the cry strangled in my throat, his innocent question causing gut-wrenching pain. Robby stacks some more Legos, his belly on the floor, legs bent at the knees, thankfully not looking at me. "She told me we could bake them together," he continues. "I really love her brownies."

I bite into my inner cheek. I attempt like hell not to let him hear me cry, but he does anyway because my suffering is too insurmountable to contain.

His large blue eyes zap to me as he instantly sits up, a single block clacking to the floor. His brows bend. "What's wrong, Aida?" He's incredibly perceptive for a seven-year-old and there's no way I'll lie to him.

"There's something we have to talk about, Robby. Something sad."

"Did—did something happen to Ms. Greco?"

My chin trembles, and I slap a palm to the middle of my chest, my eyes leaking at the corners. "Yes."

"Will—will she be okay?"

I shake my head, grabbing his hand. "I'm sorry, Robby. She had an accident…and she…she died," I whisper, strangling out the words.

He gasps, his gaze awash with his own grief. "Does that mean she isn't coming back?" His body shudders with a cry matching my own.

"That's right," I snivel. "She isn't."

With a weep, he climbs onto my lap, and together, we let each other feel the torment of losing someone we desperately loved.

I hadn't intended to see him at all, not even to bring him food, but I have no choice. Agnelo's man only shows up once a day to empty his bucket and to let Matteo shower. He won't be here to bring him food three times a day like I have, and I still love him too much to let him starve, even after what he did.

But if I have to see him, it doesn't mean we have to talk. But I need to get my feelings off my chest before they eat away at me. Once I speak my piece, I won't have anything else to say. There's no us anymore, not after this.

A heaviness encroaches into my legs as I climb down the stairs, my pulse quickening with anxiety, a bowl of rice and grilled chicken in hand.

He stands there, his eyes bloodshot, and my heart lurches.

Matteo.

It's like my soul's weeping. It's as though I've lost him too. The need to jump into his arms and stay within them is overwhelming, but I fight it. My God, it's hard to do.

"Aida, fuck! I thought something happened to you!" He runs to me but I move back, and the chain, it keeps him an inch away.

"Don't do that." His brows furrow, his eyes glistening. His breaths beat heavy as he pulls his hand to mine, the chain clanking as he fights like hell to touch me. I bite down so hard to keep myself from falling to a place where I could forgive him. But every single time I see her body fall, the blood… Nausea turns in my stomach.

"Please, talk to me," he pleads, his gaze drowning in regret. "I've been dying to tell you how sorry I am. But I had no fucking choice!"

"No choice? How dare you! You had a choice and you made

it!" I take in a calming breath, trying to still the nerves ravaging inside me. "I told you what I wanted, but you chose to murder her instead."

"You know I could never be the one to kill you. I loved her too." He sighs, defeated. "But she knew you couldn't be the one to go."

"Why not? Hmm? I wanted to die! You think I want to go through what Agnelo put me through again and again? I asked you to save me from it and you…" My eyes slam shut and I take a shaky inhale. "You chose to keep me alive because you're selfish."

"Aida…" My name is a strangled cry. "Please, I'm sorry, but I couldn't kill you." His fist slams into his chest. "I love you too damn much to be the one to end your life. You would've done the same thing."

I remain silent, sniffling back the pang of anguish beating through me. Could I be the one to put a bullet in him? Maybe I could do it if his suffering was great enough, but I don't know. Maybe it's unfair for me to feel this much disdain for what he did. Would I have chosen him over her? How could I possibly even imagine making that decision? But how could I fault him for it either? Is it even fair?

I can barely think. I need time. There's too much racing through my head. "I'll bring you food, but you and I have nothing else to talk about. You took the only parent Robby and I had and you left me to suffer in the wake of it."

"I'll die without you loving me, Aida. Don't fucking do this!" he pleads with turmoil twisting his face.

With an ache creeping up my throat, I stare into his shattered gaze, my heart breaking with it. "I didn't do a thing." I drop the food gently on the floor beside him. "You did."

I walk away, and a piece of me dies as he screams my name,

over and over until I hear it in my dreams.

MATTEO
AGE 23 – THREE WEEKS LATER

For three weeks, she's ignored me. Twenty-one days without a word from her lips, and I've counted, every damn day.

I've tried to get her to open up, and I've seen the fight on her face, wanting to talk to me, but she leaves as quickly as she comes.

How could she think I could hurt her, be the one on the other side of the bullet aimed for her? There's not an eternity where I'd be the one to kill her. Maybe she was right—I'm cruel for letting her live to endure the shit Agnelo puts her through, but even still, I couldn't do it.

Maybe I *was* selfish, but maybe I just love her too much to let her go. My world and hers has been connected from the moment we met and I'm not ready to severe the ties that've kept us tethered.

She's the only person I remember loving. Sure, I still remember my father, my brothers, but their love is distant now, blurred over time. My feelings for her are fresh, the passion in me for her still raw, still full of the future I fight not to give up on. But it seems she's given up on us already. And somehow, I still wish she'd come back to me, that somehow, I can find her again.

Ms. Greco appears to me a lot in my dreams, and in them, she holds my hand, her face bright, angelic as she smiles, telling me it's okay. I'm sure it's not her, but it brings me some comfort to know that even in death, she has forgiven my actions. She loved Aida. Of course she understood why I did it, but still it's hard to accept she's gone and that I'm the one who killed her.

Someone kicks me in the stomach, and I fall backward with a growl. This is why you don't let shit distract you when you're in the middle of fighting two guys off. Rearing back, I run at him, throwing a kick in the air that lands straight into his jaw.

"Ahh!" he screams, landing on the floor in the warehouse, as I throw punch after punch into his face, the rage filling me, tempting the beast I've become. But there's nothing holding me back, is there?

She's gone.

When the fight leaves him, I slice the knife across his neck, running after the other man, who only makes it to the corner.

There's nowhere to run. No place to hide. There are six of Bianchi's men in this shithole. They've come here for a show. They expect a worthy fucking performance, so I give it to them.

The handle of the knife digs into my palm as I ready to puncture the throat of the man begging for my mercy.

"Kill him! Now!" Drew stresses.

My feet trudge closer until I'm right in front of the guy's face. The kick across his calf comes quick, and he drops to the floor with a loud thump. I settle over him and he grows rigid, his body readying to die, his eyes round and full of fear.

There's something about killing someone when they stare at you. It's worse. It's haunting. I see them sometimes, all the people I've killed. I can picture their faces. The way they stared at me. Their voices as they begged.

And when I remember them, fuck, the emotions in the pit of my stomach gnaw, reminding me what a bastard I am. But was there ever a choice? I was bound to become a monster. That's what they've always wanted.

With Aida by my side, I was a little more human, a little more accepted, but now that she's stopped seeing me the way she once did, I don't know what I have to live for anymore.

"Please, man," the guy no older than me pleads. "I don't wanna die. I did nothin'."

I lift the knife in the air, right above him. "Neither did I." I let the blade slide all the way into his neck, blood spurting out, coating my hand, drops landing on my face.

It doesn't take him long to die, and once he does, I get to my feet, wiping the result of my sin from my cheek. The knife drops beside him, and two men take the body away.

This place holds so many ghosts, I wonder if they haunt it.

Will I die here too?

Twenty-Four

These have been the hardest weeks of my life. Every day I see him, I want to forgive him, but then something stops me. The memories of being raped, Ms. Greco, it all comes back, and that's when I find it hard to look at him.

So I leave, and I cry alone against my pillow, remembering our fantasy of Corvo Island and wishing we could return to the days where we'd dream about the life we could build together. But it's too late now.

He's finally returned from wherever they take him, and I climb down the stairs to bring him dinner, my heart beating so fast, I almost drop the bowl from my quivering hands.

He peers up at me from the mattress, his face tucked into a palm. His jaw pulses when he drags his hand away, his gaze falling from my face, down to the rest of me. And I suddenly shiver. The way he just looked at me, I felt it everywhere and suddenly I'm self-conscious. I know he's touched me, and it never happened again, but still, he's never actually seen me naked…except when he saw me at the club. My stomach churns at the memory, my throat closing in.

I try to fight myself from looking back at him, but it's a losing battle. I get lost in his eyes, like I always do. They've always been what's kept me safe and grounded.

"Aida, I miss you. Please, talk to me. I'll do anything to just hold you."

My chest rises and falls, faster and faster, my hands tingling, my eyes shuttering, the familiar pain behind them growing.

I miss you too. So much. Talk to him. What the hell is wrong with you? Haven't you punished him and yourself enough? You need him and he needs you too.

"I—" That's all that comes out.

"That's a start." His mouth quirks up at the corner.

"Matteo, I don't know how to do this anymore."

"Do you still love me?" His tone hovers just above a whisper, and the thought of him thinking I don't is like a dagger to my heart.

"Of course I do."

"Then that's where we start. Because I'll never stop loving you."

"Matteo," I choke out on my tears.

"Come here," he calls, his hand reaching for mine.

And slowly, I go. Because with him, I've always been home. Ms. Greco would've wanted me to forgive him. She wouldn't have wanted us to be apart. I have to let my anger go. For her. For me.

For us. It's the only way to survive.

I can still miss her, hate Agnelo for this, because it is ultimately his fault, and I can stop holding Matteo accountable. He did what he thought he had to, and I probably would've done the same.

I cut through the distance between us, jumping into his arms. A sob crawls out of my throat, and my palms clasp his face, my eyes staring into the man who's loved me even while he shouldn't. Tenderly, I lower my lips to his and I kiss him, testing the water, seeing if I could paint over what's been done to me.

He groans, his mouth desperate, craving, his hand riding up my spine, fisting my hair as his mouth fits over mine so perfectly as though we've been created for one another.

But then it comes. The men. I see them. Feel them. I yank back with a frantic gasp, my chin trembling.

His breathing labors as he pulls away just a fraction, clutching the back of my neck in the wide span of his palm. "Fuck, I'm sorry. We don't have to do anything." He pins his forehead to mine, and together we stay that way as seconds drift by until he speaks again. "I love you, Aida. I know what I took from you, and for that I'm sorry. I truly am."

"I know you are," I breathe, tears trailing my voice. "I'm sorry too. I blamed you for it all and that wasn't right. My anger should've been directed at him, not you."

"Swear you'll never leave me again." His words strain with desperation and I hate that I did that. With everything he's been through, I despise being the source of more of his anguish.

"I swear it." I cup his cheek, planting a kiss to the corner of his mouth. "Never again."

He drags in a long inhale, his eyes shutting, an arm twining around my lower back and he tugs me close. Chest to chest, we sit together for however long, I don't know, but it's been a while since

I've been so at peace.

With him, I seem to always find the hope of forever lying beneath the ruins.

TWO WEEKS LATER

"Uno!" Robby shouts as we play in the basement with Matteo. It's a game Ms. Greco had left behind. Playing it, knowing it was hers, makes me feel closer to her somehow.

"Yay! I win!" Robby jumps up, pumping a fist in the air.

"How the heck are you always winning?" Matteo asks playfully. "You cheating? Are you hiding cards back there?" He gets up, scooping him up and checking his hands while Robby giggles.

"I'm just better than you," Robby quirks back, while I watch them with my heart ready to explode. Is this what it feels like to have a family? To love them so much, you'll die for them? Because I'd die for both of them.

"Hey, you at least won one round," I sass. "I have won no games at all." I pout and Robby and Matteo both look at me.

"She's really bad at this game, isn't she?" Matteo asks Robby, who nods with a laugh.

"Wow, guys, way to gang up on me. Remember who cooks your meals. I can very well make you eat spinach for dinner."

Matteo makes a gagging face while Robby imitates. "I think we gotta let her win now, Robby."

"Yeah, we'll let you win, Aida. I promise." Robby grips me in a tight hug.

"Well, now I suddenly feel a whole lot better." My arms circle him and I hold him even closer.

"I always have fun with you."

"I always have the best time with you too." With a whip of pain across my heart, I realize, he's not my brother anymore. I stifle a cry. I can't believe I haven't realized that until now. In all this time, I blocked it out. And though we don't need blood to be family, it still makes me sad. I seem to be losing everyone one way or another.

"You okay, Aida?" Matteo narrows his gaze, and I nod, fighting the encroaching tears.

"I'll be okay. Some days are just harder than others."

While I still hold on to Robby, Matteo finds my hand and brings it to his mouth, kissing my fingers. "It's okay not to be okay. We'll make it through it. Together." He places my palm against his heart, then hooks our pinkies together. "Pinky swear."

Then, just like that, I smile again.

AIDA
TWO WEEKS LATER

The last couple of weeks have been uneventful, which for us is a good thing. I'm still dealing with my nightmares, unable to do anything with Matteo other than kiss him. He's patient and kind. Too good to me.

The loss of Ms. Greco still haunts me, but we all try to deal with it the best we can. I vow to find her family and tell them what happened and how much she meant to me.

I don't know where Agnelo threw her body, and I doubt anyone had informed her mom or sister that she's gone. I could just imagine how upset they are, not knowing where she is.

Her family probably has already assumed the worst, knowing

who she works for. But even still, they deserve closure. They need to hear it from me, someone who actually saw her die.

Her sacrifice for me, even in her final moments, is nothing but heroic. She always stood up for me in one way or another, and even while facing death, she fought for me—the daughter of her tormentor.

Sitting in the kitchen with Robby, we munch on some leftover baked ziti I had made yesterday. "I love ziti." He coughs suddenly, placing his fork down as he's unable to catch his breath.

I'm instantly on my feet, opening his bottle of water, stroking his back as he continues to cough. Once the coughing fit eases, I hand him the bottle. "Drink a few sips, buddy."

He slowly does, his eyes watery as he looks up at me. Once he's done, he hands it back and coughs again.

"Do you feel sick?" My brows huddle.

"I think so. My throat hurt me a little yesterday."

"Robby, why didn't you tell me? I would've gotten you medicine."

"I'm sorry." He frowns. "I didn't want you to get into trouble."

"Why would I get into trouble?"

"Because he's always yelling at you."

I let out a sharp breath, a bout of sadness gripping my heart. "Oh, Robby. I love you. Don't ever hide when you don't feel well, okay?"

"Okay."

"Try to eat if you can."

He nods, picking up his fork, taking a few bites as I take my seat across from him at the kitchen table.

As though knowing we're having a nice time, Agnelo comes stomping in, scratching the side of his gray hair.

"Where's my fucking lunch?" he barks, his fist hitting the

counter, causing my plate to rattle, some sauce spilling over.

Robby's fork clatters against the ceramic plate, his hand clutching my thigh, those small fingers digging into me, his face hiding in my side. Fear, that's all this poor child has ever known. He would've been better off with someone else. I'm almost sure of that.

"Fridge," I answer firmly, picking up my fork and continuing to eat. The next thing I know, my plate is swiped from the counter, cracking into pieces scattered across the floor.

"What the hell?" I grit.

"You stupid little bitch! I ask you for food and that's your answer?" He reaches for my throat, clasping it tight as he lifts me off the chair. "You still don't know any better, do you? You've learned nothing," he grits.

My throat aches, and I cling to every tiny fragment of a breath he allows, but his grip only tightens. "You should've gotten off your lazy ass and served me the food that I buy." He spits in my face.

"Aida!" Robby cries, and I try to twist to look at him, but it's impossible.

"You're a monster," I croak out, but it sounds like whispered words.

A sly grin pulls at his mouth. "And you're about to find out just how much of a monster I really am." He pulls me toward the basement by my throat, my feet dragging. I fight him, my fingers trying to pry his hand off me as I stare at a terrified Robby, his sobs louder the further I'm pulled away.

My fa—Agnelo yanks me forward even faster. "Your big mouth always gets you into trouble. Just like your whore mother."

My mother wasn't a whore.

He pulls the basement door open.

"Aida, what's goin' on?" The alarm in Matteo's voice is evident. I can just see him jumping to his feet, readying for a fight.

"She came to say hello," Agnelo answers, mockery dripping.

"Aida, talk to me."

But I can't, even as Agnelo's hand drops from my aching throat and he pushes at my back to head down.

When we reach the bottom, Matteo's there, hands balled at his sides, teeth bared. "What's going on? Why are you here?" He zeroes in his attention at Agnelo.

"You know…" Agnelo eyes me, then Matteo. "I've got a lot of regrets in my life." And the way he talks, it's as though he's giving us great news. "Two of them are not getting rid of you both when I had the chance. That kid upstairs too. I have no reason to keep any of you, and today—"

"No!" I instantly turn to him, my head shaking, my pulse jumping. "Do whatever you want to me, but don't hurt Robby. Please! Give him to his mother or her family, just don't kill him!"

"Oh." He chuckles. "I'm not gonna kill him. But he'll want to die when I send him to the club."

I gasp, my stomach stirring. "No, please." The tears swell, the back of my throat closing. "Don't hurt him. He's a child."

"We've all been children once. But I have some good news." He folds his arms across his chest. "I'll give you a choice like I did Matteo here once upon a time."

Before I could wonder what choice I could possibly make, he removes a gun from his waistband. My eyes expand, my world growing dizzy. It's like I've been yanked from gravity and thrown into the pits of hell.

"Your choice is pretty simple. Save one. Kill the other."

"R-Robby or Matteo?" I pant, staring at the gun. I can't kill the man I love or the boy who's like my own! "Oh God." I tremble, slapping a hand to my mouth, vomit slinking up my throat. Fear creeps up my body like a hungry ghost ready to possess me.

The weapon in his palm nears me. "Decide. Which one will it be? The kid? Or your boyfriend?"

"No! Please!" I drop to the floor and beg for his mercy, the pain in my heart unbearable. Every inch of me feels as though it's been sliced open. "I can't!" I yank at my hair.

Large tears roll down my face. Faster. Faster. Unending. The agony. I can't lose either of them. My hands claw at my chest.

I can't breathe. I'm taking shallow breaths.

"Kill me!" I implore him. "Just let me take their place. You never loved me. Let me be the one to die."

"No fucking way!" Matteo fires. "Aida, look at me." But I can't seem to do it. If I do, I'll break more than I'm already broken. His eyes, they always seem to carry me away to a place I wanted to one day share with him. But now—I choke on a sob—that will never happen. "You know it has to be me," he continues, his voice dripping with emotion, and I crack with every syllable. But it can't be him. It can't be Robby either. I have to be the one to die.

My eyes reluctantly fall to his, and I burst into tears, barely able to catch my breath. "I c-can't." I weep louder. It hurts so bad. I don't want to hurt anymore.

I turn to Agnelo. "Please, I'll do *anything*. The club. Take me there for good." I sniffle, my body shuddering.

"*This* is what I want." He hits me with a cold glare. "You will choose one. Right now, or I will take both."

"You're a sick fuck!" Matteo roars as I get to my feet.

"Maybe." He cackles. "But now you'll both be killers. Take the fucking gun!"

"I can't do this!" Every inch of me swarms with an icy chill.

"Take it!" He points the gun to my chest, and my inhales come faster than my exhales.

"No!" I yell, but he pushes it into me.

"Take the fucking gun!"

"Pl-please, d-d-don't do this!" My every word is a strangled mess, splintering out of me.

"If you don't shoot him…" He pivots the weapon toward Matteo. "Then I'll kill him and that other bastard. Choose."

"Coward," Matteo sneers. "You were always such a damn coward. Kill me yourself. I dare you."

The room swells with Agnelo's sinister laughter. "You think you're better than me, huh? You know…" He sighs like he's bored. "Once upon a time, your dear old daddy thought he was too and look where it got him."

Matteo snarls, pulling at the chain, attempting to come at Agnelo, who only chuckles harder.

He turns to me with a depthless stare. "You have on the count of three, then both of their deaths will be on your head."

My gaze finally lands on Matteo, this beautiful man who's never had a life thanks to this monster. Within his eyes, I picture us older, a bunch of kids running around like I once dreamed about, but it's over now, isn't it? Because I'll be the one to kill him.

I get it now, the weight of his decision. It wasn't easy killing Ms. Greco. He did what he thought he had to, just like I do.

I can't kill Robby. I know that. But killing Matteo…

I choke on my breaths, the tears coming heavy. I can't lose him.

"One." Agnelo's thumb presses on the trigger.

My heartbeats thrash within me, my chest tightening.

"Pl-please," I manage, looking at the man who stole everything from me. There's nothing redeeming about him, and yet, I wish he had an ounce of humanity.

"Two." With the gun pointed to the man I love, his glare drops to mine.

"Leave her alone!" Matteo says roughly.

"I'd have killed you already," Agnelo tells him. "But having her do it, knowing I can make her… Well, that's a lot better." He slams those cruel eyes to mine. "Your time is almost up."

"It's okay." Matteo softly smiles. "I love you. I'd never hold it against you. Do it. I'm ready."

"I'm so sorry." The tremor in my voice rolls down my spine, and my heart is practically being wrenched from my chest. "This was never how it was supposed to be for you and me."

We made promises. We wanted to have a life. A beautiful one. But deep down, we knew it'd never happen. We lived in our fantasy and now we've finally woken up.

"Remember us and the life we swore we'd have," Matteo says, the tears carving a path down his cheeks even as he fights them. "Live it. For me."

"No! Please! I can't say goodbye!"

"It's not goodbye," Matteo promises. "It's I'll see you later."

But it is goodbye. And it's forever.

"Pinky swear?" The words come in a pant.

"Always." His grin is wide, the glow within his gaze flickering, and I'll be the one to shut it off completely.

"I'll never forget you," I cry. "I couldn't even if I tried." How could I let go of him? How could I live a second, a minute, an hour without him? "You're the moon and the stars, the sun when it rises, the warmth when it sets," I tell him, the waves of agony rocking the very core of me.

"You were always so much better with words." His smile tethers with brokenness. There's so much of it on his face, and my heart twists with unimaginable grief.

Maybe death is the only way one can escape Agnelo. And that

is the saddest thing of all—not really living, counting down to your own death.

"I—I'm sorry," I say. "I love you!"

"Thr—"

I rip the weapon from Agnelo's clutches, and without another moment's thought, I pull the trigger.

Pop.

"No! Matteo!" His body slumps backward and my ears drown with my own screams, calling his name as I crawl to him, tears seeping down my face. But I don't get far, Agnelo's grip holding me back.

"It's time to say goodbye. To him. This house. This life. It's over for you." He yanks me backward toward the stairs.

But I ignore him, my eyes still fastened to Matteo, just lying there. Helpless.

Dead.

Oh my God, he's dead!

I break with another wave of sobbing.

I killed him.

Suddenly, we're not alone. Multiple people rush down the stairs, and the next thing I know, one of them hauls me from behind, while another heads for Matteo, whacking him hard on the top of his head with a gun.

"Matteo!" I scream, unable to stop calling for him, my fingertips fighting to touch him, just one more time.

"You know where to take her," Agnelo tells one of the men.

"Wha—?" I breathe heavy, my eyes widening. "Whe-where am I going? What are you doing? Where's Robby?"

"He's not your concern anymore," he calmly tosses.

"No! I won't go! I'll be good. Please." I fight and scratch at the burly, tall man who's already dragging me up the stairs by my arm, and Agnelo falls out of view.

The man stops, gripping my throat, bashing the back of my head into the wall. "Don't make me knock you out, girl." My temples throb as he once again tugs me up and into the main floor, heading for the door.

"Robby!" I call for him. "Where are you?" Oh my God, did they hurt him? Is he dead? My pulse knocks in my ears. "Robby!" I scream until my throat aches, but there's no sign of him. "I need my shoes!" Anything to kill time, to find him.

"You don't need no shoes where you're goin'." The man's callous tone grates up my flesh, like a scratch across a chalkboard.

He drags me out the door, the concrete grinding beneath my bare feet, to a fate far worse than I've yet to know.

MATTEO

"Drug—burrry hi—" There's a flash of voices that filter in and out, the light in my eyes flickering, like I'm fighting to stay alive. My head buzzes with a sound and my shoulder throbs. But I'm still breathing. I know that much.

"Yes, sir," someone says, a hand around my neck, then hands grab my ankles. I can feel them pressing into me, dragging me away.

"Lift—up—stairs."

Then I'm off the ground, being hauled in the air. I keep my eyes shut, needing them to think I'm out cold.

We're upstairs now, and someone opens the door, cool air hitting me. From the corner of my eye, I can see a white van, then I'm being thrown in it.

Fuck!

I grind my teeth, my shoulder hurting like hell, and I grow less out of it.

The van pulls out. "You got the shit?" one of them asks.

"Yeah, I got it. You gonna do it?"

"I guess." There's silence for a moment until he talks again. "Can't believe he sent his own daughter out to the buyer."

"He's a sick fuck. Don't tell him I said that though."

He's selling her? Fucking hell!

The desperation to find her grows by the second. If I'm too late, she could be on a plane to the other side of the world. My pulse pounds with a deafening beat.

"I won't say shit. By the way, the wife asked if you wanted to come over for dinner. She's making chicken casserole."

"Cool. I'll be there."

These assholes are talking dinner when Aida is who knows where? I can't wait to fucking kill them.

I don't know how long we drive before they stop and get out, their footfalls crunching, then both lug me out, one grabbing my feet, the other my arms.

Playing dead or unconscious is easy. I'm sure they checked my pulse and know I'm still in there. His wife will be serving dinner to their corpses.

They throw me onto the ground. My fingertips flicker against the dirt beneath. I fight the need to jump and rip their throats out. But I'm good at waiting. I've been waiting for so long.

"I gotta go get the shovels. Agnelo said to drug him if he wakes up."

"Yeah, I know. Hurry up. It's damn creepy here."

One runs off, while the other beside me mutters shit I can't make out. A minute later, they start to dig.

"Fuck, I never realized how hard it was digging a grave."

"I'm sweating balls."

"Me too, man. Poor guy's gonna get buried alive. You can't piss off the Bianchis."

"So young too. Wonder what he did to end up in that basement."

"Who the hell knows? Look at Agnelo the wrong way?"

They both laugh.

Won't be giggling soon, motherfuckers.

Sometime later, they're finally done. "All right. Let's do this shit," one says as I open my eyes just enough to see them, their feet nearing, the shovels just an inch or two away, swaying in their grasp.

As soon as one grabs my arm, I kick my legs out, hitting them both square in the chest. Lucky I had my sneakers on when they took me.

"Get the gun!" one shouts as he falls.

But it's too late. I flip up to my feet, ignoring the pain radiating through my arm, the blood dripping down the length of it, and I retrieve both shovels, snapping one across the neck of the guy before me. His mouth drops open, his hands falling to his throat, now spilling with blood.

"Al! Fuck!" the other asshole screams. "Stay back! I got a gun." His hand trembles as it falls to his waistband.

I throw one of the shovels away. "A little tip." A callous smile wraps around my mouth as I near. "Next time you wanna bury a man alive, make sure he's actually unconscious." I swing the shovel and it lands hard on the top of his head. He drops heavily on the ground, groaning, the gun slipping out of his pants. I kick it away, lowering on top of him, a knee pushing into his chest.

Raising the shovel, I bury it hard into his neck and watch as it sinks into him, blood spouting out. Sudden rage overcomes me, and the next thing I know, I'm on my feet, the shovel slamming into his neck over and over as I scream with all the fury sitting dormant within me, my face covered in blood. I can taste it on my tongue as drops land past my lips. When I'm finally done, his head is barely hanging onto his body.

My breathing erupts out of me as I stare down at what I did, and I don't feel an ounce of remorse.

When my inhales calm, I get their guns, their phones, and their keys, before removing one of their shirts and tying it the best I can around the wound at my shoulder, using my teeth and my free hand. It looks like the bullet only grazed me, but the gash is still bleeding some.

I wince as I roll their bodies into the grave they nicely dug for me. Picking up the shovel, I start to throw dirt over their bodies until they're no longer visible, until it's piled high. I push through the burning pain, the adrenaline keeping me working, knowing there's no other choice. I have to find her and I won't stop until I do.

Once I'm done, I hold on to the shovel, intending to take both with me. But as I march a step, my head gets dizzy. "Shit." I grab a nearby tree trunk, fighting to stay awake, but it's too late. My body sways, growing heavy, until I crumble to the ground, the light flickering out of my eyes.

MATTEO

My eyes pop open, but the sky is no longer blue, but black, stars swimming in the night sky.

"Fuck!" I try to jump to my feet, but still feel like I'm in a damn fog. I take a minute to close my eyes, then I get up, stumbling as I do. I can't waste any more time. Who the hell knows how long I've been down and where Aida is right now?

I look around for the stuff that belonged to the men I killed. Once I locate it all, I stuff the keys and phones into my pockets, and shove both weapons into my waistband.

The shovels are next as I grab both, dragging them down to where I know the van is still parked. Once I get the damn thing started, I'm on the road, doing my best to maintain control of the wheel.

Thanks to the GPS they have in here, I know where I'm going, though I'm going slower than I should be. But not killing myself is high on the agenda.

Once I get back to the house, I jump out, finding the driveway empty, and rush toward the door. It's open.

Slowly, I push it open further, not finding anyone there.

"Hello?" I rush inside. "Robby?"

The lights are still on, but the house is definitely empty. I have to make sure Robby isn't hiding somewhere.

I head for the bathroom first though, finding a towel and wetting it in the sink as I stare at myself, blood covering my forehead, and staining my cheeks and jaw. I wipe it all away, knowing I have to also change my clothes before Robby and I get out of here. If the cops stop me, they're really going to love the bloodied clothes. Who'd believe I'm some kid who's been locked in a basement since I was eight? They'll just see a man with blood on his clothing.

"Robby, buddy. It's Matteo. We gotta go!" I shout. If he's near enough, maybe he'll hear me and come out. Aida once told me he liked to hide when he was scared. He could be anywhere. I can't leave until I search every inch of this place.

Once I'm finally clean, I march into the kitchen. "Robby? Come on, dude."

I keep moving, not seeing him anywhere. "Robby?" I run all over—the dining room, the living room, checking behind the couches. "Fuck!"

I hurry up the stairs, combing through every damn room, under beds, but he's nowhere. When I get to Agnelo's bedroom, I grab one of his black zip-up hoodies from the closet and leave my shirt on his goddamn floor.

Running back out, I continue searching, not finding Robby anywhere. They must've taken him. They had to have. I have to find him too. I'm ready to bail, marching toward the stairs when a screech of tires wails in the distance, until they stop.

"Damn it!" I whisper, removing a gun from my waistband. The vehicle had a shit ton of weapons to keep me company.

"He's here!" someone shouts, then multiple footsteps slam against the floor. I slowly move out of the room and the floorboards creek.

Fuck!

"He's upstairs!" a man whispers. "Move in."

My pulse pounds heavy in my throat as I hide behind the wall right to the side of the stairs, hoping to catch them off guard.

They climb. Slowly. The stairs squeaking louder as they go up.

Closer.

Closer.

Pop.

I get one straight in the temple as he falls on top of another guy. I come out of hiding, firing a bullet into the chest of another until there's only one left.

One I know well.

"Well, kid"—Louis Esposito grins—"can't say you're not clever. Nice to see you out of that chain."

I snicker. "I did promise I'd kill you when I was eight."

"Well, let's see what you've got." He raises his gun and fires.

I duck, rolling onto the floor before I shoot, hitting him in the calf.

"Fuck!" he howls as I rise, treading to him, weapon drawn. "You're not as young as you once were."

"I can still fuck you up." He drags himself to the corner of the wall, separating the space between the two sets of stairs.

I kick over the two dead men as I climb down, and they topple before his feet. He points his pistol at me.

"You won't be able to kill me, old man."

But he tries with a shaky hand, the bullet whizzing past me, hitting the wall. Just as quickly, my finger on the trigger, I shoot, the bullet ripping into his hand, the weapon in it slipping out.

His scream turns into bitter laughter, the pain on his face evident, even as he tries to fight it.

"Where's Agnelo?" I ask, now standing right before him.

"I don't fucking know," he grits. "He sent me here as soon as he realized his men haven't checked in. He figured you must've escaped. The tracker on the van told him you were here."

"Tracker, huh?" My foot comes on top of his hand and I grind it. Hard.

"Ahhh! Fuck!"

"Where's the tracker? How do I get rid of it?"

"Go to hell," he grunts.

I press even harder. "I can kill you slow or I can kill you quick. Pick one."

"You son of a—"

"Call my mother a bitch and I'll rip off your dick and feed it to you."

His eyes go wide. He should know I don't kid. If he doesn't, I'd be glad to demonstrate.

"Under the trunk, by—by the wheel! Just toss it."

"Thanks." I grin, letting his hand free. Kneeling, I press the barrel of my gun to his forehead. "So, Agnelo, where the hell is he?"

"He didn't tell me."

"Think harder!" I roar. "Where does he usually go?"

"The…ahh…there's a cigar shop they go to. Try there, okay?"

"Address?"

He shoots it off.

"Do you know where he sent Aida and the boy?" When he doesn't say a word, I get to my feet, trampling his hand again, the heel of my shoe digging into his wound. "Speak!"

"H-he sold her. I—I don't know to who."

"And Robby?"

"Don't…" His breathing grows tattered. "Don't know who took the boy," he grits. "He only tells us what we need to know. The Bianchis are careful."

Lifting my gun, I stare hard into the man who treated me like shit. "I hope you have no kids. Be a shame to think you're raising any."

"No! Please!"

Pop.

A bullet enters his chest, another landing in his forehead.

I remember everything he's done, the way he spoke to me. I was just a boy, with no one to help me.

Now, he won't do that to anyone else.

AIDA

The gravel beneath my feet has been replaced with a cold steel floor. My loud breaths tighten around in the small space of the cage I share with another woman.

Her long raven-black hair is caked to her face, the ends matted, her dark denim jeans stained with brown at her knees. She hasn't spoken a word since I was thrown beside her, maybe an hour ago or longer.

When did she arrive here? What will they do to us?

My heart pounds and fear creeps up my throat until panic sets in with a heavy fist. I'm alive. For now.

My arms circle my knees and all I see is Matteo. His body falling as I shot him.

I killed him!

Agnelo forced me to kill the man I love. I'll never get over it. I'll never move on. He'll be with me for as long as I'm alive. The tormenting loss, it feasts on my soul until it's all I can feel. I can't think about him without dying inside.

The stinging within my eyes builds until the tears swarm, drifting down my cheeks. And Robby? My sweet Robby! I tuck my head against my knees and quietly sob, hoping those bastards don't hear us.

There are two of them—tall, huge, standing yards in front, rifles slung over their backs. We don't stand a chance against them.

The place is filled with piles of wood. It seems like some kind of factory or something. The woman glances quickly at me before zipping her eyes away to the men, dried black mascara running down from her bottom lashes.

How could people hurt one another this way? We're worse than animals, aren't we? We don't do things for mere survival, we do them to hurt each other, and we don't even bat an eye.

"What you lookin' at, bitch?" the long-bearded man yells at her. She instantly stiffens, hiding her face in her lap, her heavy breathing causing her shoulders to tremble.

I instantly feel sorry for her, my own pain shelved to the side. "Hey," I whisper, scooting closer. "I'm Aida. What's your name?" But instead of answering, she continues to hide.

"I know you're scared." I gently place my hand on top of hers and she flinches. "I'm sorry. I shouldn't have done that." I edge my palm away. "It's okay if you don't want to talk, but I figured we can maybe keep each other sane here, you know?"

She's not much older than me, maybe even younger. Whenever

I remember the club, all those faces there, the kids, the young women? I instantly feel ill.

With a sigh, I move back to my corner. I can't force her to speak to me nor do I blame her for not wanting to.

A few minutes pass, and when I close my eyes, my head slanting back gently against the cage, she speaks.

"A-Ava." The word falls in a hush of silence. "I'm Ava."

"Ava. It's nice to meet you, though I wish it were somewhere better." I give her a sad smile. "Have you been here long?"

She moves closer to me. "Two days. Maybe more. I don't know. I'm so hungry." Her brows tighten. "They won't feed me."

"What?"

"Yeah." She bows her head.

There are empty water bottles scattered around us, and a full one next to me I haven't yet touched. This poor woman. What savages!

I'm glad I don't share Bianchi blood, and then I think about my cousins Raquel and Chiara. They're not my cousins anymore either. Stabbing pain plants itself in my chest. I really have no one.

"You okay?" Ava asks, her fingers attempting to swat away the strands of hair glued to her forehead from the sweat.

"No," I say, and she nods because she isn't either. How could we be?

"Shut up over there." One of them comes rushing, banging his rifle over the top of the cage.

"Fuck you!" I snarl, the words slipping suddenly, and that's when my eyes bulge.

"Shh!" Ava hums, but it's too late, a vicious sneer grows on his face.

"Really?" His hand lands on the lock that keeps us prisoner. "You wanna fuck me, huh?" My heart skips a beat, sending fear riddling down my body in waves.

Why did I just do that?

"Yo, Ethan. The girls wanna fuck."

Ava cries, her body shuddering, and my hand crawls to hers, holding it tight.

"Oh, yeah?" His lips jerk as Ethan marches over, throwing the rifle down as his stare runs past both of our bodies. "Get them out, then."

No! No! No! Why didn't I keep my mouth shut?

The air grows thick in my throat, dread pulsing from within.

He undoes the lock and the men yank us out by our hair, me first, then Ava. They throw us onto the icy floor, holding us down with their knees to the middle of our backs as they drag our pants down.

The man above me lowers his face to my ear, his voice gruff, his breaths heavy, sending bile turning in my stomach. "You're gonna soon learn, little whores don't get to open their mouths without being punished."

His hands are everywhere, under my shirt, inside me. I break with a quiet sob, lying there, my eyes holding on to Ava's, her tears matching mine. In the darkness of shared misery, all we can do is hold on to each other the only way we can.

With our bodies pressed deep into the floor, while the men violate us, the tears falling down our cheeks, I reach my hand for hers, our fingertips almost touching. I did this. Me and my big mouth. It's all my fault.

She screams as the man continues, slapping her hard across the cheek for making a sound. The one behind me grunts, pushing faster, and I pray for it to be over.

Just let them stop!

I cry in silence, not wanting them to revel in my pain, but

I'm sure they are anyway. I'm sure it doesn't matter to them that they're destroying us.

When they're done, they both climb to their feet. But Ava and I, we just lie there, sobbing in voiceless despair, our gazes locked. *I'm sorry*, I mouth. Because I am.

Her lips start to move, and before she can say a word, a bullet rips into the back of her head. And the shock in her eyes, I'll never forget it, even as they drag me away, kicking and screaming her name as the blood pools around her face.

Twenty-Seven

MATTEO

I couldn't even enjoy killing that asshole, Louis, because all I could think about was finding her, finding Robby. If she's dead, I may as well be too.

I'm back in the van, the night still fitted over the sky as I drive on a long, empty stretch of the road, the tracker long abandoned. The light changes to green and I turn a sharp right, too sharp, almost crashing into a tree I didn't see.

I curse under my breath as the van jerks, before I step on the gas, a black pickup truck honking at me from behind. I stop, letting him pass, and he throws me a middle finger.

I drive on, the cigar shop only half a mile away according to the GPS. I've got more fire power than I could ever need, and with my fighting skills, I hope I can take whoever is holed up there. I'm wishing it's Faro and Agnelo so I can kill them both.

A few minutes later and I've arrived, driving around the block once I see the place. It's on a corner, huge empty lot, and the only other place in the area is a closed deli across the two-way street.

Parking half a block away, I step out of the van, lifting my hoodie and keeping my head down as I walk, hoping no one recognizes me.

Heading into the parking lot, I find two white vans and a black SUV parked all the way at the end. The place is pitch black, except for one streetlamp illuminating the lot. I step around the cigar shop, peering through the small window, seeing three faces inside, but no one I know. Two of them count a large stack of cash, while another is smoking.

My hand grips the door handle, trying to see if it'll turn. Once it does, I let go. Removing a pistol from my waistband and a flip knife from my pocket, I keep both close as I look through the window again. Aiming the gun at the one smoking, I slowly pull the trigger until the bullet cracks through the glass, puncturing him right in the temple.

"What the… Sonny?"

That's when I rush in.

Pop.

Pop.

They fall fast, their bodies hitting the floor, the faint sound of my footsteps near them. One is dead, blood seeping from the center of his chest, while the third stares up at me with fear in his eyes, his hand trembling with the gun in his palm. A round circle of crimson saturates his white t-shirt around his stomach.

"Who a-are you?" he asks.

"A friend." A smirk pulls at my mouth.

When he fires a shot at me, I duck, hitting him with one in the thigh.

"Ahhh!" His weapon clacks to the ground and he attempts to cover the hole in his leg, trying desperately to cling to the life he'll no longer see.

"Where's Aida? Where did Agnelo send her?"

"I—ahh…" he stammers with a jerk of his body.

"Tell me!" I growl, stamping into his leg wound.

"S-sold her to someone. No names. Didn't tell us."

"Has he been here? And don't fucking lie!" I dig my heel into him.

"No, man. I s-swear."

"Fuck!" I roar, smashing a fist into my temple.

"I need to know where the hell Agnelo is, and if you don't tell me…" I stomp my sneaker over his hand, pushing so hard, he screams. "Things are gonna start getting even worse for you."

He cries, unable to catch his breath as I remove my foot.

"Okay, then." I pop him with another bullet into the other thigh. "I can do this all fucking day. They have no idea I'm here. So talk or I keep shooting." I flip the knife in my hand. "Or cutting." I lower the tip of the blade into his dick. "I'd do anything for her, so you better tell me where the hell your boss is, or I'm gonna start cutting."

The blade pierces his balls and he gasps with desperate inhales.

"W-warehouse. Hiding. Please, don't cut my dick."

"Address."

"Fifty-six Main Street, right on the corner of Smith. Ca-can't miss it," he stammers, lost to the pain.

"You better be telling the truth."

"I am, man. Please let me g—"

"The only place you're going is hell." With a single bullet into his head, he stops talking.

I gather all the money, stuffing it back into the black bag beside it, taking it with me, along with the weapons.

If I can take everything from the Bianchis, I will. I'll start with their lives. It's time the reaper pays them a visit.

When I get to the warehouse, the last thing I expected was to join a gunfight that had already started. The only good thing about that is no one notices me. I blend well with the men here, some of them in black hoodies like me. There are two women here too, and I can see Agnelo holding one around her throat. Figures the coward would get some innocent woman involved in his war.

A man comes at me and I kick him in the stomach, dropping him with a bullet in his chest. I have no fucking time to figure out who the hell anyone is. If they come at me, they're getting killed.

I find a spot behind a steel beam and watch the rest of the fight, waiting for my chance to get Agnelo. That's all I'm here for. But I won't kill him. Not yet. Not until Aida and Robby are safe.

One of the guys in the hoodie throws a man off him, his green eyes so damn bright, for one second, it's like I'm staring at my big brother Dom. He and Enzo, they had the same colored eyes. The greenest shit you'd ever seen. Damn coincidence.

"Don't, Jade!" another shouts, and before I realize why, a bullet fires from a tall blonde woman's weapon, aimed at Agnelo.

"Fuck!" I groan, hoping the bastard doesn't die. But instead, it hits the woman trapped in Agnelo's grasp. She falls, just as Agnelo runs, pointing his pistol at the guy who now has eyes set on him.

But he won't get him because I will. Once he kicks Agnelo's weapon away, throwing him to the ground, he plants a foot over the asshole's stomach.

"Finally. I get to kill you," he tells the man who tortured Aida and me our whole lives. This is our kill though. It doesn't belong to whoever the hell this guy is.

Without anyone noticing me, I come out, the barrel of my gun pressing into the back of the guy's head. "Put your gun down. He's mine."

He snickers. "Nah, man. You must be confused." He pivots to me in one quick motion, like he's not afraid to die. And his eyes, they're the same color green as the other ones.

I ignore the unnerving feeling punching me in the gut, concentrating on what I need to do to find Aida.

Annoyance settles behind my eyes, and fuck, I wanna kill this guy bad. He's smug as hell and I'd love to rearrange his face until he stops looking at me like he is right now. Like he can take me.

But something suddenly shifts, his brows bending as he focuses his entire attention on me. He stares like he's trying to piece something together that doesn't fit right, like when Aida and I would do those crossword puzzles she loves.

"Who the hell are you?" His question splits open the silence as his eyes grow large, as though he knows the answer to his own question. But that would be crazy. No one knows who I am. I'm a kid long forgotten, erased from history. Memories of me long vanished like I never existed at all. I matter to no one but her, and now, I've lost her too.

I suck in a slow inhale, and my eyes revert to the man I'm truly after. Agnelo. My gun rises toward his head.

"Ahh, there he is," Agnelo taunts with a sneer. "I've been looking for you."

"Well, you found me." My reply is calm, but inside, the wrath pounds as though trying to escape the cage I've built around it, needing to satiate its desire for revenge against the man who took everything from me.

Once I find her, I'll rip him limb by limb. He's going to know what suffering is, and he'll die while enduring it. Sometimes, an eye for an eye is the best medicine.

"Tell me where she is," I whisper-shout. "Where the hell did you send her?"

I tune the others out, now coming to stand around us. There are four of them in all, plus the two women.

Who the fuck are these guys?

"Tsk, tsk." Agnelo chuckles, and even on the ground, this fuck thinks he's got the upper hand. "You'll never find her. Stupid kid. I told you, she'll never be yours. When will you finally listen?"

I roar with a growl, the butt of my gun popping him right in his temple. "She's your fucking daughter and you sold her? To who?" I know he's not her father, but she was his daughter in every sense of the word. He was supposed to protect her. She was just a child when he stole everything from her. The least he could've done was keep her safe, but Agnelo is the devil, and the devil has no soul.

"Are you looking for Aida?" the guy asks, and I instantly look at him again, my pulse racing.

"How the hell do you know her? Have you seen her?"

"No, man. I'm sorry. But if you need help, my brothers and I, we can help you find her."

Brothers. I once had those too.

I stiffen my jaw. "I work alone."

Staring back at Agnelo, I'm ready to get him out of here so he can tell me where the hell Aida is.

"This is so beautiful." A synthetic smile crosses Agnelo's face. "Reunited at last and they have no idea. I only wish my brothers were still alive to witness this miracle."

My body breaks with a cold wave, a subtle awareness filling the space around me.

What is he talking about? Who are they? His brothers are dead?

"What the fuck is going on?" the guy asks, equally confused.

"Why don't you tell them who you are?" Agnelo stares hard at me before glancing at each of the people here.

Suddenly, the other one, who I first saw with the green eyes, he's in front of me, his gaze narrowing as he circles me.

My heart throbs in my chest and that strong desire I had to kill them all just to get the man I want, is slowly fading. The more I look at him, the more I realize something I never for one moment thought I'd find again.

Brother? Raw emotions clog up my throat. How's this even possible? Is this really him?

Dom?

The questions spin in my head. Fuck. It's like I'm back to being that little kid again, wanting his big brother to hold his hand and tell him he's going to always protect him. Because that's what Dom did for me. He protected me with everything he had. At school, at the playground, he was ready to beat anyone who messed with me.

And here he is after fifteen fucking years. But I can't seem to ask, how after protecting me for so long, how he could give up on me. How could he trade me for his own safety? Because that's not the brother I remember.

"No…" His intake of breath sharpens with the slow shake of his head. It hits him then, who I am. His face twists with a bout of sadness, his brows furrowing. "It can't be." A palm runs over his mouth while his eyes don't leave mine. "I watched you d—"

I attempt to steady my nerves, my breaths intensifying the more he stares. When I dart my gaze to the others, a heaviness sinks into me. The other guy with the green eyes… I can't believe I hadn't realized it as soon as I saw him.

Enzo.

I push down all these damn feelings clawing at me. I can't be weak. I can't let them know how much they hurt me, what abandoning me had done.

I cock the pistol at Agnelo.

"Who is that, Dom?" the dark-eyed one asks, swiping his hair away from his forehead.

I drag in a breath, my heartbeats slamming into my rib cage, realizing the man who just spoke is Dante. He has to be. He's a lot bigger, but if I look at him enough, I can see it. It's him.

They're all here. But why?

"Don't you recognize your own brother?" Agnelo sniggers, his shoulders rocking.

"Br-brother?" Enzo speaks low. "It can't be." He looks straight into my eyes and I can see the realization branding on his features. "Fucking hell."

Dante comes over to stand beside Dom, his jaw straining as he examines me up and down, muttering a curse.

"Matteo?" Dom's voice curls with a strain. "Is that really you?"

"Surprise!" Agnelo announces, flipping his hands in the air.

"H-how could you be here this whole time? Where have you been?" Dom stutters, his eyes still on me.

I try not to stare back. My heart, it can't fucking take it. After all this time, seeing them again, it unravels me. They have no idea how damn hard it is not to ask them why? Why didn't they search for me?

"He's been with me this whole time," Agnelo interrupts. "Isn't that right, kid?"

"Tell me where she is!" I roar. That's what matters now. Aida and Robby.

"You're like a sad, little puppy." He narrows his eyes with a harsh squint, trying to sit up but some other guy I don't know pushes him back down. "She's long gone by now. Probably in a different country."

I let out a deep-chested growl, forcing the muzzle of the pistol to my own forehead.

She can't be gone!

"Good luck finding her by yourself," Agnelo tosses. "But if you want a shot at saving her, well, you're going to have to take me out of here before your brothers end your chance of ever getting to her in time."

Did you actually think I'd leave you here? Believe me, the stuff I'll do to you will be far worse than whatever my brothers are capable of.

"Matteo, please," Dom pleads. "Let us help you. Don't fucking listen to him. All he ever does is lie."

But I ignore him.

"Goddamn, Matteo. We're your brothers." Dante clasps me on the shoulder, but I shove it away. "We'll help you find her."

"I have no brothers." I pierce him with a deadpan look. The words slip out before I have a chance to realize if I even mean them. But after so long of being alone, knowing I had no family who loved me enough to fight for me, I can't pretend we're family now. "The best thing you can do is forget you ever saw me. I'm still dead where it matters."

I draw my gun at the one holding Agnelo down. "Tell your friend to move," I tell Dom. "Agnelo is coming with me."

With Dom's permission, the guy steps back, letting Agnelo get up. I gradually edge toward him, clasping my arm around the back of his neck, the barrel of the gun against his temple.

When I drag him away, Enzo yells, "Wait! Don't go. We love you, man. We never would've given up finding you if we knew you were alive."

I jerk back at that confession, the weight of it slamming into me, my legs growing heavy. Unable to move. To breathe. They thought I…I was dead? I glance at each one of them.

My brothers.

And though that little boy inside me wants so badly to stay, to know the truth, the man I am now, he wants to save the love of his life more than he wants his family.

"I'm sorry." Dom's voice wavers. His expression is as broken as my heart, cracked to the very bone.

With one last glimpse at them, I bolt out of there, knowing if I stay another moment, I won't be able to hold on to the mask of fury that's keeping me from remembering how much I still love them.

Twenty-Eight

MATTEO

"Tell me where they are!" I slam a fist into his stomach, both of us now back in that basement I wasted away in for years.

"I don't know." He coughs out blood, keeling over, his hands holding on to his midsection. It's been half a fucking day since we've been here, and he's not told me one damn thing, even with a bullet in his thigh. I don't know how much more I can hurt him without completely killing him. If he dies, so does she.

I dangle the set of keys I got from his wallet on my index finger. There are probably over twenty keys here. I could only imagine what each one is for, how many damn prisons they can open, hostages they can let out. When he still doesn't answer, I land a punch to his jaw.

"Don't fucking lie to me. I'll shoot every one of your limbs until you tell me." He groans, the chain he once used on me, now cutting into his own wrist.

"Goddamn it." He palms his face. "I think you broke something."

"Start talking or I start breaking all your bones." A sneer slithers to my mouth as I kneel over to grab his shirt in my fist, glaring into the eyes of the devil, unable to wait until I send him back to hell.

I right myself, readying to slam him with another punch to his face.

"I gotta tell you, kid." He moves his chin side to side with his hand. "I'm proud of you. Look how far you've come. It's too bad after all is said and done, I *will* have to kill you. I'm sure you understand."

I give him a sinister smile, and my face nears his until only a hand separates us. "You don't get it, do you? You're gonna die. I'll kill you, and I'll enjoy it. And she and I, we'll make a life together and we'll put everything you've done behind us while you're rotting away."

He chuckles, his head falling back. "And what will you do when more of my men come? You gonna kill them all? By yourself?" His face twists with mockery, dismissing my power. My strength.

"I've killed many so far, and I'll do it for as long as I need to find her. If you won't tell me where she is, I'll make sure you die so slowly, you'll beg for me to make it faster." My lips jerk with a snicker. "You forget you made me." I right myself, heading to retrieve one of the knives on the floor a few feet away. "Give yourself some credit."

When I pivot around, he eyes the blade in my hand, darting his wild stare back to me with a nervous grin. I can practically see his lips shaking. "What are you gonna do with that thing?"

"Well…" I flip the knife in my hand. "First, I'm gonna carve our names on your skin so that even as your flesh joins the dirt you belong in, you'll never forget us."

The quick jerk of his breath is small, but enough for me to catch it. A triumphant smile appears on my face, finally feeling like I've got the upper hand. After so long of being the captive, I'm now the one who holds the key. Literally.

"I'm done playing games. Who has her?" I clutch the black handle of the small knife, its blade glistening in the drops of light flickering against its sharp edges.

I prod slowly, back to the man who holds all the answers. Who's taken everything and everyone from me.

I want to hurt him so damn bad, I'm literally vibrating with the need. I want him to suffer. I want him to bleed until he's dead.

"You gotta let me go for me to tell you that," he jeers with a flick of his thick, dark brows.

"You still think you're in charge, don't you?" Standing before him, I let the blade crawl down his chest until it reaches his stomach, and slowly, meticulously, without taking my eyes off his, I let the very tip of it puncture his skin.

He groans, his teeth gritted as he stares hard into me. "Fuck you."

"How does it feel?" I continue to cut into him with a glare. "Not to be the one who hurts, but the one to hurt instead?"

"You can't do shit to me, kid." His nostrils expand. "I'm Agnelo fucking Bianchi. You hear me?"

"Yeah." I shrug my shoulders. "I hear you."

Before he can even pull in a breath, I stab his palm so hard, the blade makes it to the other side.

"Ahhh! You son of a biiiitch!" he screams, but I ignore it, pulling up his shirt in the front. Painstakingly, I cut her name across his chest in big letters.

"I'm g-gonna kill you," he screams, trying to stop me with his working hand, no longer able to keep the brave front he's been trying to hold on to.

"You really shouldn't disturb an artist when he's working." I raise the knife in the air and stab that hand, once, twice, maybe more. I've lost count from the seething blaze burning inside me.

He grunts. He screams. He cries. I've waited years to hear that son of a bitch cry. If only Aida was here. We could do this together.

"Now that you're better behaved," I taunt. "I can continue."

Right under her name, I cut out mine.

There's so much blood dripping down, I don't realize it until I'm done.

"Had enough yet?" My laughter bites with a cold rush of emotions.

He coughs as he tries to calm his breathing, his chest swelling up with force.

"No? Fine. Have it your way." I march back to the stash of weapons I found in the van, lowering to the floor to pick up one of the nines. "I'm gonna hurt you every fucking way I can, but I won't let you die. Because I need you alive. For now. But how you die"—I lift the weapon aiming it at his hand, the one chained—"well, that's on you."

Pop.

He screams loudly as the bullet enters another part of his hand, and it's like music. I shut my eyes, breathing softly, enjoying his suffering. Does that make me a monster? Maybe. But I'm okay with that.

"Where're Aida and Robby?" I ask calmly, yet my pulse is increasing every second. I need to find them. Fast. This is taking too long.

Gradually, his face lifts up to mine, his body shuddering as his eyes still spill with venom.

"Still won't tell me? Okay." Without a blink, I pop a bullet into the top of his foot and the deafening shouting of a coward is what I hear next. "I'll keep doing this until you break. And you *will* break, Agnelo. I promise."

I'm on top of him in an instant, and I let the knife fall across his flesh like it's possessed, like it needs his pain for survival, as much as I do.

"Tell me!" I roar as the blade slices across his cheek, his forehead. "Fucking say it! Where are they?"

He fights it—the desire to tell me what I need to know. He fights it with every cut, every slice of his skin until he can't fight anymore. Until his blood is all he sees around him.

Drip.

Drip.

It dances like the rain, slowly trickling from the slashes on his thighs, his calves. Anywhere I can hurt him, I do.

"I—" he stammers. "I—I'll—I'll tell you. Fuuuuck." He cries real tears.

"Better do it quick." The tip of the knife nears the spot under his chin, raising his face to mine, nicking him.

"You're gonna kill me anyway," he breathes, trying to mask the pain, but it shows. He can't hide from it. "S-s-so why should I help you?"

"Because if you don't"—I push the knife deeper—"I'm going to hurt you for weeks, killing you slowly. At least if you tell me, I'll kill you faster."

He coughs to catch his breath. "If I didn't hate your family, I'd actually like you."

"I won't take that as a compliment." I stand straight. "Address. Now."

With a deep inhale, he speaks. "Carlito, his…" He coughs… "His family owns a factory. They're there." He gives me the address and I keep repeating it in my head so I don't forget it.

Running over to the weapons, I pack them up, grabbing the handle of the bag as I head for the stairs.

"A-at-at least I let you piss in a bucket," he calls when I'm a few steps up. "Wha-what will I do if I gotta go?"

"Piss yourself." I'm out the door, hoping I'm not too late to save her.

AIDA

"Such a pretty thing, isn't she?" Ethan hisses, grunting while inside me.

"Get off, it's my fucking turn."

"I'm not done yet." He pumps faster as he robs me of my dignity, taking something that doesn't belong to him. I close my eyes, wishing to die.

It's been hours of this, using me whenever they see fit, while her body is still on the floor.

Pale. Dead.

Ava.

Is there someone who misses her? Will they ever know what happened?

The ache behind my eyes comes swiftly the more I look at her face—too young to die when she never even lived.

Am I next? Will they kill me after they're done using my body? Maybe it's better if I do die, then I could be with Matteo. At the thought of his name, there's a clenching in my chest.

The raw anguish. It's too much. The space he once filled in my heart, now devoid of anything at all, the pain from his loss bound to my soul like a tattoo.

I attempt to recall every second of our last few moments. What he said. How he looked. But it all flies by in a flash and I can't quite seem to grasp it. Every inch of me fights to remember him—everything about every single moment of our life together, from when I first saw that little boy, his eyes grasping mine as he lay on that gurney bleeding, to the man who has grown to show me what love truly is.

He owns me. Even in death.

I miss you so much. I'll never stop loving you.

And it's true. There's no way to forget the only man who holds a piece of my heart no one else knows even exists. He'll be the first. The last. The always wrapped in forever. "Pinky swear," I whisper as though somehow, he could hear my promise, but how could he?

"Did you say you like my cock?" Venom in the man's voice hisses past my ear, and as my eyes open, I find someone standing behind him and I gasp.

My mouth tries to move, to say even a single syllable, but it can't. Old tears distort my vision and I know I must be imagining him standing there. It's a hallucination, or maybe I'm dead and this is a dream.

A finger lifts in the air, landing across his lips, telling me to quiet. And I do, even as I stare hard, even as every hair on my body stands up. Surely, Matteo isn't here at all.

But then he vanishes like he wasn't there. I knew it. My mind is playing tricks.

"What a good whore," the man groans, still in me, but I barely feel a thing.

My heart tightens, new tears springing into my eyes.

Please come back. Let me see you, just one more time.

"What the fuck? Why are you touching my ass, man?" Ethan instantly pops off me, glancing behind him. As he does, I quickly sit up, pulling my pants back over my hips, scooting backward as far as I can go. I realize I wasn't hallucinating at all.

"Oh my God!" A shaky hand clamps over my mouth as the tears make a path down my cheeks. "You're here!" I cry, seeing the other man already dead, his body at his friend's feet.

"Of course I am, Aida. I'll always come back for you." He points his gun down at his side.

Ethan looks confused, jerking his eyes from Matteo to me. Before he has a chance to react, Matteo fires into his chest. Once. Then again, and again, my attacker stumbling backward until he lands on the ground.

My heartbeats ripple through me as I look at the carnage, then stare at the one who caused it.

Matteo's gaze snaps to mine in an instant, and I get to my feet, unable to rip my eyes away from his. He assesses me as I tread toward him slowly, like I'm still unsure if I'm seeing his ghost. "Matteo, is—is that really you?"

He walks just as slowly at first, until his feet pick up pace, and mine do too, both of us running the short distance between us, both of us breathing hard as we come to stand before one another. My brows tighten, moisture building behind my eyes, his gaze filling with his own emotion.

"I thought I killed you." Tears fill the space between my words, my palm cradling his cheek.

He clamps his hand over mine, his thumb rubbing my skin. "Thankfully you've got a crappy shot." A grin spreads across his face, his eyes glistening.

My laugh comes out strangled with a sob. "Matteo…" I rise on my toes, leaning in close, my lips hovering over his. Our breaths mingle with aching desperation, his hands clinging to the back of my head, gripping tight enough to keep me tied to him for eternity.

"I know." His forehead falls to mine. "God, I thought you were gone for good."

"When I'm lost, you always seem to find me."

"And I always will," he breathes, his lips brushing tenderly with mine.

"Pinky swear?" A sob escapes me, my free hand tightening on his shoulder, my fingernails sinking into hard muscle.

"Pinky swear." He scoops me into his arms and I kiss him, my hands crawling to his back, holding on with a ferocious desperation. If this isn't real, if I somehow imagined this moment, I don't care. Just the mere thought of being with him again is enough. My head falls against his chest as he carries me out of this nightmare.

"We have to get out of here before more of them come," he says as we step outside.

I nod. "We have to go back to the house and get Robby, then go somewhere far away. Just us three."

But instead of agreeing with me, his gaze turns clouded and his jaw twitches.

"Matteo?" A shudder slinks up my spine as he settles me inside the back of a van. "Where's Robby?" My pulse throbs at my neck.

"I don't know. I thought he was here. That's what that fucking bastard said."

"No." I shake my head with a tremor in my voice. "It was just Ava, the girl they killed, and me." I suddenly feel sick to my stomach. "Wait, what bastard?"

"Agnelo. I have him chained up in the basement."

My gaze widens. "Take me to him. I need to see him. He knows where Robby is. I'm sure of it."

Twenty-Nine

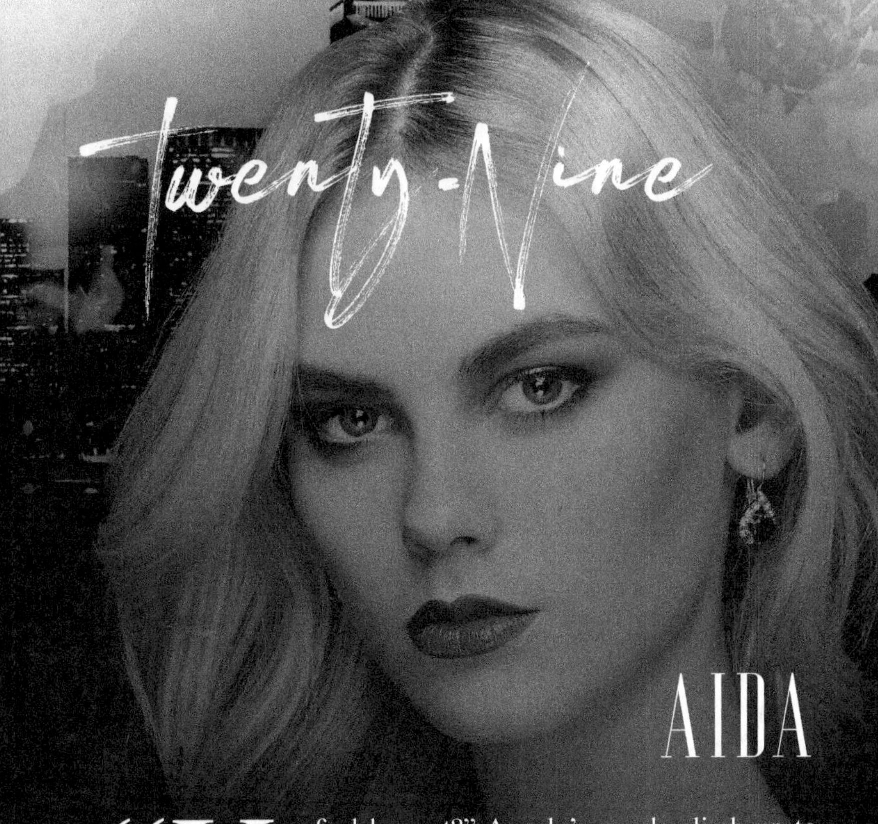

AIDA

"**Y**ou find her yet?" Agnelo's words climb up to greet me as soon as the basement door opens and my feet move down the steps. "C-c-come on now, don't keep me in suspense," he continues.

Even as he sounds weak, he still has the strength to mock us. I've never had this visceral desire to end someone's life before, but his, I'll do it gladly.

Matteo tucks my small hand in his bigger one as we descend together to face the monster children should only know from stories, but he made all our nightmares come true.

"Did you piss yourself, yet?" Matteo asks as we make it down the final step. And when our eyes zip to his pants, we realize he did.

"Need a diaper?" I snicker. Seeing him covered in wounds brings me a satisfaction I can't describe.

He laughs with a cough. "Th-there sh-she is. I've missed you, Glad to see you in…fuck"—he winces as he shifts on the mattress—"one piece."

Without hesitation, I rush to him. "I'll kill you right now if you don't tell me where Robby is."

"Oh." He feigns a frown. "Was the boy not there? My memory is getting rusty." He coughs, spitting up blood.

My breaths rush past me in a panic, my pulse thrashing. "Where is he?" I shout, turning back to Matteo. "Give me your gun." I stretch out a hand, and he takes out the one in his waistband and gives it to me.

"Now." I turn to Agnelo. "Should I continue to hurt you? Seems like Matteo did a fine job so far."

His eyelids flicker, like he's trying to stay awake, but he keeps going. "Not afraid of…" He pauses, trying to control his pain. "A bunch of pathetic kids," he spits out, biting down on his teeth. "I've been through worse."

A laugh weaves out of me, and before he can utter another word, I slam the gun into his hand. And I don't stop. I scream with all the pent-up anger laid buried, hitting him again and again—his head, his neck, his arms. I pound him with furious blows, my body buzzing and tingling with the desire to watch the life slip out of his lungs. I see Ms. Greco, remembering her death, Matteo shot, falling on this very mattress, my attacks, the constant fear in Robby's eyes—it all flashes before me, like a movie.

Arms wrap around me from behind, and Matteo's voice lulls me, keeping the ghosts of my scars from continuing to own me.

"It's okay, my love. Shh. I've got you." With a cry, I twist into his arms and wrap mine around his neck, sobbing into his chest as he holds me. "I promise, you can do whatever you want to him, but after we find Robby."

"Okay," I sniffle as I pitch back. His thumbs swipe under both my eyes. "Thank you for not giving up on me. I blamed you for her death and I'm so sorry for that. Please, forgive me."

"You never needed my forgiveness for a single damn thing, but if you need me to say it, then yeah, I forgive you."

Agnelo coughs and moans behind us, and our attention is back to him. "You ready to talk yet?" I ask. "Or should I continue?"

"His mo-mother." He spits up blood. "The mother and the Cavaleris, they…" he whimpers, "…got him."

Matteo stiffens beside me, his expression tight.

"So, his mother, she wasn't in jail, huh?" I shake my head, disgust coming over my face. "You took him too, didn't you?"

"He's *my* fucking kid." His eyes harden even as he slowly dies. "My kin. Not like you." His upper lip curls, blood running in between his teeth.

"The best thing to ever happen to me was to find out we're not related. And don't worry, Robby will never know who you truly are."

When he doesn't say anything, just stares at me with boldness, I raise the gun in my hand, readying to bash it into his skull.

"Who was my father?" I ask. "What was my mother's name?"

"Wa-wallet," he says, lifting his unchained hand to cover his face. "Her wallet's in the office, bottom drawer. D-don't know who your father is but got her name on her license."

Not wasting a second, we rush up the stairs, a chill skittering up my arms.

"Robby's mom," Matteo says as we make it to the office. "She's with my brothers."

"Your brothers?" Confusion settles over me as I pull open the drawer.

"Cavaleri. That's me. Matteo Cavaleri."

My mouth falls open. He's never told me his full name, even when I had asked.

"I saw them," he admits, and I witness the hurt in his eyes. "When I was out looking for you."

"What? Oh my God!" I rummage through the drawer, my attention jumping between him and my mission to find my mother's wallet. "Do you know where they live? Why they left you? Agnelo could've been lying about it all. I know you wanted to believe he wasn't, that you had no one, but what if they never stopped looking for you? What if there's more to the story?"

Matteo appears as though he's considering what I'm saying, while I throw all the papers in the cabinet onto the floor. Finally, I see it—a rectangular brown wallet, the leather still soft beneath my fingertips.

My heart races as I stare down at it, Matteo's footfalls inching closer, until he appears beside me.

"Open it," he murmurs.

But I can't.

"I'm afraid." I swallow over the words, the trepidation churning in my stomach. "For so long, I had wondered about her. And now, I don't know if I'm ready to know her, because she'll never be my mother, Matteo." Tears fill my eyes, so heavy they crash over me like a tidal wave. "She'll never get to love me. She'll…" I burst into a sob. "She'll never know me."

Instantly, he cups my face, kissing the very tip of my nose. "But you can know her. In some way, you'll have her like you never did before. And believe me, I know how it is losing those you love. But she wanted you. She protected you." He lifts my chin in between two fingers. "Open it, Aida. Tell me her name."

Nerves roll down my body, and with a shaky hand, I pop the button, lifting the flap…and there she is.

Her smile is wide, her hair blonde and wavy. She's exactly how I remember her in my dreams, as though I plucked her out and placed her within them.

"She's so beautiful," I whisper.

"She is. Like you." His arm drapes around my shoulder and he tucks me into his side, kissing the top of my head as we both gaze at her.

"Cecilia Robinson," I say. "Does that mean I'm Aida Robinson? Is that even my name or did he change it?"

"Let's go ask him," he tells me. "Then we'll go and find my brothers to make sure Robby is really safe."

"I hope he is. I hope that one of us was able to get their family back." A sharp pang hits my chest. "Will you talk to them?" I look up at him, pulling away a fraction.

"I don't know." His gaze jumps to the floor. "Too much time has passed. I doubt they really care."

"I bet you anything they still love you." I trail my knuckles down his cheek, and his eyes return to mine. "Wishing every day that you were still alive. You have a chance, Matteo. Something I'll never get with my mother."

I grasp his hand, squeezing. "We'll find Robby and then you'll talk to them. For me." But it's for him. He needs this. His pain is still so fresh, even after all these years. He needs the truth about his life as much as I do.

He doesn't say anything as I close the drawer, taking the wallet with me. But before we go back down, my attention swivels toward the baseball bat Agnelo has always kept here, right in the corner of the room. I'm sure he's used it plenty of times, and not in the way it was intended.

"One second," I say, going to grab it.

"What are you going to do with that?"

"I'm gonna kill him with it."

He pauses, clasping the back of my neck in his palm, his eyes boring deeply. "I won't stand in your way."

We start for the basement, ready to end this once and for all. But I suddenly remember we can't leave this horror of a place until we get everything I've kept hidden. "The pictures you made me, your photo of your family, we have to get them."

"Shit, yeah."

We hurry up the stairs, and once we're in my room, he lifts the mattress as I snatch up all the pieces of us we held on to—the sketches of me he drew, my diary, the picture of his once happy family. It's ours now. Agnelo can't take it away.

He takes the photo from my hand and stares at it with deep concentration.

"They love you," I reassure, stroking his back, knowing it has to be true. "They love you so much. Their baby brother."

His shoulders rise higher with each one of his inhales. "Maybe." He sighs, and the way he says that, it cuts into my heart. The vulnerability within him is so beautiful, I ache to hold him and never let him go.

He's strong, yet tender. Still broken, yet not bruised enough to give up. And that's what he's been doing from the moment we met—fighting. But maybe the fight can finally be over. Maybe we can win.

He slips the photo into his pocket, and together, we return to the basement.

Agnelo doesn't say a word this time when he hears us, his coughing getting worse.

"Was my name Aida?" I stride up to him. "Or is that another

lie?"

"It's wha—sh-she called you," he flusters, finding it difficult to speak.

"Kill m-me." With his eyes streaked red, he lifts a defeated look at Matteo, whose footsteps lightly pad the floor before he takes the space behind me.

"I'm not gonna kill you. She is."

With a shout, I lift the bat in the air. "This is for my mother!" It swings across his neck with so much force, my body shakes.

He groans, still very much alive, and I'm glad for it.

"This is for Ms. Greco!" I smash another hard blow into the back of his head. "For Robby!" I hit him two more times, his skull giving way, pushing into his brain. But I don't stop. "For Matteo. For his family. For what those men did to me! For Ava! Ahhh!" A scream tears from the depths of my despair as I continue to rain down on him with the wrath that's been building through the years, for the pain I endured when those men pulled me out of the cage and did what they wanted. But I won't let him hold me back from a life anymore. I won't allow him to claim my freedom too. He can't have me anymore. I'm not his.

"He's dead now." Matteo clasps a hand to my shoulder and I slow my movements, my exhales rough as I stare at what I've done. Agnelo is no longer recognizable, his skull caved in, blood and pieces of who he once was spread across the mattress. The bat drops with a loud clank, and with heavy weeping, I shatter in Matteo's loving arms.

"It's over," he says. "We're finally free."

MATTEO

We watch the house burn, embers greeting the midday sun as they echo into the air, drifting slowly onto the ground.

There are fragments of us in that home, things that weren't all bad, like holding her hand as she lay beside me, talking about better days, imagining a future that now could very well be ours. But most of all, it was nothing but a prison, and everything in it was a nightmare masked in the slightest of dreams.

He's finally dead. His flesh and bones set ablaze. There's some semblance of comfort knowing he can't hurt us anymore, can't hurt anyone.

After she beat him to death, we untied him, grabbing matches from the kitchen before setting the house on fire. We left a gun beside his body, along with a box with the rest of the matches, hoping it's enough proof for the fire department to think he did it.

Holding her beside me, her eyes are transfixed to the fiery flames that remind me of her madness as she killed him.

Fuck, it was hard to watch. Not because I gave a shit about the gore, but I got a true glimpse of all the trauma she was holding on to.

We didn't talk about it after. I just held her. Let her cry. And I think that was enough for her to know she wasn't alone. That she'll never be again. I'm not chained anymore. I'll always be right by her side. No one will keep us apart again.

Tires squeal against the pavement and instantly my hand is on the gun, removing it from my waistband. "Find cover," I tell her. "It's Agnelo's men, and they won't hesitate to kill you."

"I can fight them," she tells me.

"I know you can, but I'd fight better, knowing you're safe."

She nods, kissing me quickly as the cars get closer, running to hide behind one of the columns on the far right of the house.

Retrieving another weapon from my ankle, I face the incoming vehicles, ready to take them all on.

Three black SUVs rush up the driveway, and I shoot a warning shot into the front of one, taking out a headlight. They pause, just sitting there, the windows tinted so I can't see who the hell is inside.

"Whoa," one of the guys says, rolling down the window enough for me to hear him, but not see him. "We aren't here to kill you, baby bro."

I shudder back a step, my heart rate kicking up.

When I don't say anything, he continues, "So like, can we come out now or are you still not sure if you're gonna ice us?"

With a shaky hand, I lower my weapon, and doors open. One by one, they shuffle out, the guys from the warehouse.

My brothers.

My lungs grow heavy with the breaths I can't seem to take, not believing that I'm seeing them again.

Why did they come?

"I like what you did there." Enzo lifts his chin toward the burning house, and I realize it was him talking to me from the car. "But we probably should get you both out of here before someone sees the fire and calls the po-po."

Dom and Dante are right next to him, their faces grim.

Aida comes out, stepping almost silently until she's holding my hand, sticking out her free one to them. "I'm Aida," she tells Enzo. "You're Matteo's brothers I hear."

"Wow, the famous Aida," Dante says. "Raquel and Chiara are really worried about you. They're waiting for you at the house."

"Is Robby with you?" Aida's tone swells with hope.

"Yeah," Enzo tells her. "He's with Jade, his mom. He's safe."

She lets out a huge sigh of relief, her body practically sagging. "Thank God. I was worried he lied about that too."

"Nah." Enzo smirks. "We found him before that son of a bitch could hurt him."

She peers up at me with a radiant smile. "He's safe," she trembles out. "We did it."

"Yeah." I brush her cheek with my knuckles. "We did."

"Look," Dante throws in. "The girls hope you can come back to the house with us." He stares at me now. "Both of you." There's a pause in his words. "Matteo…I'm so damn sorry. Fuck," he strains, turning away, clasping his hands around the back of his neck.

Dom steps up to me. "There's so much I want to say to you." Grief thickens his voice. "But if I ever thought you were alive, I wouldn't have stopped looking for you. Never. I would've raised *hell* to find you." His eyes drift to a momentary close before he opens them again. "Every day, it's like I saw you get shot all over again."

"You were there?" I finally manage. "With Dad and me?"

"Yeah." He nods. "I was there hiding, and when I heard Faro threaten us all, I ran home and we left. But I thought you were gone. I had no idea you survived." His jaw flexes. "I'll always regret not staying long enough to see whether you were still breathing."

"So you never traded my life for all of yours?"

He cants his head. "That's what he told you?" A fist forms at his side. "Son of a bitch." He takes a second to control his plundering breaths. "You think I'd ever leave the only brother I actually liked?"

"Fuck you, man." Enzo elbows him from behind.

An invisible pull slices into the back of my throat. Part of me wants to fight it and the other part wants to let go.

Dom clasps a palm on my shoulder, desperation for me to believe him clinging to his eyes. And I do believe him. When I look to him, I find the same broken man reflected back at me. We may have had different paths in life, but it didn't leave one better than the other. Agnelo had lied. He has spent his life lying. To himself. To us. To everyone.

"We fucking love you," he promises. "We always have." Dom's arms fasten around me hard, and I let my arms hook around him too.

This heaviness in my body that I've worn since the moment our father died, it just vanishes.

As he holds me, it brings me back to that boy I once was. The one who'd run to his brother for a hug, who'd look up to him above anyone else.

And I let go. Of the hurt. The anger. The gripping fear. I let go of it all, like I've burned away the last of my chains.

"It's okay, baby bro," Dom says, the way he once did. "I've got you. You're home now."

And I do something I haven't done since I was a child.

I cry.

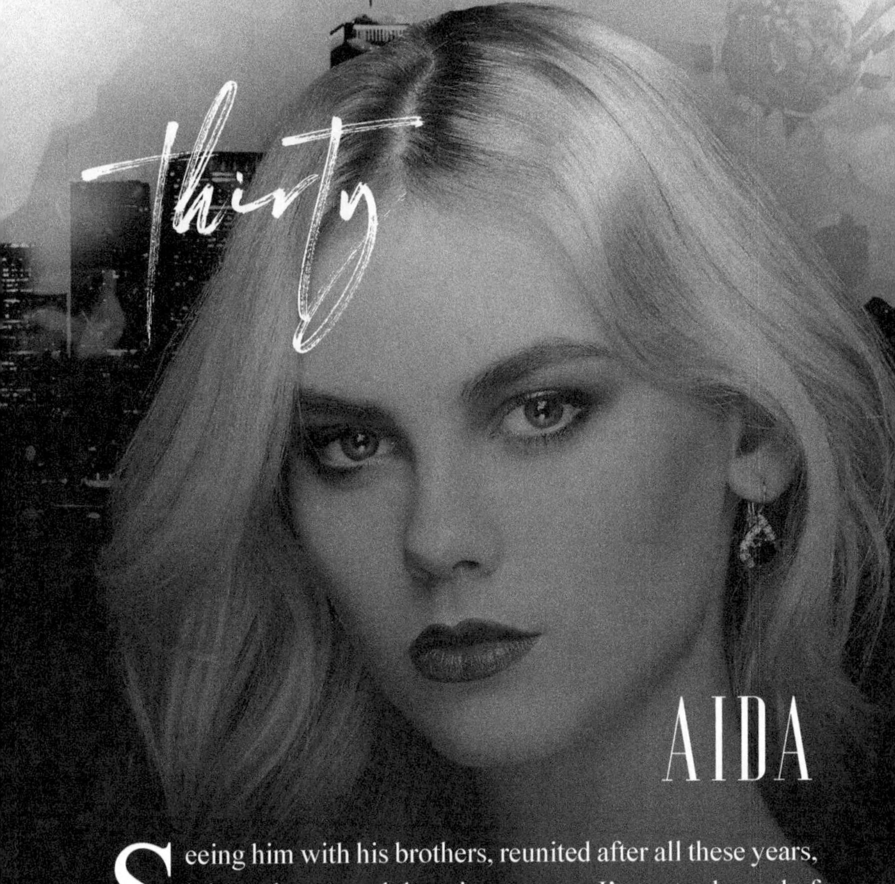

Thirty

AIDA

Seeing him with his brothers, reunited after all these years, it brought so much happiness to me. I'm not ashamed of how heavy the tears ran down my face as each one of his brothers hugged him.

On the drive to Enzo's home, Dom told us what they had been through since they lost their father and Matteo. I can't imagine being on my own so young, living on the street and then homeless shelters. He also explained how he knew Chiara, that he loved her, that Dante and Raquel were together too, as well as Robby's mom and Enzo. It's nice to know both of my cousins have found men who care for them.

Dom parks his SUV in the driveway of a sprawling mansion. Here I thought Agnelo's home was big. This is like three of them.

Nerves etch away in my stomach, and I shiver at the thought of seeing my cousins, telling them what I've been through and why I wasn't allowed to see them.

It all makes sense now, why he kept me hidden. He was worried the truth of my real identity would be revealed. But even with all the worry at seeing them, I can't wait to hold Robby in my arms, to know he's really there.

"You ready?" Matteo whispers into my ear, the cadence of his voice soothing away my fears.

"No. But I'll have to be. And having you with me"—I angle my body toward him—"it makes everything possible."

"I love you, Aida." His eyes deepen as he plants a kiss to my forehead. "I've loved you then. I love you now. And I'll love you in every space in between." My heart practically jumps in my throat, my hand grasping his. It's still going to take me time to finally realize that we're free. Agnelo won't break us anymore. Our bond, it's forever.

We exit the car and walk hand in hand behind his brothers. I shudder with a breath, leaning into his side, his arm rounded around me, tugging me closer as we enter the home.

"Aida!" Robby shouts as soon as he sees me, and I burst into tears, kneeling, gasping with a sob as he runs into my outstretched arms. "You're okay!" He coughs, wheezing a bit, and I remember he was sick the last time I saw him.

"I'm okay," I pant, tears streaking down my face. "How are you feeling?"

"I feel better." He pushes back to look at me. "I got medicine at the hospital."

The hospital? Oh God.

I try not to react, forcing a smile. "Oh, buddy. I'm glad they took care of you there."

"I'm so happy you're here!" He grins, hugging me again. "I missed you, Aida."

"I missed you so much." My eyelids press into a tight close for a few seconds as I hold him. I happen a glance behind him, finding both of my cousins, their expressions soft, the tears warping their gazes too. Beside them is a tall, blonde woman. The kindness in her smile, those eyes—that's Robby's mother. My heart lurches from fear that she'll hate me for taking her son.

With Robby holding my hand, I stand up, making my way to them. "I'm sorry," I immediately tell her, biting into my lower lip.

"Sorry?" Her brows knit. "For what?"

"For having him, for…I—I don't know."

"Oh, no." She shakes her head, her gaze gleaming. "If it weren't for you, my son would never have known what it meant to be loved, and you loved him when I wasn't there to do it. For that, I'll always be thankful." She swipes a finger under her eyes. "And Ms. Greco, is she here too? I'd like to properly thank her."

My eyes drop to my feet.

"Oh," she whispers. "I'm sorry." Her hand seeks mine, gently clasping it.

Kissing the back of Robby's hand, I let it go, and he runs to his mother's side, clasping his arms around her thigh. That's where he should be. I've had him long enough.

Chiara and Raquel both come to me now. "You don't know how happy we are to see you." Raquel throws herself at me, hugging me tight.

"We've been so worried with everything going on," Chiara adds. "Once Dom told me Matteo was looking for you, fuck, I wanted to go after you myself."

"And she would've." Raquel pulls back, saying, "If it weren't for the guys stopping her, she'd go fighting."

Chiara shrugs, tipping up the edge of her mouth. "I killed my father after all."

My eyes round. "Faro is dead?"

"Oh, girlfriend." Chiara throws an arm around my shoulder, moving us to the sofa. "We have so much to catch up on."

And we do. They fill me in on the fact that the Bianchi men are now all dead, and at the news, Matteo and I look at each other and smile. It's really over. They'll never hurt us anymore. But for the first time, I'm sad not to belong to this family.

"I should tell you…" I turn to the girls on the other side of me. "I'm not your cousin. Agnelo…" I take in a shallow breath. "He kidnapped my mother and me, so we're not—"

"Not what?" Chiara folds her arms, tilting up her chin. "Not family? Because let me stop you right there. We may not have been close growing up because of him, but you'll always be our family. Blood isn't always thicker than water, cuz. We all should know that better than anyone. So…" She throws a palm to my knee. "You're stuck with us."

Raquel nods from behind her with a soft smile. I find it hard to speak, and it seems all I can do is cry, not knowing how to express the amount of appreciation and love I feel in this moment. We may not have grown up close, but to them it doesn't matter. They've accepted me as one of their own, and for that I'll always be grateful.

Chiara scoots closer, enveloping me in her arms. "If anyone ever messes with you again, you tell me, and I'll make sure they regret it."

"I don't know," Matteo interrupts. "With the way she killed Agnelo, you may need her to defend you." Our eyes meet and he looks at me proudly.

"Really, now?" Chiara backs away, her gaze narrowing. "And

you were saying we're not family."

MATTEO

After Raquel took care of my bullet wound and patched me up, we headed toward the bar in the corner while the ladies continued to catch up. Raquel said I was lucky the shot only grazed me. I honestly forgot all about it until my brothers noticed it.

"What the hell is this?" I smell the honey-colored liquid in my glass, looking curiously at Enzo. "You realize I've been in a basement for fifteen years, right?"

Enzo and Dante chuckle, downing their own drinks.

"Damn showoffs," I say under my breath.

"Give it a week, you'll be drinking just as easy as us." Enzo slaps me on the shoulder.

"Fine, fuck it." I take a swig and… "Shit! This tastes like ass. What the hell?"

"I'll get you a beer." Dom laughs, his whole body rocking as he lowers to get one from the mini fridge.

"Baby bro is a lightweight. We gotta start him slow," Dante throws in.

Dom pops the cap off and hands me a cold bottle. This time when I take a sip, I don't feel like I want to toss that crap in the garbage.

"Look," Dom says to me, suddenly appearing serious. "We want you to know you never have to worry about a thing as far as money and everything. We've got plenty of it now. What's ours is yours."

"That's right," Enzo says. "Except my cars. You can't touch that shit."

"Yeah, he's right," Dante adds. "That's sacred territory."

"When do I get one of those?" I swallow another swig of the beer, only half-kidding around. It'd be good to have one so I can take Aida on all the dates I once promised myself I would take her on.

"Oh, we'll hook you up." Enzo drapes his arm over my shoulder. "Any kind you want. Hell, I'll buy you three."

"One is good." I chuckle.

They tell me more about what they do for work and how they got to be where they are. I'm glad they got something out of this, not that it'd replace anything they had gone through, but at least they didn't struggle for the rest of their lives.

"If there's anything you ever need," Enzo says, "we'll make it happen."

"Yeah." Dom nods. "We can buy you two your own place once you're ready for that, but feel free to stay with Chiara and me for as long as you want." He had offered his place to us earlier, and we agreed to stay.

"Thank you." A lump lodges in my throat. I can't believe I'm actually here. It feels like a dream. "There's something you can maybe do for us."

"Anything." Dom's stare grows hard.

"This woman, Alison Greco, they killed her. We want to find her family. It'd mean a lot to Aida." I could never tell anyone I killed her. It's something only Aida and I will know.

"Done. I can get my men on it right now." He takes out his cell.

As he types into it, I continue, "There's another person she's trying to find. Her biological dad. We don't know his name, but her mom's name was Cecilia Robinson."

"Got it. I promise to get you their addresses by tomorrow."

"Thanks." I remember that in my pocket is the photo of us with

Dad. My hand reaches in, and carefully, I pull it out.

Enzo's arm falls away as he sees what's in my hand.

"Shit," he mutters. "You still have that?"

My other brothers hover closer and their eyes go to the photo too.

"Damn, look how stupid we look." Dante laughs.

"Yeah, you do. Me? I look goood." Enzo wags his brows, and I shake my head. They haven't changed much.

"Mom and Dad would be happy to see us back together," Dom says.

"You think they can see us?" I ask.

Dante sighs. "I'd like to think they can."

We're alone now, just Aida and me, in one of the empty bedrooms in Dom's house. He left me some clothes, and it seems like we're basically the same size.

Chiara had given Aida some stuff to sleep in too, and she's in the bathroom changing while I'm out here, fiddling with my damn fingers like a scared little kid. How am I supposed to share a bed with her and not get hard? It's impossible and wrong after everything she's been through.

The mattress is big enough where I could move away, but what if she wants to be close?

The bathroom door opens, and my eyes sweep to her. She comes out in a long white t-shirt, touching the top of her thighs, a hint of shorts under it. I never thought a simple shirt could look this good on a person.

Yeah, this is bad.

"Does this look okay?" She twists her mouth nervously.

The unease, it brings me back to when she doubted how

beautiful she was, and I instantly want to reassure her. "You look stunning," I say, rising off the mattress, stepping up to her, a finger brushing down from her shoulder to the very tip of her fingers. I could feel the goose bumps I'm leaving behind.

Her breaths hitch as she swallows, her eyes meeting mine. She reaches a palm to my face, holding me still. "I want us to have everything together," she says. "I want to be with you, all the way, but…" Her brows snap as she inhales deeply.

"Hey…" I tighten her hand in mine. "Whatever it is, I promise it's okay. Don't be afraid to tell me."

She nods. "I'm just scared, Matteo. Scared that when you make love to me for the first time, I'll see their faces."

Fuck. My damn heart…

"I'll wait until you're ready." I stare deep into her eyes, hoping she knows how true that is. "As long as it takes, even if it never happens at all. You are all that matters to me, Aida. Always."

"I love you, Matteo." Her voice grows wispy and low, breaking with emotion as she rises on her feet, her lips growing closer to mine. I lower my face at the same time and tenderly she captures my lips with hers.

I kiss her like I want to remember every second, the feel of her, the taste. I kiss her slow, like it's the very first time I've ever gotten to do it, my palms slowly climbing up from her back, up to the thick, soft strands of her hair.

She moans as she kisses me deeper, her fingers reaching under my white t-shirt, and I flinch away from her touch, not realizing I did it until I completely pull away.

"What's wrong?" She wraps her hands around herself, uncertainty riddled on her face.

"It's not you. It's just—" How do I tell her that the scars on my back from the beating I took while I hung on that beam may repulse her?

"Matteo, it's me." Her gaze cuts through my self-doubt and she places a hand to the center of my chest. "You can tell me anything too."

"I know I can." I peer down at her touch, my heart beating with renewed passion. "There are ugly scars on my back. I don't want you to have to see them." I've never actually looked, but I can feel them when I run my hands there.

"Oh, Matteo…" She reaches a palm to my cheek, holding me in its warmth. "I don't care about scars. We all have them." Her hand returns to my back once more, her palm running up the ugliness seeped into my flesh. "They'd never scare me away, no matter where they are."

I release a long, shaky huff, then I turn around, yanking the shirt up my back so she can finally see them for herself. Her hands touch me there, running down my marred skin.

"I love you," she says, her cheek falling to the scars, her arms surrounding me.

I shut my eyes, reveling in the feel of her—just being this close, no chains, no walls keeping us apart. It's something I'll never take for granted.

"I can't believe they're all dead." She sighs, her hands coming to rest at my chest.

"You can stop looking over your shoulder now. There's no one there anymore."

"Yeah…" Her voice drifts. "We can have a life now, Matteo. It's ours." She burrows her face further into my back, her lips landing over my mutilated skin.

Fuck, I love her so damn much, but am I capable of giving her the kind of life she's always deserved? Knowing all the things I've done in the past, do I even deserve it?

"Where do we go from here?" I ask her.

"I don't know…" She holds me tighter. "But wherever we go, we do it together."

Thirty-One

AIDA

The following day, one of Dom's drivers takes Matteo and me to Ms. Greco's mother's home. I had wanted to visit them to pay my respects, and to meet them, to know where she came from. If anything, I knew they had to be wonderful from the way she'd spoken about them. The sisters spent their time taking care of their mother, while also trying to live their lives. She has two nieces, and her sister is divorced from what I remember.

Matteo sits beside me, both of us staring out the window, embracing the world and each other. It's different when you've been locked away. Everything seems brighter, flashier, the colors practically glowing. We take it all in. Every little detail everyone else probably takes for granted.

We were both Agnelo's hostages. One a prisoner in the basement, the other a prisoner in the house. If I had no yard, I wouldn't even know what it felt like to breathe in fresh air. It's something Matteo never had and something I'm grateful for. I could imagine how many others like us are out there, locked away, nothing but darkness. But at least I had Matteo and Ms. Greco. How many don't even have that?

"You okay?" he asks, his lips lowering to my temple with a warm kiss.

"Yeah." My heart swells with a smile. "Just thinking how lucky I am that I have you."

"I think I'm the lucky one, Aida," he whispers. "You kept me sane. All the shit I did…"

He told me about it all last night as we lay down in bed together, and I reassured him, it made no difference to me. He was still the man I love. "It doesn't matter," I remind him. "I'm sorry those people died, but you had no choice."

He nods, his gaze falling downcast, and I can tell he doesn't agree. He blames himself for it all—the murders, the beatings. But he was just a child, learning to kill.

"It's hard," he admits, gazing up at me. "To see myself the way you do."

With my eyes boring into his, I cup his face. "For all the days you forget who you truly are, I'll be there to remind you."

He quickly curls an arm around me, holding me against his chest, his breathing hitching as the car sways.

A few minutes later, we pull up to a two-story pale blue house, a cheerful garden gnome with a green hat in front of the freshly cut grass. You can smell it from the whiff of air rising through the slit in the window.

"You ready?" he asks, as he grips the door handle.

"I don't think I'll ever be ready for this."

"We'll tell them together."

My gut churns. "How do we tell them she's dead?" Tears spring into my eyes.

"I don't know." His Adam's apple bobs, and he opens the door.

"Take your time," the driver says as he turns, and we shut the door behind us.

I stare at the brown, unassuming door, my heartbeats drumming so loud, I almost lose the courage to go up the steps and knock.

But he must notice how nervous I am, because his hand slips into mine and he brings it to his mouth, kissing the top of it. "It'll be hard," he admits. "But we'll make it through, and so will they."

"Okay." I shudder with a breath. "Let's go." And we do, walking side by side toward the door, his hand knocking gently.

"One second!" someone shouts—a female voice. Then it opens, and two little girls look up at us.

"Hi there." I kneel.

"Who are you?" The girls look questioningly at us, squinting through a set of dark blue eyes. They're most definitely twins from all appearances, and identical at that. One of the girls pops a hand on her hip, the other twisting a curl of brown hair at her shoulder.

"Girls! What are you doing?" A woman hurries to the door, seemingly out of breath, her black hair coiled up high in a messy bun, her black t-shirt covered in red stains.

"I'm sorry." She looks down at herself. "I was cleaning the kitchen. These girls made an absolute mess. How can I help you?"

We stare at her with an understanding smile. "We're friends of Alison's," I say, feeling that familiar twinge in my heart whenever I think about her.

"Oh my! Where is she? Mom and I've been calling her nonstop for almost two months. Please tell me you know where she is. We wanted to call the cops but ahh—" Fear greets her gaze before her face twitches. "I need to know where my sister is. Please just tell me."

My breathing turns heavy and I'm ready to burst into tears, but he's there, holding me steady, like he always does.

"Would it be okay if we came in?" Matteo asks.

That gets her expression turning serious. "I—ahh—I don't know."

"We're not with the Bianchis. I promise." I hope to reassure her.

Her eyes pop wide and she nods, stepping out of our way so we can stroll inside. The girls stand beside their mother, before they run into another room.

"You can come in here." She gestures with a hand toward the two black leather sofas. "Mom is taking a nap."

"I'm most definitely not," a distant voice says, and we all turn to find an older lady, short gray hair reaching her chin as she carefully climbs down the stairs, holding tightly to the banister.

"Who may you two be?" Her glance moves quickly between us, her kindness showing in the softness of her gaze.

"They're friends of Alison, Mom. I'm Dora, by the way," she quickly says before going to help her mother settle on the couch.

"Sit, you two," Alison's mom says, and we take a spot at the end of the sofa, opposite from her while Dora takes a seat to the right.

"So where's my daughter? Did something happen to her?"

"Mom!"

"I don't want to think it either, honey, but she hasn't called or visited in weeks, and it's not like we can call those bastards and ask."

Dora peers into her lap, her fingers playing with the strings of her sweatpants. She's pretty, just like Alison was. I can clearly see the resemblance.

"There's no easy way to say this…" As I try to get the words out, a sob slips out.

"No!" Dora cries, slapping a hand to her mouth.

"They killed her, didn't they? Those fucking Bianchis, they killed my baby?" Her mom's emotions slice through her words as she looks straight into my eyes, waiting for me to confirm it.

"I'm so sorry." An ache clogs my throat. "But she's gone."

"No!" Dora cries, jumping to her feet. "I won't accept that!"

"My poor baby," her mom snivels. I let them take all the time they need, my tears leaking along with theirs. There's a heavy wave of mourning crawling up every wall.

Matteo holds me, and I know he feels it too. She mattered to him. He loved her. But we can't tell them he shot her. It's something we'll take to our graves.

"Did she suffer?" Alison's mom asks.

"No." Matteo's voice is forceful, and she nods, as though that small sliver of information brings her peace.

"Do you know where they put her body?"

"I'm sorry, we don't," I tell her. "But we want you to know we loved her." I look up at Matteo. "Both of us."

"You're her, aren't you? Aida?" The mother swipes under her eyes. "She talked about you all the time."

My heart warms to know she had. That just like she meant a lot to me, I meant the same to her. "I am. Your daughter saved me. Every day."

"She was a hero to us," Matteo adds. "We'll never forget her."

"She loved you," Dora says in a teary tone. "You were like a daughter to her."

"And she was every bit the mother to me." I blink back tears, my chin trembling.

"We have something for you." Dora stands, swiping at her eyes, as more tears come. "Years ago, she had us hide something for her, something that she said belonged to your mother."

"What?" My pulse jumps.

"Oh my, I forgot all about that," her mom whispers. "Go get it, honey. I'll tell her the story."

Dora nods as she passes her mother, going up the stairs. We all sit quietly, not sure what to say to a woman who just found out her daughter died.

"When Alison first met your mother, she gave Alison a handbag. She told her to keep it safe just in case. Alison brought it here and told us to hide it. And to this day, it's been here, waiting for you."

Hope grows in my heart, like a root taking shape, nourished by the thought that maybe in that bag is more of my mom, something that'll give me more of the shreds of who she was.

"Thank you," I tell her. "I'm grateful you kept it."

"Of course we did, child. Alison would kill us if we hadn't." She laughs dolefully. "The way she spoke about you..." Her eyes shimmer as she stares past me as though recollections find her deep in her mind. "She'd tell me how smart you were." Her gaze lands to me again. "That you were the sweetest child, so polite, even with that deranged criminal who kept you locked away in that house." Her eyes go to Matteo. "Did you live there too? And I use that term loosely."

"Yes," he says.

"Oh goodness." She shakes her head, her gray brows tucking tight. "She never talked about anyone else in that house, but I always suspected something else was going on. I know she was scared. She probably would never have told me about Aida either, but when she gave us the bag, she broke down." She settles further against the sofa. "The way she poured her heart out when she told me what he was doing. The kinds of evil that family was capable of… I can't even think about it." Her bottom lip quivers. "I'm gonna miss her."

"Me too," I breathe. "If it brings you any comfort, I want you to know the Bianchis, they're all dead now."

"Good." And the glare that fits her face doesn't seem to quite suit her.

"Here it is." Dora returns with a simple black satchel. "This was your mom's." She hands it to me.

My fingers run past the soft material, so well kept, like it's been treasured. How could I ever repay Ms. Greco for this? I hope wherever she is, she realizes what a gift she has bestowed upon me. I fumble with the button, the room silent as I drag up the flap, and gradually, I reach a hand inside, finding a notepad, a pen, and a stack of… "Photos," I practically cry, when I retrieve them.

There are lots of them, small enough to fit into a wallet. I realize, she must've taken them out before they took her wallet and put it inside here so Agnelo couldn't get rid of them.

I glance at the first one, and it's of her and me, both of us grinning with silly faces. Tears track over my cheeks, stumbling down my face. I wipe them away, not wanting to ruin the photo.

The next photo is of just me, or at least I think it is, because in it, I appear to be a newborn. Another is of Mom in the hospital, holding me, her grin wide as she gazes at me like I hold the answers to all of her problems.

Little did we know that only years later, our lives would be forever shattered. I sift through each photo, and once I find the last one, I see someone else in it—a man, and his eyes are the exact shade of hazel as mine.

"Dad," I whisper, a finger running over them both. He has an arm flung over my mother while he holds me at his side.

My parents. The two people I can't seem to remember, not unless I'm dreaming of my mother, and even still, I don't see her anymore. And I want to, so badly.

"I have to find him," I tell Matteo. "I have to try."

"I know, and we will. I told Dom, and this morning he told me he's found his address."

I gasp, not believing he had done that for me already.

"We can go whenever you're ready."

I throw myself into his arms. "I want to go as soon as possible."

"Then that's what we'll do."

We separate, peering over at the two women. "I'm sorry about everything," I say. "We didn't want to hurt you this way, but I couldn't allow you to live not knowing."

"I appreciate it, dear girl." Alison's mom purses her lips, while Dora's face is practically ashen. "You two are welcome anytime, you hear. Anytime."

"Thank you." We both rise, readying to go.

I give the old woman a hug, and she tucks me tighter to her, patting my back. "Bye, now."

Dora takes us to the door, and she's no longer the same woman who first opened it. Without even a goodbye, she closes the door behind us. The next thing we hear are the echoes of her sobs as they drift through the space and into my already broken heart.

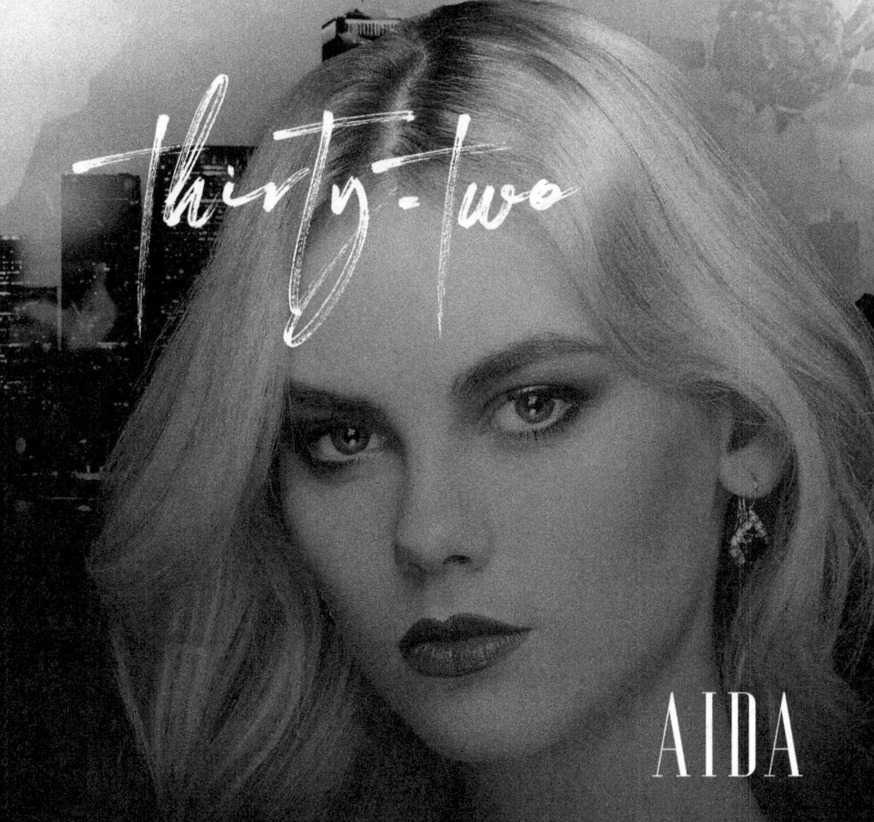

The next morning, while Matteo and his brothers spend quality time together, the girls and I do the same. Chiara and Raquel are in the kitchen, Raquel making coffee and cooking breakfast while Robby is planted in between Jade and me on the sofa.

I think they wanted us to have some alone time together and are taking longer on purpose, which I appreciate. There's so much to say to her, yet at the same time, I don't know what I could say to make any of this better. She lost her son, while I had him.

Earlier, before Robby woke up, she'd told me about what she's been through and what her life has been like. She was abused. Raped repeatedly. Property of the Bianchis like many of the other women. I was lucky compared to her. She had no one. But I did. I had people that loved me.

She strokes Robby's hair while he holds both of our hands, watching television. Agnelo never allowed me to watch television, so I have no idea what's on.

"Mommy said you're going to see your daddy tomorrow," Robby says, glancing my way.

"Yeah, Matteo and I are going to go together." I gaze into his innocent eyes, full of wonder and forgiveness. That's one thing kids can do better than us—they can forgive. They can grow and adapt, while we stay stagnant.

It's hard to bounce back from something that's been so embedded in my life. I find the torture of the club in my nightmares, waking up to realize I'm not actually there at all. I hate that it's still there in my subconscious. I've waited so long to live my life, to love Matteo, and I can't even do that. I know it'll take time and that I have to be patient, but I've waited long enough.

"Are you scared?" he asks.

"A little."

"Well, you shouldn't be. He's going to think you're great." He grins. "Like I do."

"Oh, Robby." I hold back the emotions this sweet child brings out. "I hope you're right."

"He's absolutely right," Jade agrees, her eyes landing on me with a warm smile. "He's going to be happy to see you after all this time." She grabs my hand, squeezing reassuringly. "You'll see."

I nod nervously, trying to look excited, but really my insides are flipping and stirring like they're having their own party. How do I just show up to his house after all this time and say, *"Hey, I'm your long-lost daughter. How you been?"*

"I keep agonizing about what to wear. The girls gave me options and I have yet to decide."

She laughs. "I get it. It's a big deal."

"Yeah." I inhale long and deep. "I think I'm going to try all the outfits again." I scrunch my nose.

"Put it on for us!" Robby chimes. "We can help you pick!"

"I don't know…" I pull my lips back.

"Only if you want to," Jade adds, ruffling his hair with her fingers.

"Want to what?" Chiara comes out with Raquel carrying a tray. For someone who was shot only days ago, I've not seen Chiara sit and rest for more than a few minutes.

"Robby suggested I try on the clothes for you guys so you can help me choose what to wear when I go see my father."

"You'll look great in whatever you wear," Chiara says, nestling into the armchair next to me as she winces.

"You okay?" I ask, grabbing a cup of coffee, adding milk and sugar.

"Good as new." She winks, but I can tell she's still in a bit of pain.

"Come on, buddy," Jade tells Robby. "You have to eat."

"Okay, Mommy." He kisses her on the cheek and gives her a hug, his face brightening with a beaming smile. And I'm instantly warm and fuzzy all over.

I'd love to have kids of my own someday, lots of them, with Matteo. I know we have a lot to overcome but I know we can have what we always dreamed of.

Robby plants himself in front of the table, grabbing a paper plate, and fills it with pancakes, then squirts syrup on them.

"He's so going to mess up your floor," Jade whispers to Chiara.

She waves a dismissive hand. "I don't care. We'll clean it."

"So," Raquel offers. "Chiara and I were thinking, once she's better, maybe we can take you girls shopping, then maybe get our nails done." She pauses as I peer up.

"I'm fine." Chiara rolls her eyes, but Raquel gives her a stern look, causing her to roll her eyes even harder.

I laugh, considering it. Is that what normal women do? Am I normal? Probably not. Maybe I'll never be, but maybe this is a step forward. "I think I'd like that." I grin ear to ear. "I think it'd be good for me."

"It's a date, then." Chiara winks. "You know, whenever Doctor Raquel allows it."

"Sounds perfect."

MATTEO

It was hard to separate from Aida today. We've been attached to each other for so long, it's unnatural to be without her. Sure, I left the basement when I had to kill, but that's not the same thing. But what my brothers and I have to do today is necessary, something we've all thought about, but found hard to do—returning to our childhood home. It was a place filled with timeless memories, of the days when cruelty didn't exist, when our laughter, and that of our parents, was all we heard. All we remembered.

When I was stuck in that basement, I thought about our house, and dreamed about returning there someday. The child. The dreamer. But with age, the dreams faded, and soon I forgot that place where I was truly happy.

Sitting in Dom's car, driving back there again, I find myself remembering the dreams held by that child I once was, the child who was ripped apart seam by seam, until he no longer recognized himself.

"You okay?" Dom asks, switching lanes as my foot bounces on

the floor, Dante and Enzo driving behind us. I think they wanted to give Dom and me some time to talk alone.

"I don't know." My admission is filled with truth. There are feelings in me I can't even put into words, too great to speak them out loud.

Dom says the house we grew up in is still there. Though they never went back, it was too difficult he said, he still would check on the property.

"Yeah, I get it," Dom finally says. "I never thought I'd go back to that block ever again. I just—fuck…" He tightens his hand around the wheel. "I can't even believe you're in my car right now." He pauses, his tone edged in the hurt piercing down to my very bones. "You don't know how much I missed you."

I draw in a breath, swallowed up by the pain in his voice.

"I hated you all for a long time," I say. "I didn't want to believe you guys forgot me, but over time, that's exactly what I ended up believing."

His stare on me is hard as we stop at a red light. "Never." A palm buckles over my shoulder. "I would *never* abandon my brother."

"I know that now."

His hand returns to his thigh as we continue on. "Shit. We're here." The car lurches to a stop, and instantly I'm bombarded with the memories. It's exactly the same, except the fence. It's taller and white. But the house, it's as though it's been picked right out of my mind. Though I was small, I remember the dark brick home, down to the black door.

Dom slowly climbs out of the car. I follow, my other two brothers jumping out of Dante's vehicle and walking to us. We stand beside one another, eyeing the house from the curb.

"Damn. It's exactly the same," Dante says under his breath.

"Should we knock?" Enzo asks. "You think whoever lives there would let us see inside?"

"If they're even home," Dom says.

"Remember when we'd play basketball in the front, and the ball would end up at Connor's next door?" I chuckle.

"We were lucky his mom was so nice." Dante's own laughter comes alive. "Do they still live there?" We peer over at what once was our neighbor's home. Connor was in Dante's grade, and one of the few kids on our block. We'd sometimes hang out at their house. Our moms were kind of close back then.

"Let's find out." Enzo's already taking steps there.

"Wait," Dom calls and Enzo turns. "What the hell are we gonna tell them?"

"We'll figure it out." He shrugs, continuing toward the door, knocking once.

"Hold on!" a woman yells.

"Shit," Dom mutters. Together, we wait, my heart pounding, as the door quickly opens and a lady with short black hair, resembling an older version of the woman I kind of recall, appears.

"Ahh…" Her attention bounces to each of us, and the nerves scatter in her gaze. "How can I help you boys?"

"Mrs. Cuzamano. Forget us already?" Enzo grins.

She squints, her face moving closer to my brother before her gaze grows large, then she's staring at all of us again.

"Oh my God!" She gasps. "Is that really—"

"The Cavaleri brothers in the flesh?" Enzo stretches out his hands.

Her palm hits her mouth, large tears filling her eyes. Fingers flutter past her mouth as she shakes her head incredulously. "I can't believe this," she whispers. "I never thought I'd see any of you again." Her exhale comes rough as she moves aside. "Please, come in. I—ahh—I have something to show you."

I glimpse over at Dom, who matches my curiosity, and one by one, we shuffle inside.

"Have a seat." She gestures to the brown leather sectional, and we settle on it, a simple round glass table at the center with a vase full of yellow roses, the walls a cream color.

She stands over us, the shock having not worn off. "I don't even know what to ask." There's wonder in the way she stares at each of us. "The police gave up. They stopped searching for all of you. But deep down, I hoped you were all alive, that you ran from trouble or something."

"We're not gonna lie to you," Dom says. "But we can't tell you everything either."

She nods slowly. "And your father? Is he—"

"No," Dom throws in. "He died."

"Oh no." Her brows huddle. "I'm so sorry." A breath whooshes out. "Your parents were the best of us. I hope you know how much they meant to me, and that I miss your mother's friendship dearly."

"I'm sure she'd say the same." Dante speaks this time. "How's Connor?"

Her smile is soft, her fingers brushing away the hair sitting against her cheek. "He's great. An accountant now. Married. Three kids." She laughs, fondness etched in her gaze.

"Good for him," Dante adds. "Tell him we said hello."

"I will," she murmurs, silence falling for long seconds.

"You had something for us?" I jump in, wondering what in the world she'd ever have that we'd want.

"Oh, yes." Her words come quick. "Give me a minute to get it." She runs up the stairs, and Enzo shifts toward us. "You think she knows who lives in our house?"

"We'll ask her," Dom says as she rushes back down the stairs, carrying a shoebox.

"When the police were done investigating, they let me take some stuff from your home. I—I thought maybe by some miracle you guys would return and I could give this to you." Her voice breaks as tears slowly journey down her cheeks. "And here you are"—she wipes under her eyes with the back of her hand—"in my house again."

"What's in the box, Mrs. Cuzamano?" Dante stands, growing closer, a hand on her arm.

"Pictures." She smiles.

Dante's hand drops away, his chest expanding with a sharp inhale.

"I saved every photo your mother kept in that house," she explains. "Baby pictures. Family photos. Everything is here." She sniffles, lifting the box in her grip. "I knew exactly where she put them." Her laugh is filled with a sweet sadness. "After all, she loved showing me your baby photos when I'd stop by for coffee. She was so proud of her boys." Her hands extend and Dante takes the box from her.

"Fuck." Dom rises while I'm unable to move, something tightening and burning in the back of my throat. "Open it."

Dante gradually removes the top, then they're sitting back down between Enzo and me. Their hands dig into the box, finding photo after photo of the family we had once been.

"Mom…" Enzo chokes out, and slowly my hand finds a photo too, staring at one with all of us at a carnival in town. I was maybe a few years old, planted on Mom's hip, my dad's arm around her, my three brothers in front, holding ice cream cones. My face is smeared with chocolate, and the smile on it is pure happiness. My vision blurs, and shit…this is hard.

Quiet blankets the room, each of us gripped with more emotions than we can probably handle in her presence.

"Thank you." Dom's words are laced with sadness as he peers up at her.

"Nothing to thank me for." She moves to sit on a love seat. "I'm glad I managed to save that part of your family for you. It was my hope I'd get to share them with you one day."

We continue shuffling through picture after picture, and I can't seem to stop. My heart, it fucking hurts, because I'd do anything to have them back. Just one last hug. A kiss. Anything. Even to hear their voices. But there's only silence that beats where their hearts once did.

"You think the people next door would let us look around?" Dom asks, putting the photos in his hand back inside.

"Oh yes. She's very nice. I'll come with you if you want."

"That'd be great." He nods.

My fingers don't want to let the photo go, as I stare at it again, wishing I could remember that day. Remember us this way. But I can't. The darkness has stolen any bit of light I once knew.

"This is damn weird," Enzo whispers as we wander into what was our dining room.

"Tell me about it." Dante scoffs. "It's like we're haunting a place we once knew."

I trek beside Dom, behind our two brothers, my eyes wandering to every inch of this place. Enzo is right. Being here is strange and kinda sad. It's different now. Our house. And not just the furniture or paint colors. The walls aren't filled with photos of us. They're bare, like we've been washed off. My mother's pink, fuzzy slippers aren't lying by the kitchen rug before the sink. That cotton candy machine she used to use isn't on the counter either. It was my favorite thing, blue and pink cotton candy sticking to my fingers.

But it's like a ghost town here, nothing that would remind me of us.

We make it to the dining room, Mrs. Cuzamano and Betsy, the owner, talking quietly in the hallway. She was more than willing to let us wander around her home, even while knowing nothing about us. Her husband and daughter once lived with her, but then her husband died, and her daughter got re-married. She's all alone in this house.

Taking our time, we climb up the creaking wooden steps, reaching the bedrooms we once called ours.

No toys left scattered across the hall, nor the voice of our mother yelling for us to clean it up.

Dante pushes open the door to a room he once shared with Dom, but there are no bunk beds here anymore. It's been replaced by a small four-poster bed with a white flowery blanket on top, pale pink walls, the only thing that reminds me of my mother and her favorite color.

"We have photos now," I say. "We can restore our memories. Like an old painting. Make them brighter."

Enzo throws an arm over my shoulder. "You still know how to draw?"

I chuckle, remembering all the times I did for Aida. "Of course I do."

"You should draw us. The family. Maybe from one of the pictures."

I close my eyes, pulling in a breath. "I think I will."

"I want one too," Dante adds, closing the door as we move to the room that was once Enzo's and mine.

"Then I'll draw one for each of us," I tell them. "So that way, we never forget."

"Forget what?" Dom asks.

"What it was supposed to be like."

AIDA

The drive to my father's home the next day didn't take but thirty minutes, and they were the fastest thirty minutes of my life. The car is parked at the curb, my eyes paralyzed on the white door, the only thing keeping me away from meeting the man my mother was in love with. Or at least I hope she was.

Matteo's brothers were able to show me the articles about my disappearance, my dad's pleas to find us, offering money to get us back. As the years dwindled away, so did the trail of our existence. We were forgotten by the world, but I hope not by him.

"We can stay here for as long as you want," Matteo says, clutching a hand around me in the back of one of Dom's SUVs, the same driver who took us to Alison's mother at the wheel.

"What if he hates me? What if I ruin his life by showing up?"

"No way. I don't think any parent would feel that way. And if he says that, I'll gladly punch him."

A grin wraps around his face. I know he's only half-kidding.

"I'll be there with you every step of the way, baby. You just have to be the one to take the first step."

My heart instantly jumps from the term of endearment. He's never called me that before. I've heard his brothers call the girls that. I'm sure that's where he picked it up, and I kinda like it. A lot.

"Okay," I tell him. "But if you don't open the door and get out, I never will." My tumultuous pulse practically somersaults in my throat, drumming like the gallop of horses.

He chuckles, grabbing the door handle and pushing it open. "Let's do this." Exiting first, he gives me his hand, helping me climb out. Once we're both on our feet, he continues to hold me, guiding us toward the small colonial house. If it wasn't for him, I'd probably bolt.

The heaviness of my breathing causes my entire body to break into a tremor. Without me even asking, he circles an arm around me and keeps me close, kissing my temple.

"You're going to be great. I've got you."

"I need to stop being so nervous. If he doesn't like me, then it's okay. At least I tried." But that's a lie. If he turns me away, I'll die inside.

"I can always kill him."

I push him with a shoulder, laughing quietly. "Don't do that. Okay, maybe you can hurt him. A little."

"Deal."

We're now right in front of the door, and my hand hovers as I try to knock. Matteo does it for me instead. "I've got you," he assures once more, and it's as though the reassurance gives me the courage I need.

Closing my eyes, I take in a single long breath, and I look back at the door, the sound of faint footsteps getting closer until the door opens. A woman with short brown hair and matching eyes greets us with a curious smile.

Who the hell is that?

"Hi there!" she chirps brightly, a set of white teeth on display. "May I help you?"

"Um—I—ahh. Never mind," I fluster, turning back around.

"Baby," Matteo calls softly, a hand gently grazing my shoulder.

With a defeated sigh, I pivot, my mouth bending in a smile that probably looks like it belongs on a crazy woman.

"Is Clark available?" Matteo asks.

She observes us intriguingly. "Who may I say is asking?"

"Mom, who's there?" someone calls, and a young boy is suddenly there. He appears older than Robby, probably by a few years, and his eyes are like mine—like Dad's.

Oh crap. This is his new family.

"Um, you know what, never mind." I shake my head, my eyes going downcast to try and hide the tears that have already come.

"Oh my God," the woman whispers, her voice full of bewilderment. "You're…you're her, aren't you?"

Her eyes round, a hand flying to her mouth. The shock on her face has her staring at me so hard, my body breaks into a wave of tingles.

"Clark!" she yells. "Clark, get over here. Right now."

"What's wrong, Emma?" A male voice drifts over. "Can a man eat?" And the way he says that, it's not with anger, it's with jest.

He loves her. He's forgotten us.

"Just get over here!" She can't separate her eyes from me, like a deer in the headlights.

"I'm here, honey." He shows up right behind her, looking at me, then Matteo.

That's my father. Oh God.

Grief plants itself into my heart and I rub at the pain. How different would I be if I were raised by him?

"Who are you folks?" he finally asks, scratching the side of his light brown hair, sprinkled with a bit of gray. There is kindness written all over his face. You can practically feel it. "Because whatever you're selling, we ain't buyin', unless you got some fishing hooks, I do need some of those." There's a twinkle in his gaze and I can't stop staring.

Emma doesn't say a word as she slowly pivots her head to him. When he sees her expression, he stares deeply at her for a second, before he drifts his attention back to us.

"Who—who are you?" His stare narrows. But then he prods past her, nearing me, his head tilting sideways, and his tears form hard and fast, like a puddle growing larger from the sudden pouring of the sky.

"No…" he whispers, stumbling back, and Emma is there, her hand on his shoulder. "A-Aida? God. No. It can't be. After all this… Is this real?"

I pant, wetness coating the rims of my lower lashes as I nod, breaking into a silent sob. "It's me, Dad."

"Aida!" he cries. In a flash, he clasps me in his arms and holds me as we both cry. For minutes. For hours. I don't know. Right now, it doesn't matter because I found my father and he's never forgotten me after all.

We're actually here. In my *dad's* home. I have a father. A real one. A kind one. The shock will take a while to wear off.

"This was when you were one and started walking," he explains, twenty minutes later, opening a photo album he's kept with photos of us. Mom, me—our family. We seemed so happy. I swipe a tear from my eye, grinning as I look at every single picture.

Matteo sits quietly next to me, while Emma places some tea and coffee on the end table beside my…my dad. My God, I'll never get used to it. I've come from having a monster for a father to meeting this man, who's actually how a dad should be. I can tell how fond Noah, his only other child, is of him. He's eleven and has his mother's hair.

Noah bites into a muffin, crumbs flying out everywhere as he sits in the same love seat as his mom.

Emma tsks. "There are plates right on the table."

He reaches for one. "Sorry, Ma."

"Please don't judge me based on this animal I raised. You'd think he was raised by wolves."

I laugh. "I think he's sweet. I'm happy to have a brother." Here I thought I'd never have a biological sibling after finding out that Robby and I weren't related, but here I am in the same room with one.

"See, Ma?" He chews, crumbs stuck to his teeth. "Sweet."

She rolls her eyes on a laugh. "Let's go get you cleaned up."

"Fiiine!" He gets up, and they leave me with Dad and Matteo.

Once they're out of sight, Dad sighs. "Your mom is gone, isn't she?"

"Yeah, she's gone." The heartache, it catches me again, and I miss her even though I don't really remember her.

"I tried so hard to find you two." He faces me, leaving the album on his lap. "But there were no cameras that caught what happened. Nothing to go on, the cops said. Just Mom's car with no fingerprints besides hers." He places both of his palms on mine.

"What happened to you, sweetheart? Who took you?"

"Believe me, you don't want to hear that. It's enough to know we were taken by very bad people, who did very bad things."

With those simple words, he breaks down, his body rocking with a deepened cry, a hand covering his face while the other is still holding on to me—the daughter he lost but the one who found him.

After a few more moments, he clears his throat and wipes at his eyes. "I'm *so* sorry." He sniffles. "We have to report this to the police."

"We can't, Da-Dad," I breathe, swallowing the nerves lodged in my throat.

He seems to like me calling him that because his face brightens.

"The mob is involved, sir," Matteo explains. "It'd be too dangerous. But we took care of it. It's over."

He shakes his head with disgust, his expression hardening with a loud exhale, and he's not a hard man to begin with. "I wish there was something, anything I could do."

"Just finding you is enough, Dad." My tearful words echo into his heart, mirroring our pain reflected in his eyes.

When we first came inside, we told them who we were, and that Matteo's brothers helped us find him. I didn't want to say too much with Noah there, and I think that's why Emma took him away. She knew we needed the time to speak openly.

"So, Emma knows everything about Mom and me?" I ask.

"Oh, yeah, I had told her fairly quickly once we met years after you two were gone. I was so heartbroken, just a wreck…" His face falls. "She found me drunk in a bar, to the point I couldn't even walk. She made sure I got home safe." He nods slowly. "I did that a lot back then. You know? She helped me cope."

"I'm sorry." My brows bunch.

He pats my hand, his eyes that of a broken man, bruised by the loss he's had to endure. "You and your mom, that's who I'm sorry for." A defeated sigh falls out of him. "I'll always love your mom. She was a wonderful woman, and she loved you *very* much."

"Thanks for that, and for these pictures." I can't manage to stop smiling. "You sure I'm allowed to keep them?"

"Oh, yeah. They're yours." He pauses, his eyes searching mine. "You think you could come by tomorrow too?"

"Yeah, Dad…" I throw my arms around him. "I'd love that."

"Good. Good." He squeezes me tight. "Oh, I just remembered." He grins as he pitches back. "I've got some videos of you and your mom that you just have to see! Give me a minute to get them." He stands, clapping his hands. "Don't go, okay?" He observes me nervously.

"I'll be right here. I'm not going anywhere."

He exhales hard and fast, like an invisible weight lifting off his shoulders, then he turns and walks out of the room.

"Told you he'd love you," Matteo says, his eyes radiating through me. "You look happy, Aida."

I slide my hand over, my fingertips flirting with his, and with a deep look into his eyes, I confess something I never thought I would. "I think I am, Matteo. I think I'm finally happy."

Thirty-Four

MATTEO

"**I** don't know what the hell I'm doing," I tell my brothers two days later, the car jerking as I try to drive the SUV they surprised me with yesterday. It's exactly like theirs. Enzo said it officially made me part of the family. I know he was only kidding, but I like having the same one. It makes me feel closer to them.

The parking lot at one of their nightclubs is huge and abandoned at this time of day, making it the perfect spot for learning how to properly drive.

Enzo chuckles from the back seat, clasping me on the shoulder. "Bro, how the hell did you manage to drive the van and shit?"

Putting the car in park, I twist over to him. "I don't fucking know. Adrenaline?"

"Don't worry," Dom says from the passenger side. "You'll get it. You had to see how bad Enzo drove when he first started."

Enzo scoffs, flipping Dom off.

"You sucked," Dante tells him, chuckling, seated beside him. "You almost crashed into a tree once. Or did you forget?"

"Damn, you two are trying to ruin my very fine reputation here." He fixes the collar of his blue button-down shirt.

"So how bad were you, really?" My brow pops, my mouth curling at the corner.

"Fine." He throws a hand in the air. "I was terrible. I don't know how they ever gave me a license."

That has me shaking with a laugh.

"Truth?" he continues. "You're way better than I was."

"I have to be." I let out a harsh sigh. "There's so much I promised Aida we'd do if we ever got out and I want to do it all with her, without some driver taking us places." My chest tightens, recalling the days in the basement, dreaming of a better life, one we could share. Now I can actually give her that.

I wonder if she's having a good time out with her cousins and Jade. They took her on a girls' day, whatever that means. She needed that. Family is important.

Reuniting with my brothers has been a gift. I was lost, abandoned, at least I thought I was, until I saw them again and learned the truth. They never forgot me, and I'm ashamed I ever believed they did.

"You will," Dante says. "You two will have everything you have ever wanted and more. We'll make sure of it." His brows bend with reverence. "We can't undo what's been done, but we can give you guys new memories. A fresh start."

"Yeah." My mouth falls into a thin smile. "I'd like that. Now, if you guys could get me license ready in five days so I can surprise her with that date, I'd be grateful."

"Shit." Enzo leans back into his seat with a wide grin. "Never said we could work miracles."

After an hour of teaching me how to drive, we arrive at some store that sells suits. "What are we doing here?" I ask them as we strut inside.

"Every man needs a suit, especially when he plans to take out the woman he loves." Dom's voice is low, as a guy in a black suit comes out from behind the counter to greet us.

"Hello, nice to see you all again," he tells my brothers with a curt nod. "What can I do for you guys today?"

"This is my other brother, Matteo." Dom gestures to me with a tilt of his head. "He needs everything."

That gets the man's brown eyes lighting up.

"All right, sir." He looks at me this time. "Come with me. I'll take your measurements and we'll set you up with everything you need."

He starts toward the back room while I glance at Dom, scratching my temple.

"Go. You deserve this." He nods.

My palm runs down my face as I dart my attention to each of my brothers, and there's love on their faces. For me. "It's weird," I say. "Being out here like I'm normal. I—I don't know. I can't explain it." My eyes lower to my feet.

"Hey." Dante clasps a hand over my shoulder. "It's okay. We get it. Take your time. If something doesn't feel right, tell us."

"Yeah," Enzo adds. "Like when we take you underwear shopping. I'm warning you now, I ain't seeing you model that shit."

I let out a deep laugh. This is nice. This is real. And it's my life now, one I'm never letting go.

AIDA

"Guys, this is too much," I tell my cousins as they continue helping me find more clothes. We've been at it for a couple of hours, going from store to store. Chiara's SUV is piled with bags, all for me and Jade.

"You're doing this for me," Chiara says, picking up a baby-blue off-the-shoulder flared dress. "I'm sick of sitting around at home. I want to treat you two. Think of it as being part of my recovery. So, indulge me and try this one on."

I shake my head with laughter. "Okay. I do kind of like it." My fingertips run down the soft material, imagining Matteo seeing me in it. There were so many things we once wanted to do together—picnics and restaurants, dancing as the stars twinkled above us, the water at our feet, making love on the sand. I want that with him so badly.

Earlier today, I had opened up to Jade about what's holding me back from sleeping with Matteo. She's the only other person who knows what any of this feels like. I asked if she was once afraid to be with Enzo and she told me she was at first. But Enzo's acceptance and love, made it easier over time. She's still dealing with her trauma and is even looking into therapy. She asked if I'd like to join her, so I agreed. Maybe that's what I need. I want to be ready, but I'm just afraid that if we go that far, I'll make him stop and ruin everything.

In that instant, Jade comes out of the dressing room with a long, flowy red dress, with thin straps over her shoulders. "What do you guys think?" she asks us, doing a little twirl.

"Wow," I say. "You're so pretty."

She waves off the compliment, even as my cousins tell her the same.

Robby sits in the velvet sofa, eating a cheese sandwich, staring at his mother in awe. "You're beautiful, Mommy. You too, Aida." He grins at me.

"Aww, you're just the sweetest boy alive, aren't you?" I walk over to him, kissing the top of his head.

"I wish Ms. Greco was with us too," he tells me, his mouth twisting sideways.

"Me too." I take a seat beside him, and tuck him close, a hand wrapped around his small frame. "But I know she's watching us, and I know she's happy."

Thirty-Five

AIDA
FIVE DAYS LATER

The girls have been dolling me up for the past hour. Shoes are scattered across the room I share with Matteo in Chiara's house, while Raquel does my makeup. I don't exactly know what I'm being made up for and none of them will tell me.

I have a sneaking suspicion they're planning something, especially with Matteo being gone, coincidently running errands with his brothers.

I bet he's in on it. Butterflies flutter in the pit of my stomach, a smile dancing over my lips as I start to wonder what's waiting for me.

When Raquel starts on my cheeks, memories of the past come barraging in—Destiny's face flashing before my eyes. I drag in a breath, holding it as I count to three, a coping mechanism I had learned from my new therapist.

I picture myself going inside my head, picking out the awful reminders and flushing them down the toilet, replacing them with the present moments. The good ones. It sounds silly, but it works. And that's all I could hope for—to get better every day. To remove myself from the horrors of my previous existence.

"I think she's ready," Raquel announces. Moving aside, the rest of them examine me on the chair I'm seated in. It's as though I'm a display at those fancy museums I've read about in my books.

"You look gorgeous," Jade gushes, clasping her palms together at her chest, her brows knitting.

"Wow. Seriously, wow," Chiara adds, picking up a pair of gold satin flats in a V-shape at the front. "Stand up. I want to see how the dress will look with these shoes."

I rise as she places them before me, stepping into them. They're one of the many things she had graciously purchased for me the day we all went shopping.

Both Matteo and I have had everything we could ever want. I almost feel undeserving of it all, like I'm not supposed to have any of these nice things. But they keep reminding me that I do, that I matter to them.

"Aren't you glad you listened to me?" Chiara pops a hand on her hip. "That dress is hot."

As I look at myself in the full-length mirror, I have to agree. The baby-blue dress she had spotted flatters my body well. Hopefully, Matteo returns soon so I can show him. He's never seen me done up before. I wonder what he'll think. Raquel didn't go crazy with my makeup. I still look like me and that's exactly who I want to be.

"Are you ready?" Chiara swings her arm around my shoulders.

"Ready for what?" I squint a gaze at her.

"You'll see." She shrugs, darting her eyes away with a curious turn of her mouth.

"What did you guys do?" I happen a glance at each of them and they suddenly all look suspicious.

"Trust me, you'll love this surprise," Raquel adds, walking toward the door with Jade and opening it for us.

We make it down the stairs, just as the doorbell rings.

"I wonder who that could be." Jade laughs, biting the corner of her bottom lip, moving toward the door. With her hand on the doorknob, she looks at me, her eyes glistening, and my pulse kicks up, almost climbing out of my throat.

"Open it," I whisper just as Chiara parts from me, and I stand there alone, staring at the door, wishing that the man I love is on the other side of it.

Jade pulls it open, and I see him…

Matteo.

Goose bumps skitter up my arms, my breath stilling in my lungs as I take him in, a bouquet of bright pink roses in his hand, a gray suit wrapped around his body. But the most beautiful thing about him is the dreamy smile he wears just for me.

My feet tread slowly toward him as he stands there, and in his eyes are the same flame of emotions burning in mine. This man, my man—my God, he's beautiful.

His wide chest rocks up and down the more I stare at him, the more he stares at me, unable to peel our gaze off of one another. I'm drowning in the weight of my tumultuous emotions.

Tears form in my eyes, and I try not to cry. I try not to ruin my makeup, but I fail. Because it's impossible to contain it all right now, and I don't want to.

"Matteo…" I whisper, walking faster now, and he does too, practically running to me, throwing his arms around my back while mine envelop his neck.

"You look so damn beautiful," he softly says against my ear, sending a jolt down my spine. I can't believe this is even happening. That we're together.

Finally.

We can go on as many dates as we want. Do whatever we want. No one will stop us.

My goodness. Is it truly over? After all this time? Is he really mine?

I pull back so I can find his eyes, needing them right now. "What is this?" I ask as he cups my cheek, the flowers in his other hand.

"There was so much I've wanted to do with you one day. And I don't want to wait anymore, baby. I want us to start today." His throat bobs as he continues, never separating his eyes from mine. "I don't want to live in the past, I want to live in the now, in the future." He pauses, slanting his forehead to mine. "I love you more than I could ever describe, and I don't think I'll ever deserve someone as amazing as you, but there's no way in hell I'll ever let you go." His voice crumbles with a deep ache, and I feel it right in my chest. This love, this connection we share, no one will ever break it.

"How many times do I have to tell you?" I draw back, wanting him to see me, really see me. "You're the most wonderful man I could ever meet. You did what you had to do to survive. You're not them, Matteo. Do you hear me?"

He nods.

"Say it," I tell him. "Say it for me."

The back of his hand brushes down my cheek as his mouth forms a genuine smile. "I'm not them. I never will be."

"That's right. Now"—I place my hand on his other—"may I have my flowers, please?"

"Yes, my lady." He hands me the bouquet with a bow and a giggle jumps out of me.

"So…" I take his hand and hold it tight. "Where are we going exactly?"

"Oh, you'll see." He tugs me out the door just as I turn back to wave at the three women who are all giddy with excitement.

As we exit, I see his brothers, waiting by a black SUV. Are they all taking us? I definitely can't drive yet. Chiara has been teaching me though, but I'm still a little nervous.

"Have fun, you two." Enzo throws a set of keys at Matteo who easily catches it.

"Wait, what?" I jerk my head back at Matteo whose only response is a tiny, crooked smirk, refusing to make eye contact. He opens the passenger side door. "Are you driving?" I ask while he helps me to my seat.

"Yes, baby, I am." My stomach rolls. I'll never get sick of hearing him call me that. He puts on my seat belt with a laugh. "Are you scared?"

"Ahhh…" I pull my lips back in a grimace. "Kinda?"

"Don't be," Enzo shouts. "He's a natural. Just watch for the turns. May wanna hold on."

"Shut up." Dante swats him on the chest, but that only gets Enzo chuckling.

Matteo makes it around the car and hops in, pulling on his own seat belt.

"When did you get your license?" I ask him, placing the bouquet on my lap.

He puts the car in drive and we're pulling away. "Today." He grins. "I wanted to surprise you. Are you surprised?"

I lean back into the leather, unable to take the smile off my face even if I tried. "Just a little."

"Good, because I'm not done yet."

MATTEO

We arrive at a park my brothers had said would be the perfect spot for what I had planned. It isn't grand, but it's ours, something we wanted long ago.

There was a time I stopped believing in hope and a better tomorrow, that days like this would never be possible. But here we are. We made it out. And every day, I swear to make her life better than the day before. Because I'm hers and she's mine, and it's my job to make her happy.

She gasps, her eyes taking in the beauty of nature. "Is this a meadow?" she asks with awe basking in her voice.

"It is." I lift our joint hands to my mouth, kissing the top of hers.

"Wow," she breathes, her gaze wandering to the bright-colored flowers we walk through. Purple, yellow, orange—it's like every color of the world is right here beneath our feet. Ours to touch. To feel.

I take her to the spot I had already arranged. My eyes catch sight of the picnic blanket and large basket my brothers had given me, along with a CD player that looks almost like the one she had in the basement. Everyone was in on it. I wanted to do something special for her and I hope I succeeded.

"Matteo…" She stills, blinking back tears as she glances at me, a hand against her chest when she finally sees the stuff on the grass. "This is the sweetest thing anyone has ever done for me."

"It's not enough." I face her, pulling her body to mine. "You deserve it all, baby. And I'm going to make sure I give it to you."

Her warm exhales skim across my lips as our mutual gaze deepens, the air thickening with the power of our love.

My cock grows hard the more she stares, the more she rises on her feet, leaning into my mouth, her lips hovering against mine, panting heavily. With another rush of a breath, she kisses me desperately.

My heavy growl slices through the air as I grab the back of her head, her soft strands slicing in between my fingers. I kiss her roughly, groaning when her nails dig into my back.

My tongue invades her mouth, snaking around hers, those little whimpers only making me want her more.

With a quick move, I lift her into the air, my arms under her ass, hers holding on to me around my neck as I take us to the blanket. I lay her body down, mine over hers, our mouths still ravaging.

Harshly, she yanks my shirt up, her hands falling to my scars. Feeling her touch me there, accepting them, it does something to me. My hunger for her grows and I fight to steady it, to take my time and let her tell me what she wants. I know she's been struggling. I'd never push.

My lips fall to her neck, kissing her there as she grinds her hips into my knee, rubbing herself on me.

"Touch me." She sighs with a tremble. "With your fingers." She swallows her bottom lip into her mouth as I glimpse at her.

Fear tugs at me, wanting to please her, yet afraid I may not know how. But I've done this before. I can make her come like that again.

My mouth returns to her neck, leaving tiny kisses down to her shoulder, my fingers stroking past her hip, my hand falling to her inner thigh as I part her legs wide. There's no one here to see us.

The park is private, and Dom ensured no one would step foot in it besides us.

She rocks her hips, her eyes shut, as though anticipating my touch, as though wanting it, like I deserve it. I brush my fingers up and down the skin of her inner thigh, teasing her, watching her as she squirms, a moan slipping past her full parted lips.

I let her feel my touch right over her panties, damp and warm. Propping myself on my elbow, I observe her in the throes of ecstasy, never seeing anything as beautiful.

"Matteo…" she rasps, her hand biting into my back as I part her panties to reveal the softness beneath. My fingers run in between her wet slit, barely touching her as she cries, her lashes fluttering, the sounds coming out of her so sensual, I want to hear more. I never want to stop hearing her say my name when she's this way.

Eagerly, I sink the tip of my finger inside her, rolling it back up to her clit, rubbing her there as she bows her hips on a breathy cry.

"Yesss, that feels good," she pants, and I do more, letting my thumb rub her there while my other finger thrusts all the way inside.

She clamps around me, pulling me in deeper. To know I'm doing that to her, that I can feel her become this free, fuck, I never felt this big. This powerful.

"Yes, yes… Oh God…"

"Your pussy is so wet, baby. I like knowing I did that," I tell her, adding a second finger inside her, slowly sliding in and out.

"Please," she groans. "I need…"

My cock throbs to feel her, even knowing I never felt it before. But it's a natural feeling I can't describe, this want—this desire.

"I'll give you what you need. I always will."

When I drive my fingers deeper, when my thumb swirls around her clit faster, she screams out my name over and over, her back arching, her body shuddering, her hands sinking into my flesh, so hard, I want to bleed for her.

"Matteo, yes, yes…!" She keeps going, wave after wave, until her body slows from the high, until her eyes open again, and the cutest smile makes it to her lips.

"Did we just do that outside?" She breathes all heady, her cheeks flushed pink, her chest rising up and down with her rough breathing.

"We did," I say, unable to keep the smirk off my face even if I wanted to. Sitting up, I fix her panties, making sure she's covered before I hold her against me, her back to my chest. I don't know how long we stay that way, the cool air rustling around us, the world perfectly still.

"This has been the best day of my life," she hums sweetly.

I kiss the back of her head. "And I'll give you more of them, more of this. Forever."

"I love you, Matteo Cavaleri, more than my whole heart."

"Well, you *are* my heart, Aida Robinson. My heart and soul."

And when she's ready to take the next step, I'll show her exactly how much of my heart and soul she really owns.

Thirty-Six

MATTEO
ONE WEEK LATER

"So you gonna show me what you got or what?" Enzo shoves me with his shoulder as we all stand in the middle of the gym Dom has in his basement. It's like a whole house down here.

"Really, Enzo?" Dante throws out. "He spent years being forced to murder and beat people up, and you want him to fight you?" He swats him on the head. "Leave the kid alone."

Dom shakes his head at Enzo, who throws his hands in the air. "Fine. Shit. I'm sorry, man," he tells me, looking ashamed. "I was just fuckin' around."

But just as he loses his focus, turning away, I grab him around his midsection and flip him in the air and onto the ground.

"Fuckin' hell!" He groans with a chuckle as I press my knee gently into his stomach.

"Never hesitate." I smirk in return as I rise, giving him my palm, and he jumps to his feet.

"Fuck that. It's on now, baby bro." He raises his fists. This time when I fight someone, I know they're not going to end up dead at the end.

We throw each other around for a bit while Dante and Dom work out. It's still strange to be in the same room as them. I don't know when it'll stop feeling this way.

With every day since we've reunited, I wonder if any of this is even real. What if I had hit my head too hard, and this is all a hallucination? Because after everything, how could things be this good for me?

Once we're done, Enzo pulls me to the side, clasping a hand on my shoulder. "So…" He concentrates on my face real hard and lifts a brow. "As your big brother, it's my duty to give you some advice on the ladies."

"Ahh…" I rub the back of my neck. "Yeah, no, thanks. I don't need…that."

"Trust me…" He narrows a gaze, nodding slow. "You will."

This is damn near awkward. Sure, I can use the advice on this shit, but not from my brothers. Maybe a book or something. Or a video. Hell, the shit they've showed me on the internet is wild. You can literally look up anything, even on a phone. That's crazy.

He reaches into his pocket, handing me a box.

"What the hell is this?" I question, grabbing to inspect it.

"Condoms. You slip it on your dick, like a jacket. Keeps all the diseases away and the babies too."

"I know what a condom is, jackass. I'm asking why I need a

whole box." When Aida and I would have our lessons, this was on there. Unfortunately.

He chuckles. "Because you're gonna like fucking. A lot. Believe me."

I clamp my jaw. Yeah, this is getting worse by the minute. What is more uncomfortable than your brother giving you sex advice? When the girl you like is teaching it to you.

"Okay, so some pointers," he continues as I groan, glancing down, my eyes covered with a hand. "Use your fingers and mouth on her first…you know, down there. And touch her breasts too, but don't squeeze the nipples too hard, well…" He smirks. "Unless she likes that shit."

"Oh my God." My gaze drifts to the ceiling.

"I'm just trying to help you out, bro, for whenever you two are ready, assuming you haven't already…"

"We haven't." He doesn't need to know the details of what we've actually done.

"See, there ya go!" He flips his hands in the air. "I'm just looking out." He grows serious again. "Alright, so make her come a few times, get her real wet and hot for you before you stick your dick in her. And follow her lead. See what she likes by the way her body responds, the sounds she makes."

"Yeah, I'm done." I start to walk away.

"There's nothing to be ashamed of!" he shouts behind me, causing my brothers to stop working out.

"Ashamed of what?" Dante asks, removing his boxing gloves and throwing them on the floor.

"I was giving our bro some lessons on the ladies." Enzo wags his brows.

"Poor kid." Dom shakes his head. "I'm sorry," he says to me, getting off from the bench where he was lifting weights.

We kid around for a few minutes and I'm relieved that Enzo has stopped giving any further talks on that subject.

"If Pops were here, he'd love this," Enzo says from beside me. "To see his boys together."

Dom clenches his jaw. "Yeah…" With a long breath, he looks up to the ceiling, staring hard. "I hope he knows Faro never took us out. That we're okay."

"I *know* he does." Dante clasps him on the shoulder, looking straight at him. "And you, you can let go of it, that guilt you carry." Dom's mouth goes tight. "You saved us. We got Matteo back, even when we thought that was impossible. You've got nothing to feel guilty about anymore, brother. You're done now."

Dom's throat bobs, and Enzo and I come to stand beside our two brothers.

"The Cavaleri brothers," Enzo adds. "We're back, baby."

"What the hell does that even mean?" Dom grimaces.

"I don't fucking know." He shrugs. "But it sounded good."

Then we're all laughing like nothing has changed, like the years weren't stolen, like our world hasn't been turned upside down, because sometimes, that's what you have to do to survive.

The past couple of weeks have been everything both of us could've ever imagined. She has a father, and a new family. And I have mine, however broken it is.

Aida's been dealing with her trauma with the help of Jade. In fact, they've gotten very close and have been seeing a therapist together. Jade even accompanied her to the doctor to get checked out after everything she went through.

I'm grateful she has someone to help her, because no matter how badly I want to, I can't. It didn't happen to me. I could comfort her, but I can't do much more than that. With Jade, she has someone she can relate to. And together, I know they'll get through this. I could already see small changes in Aida—the way she laughs, the way she looks at me. It's like those scars are slowly healing, like the ones on my back have.

Aida groans with a smile in her voice as she yawns and stretches. While I do my best not to stare, it's nearly impossible not to notice how hard and damn beautiful her nipples are.

My cock stiffens at the very sight of her, wanting to feel her coming while she's wrapped around my cock. I touch her when she lets me, when she tells me it's okay. The first time we sleep together, I hope I manage not to fuck it up. What if I suck at it? What if I hurt her? How the hell do people do this for the first time? But my body, damn it wants her bad.

My breathing grows heavy as she continues to stretch, her thigh rubbing against my inner one, and if she moves just a fraction, she'll notice how much I want her.

The comforter crawls down her body when she reaches her arms up with another yawn, falling past her stomach. I bet anything she doesn't even realize how damn seductive she is.

When she finally stops, she catches me staring and holds my gaze. I don't know if she notices something in my eyes, but I notice something in hers, like she feels this too—this maddening desire. Her lips part, her breathing turning harsher, my gaze falling to her mouth.

My jaw pulses, her chest rising and falling to the tempo of my heartbeats. "Matteo…" she whispers as though sensing the battle in my head. "I want this." There's confidence in those words and I'm not sure if she wants what I think she does.

"Are you saying…"

She nods, and my gut tightens with knots. I need this to be

perfect for her. How the hell can I do that?

"Baby…" I let my hand reach the delicate outline of her face, my knuckles brushing down from her temple to the tip of her chin. "I don't know how to love you."

Her brows tighten, her eyes fastened to mine. "You've been loving me your entire life, Matteo. Just keep doing that."

Slowly, I allow my hand to fall. Lower. Sailing along her neck, her pulse racing beneath my skin, until it falls between her breasts.

I flip the comforter off of us completely, allowing me free rein of her body. When one of my fingers strokes over her taut nipples, her back arches and the most erotic moan finds its way out.

It's the only encouragement I need to rip past the last bit of fear holding me back, both my hands around her hips, my cock heavy and throbbing. My mouth replaces where my finger had just been, and I suck her into my mouth through the soft silk, the tip of my tongue circling over her beaded flesh as I watch her watching me. My cock jerks in my sweats, aching to feel her.

"Yes," she pants, a hand flying to the back of my head, clutching deeper. I pull back, needing my gaze to drink in every line, every curve, every valley I've yet to discover. I can't wait to discover more of her in every year to come.

"Are you sure?" The pitch of my voice is consumed with hoarse uncertainty, dripping with temptation, wanting to make sure she's ready for this after everything she was forced to endure. And selfishly, I want to also hear her say she wants me, that I'm enough for a woman like her. Someone good.

With Aida, I realize all the stuff I was forced to do doesn't define me. My love for her, her love for me, that's what matters.

She nods, her gaze searching mine. "I am. You're my sanctuary, Matteo. The only time I ever felt safe was with you. This is no different. Not for me. Not anymore." Her eyes squeeze shut for a brief moment before she looks to me again. "I need this. It's how I continue to heal." She takes my hand to her mouth, kissing the center of my palm. "I'm ready now. I want you, only you." And there in the rasp slipping between her words, I can hear the truth just as much as I can see it in her eyes.

Without letting another second pass us by, I rise to my knees, my hands reaching the thin straps at her shoulders, and gradually, I glide her gown down her arms until her breasts fall free, roughly yanking the rest of it past her thighs and onto the floor.

She's completely bare. For me. A man who doesn't deserve this level of trust. But here she is, giving it to me anyway.

"Aida," I groan, unable to stop staring at how beautiful she is as she writhes, hunger piercing her gaze.

I commit every inch of her to memory. She's like a piece of art, and one day, I'm going to draw her, just like this.

My hands lower to her body, starting at her breasts, roaming down with care, falling to her stomach, her hips, her thighs as she parts a little, enough to show me all of her.

My fingertips brush the inside of her thigh, rolling my fingers up and down each one, and her exhales grow rough, her ass circling against the bed, her eyes on me.

"You're the most beautiful thing I've ever seen, and I'm gonna love you, Aida, like no one ever has before."

Her eyes shimmer, and I'm on her in an instant, my body pressing over hers, my kisses rough, her hands against my back rougher, pushing me deeper into her.

I make love to her mouth, and it's just that easy. I pour everything I have into that kiss. Every feeling. Every word. Every promise. It's hers. I belong to this woman.

Cradling the back of her head, I grab a handful of her breast with my other hand, thumb stroking her nipple. When her cry of pleasure vibrates around my tongue, I arch my cock against her center, making her quiver beneath me.

"Do you feel how badly I want you?" A growl slips out as she pants the more I rock into her pussy, but I won't make her come this way, not yet.

Reluctantly, I pull away, wanting to taste her everywhere. And I do just that, peppering her with kisses, from her neck, further until my mouth hungrily drops in between her chest. I swallow a nipple into my mouth, sucking harder, my tongue sweeping past one, before I take the other.

"Matteo!" she gasps, and the way her nails dig into my scalp makes me want to never stop.

I draw back, just for a moment, just so I can look at her one more second, and every time that I do, it feels as though I'm looking at her for the very first time. My thumb runs across her lips. "I promise to take care of you. Every single day."

"I promise to take care of you too, Matteo." She holds my face in her hands, her eyes swimming with unshed tears.

When she touches me like this, so damn tenderly, it seeps into the marrow of my bones. Her love is everywhere, soaking into me, and nothing has ever felt this pure. This good.

"I love you," I softly exhale as my face falls to her throat, a hand drifting down the side of her body, wanting to touch her.

I peer up at her as my finger gradually lowers over her most intimate place. She's wet and warm as I swipe up in between her slit, her whimpers turning me the hell on. I keep going, slipping past, touching her deeper.

"Yes, right there," she cries, as I rub her spot, her eyes hazy with lust as I look down into them, wanting to dive in and surrender to the fall.

I glide my finger lower, sinking it inside her pussy without a hint of doubt or hesitation. Because the way she looks right now, the way she's clamping around me, I know I'm doing something right.

I thrust fast, then slow, changing up my tempo, her moans growing louder. My teeth graze the underside of her jaw as she cries my name, her nails slicing up my back as I dip in and out of her, going deeper every time I'm all the way inside.

She's soaked around me, and goddamn tight.

Would I even fit? Could I hurt her? Fuck. How will we even do this?

Her walls tighten around me the faster I pump, her panting growing heavier, her moans entwining into one frenzied sound.

"Matteo!" Her gaze locks to mine, her mouth parting, brows drawn, and when I work her harder, ramming faster, she screams my name, hiding her face in my shoulder, biting into my flesh as her thighs tremble and her body shudders underneath me.

I don't stop until she does. I want all of it. Everything she has to give me. Because it's mine. Once her body stills, her heart racing to the beat of my tumultuous one, I kiss her slow, groaning as my cock rocks in between her thighs, wanting to come undone and watch her do that again.

Quickly, I move to retrieve one of the condoms Enzo had given me from the drawer in the nightstand. I settle on my knees, and her eyes fall sharply to the square in my hand.

Those rosy nipples shudder from her chaotic breaths. "Open it," she whispers. "Please."

I nod, without looking away, knowing I'd agree to just about anything to make love to her. Calling it fucking just doesn't feel right, not with her. Not for us.

My cock aches so violently, I'm afraid I'll tear her body to shreds. But I want to love her slow, to remember every detail of our first time—from the way she sounds, to the way she moves, to the way we feel together.

Dropping the condom beside me, I pull my white t-shirt off, my hands then landing on the waistband of my sweats, gradually pulling them down.

My cock springs out, and her eyes instantly widen. Hell, I hope that means she likes it.

"Could I…?" Her fingers reach out, hesitantly drawing them near the tip of my length, her gaze dancing between my eyes and my cock.

"Yes, touch me, baby." I grab her wrist, leading her all the way to where she wants to be. "It's yours."

"Matteo…" she breathes. She runs two fingers around the crown before fisting me gently, like she's afraid it'll hurt.

"Tighter." I clench my teeth, throwing my head back with a growl as her hand squeezes me, and I jerk when she slides it up and down.

My balls ache, a jolt zapping through my back the faster she moves. That need to explode comes barraging, and once I feel it, I stop her, grabbing her wrist and gently pushing it back against the bed. "I'm gonna come if you keep doing that, baby, and I wanna come inside you."

She sucks her lower lip with a whimper, her thighs rubbing against one another. My eyes take it all in as I rip the packet and slip into the condom.

I drape my body over hers, loving her curves wrapped around me.

"Your hands are too good for a man like me." I grip my cock in my fist, lining it at her pussy. "Every single part of you is." The tip slips just past her entrance and I lower my face close to hers, her lips perched over mine, her exhales shuddering, mingled with my own. "Am I hurting you?" I tremble out, staying still until she tells me she wants more.

"No." Her hands fall to my ass. "Keep going and don't stop." And I don't. With every inch, I sink inside her, so wet and willing, so breathtaking. I never want to stop looking at her body. But her heart, that's the most beautiful of all.

"I love you, Matteo." Her gasping is whispery and rough as my forehead falls to hers for seconds before I pitch back.

With her palm fitted over my cheek, and mine over hers, I sink all the way inside, our eyes so connected, my soul rattles.

Vulnerable. Yet strong. Soft. Yet hard. A lover. But a fighter too. I'm all of those things in her arms. And I'll fight every damn day to deserve her.

My cock surges, stretching her as I thrust, and she makes the sexiest noises I've ever heard. My strokes turn faster as I scatter kisses past her neck, her breasts, her hands gripping the sheets.

When I look down, her gaze is full of the same emotions I see reflected at me. This time, our kiss, it's filled with promises— of unhurried love, enduring devotion, of a life filled with firsts. Together, we will have many of them and no one will stop us. Not this time.

With another slam of my hips, I feel it—a swell, this extreme tingling at the base of my spine. I pump faster, needing her eyes on me as I experience this intensity with her, with this woman who's been my everything from the very first day. I can't even put into words how good I'm feeling. It's like we're connected, our souls as one.

Her hands claim my back, her fingers biting into my flesh every time my hips drive harder, the sound of skin on skin blending with the sounds of our pleasure. When she squeezes my cock, crying out my name, her back arching, I'm right there too, the fire she set burning me as I spill with every drop.

"Fuuuck!" I groan, thrusting harder until there's nothing left to give.

"Matteo…" she exhales roughly once her spasming ends, but I don't move, staying inside her, not wanting to separate. "That was…wow."

"You're incredible," I tell her, my chest on fire from my heavy breathing, our legs tangled in a chaotic heap.

I've never been this naked with anyone. Never bled this much of myself into another person. But somehow, with her, it feels right.

We stay that way for long winding minutes until I slip out of her, discarding the condom into the trash bin, before holding her body against mine, feeling the wave of her heartbeats drumming over my fingertips.

I kiss the back of her head, pulling the blanket back over us as she yawns. "Close your eyes, baby. I'll find you in your dreams."

Thirty-Seven

MATTEO

"Yes, yes, don't stop," she cries the following morning, bent over, her palms against the shower wall after I soaped her up and washed her off. My cock slides easily into her drenched pussy, the water spraying over my head, her hair tangled in my fist.

I reach down, gliding my fingers past her stomach, finding her clit, rubbing her faster. Her hand snaps to my wrist, and she grasps tight, her moaning loud and all mine.

After last night, my confidence grew, and while showering together, things just kind of happened. I should probably thank Enzo for the box of condoms right about now.

"Oh God, Matteo…" I draw circles over her clit, thrusting roughly as her pussy tightens, letting me know she's close.

A deep-chested groan escapes from my lungs as I pound my hips into her, her body still wet while water rains down my back.

"So beautiful," I grunt, my balls burning for release, my other hand letting go of her hair only to squeeze her ass in my palm.

When I drive inside her deep this time, her cries of pleasure spill from her lips as she lets go and lets me have that part of her. I join her, my hips slamming, every inch of my thick cock inside her warmth, giving her every drop of me in return.

After we showered, we put on clothes and ready to head downstairs for breakfast. Sex in the shower was another thing I crossed off my very long bucket list. It's something Enzo said I needed to have.

"I can really get used to this," Aida says with a smile curling over her mouth, her hand holding mine as we climb down the stairs.

"Which part?" I smirk.

"All of it?" She bites into the edge of her lower lip.

"I like all of it too." With a thumb, I rub a circle over the top of her hand, unable to stop looking at this woman who gave me a new life. A new purpose. A drive to live.

As we make it down, we hear the distant voice of Dom, and he sounds angry. Aida looks up at me with a narrowing of her gaze.

"Let's go check it out," I tell her.

We find my brothers gathered in the dining room.

"We'll get Elsie back," Dom says to Jade. Everyone seems to be here too, along with multiple men who work for my brothers.

As soon as Dom sees me, our eyes meet, and I can immediately tell he doesn't want us here.

"Who's Elsie?" I ask, and in a flash, all eyes are on us. I hope they realize, if they're going to be looking for someone, they won't be doing it without me.

"Hey!" Enzo breaks the awkwardness. "Baby bro is here!" He comes over, giving Aida a hug, then clapping me on the shoulder before leaning into my ear. "You need any more condoms yet?"

I smirk.

He chuckles low. "I got you, killer." He smacks me on my back before he pushes a step away.

"We're just talking business," Dom explains. "Nothing for you to worry about."

"I'm not eight anymore," I tell him, glancing at each one of my brothers. "You don't have to treat me like I am." With gradual steps, I move toward the center of the room, my woman beside me. "Whatever you got going on, I want in, especially if it has to do with those bastards."

"Matteo…" Dom runs a hand over the top of his short-trimmed hair. "I'm just trying to keep you alive. I can't fucking lose you again. This fight, it's not yours." He treads toward me. "You two have been through enough. You should be here, enjoying your lives."

"I know you're trying to protect me," I say. "And I understand why. But look, the shit that I saw at that club…" I flex my jaw. "One thing I know how to do is hurt people, so let me hurt those who deserve it, for once in my life."

Dom gives me an unsure stare, the indecision weighing heavy in it.

"Who's Elsie, Dom?" I ask again, needing this. It's a way to fight back, to help innocent people for once, instead of hurting them.

He blows a breath. "She's a friend of Jade's. They were taken with another friend. Trafficked. Elsie got away, escaping into this guy Michael Marino's car. He's the son of Giancarlo, the don of the Messina crime family, and rumor has it, he's set to take over soon."

"And you're bringing the fight to him?"

"If we have to."

Dante chuckles, holding Raquel in his arms from behind. "He's probably got his panties twisted because we killed the Bianchis."

"No," Chiara adds, and Dom peers over at her. "They never liked my father or my uncles. Big surprise." She rolls her eyes. "That was the reason my father wanted me to marry Michael, to unify the two families. But I would never let that happen and Michael wasn't interested either."

Dom's attention wanders back to me. "Are you sure you want to join us if we have another enemy to fight?"

"I do. I need it." If I could help save someone else, I will.

Dom sighs, deflated. "Okay. I won't stop you." He grips both my shoulders and levels me with a stare. "But you better not die." He smiles wide and shakes his head. "I love you."

"Yeah, yeah." I shake him off with a chuckle. "Me too."

"Look, after all of this shit is over, how about you and Aida take my house in St. Tropez, have a little vacation?"

I glance over at Aida, whose face lights up.

"We have a private jet on standby that can take you guys anywhere," he adds. "It doesn't have to be there."

"Corvo Island." Aida sighs with the tilt of a smile, looking up at me with love flowing out from her gaze, like the sun pouring its light into my very heart, casting the darkness away. "That's where I want to go."

"Yeah," I say. "Corvo Island."

"Okay." Dom nods once. "Corvo Island it is." Then he's hashing out a plan to get Elsie and bring her home.

"I hope you're not upset with me for wanting to help," I whisper into her ear as I lean over.

"No, I understand. Just promise you won't die on me when we just got to living."

With my head falling over hers, I wrap an arm around the woman I love. "I promise to try."

"Pinky swear?" she asks, holding hers out for mine.

"Pinky swear, baby. Always."

I kiss her, hoping it's not the last time I get to do it.

AIDA
ONE YEAR LATER

Chiara and Raquel gush behind me, fluffing out my ivory wedding gown. Not that there's much to fluff. It's a simple chiffon dress with a thin sparkly belt.

Running my fingers over the sweetheart neckline, I can't help but smile at myself. It's really happening. I'm about to marry the one man in this world who was made for me.

It took us some time to get here, and lots of work on both of our parts. But we chose to wait, to tame our demons before we committed the rest of our lives to one another.

And our dream of living on Corvo Island? That came true too. We purchased a house here a few months ago, and thanks to the private jets Matteo's brothers own, we're able to come here whenever we'd like. It means the world to us both. We can't thank Dom and Chiara enough for making it happen.

This small island, it understands us and all the baggage we carry. Here, we can let it all go and breathe a little easier. Maybe it's because we're so far away from where it happened, or maybe it's just the magic it holds. I don't question these things. I embrace them.

After Matteo proposed to me on the same meadow where we had our very first date, we knew we had to get married here, on this tiny island I once only fantasized about. I still recall that day as though it's happening right before my eyes.

He had recreated the same scene, even used the same picnic basket and blanket. "Dizzy" by Ella Bleu played as he got down on one knee, and I had tears running down my face, overflowing with insurmountable joy. It was pure love. Everything about him is.

To be able to get here, to days filled with happiness, it's more than I imagined we'd have. Once upon a time, he told me we'd be happy one day. I couldn't see it then, but I see it now. I see our future. Our family. And I want it all with him.

I dream of it sometimes. The future. And unlike when I was in that basement with him, I don't have to hide in a make-believe world, because we're living it. Now.

We have a place of our own next to Matteo's brothers too. Once one of their neighbors moved out, Dom had purchased it for us. It was a massive surprise, but I was thrilled to be near my cousins, to gain something Agnelo took from me: a family.

"I think you're ready," Raquel says, grinning behind me, and I catch it through the mirror.

"Knock, knock," my father announces from the other side of the door to the small room we find ourselves in. "May the father of the bride enter?"

"Yes, Daddy," I laugh.

The door parts, and he's there as I face him, wearing a black tux. There's something hidden in his fist I can't yet see.

"Oh my goodness…" A finger swipes under his now-glassy eyes as he clears his throat. "You are the most beautiful bride I have seen in my life." His words have him choking up as he slowly continues to me. "You remind me of your mother on our wedding day. She had a similar dress." His cheeks deepen to a darker shade of red. "She'd be so incredibly proud of you."

He takes my hand in his, staring at me with raw emotions spilling. An ache grips the back of my throat, overwhelming me with both love and sadness. But in my life, sometimes those things go hand-in-hand.

"I have something for you," he goes on, opening his fist to reveal a charm.

But it's no ordinary charm.

"Oh, Dad…" I cry, barely able to contain the swell of my own tears, not worrying about the light coat of makeup I'll surely ruin.

I stare down at a small photo of my mother tied to a white ribbon.

He places it in my palm. "It's for you to wrap around your flowers." He reaches for my white rose bouquet, sitting on the chair beside us, and he proceeds to tie it while I hold the flowers for him. "I kept trying to figure out how to include your mom on this special day, and then Emma came up with this idea. She said she saw it on the Internet. So I found the necklace online and sent them the picture."

My heartbeats ram within my chest, and my lower lip quivers just as he finishes.

"It's the most special gift I've ever gotten, Daddy." I throw my arms around him and silently cry, holding onto the only thing I'll ever have of my mother: her photos.

"She's here with you," he tells me, pain shattering him too, slicing through his tone. "She'd never miss this, not for anything."

I perch back and he reaches for his handkerchief, gently patting my lower lashes.

"Good as new." His own eyes are full of large tears, affection spilling from his gaze.

A gentle knock has us turning toward the door.

"It's time," Chiara announces, tilting her head to the side. "If you need more time, just let me know."

My dad looks at me, placing his palms on my shoulders. "What do you say, kid? Are we ready to get you married?"

I'm a blubbering mess, soft laughter spilling free. "We're ready. I've waited long enough for this."

He peers back at Chiara. "You heard the lady. Let's get this show on the road."

She salutes him with her own carefree laugh as we follow her out the door and into my new life as Mrs. Cavaleri.

MATTEO

"Are you nervous?" Dom asks, standing at the floral aisle with me, my other brothers beside him.

"Not at all." I grin, knowing it's true. "I can't wait to make her my wife. It feels like we've been waiting forever for this. And I'm glad to finally cross this off my bucket list."

His palm hits my shoulder. "I'm proud of you."

"Yeah." I shrug off the sentiment.

"She's a great girl. I'm glad you two had one another there…"

His voice trails off.

"I'd be dead without her. There's no doubt about it."

His jaw clenches, and he drops his hand away. "I don't wanna hear that."

His breath is long and heavy, like the idea of me dead physically hurts him.

I know he loves me. I know he's been ridden with guilt over what he thought was my death. My brothers have told me how badly he took it all when they were young, and that his pain only intensified, hardening him through the years.

He's changed now, though. I can easily see the difference from when we first met and now. I like seeing the Dom I once knew. The one who took care of me, but laughed too. He never acted like I bothered him, always helping me with homework and playing with me, even when I was sure he'd rather do his own shit. But that's who Dom was, putting others before himself. He's still that way.

I glance around at the chairs filled with people. It's just my brothers and their wives here, along with Emma and Clark. Small. Simple. We didn't need the fanfare. We just wanted to get married, and here in the place she once talked about…well, that was the perfect spot.

The music changes, and the sound of a saxophone drifts in the cool, warm air.

"It's time," Dom says with a heartfelt grin.

I give the acres of greenery below the mountain a final peek, knowing the woman I've been tied to since I was eight is about to walk down the aisle.

And a moment later, there she is, rounding the corner. Her eyes flick to mine, holding them still, and my heart flips right in my chest. My throat bobs, not from nerves, but from the amount of devotion spilling through my veins.

And once she starts to stroll down to me, her off-white strapless dress drifting around her ankles, long hair billowing in the air, my throat…it fucking aches. I'm close to dropping to my knees with all the emotions wafting through me. The tie at my neck somehow feels tighter; my lungs run out of air as I stare at the only woman I want to look at for the rest of my life.

She's like an angel, and I don't know what I did to deserve her. All those people I've killed…their faces haunt me, and yet, she still loves me in spite of it.

Her smile is wide, and mine grows bigger. It takes everything in me not to run to her and take her in my arms and never let go. But I wait as she takes her time, her father proud beside her.

When she's finally right before me, I take her hands in mine and leave a soft kiss on her forehead. Her brows tighten, eyes glazing over.

"You're more beautiful than all the stars in the sky," I whisper. "And every day I wake up hoping to be a better man the day before. Because you deserve nothing less than that."

She beams at me, squeezing my hands. "And every day I hope to remind you that you already *are* that man, Matteo Cavaleri. You always were."

I smile so damn wide, because I'm used to smiling now.

And together, with our hands bound tight, we face the wedding officiant, knowing our hearts have already been bound years ago.

The End

playlist

- "The Wicked" by Andrea Wasse
- "The Killer Was a Coward" by Dermot Kennedy
- "Down" by Simon feat. Trella
- "Hurts Like Hell" by Fleurie feat. Tommee Profitt
- "Dead Man Walking" by Sam Tinnesz
- "Broken" by Jonah Kagen
- "Chains" by Claire Gurreso
- "Can You Hear Me" by UNSECRET feat. Young Summer
- "Carry You" by Ruelle feat. Fleurie
- "Darkness Falls" by UNSECRET feat. Cece and the Dark Hearts
- "Haunted" by ADONA
- "Dark Side" by Bishop Briggs
- "Never Alone" by Krigarè
- "The Storm" by Kat Leon
- "Far From Home (The Raven)" by Sam Tinnesz
- "Enemy" by Tommee Profitt feat. Beacon Light and Sam Tinnesz
- "Man or a Monster" by Sam Tinnesz feat. Zayde Wølf
- "Tomorrow We Fight" by Tommee Profitt feat. SVRCINA
- "Soldier" by Fleurie feat. Tommee Profitt
- "Game of Survival" by Ruelle
- "Everywhere Ghosts Hide" by Erin McCarley feat. UNSECRET

- "Lost It All" by Jill Andrews
- "Mad World" by UNSECRET feat. REMMI
- "Killer + The Sound" by Phoebe Bridgers feat. Noah Gundersen and Abby Gundersen
- "The Hate Inside" by Tommee Profitt feat. Sam Tinnesz
- "Up in Flames" by Ruelle
- "Something to Someone" by Dermot Kennedy
- "Prisoner" by Raphael Lake feat. Aaron Levy and Daniel Ryan Murphy
- "Watch Them Fall" by UNSECRET feat. Sam Tinnesz and Tedashii
- "Eternal Flame" by Randall Jermaine feat. Alexa Ray and Atom Music Audio
- "Dizzy" by Ella Bleu
- "Hush" by Siebold feat. Garrison Starr
- "Stuck in This Mad World" by Siebold feat. Neutopia
- "Hard Times" by Vision Vision feat. Congratulationz

Acknowledgments

Book number eight, wow. I'm eternally grateful for every single one of you who've picked up my books and gave me the courage to continue writing.

A special thanks to Robyn, Adrienne, Courtney, Kate, Leah, and Tricia for beta reading and proofing for me. This book was very scary to write, and I thank you for your advice and input. You guys are truly the best and I'm glad to have met you all.

Fragile Hearts Series

1. *Fragile Scars* (Damian & Lilah)
2. *Fragile Lies* (Jax & Lexi Part 1)
3. *Fragile Truths* (Jax & Lexi Part 2)
4. *Fragile Pieces* (Gabe & Mia)

Cavaleri Brothers Series

1. *The Devil's Deal* (Dominic & Chiara)
2. *The Devil's Pawn* (Dante & Raquel)
3. *The Devil's Secret* (Enzo & Jade)
4. *The Devil's Den* (Matteo & Aida)
5. *The Devil's Demise* (Extended Epilogue)

Messina Crime Family Series

1. *Sinful Vows* (Michael & Elsie)
2. *Cruel Lies* (Raph & Nicolette)
3. *Twisted Promises* (Gio & Iseult)
4. *Savage Wounds* (Adriel & Kayla)

Savage Kings Series

1. *Ruthless Savage* (Devlin & Eriu)
2. *Brutal Savage* (Tynan & Elara - September 6th, 2024)
3. *Wicked Savage* (Fionn - January 6th, 2025)
4. *Filthy Savage* (Cillian - May 5th, 2025)

Standalone

1. *Shattered Secrets* (Husdon & Hadleigh)

For Lilian, a love of writing began with a love of books. From *Goosebumps* to romance novels with sexy men on the cover, she loved them all. It's no surprise that at the age of eight she started writing poetry and lyrics and hasn't stopped writing since.

She was born in Azerbaijan, and currently resides in Long Island, N.Y. with her husband, three kids, and a dog named Gatorade. Even though she has a law degree, she isn't currently practicing. When she isn't writing or reading, Lilian is baking or cooking up a storm. And once the kids are in bed, there's usually a glass of red in her hand. Can't just survive on coffee alone!

Lilian would love to connect with you!
Email: lilanharrisauthor@gmail.com
Website: www.lilanharris.com
Newsletter: https://bit.ly/LilianHarrisNewsletter
Signed Paperbacks: https://bit.ly/LHSignedPB
Facebook: www.facebook.com/LilianHarrisBooks
Reader Group: www.facebook.com/groups/lilianslovlies
Instagram: www.instagram.com/lilianharrisauthor
TikTok: www.tiktok.com/@lilianharrisauthor
Twitter: www.twitter.com/authorlilian
Goodreads: https://bit.ly/LilianHarrisGR
Amazon: www.amazon.com/author/lilianharris